ALSO BY KENNEDY RYAN

BLOCK Shot

A HOOPS NOVEL

KENNEDY RYAN

Bloom books

Published by Bloom Books, an imprint of Sourcebooks
P.O. Box 4410, Naperville, Illinois 60567-4410
(630) 961-3900
sourcebooks.com

Originally self-published in 2018 by Kennedy Ryan.

Cataloging-in-Publication data is on file with the Library of Congress.

Printed and bound in the United States of America.
VP 10 9 8 7 6 5 4 3 2 1

For Jane, a woman like Banner,
with angel in her heart and warrior in her blood.
Fight. FOREVER.

AUTHOR'S NOTE

It was important that we hear Banner, the heroine, speaking Spanish, her first language. I understand many of the phrases in *Block Shot* could be translated in various ways depending on the Spanish-speaking people group and geography. I, in consultation with Spanish-speaking early readers, have chosen the translation we determined most authentic for Banner, a Mexican-American raised in California.

PART I

COLLEGE. SENIOR YEAR.

*"There is something about falling in love
with a beautiful mind…"*

—*Cindy Cherie, poetess*

CHAPTER 1
JARED

TESTOSTERONE AND ENTITLEMENT.

The air is thick with both.

And weed, which in my experience transcends all socioeconomic barriers. The everyman drug. Even this tight circle of overgrown trust-fund-baby boys draws and blows from the pile of bags I tossed onto the large mahogany table at the center of the room.

"This is good shit," Benton Carter says, proffering the joint to me. "Want some? You *did* bring it."

"You mean I fetched it," I say low enough for only him to hear. "And I'm just about over being the resident lapdog at Prescott's beck and call."

One glance to the head of the table confirms that William Prescott wears that smug, self-satisfied smirk that seems permanently tattooed on his pasty face. He catches my eye, raises his joint, and gives me a thumbs-up.

"Ask me where he can put that thumb," I tell Bent.

"That is *not* how you get in, Foster." Bent shakes his head, but an irrepressible grin tugs at the corners of his mouth. He has no more tolerance for that asshole than I do. "Prescott's the chapter president. Final say rests with him on whether you get in or not."

Getting "in" seemed like the best thing I could do for my future when Bent told me about the Pride, a secret society akin to Yale's

Skull and Bones. It's a national network of good ol' boy blue bloods who look out for one another in business and pleasure. Only Ivy League and the most elite private schools like ours, Kerrington College, have chapters. Admission only comes "through blood or bond." Either you're granted admission as a legacy connected through a family member or you get in because a member sponsors you. When Bent, whose family goes back four generations in the Pride, approached me about joining, it seemed like a fantastic idea. For someone as ambitious as I am, it was a gift from the gods. After months of doing the chapter president's bidding, I'm ready to punch that gift horse in the mouth.

"You're close," Bent whispers, casting a furtive glance around the table at the other members still smoking, drinking, and posturing to impress each other. "Perform this last rite Prescott assigns tonight, and you'll be in."

"You *do* realize last rites are generally followed by death."

"It won't be that bad. Just…" Bent stares at the table instead of at me. "Just don't lose it when he tells you what it is. Do this one thing, and you're in."

Based on the crazy shit Prescott has already had me do, *this one thing* could be anything. Breaking into a professor's office to steal his laptop and an exam. Exhuming a grave to retrieve a Prescott family heirloom. Dismantling the bell in the campus tower. Not to mention buzzing all my hair off. What any of it has to do with so-called brotherhood and character, I have no idea. I think Prescott knows every time I smile to his face I'm mentally flipping him off, so he searches for the riskiest, most asinine tasks he can come up with. By luck of birth, he ended up in this position, and from my perspective, he is the least likely to succeed without the inherent advantages of his daddy's money and the Pride's fraternal network. I'm not the most submissive lion in the so-called pride on a good day; I'm nearly at the breaking point after three months of bowing and scraping to this tool.

"Whatever he wants me to do, I hope it's quick or that it doesn't have to be done tonight." I glance at my watch. "I have a study group in less than an hour across campus."

Bent narrows his eyes at me through a cloud of smoke.

"A group?" he asks. "Or a girl?"

I stiffen and cock a brow, silently asking *what the hell*. In the smoke-filled basement of Prescott Hall with these blue bloods, Bent may be a Pride legacy and I a mere prospect, but he knows I remember him as the lanky kid I met at freshman orientation. We've been tight ever since, and I've locked the door on most of the skeletons in his closet.

My face blank, I toy with an unlit joint. "What girl?"

There's a war between reluctance and loyalty on his face before he releases a smoky sigh.

"Prescott knows you don't study at the library." The words slide from one barely open, hardly moving corner of Bent's mouth. "He knows you study at the laundromat."

His face and eyes sober.

"He knows about Banner."

The air chills around me, and a queasy feeling grips my stomach at the mention of Banner Morales. Dark, bottomless espresso-colored eyes fringed with long, thick lashes. Full lips tinted by chocolate and roses. High cheekbones and one dimple on the right side. A bold nose dusted with exactly seven freckles. I blink to clear the mental image, sharpening my focus on my best friend's worried expression.

"What does she have to do with this?" I strip my voice of the emotion struggling to break the surface. "She's just my study partner."

Bent tips his head and gives me a knowing look.

"Foster, come on. It's me."

I haven't talked to anyone about Banner. How I think about her all the time. And how she makes me laugh without even trying. How my dick gets hard when I smell her shampoo. All of this is fodder for merciless ribbing, so, no, I haven't talked to anyone about Banner except Bent, and even then not much. I maintain a blank face and level my mouth into a flat line.

"Dude, I'm clueless," I answer evenly.

"Yeah, well, you—"

"Benton, what are you and the prospect talking about?" Prescott demands from the other end of the table. "Care to share with your brothers?"

He addresses the question to Bent, but his eyes latch onto my face, and I don't look away.

"Nothing," Bent answers easily, lifting the joint to his lips. "Finals."

"Ah, finals." Prescott gives us a lopsided phony grin. "That's right. I remember from his application that our prospect is summa cum laude."

"Not yet," I remind him. "One more semester."

It's a miracle my GPA hasn't suffered with all the ridiculous errands and stunts Prescott has assigned to me.

"But it'll happen," he replies, his smile several degrees warmer than his frosty-blue eyes. "You're a smart guy. Here on scholarship, right?"

The silent implication: How else could I afford Kerrington? It's true. My dad is retired military, and my stepmother is a teacher. I wasn't raised with the luxuries these guys took for granted growing up.

But I *will* have them. Unlike these spoiled brats, I'll earn them.

All of this runs through my head while Prescott and I stare at one another, showing neither our hands nor our thoughts. Bent said Prescott "knows" about Banner, which can't be good. I'm waiting to hear what this last rite of passage is, and it better not have anything to do with her. She'd laugh in my face if she knew the idiotic shit I've been doing to get into some secret society that will supposedly pave my way in the future. Banner doesn't do shortcuts and doesn't look for fast tracks. She *is* a fast track. The girl's certified Mensa, for God's sake.

Her brain was the first thing about her that turned me on. We faced off once in our Debate & Public Speaking class. Needless to say, she shredded my every argument and ripped apart each of my rebuttals.

I could barely walk back to my seat my dick was so hard.

"Are you ready for the final rite?" Prescott asks, reminding me that unfortunately I'm still here.

"Sure."

I've found saying less is always better with Prescott. He's like a parasite leeching any word he can exploit or drain.

"You've met and exceeded every challenge so far," Prescott says. "For your final rite, you will fuck a fat girl."

A stunned silence spreads around his words like spilled milk. Really, that's not entirely accurate since I'm the only one who seems stunned. Every other face around the table reflects excitement, discomfort, curiosity, or some mixture of all three. Even Bent watches me impassively, as everyone waits for my response.

They don't have long to wait.

"What the hell?" A scowl breaks out over my face like a rash. "You want me to fuck some random fat girl? I don't understand what—"

"Not random," Prescott interrupts. "Banner Morales."

Fury sets a small blaze at my feet, licks up over my legs and the rest of my body. My heart is a lump of coal catching fire in my chest and burning until it hurts. So I'm basically a chimney with no flue.

"Repeat that." My voice drops to a deceptive quiet that doesn't bely the emotions roaring inside me.

"I said you have to fuck a fat girl," Prescott reiterates, his face an unreadable mask, but his eyes telling: vibrant, cruel blue. "Banner Morales."

I'd appreciate the irony of this final challenge being something I fully intended to do anyway if it wasn't so insulting to one of the few people I not only tolerate but really like. If it wasn't intended to hurt her.

"I won't do that."

At least not for him. When I fuck Banner, it'll be purely for me and for her.

"And she's not fat," I snap.

Prescott's abrupt laughter shatters the quiet only he and I break at intervals while everyone else watches.

"We'll say pleasingly plump if that makes you feel better, Foster." His mouth zigzags into an icicle smile. "Either way, fuck her or you won't get in."

Later, when logic and a cooler head prevail, I'll make sense of this, but right now I only know that Prescott, for some reason, wants to demean Banner and thought he would use me to do it.

"The only fucking there will be, Prescott," I grind out, "is however you manage to fuck yourself."

Bent groans behind me—the first sign that he is, unlike the rest of the waxen zombies assembled around the table, alive.

"Foster," Bent hisses at my elbow. "All you have to do—"

"Shut the hell up." I whip a look around to him. "You knew about this?"

"Good God, Foster," Prescott intones from the head of the table. "Put a bag over her head and take the top so she doesn't crush you. It'll be over before you know it."

I stand so abruptly my chair falls behind me and crashes to the floor. His words have barely polluted the air before I'm at his side and have one of his arms twisted behind his back and his face pressed to the table.

The other guys mumble and cough and protest weakly, but I spread a glare around the table in case any of them feel the need to defend this motherfucker whom *they* don't even like or respect. The Pride? Give me a damn break. These men aren't lions. They're sheep who follow and bleat.

"You're making a huge mistake, Foster," Prescott screams, straining futilely to loosen my hold on his arm and head. "No way you're in after this."

"You tiny-dick son of a bitch," I growl. "Do I *look* like I still want to be in your pathetic secret treehouse club?"

I tighten my grip on his arm, watching with satisfaction the discomfort pinching his features.

"Not only do I officially withdraw my bid for admission to this foolishness you're masquerading as a brotherhood," I bend to say in his ear, "but if I hear you've bothered or hurt Banner in any way, I'll beat you with your own belt and knock your teeth down your throat."

I release him, and he immediately surges to his feet and turns on me, stepping so close our noses almost meet. His beer-scented breath huffs into the small space separating us. I don't step back but let my rage and his wrestle in the tension-tightened air.

"Do it," I whisper, fists clenched and ready at my sides. "I'd relish beating you in front of them."

"You will regret this," he says, the side of his face I pressed to the table mottled and red. "You're throwing away the opportunity of a lifetime, and this will follow you forever. Is Chubby worth that?"

I force myself to smile instead of snarl.

"Everything I have I earned, even against the odds." I shrug carelessly. "It would be in your best interest to stay clear of me. You're an unweaned baby, still sucking on your mama's tit. If there's one thing you should have learned about me over the course of these last few months, it's that I'm a resourceful motherfucker and will do whatever is necessary to achieve my goal. If I hear you're bothering Banner Morales, I'll put you down."

I hold his stare for an extra beat so he feels the weight, the truth of my words.

"That's a promise, Prescott."

I don't wait for a response but grab my laundry bag and my backpack and ignoring the gaping faces assembled around the table—including my best friend's—take the steps from the basement two at a time. It's only when I'm standing outside Prescott Hall and drawing in a cold, bracing breath of winter air that I process what has happened. I just flushed the last three months of my life down the toilet. All the fetching of drugs and booze, completing dangerous, impossible tasks, breaking laws, and generally subjugating myself to this asshole...wasted.

Hell, I even broke up with Cindy last week, my girlfriend who looks and fucks like a porn star.

All of it gone. Poof. For nothing.

Not for nothing. For Banner.

A girl who doesn't even know I like her. Whom I've never even kissed.

"What the hell was that, Foster?"

Bent's angry question slaps at my back as I walk down the front steps.

I turn to face him, a few steps below.

"I should kick your ass." Even though my voice is quiet, he knows my anger when he sees it.

"You messed up, dude." Bent sucks his teeth and shakes his head agitatedly. "You wanna fuck her anyway. What was the harm?"

I tilt my head and consider him through the puffs of frigid air expelling from our mouths and noses.

"How do you know what I want?"

"Besides knowing you for four years and never seeing you like this about any other girl?" The stiff line of his mouth cants just a little.

"I'm not 'like' anything." My words sound defensive even to me.

"You talk about her more than you talk about Cindy. Remember Cindy? The one who actually sucks your dick? Yet all I heard was Banner is a genius. Banner kicked my ass today in debate class. Banner's a double major. Banner speaks all these languages. Banner, Banner, Banner."

"Ex," I correct softly, allowing myself a smile. I must have talked about her more than I realized.

"What'd you say?" Bent asks, blowing into his hands.

"I said ex-girlfriend. Cindy and I broke up."

"I know that, too." Any trace of a smile disappears. "We make it our business to know everything about Pride prospects."

Any ease between us withers. Tension reclaims my shoulders.

"Well, you can stay out of my business because I'm not a prospect anymore." I turn to begin the ten-minute walk to the laundromat where Banner's already studying.

"I can probably smooth things over with the rest of the group and pressure Prescott to let you in," he calls after me. "That was Prescott's thing. No one else wanted to do it."

I shake my head and keep walking, letting my middle finger raised in the air do my talking for me. After a few moments, the sound of the door slamming shut signals that Bent gave up and went back inside.

Good. I need all ten minutes to figure out what I'm going to do.

Tonight was supposed to be the night. The night I would lay my cards on the table and tell Banner how I feel.

Feel?

Is that the right word?

I don't "feel" for girls. I fuck them. And if I want to be the only one for a little while, I date them. And once I don't care if someone else has them, then I stop. But *obviously* there's a pattern.

I mean, with the fucking and all.

It's more than that with Banner, though. Prescott says she's fat. Honestly, maybe she is a little chubby. Who knows, what with the oversized sweatshirts she always wears. I love the way she looks, but that's not it. She's not my usual type. With Cindy, I knew within two minutes how I would get her. I'm a calculating motherfucker, instantly and constantly assessing weaknesses and tendencies to get what I want. Most people are simple, easy to figure out. But Banner has an algorithm I haven't solved yet.

Maybe tonight I will.

CHAPTER 2
JARED

I HAD NEVER BEEN TO A LAUNDROMAT BEFORE COLLEGE.

Growing up, Susan, my stepmother, did our laundry on the weekends. She probably spoiled us—me, my dad, and my stepbrother, August. Our clothes magically appeared in drawers and closets, washed, hung, folded, and fresh-scented. It wasn't until college that I realized what a pain in the ass it is to do your own laundry.

Banner runs a small business, taking in laundry from students like me, too busy or too lazy to do it themselves. She usually studies at Sudz, an off-campus laundromat, while her clients' clothes wash and dry. Most of the dorms have a laundry room, so Sudz doesn't see as much traffic as you'd think. Some nights she studies so late she's arranged with the owner to just sleep here on a couch in the back room. We often have the place to ourselves.

Tonight we have the place to ourselves.

I hover at the entrance of Sudz, shifting the bag of laundry on one shoulder, my backpack on the other, and observe Banner at my leisure. In a flurry of deft movements, she tames the wild tangle of whites into orderly stacks, all the while whispering to herself, the thick, sculpted arch of her dark brows dented in concentration. Earbuds in, she is rehearsing what I know to be conversational Mandarin Chinese.

Banner has a thing for languages. First day in our Debate &

Public Speaking class, Professor Albright said the power of language is how it connects us. He asked something in English, and of course we all answered. Then he asked a question in Spanish, and still many replied in kind. French, fewer, but some still answered. Italian, almost no one, a few, maybe three. When he called out a question in Russian, only one voice echoed from the very back of the huge lecture hall.

Banner Morales.

Even uttering the phlegmy, harsh Russian consonants, her voice sounded like it had been smoked over coals then left chilling on ice. Richly flavored but cool. Husky. Confident. I couldn't resist. I had to turn and see who belonged to that voice. I'm used to girls noticing me, but Banner's eyes never left Professor Albright standing down front, even though I stared up at her for a good minute. I wanted her to see me watching her, but she didn't acknowledge me. I've been trying to get her to see me ever since.

"*Hěn hào chī,*" she whispers, starting on a stack of darks.

I tap her shoulder and she jumps, screeching a little and making me laugh. It's so unlike her to screech.

"Sorry," I say, my grin unrepentant.

"You scared me half to death, Foster." Hand pressed to her chest, she rolls her eyes, but a good-natured smile tugs at those full lips. Her lips look perpetually just-kissed. She has one of those Julia Roberts mouths. Her lips, the top and bottom, are precisely the same width and fullness. There's no dip or bow, as if when they were molding Banner's features they tugged at the corners of her mouth and said *just a little wider.*

They must have thought, *"There. Perfect. That'll torture Jared Foster every time he looks at her."*

"What were you mumbling about when I walked in?" I ask.

"Working on restaurant conversation tonight." She turns off the audio on her phone.

"Oh, that'll come in *so* handy."

"More than the Latin you took in high school," she says, chuckling. "They call it a dead language for a reason. You need to learn something that'll be useful to you in business."

"Yeah, yeah. I will. Now tell me what you were saying when I came in."

"*Hĕn hào chī.*" She carefully places each syllable as though if she drops one it might break.

My lifted brows request the translation.

"Very delicious." She grins infectiously. "On my first business trip to China, I'll be able to tell the server that the meal was *hĕn hào chī.*"

"China, huh?" I drop my bag of already-clean laundry to the floor. Many of my clothes get rewashed to justify studying with Banner in a laundromat.

"Basketball is exploding in China," she says. "Yao Ming tore down the Great Wall, so to speak. The financial implications of China for the NBA are huge."

"So they tell me in our Econ class."

After having no classes with Banner at Kerrington, despite the fact that we are both sports management majors, we share two classes our last year here.

"Speaking of which, we need to study for that final," she says, tossing a dryer-warm T-shirt in my face. "And you're late. Again."

"Sorry." I toss the T-shirt back into her pile of navy blue and black cotton. "Again."

"I hope it's worth it."

I let her words settle around us for a second before answering.

"You hope what's worth it?" I ask with a quick frown.

"I'm not stupid," she says wryly.

"Obviously."

"I know what you've been up to," she says, lowering her voice conspiratorially.

Oh, shit.

"Uh…you do?"

"Of course." She hits my shoulder with her small fist. "You're pledging a fraternity."

A relieved breath rushes past my lips. "What makes you think that?"

"The buzz cut?" She points to my shorn hair. "The late hours and weird 'assignments?' It all adds up to a fraternity. I just hope they aren't asking you to do anything too outrageous. Or dangerous."

The stern line of her lips paired with the belligerent glint in her eye makes me want to divulge all the outrageous, dangerous shit I've done the last three months to get in with the Pride. Of course, every prospect signs confidentiality agreements, and even if we don't get in, we can't talk about the Pride. But if I could tell her…she looks like she would kick some ass in my defense.

"So are you in?" she asks, going back to the pile of darks and starting to fold again.

Hell no. Prescott's words "fuck a fat girl" resurface in my head, and anger grips me by the throat. I swallow several colorful curses and simply shake my head.

"I withdrew." I twist the rope on my laundry bag and avoid her stare. "They crossed the line."

"I'm sorry, Jared."

She covers my hand with hers for a second. I hated Prescott calling her fat, but she's not small. Her hands are, though. Long, slim fingers. Short unpainted nails. She's maybe five six or seven. No makeup covering her clear, olive-toned skin. Dark, wavy hair scooped into a knot and anchored with two pencils. Banner doesn't bother with the things girls often do to gain a guy's attention. Maybe she's too driven, too tunnel-visioned on her goals, but she has my attention. She's had it for months, and she either doesn't know or doesn't care. Tonight, I'm determined to find out which.

When she moves her hand to pull away, I loop my thumb around her index finger, anchoring our hands together. We share a held breath, and the only sound is water sloshing and clothes spinning in the machines. It's so quiet in the laundromat that I hear her breath hitch when I reach under to scrape her palm with my thumbnail. I don't let her go, don't let her ignore the inevitability of my interest. A frown gathers on her face, and genuine confusion clouds her eyes. She looks from our hands still pressed together to my face and then shakes her head like she's imagining something. The moment is elastic, for a few seconds thick with unspoken desires—mine and I'm pretty sure hers—and then, in an instant, snaps back to the harmless, sexless thing we usually have. She lets out a breathy laugh and pulls away.

Will I have to take out an ad? Sketch lewd pictures in her notebook? How can she not know that I'm interested in her? Hell, Bent's never even *met* Banner, and he knew. I'm not usually a subtle guy when I want someone, but I've never wanted anyone like Banner.

"We'd better get cracking," she says and walks toward the back room where we usually study.

Her books are already spread across the rickety coffee table. I pick up and flip through her Econ textbook, pulling it back a little to read notes in the margin.

"You *do* know you need glasses, right?" She moves her books to make room for mine.

"No, I don't." I scrunch my face. "That's crazy."

"Are you worried about how you'll look?"

"No," I answer honestly.

"Figures," she mutters, a small smile teasing the corner of her mouth.

"No," I repeat firmly, maybe slightly defensively because the words *do* blur a little. "I just don't need glasses."

She shrugs and laughs under her breath, flopping onto the couch and digging into her backpack for supplies. Her heavy coat is draped over the armrest of the lumpy couch. Heavy coat. Oversized sweatshirt. Baggy jeans. How's a guy supposed to know what's under all that? For the first time in…ever, I don't think I even care.

"Albright will expect you to defend your position," she says, and I realize I'd tuned out while she sat and cleared space on the table for my books. "You know what he always says."

"Convince me," we say in unison, laughing and mocking our professor's deep voice. He constantly challenges us to prove our points and to thoughtfully articulate why we believe what we say we do.

"I was so intimidated by him at the beginning of the semester," she confesses, traces of our humor lingering around her eyes and mouth.

"Didn't seem that way. You answered the man in Russian from the last row of the auditorium," I remind her. "Seemed pretty confident to me."

"It's no different from answering him in English." She pushes a stray strand of silky hair fallen from the topknot behind her ear. She does that when she feels self-conscious. For all her tells, she hasn't told me much, and I have no idea where I stand with her, unless it's firmly in the friend zone.

"Yeah, no different because you speak Russian." I dip my head and try to catch her gaze, smiling when she sketches on her notebook and refuses to look up. "And Spanish. And Italian. And soon Chinese."

"Well, Spanish was the first language I heard at home." She shrugs one shoulder. "Mama thinks it's a travesty for Hispanic people not to speak it. I grew up bilingual and realized I had a knack for picking up languages pretty easily."

"You seem to have quite a few 'knacks.' Is there anything you *don't* do well?"

A wry smile tips her mouth. "Jokes."

"Jokes?"

"Yeah, I'm really bad at them."

"Convince me," I say, using Professor Albright's signature phrase.

"What?" Eyes wide, she finally looks up from her doodling.

"Tell me one of these bad jokes."

"Oh, gosh." Faint color washes under her skin. "Okay."

She traps her bottom lip and closes one eye, concentrating before clearing her expression and looking back to me and speaking.

"Knock, knock."

"Seriously?"

"Knock," she says firmly, "knock."

I sigh and bite into a smile.

"Who's there?"

"Europe."

"Uh…Europe who?"

"No, I'm not."

I stare at her blankly in the waiting silence following her "joke."

"Are you *done*?" I ask incredulously. "That was it?"

Laughter erupts from us at the same time.

"Yeah, that's bad," I agree.

"Well, I try."

"But your horrendous joke-telling doesn't quite outweigh how awesome you seem to be at most other things."

"Ha!" She rolls her eyes and resumes doodling. "I wish my advisor agreed with you."

"What do you mean?"

"He's old school. He doesn't think women make great sports agents."

"A lot of people don't. There aren't many of them, for sure. You know you're entering a male-dominated field, but if anyone can handle it, you can."

"Thanks, Jared. His views are pretty antediluvian."

Shit. Those lips wrapping around the word "antediluvian" may as well be wrapped around my cock. Has my brain always been a sex organ, or did she do this to me?

"Did you hear me?" she asks, frowning.

"Sorry." *I was busy adjusting myself under the table.* "What'd you say?"

"He keeps spouting survival of the fittest. He thinks women lack the killer instinct required to be truly successful sports agents."

"He's not wrong."

The look she shoots me could cut the rest of my hair off.

"Whoa." I raise my hands to ward off all that ire. "Not about women's inability to succeed in this field."

Her expression eases a fraction.

"But he's not wrong about survival of the fittest," I clarify. "That's real. Most sports agents are assholes. Mercenary. Cutthroat. Ruthless. I'm perfectly suited for it and plan to be the best asshole in the game."

She smiles, uncertainty in the barely curved lips and searching eyes. "You don't mean that."

"I do." We stare at each other for a few seconds, and I let her see the truth of what I've said.

My dad, with all his military training and knowledge of how to kill people in a hundred different ways, is a kind man. My stepmother and stepbrother, good people with good hearts.

And then there's me.

I never felt as nice as the rest of my family. It wasn't until I started here at Kerrington that I realized it's not that I'm not as nice, I just see people more clearly. I spy their twisted motives and ill intentions. The entitled brats here only honed that sense, only deepened my conviction that, by and large, people look out for themselves. If they're gonna suck, I'm gonna manipulate them to my own ends. Thus my choice of profession.

"I'm made for this job," I tell her.

"So am I," she fires back, her voice defensive. "My advisor says survival of the fittest, but I don't think about life in terms of Darwin."

"You mean science? Facts? Truth?"

"No, I mean in terms of the last man...*person*...standing...in terms of having to eliminate everyone else so that you come out on top. A food chain culture that thrives on atavism."

That sounds like life to me, but I let her keep talking.

"I think less Darwin, more"—her eyes search the room as if the answer might be painted on the laundromat's Pepto-pink walls—"Maslow."

"Maslow?" I ask. "Two completely different schools of thought."

"Yes, but both predictive of human behavior." She leans toward me, warming to the subject. "Darwin used evolution, our most base biology, and Maslow used psychology, but both sought to understand why humans do what they do and how we end up with the best of the best."

"And you think Maslow has it right?" I ask skeptically. "Convince me."

She quirks her lips at my continued nod to Professor Albright.

"I think Maslow is at least another way to approach it. Darwin's approach considers us no better than animals."

"We *are* animals."

"*We* are human," she asserts pointedly. "We're higher functioning, not only intellectually but emotionally. Darwin assumes evolutionary competition leads to survival. Maslow believes that survival is a need, and if that need is met, we have the emotional margin for compassion and cooperation to meet the needs of others, too. With Darwin, there is a last man standing. With Maslow, we could *all* be left standing."

She tucks her hair behind an ear again, sliding her eyes away. "Guess this is why my advisor thinks I don't have that killer instinct."

"Maybe you're the killer with a heart." I lift her chin with one finger. "Maybe you'll take all that caring shit and use it to win clients over. Leave the heartless, ruthless stuff to people like me."

When she glances up, her dark eyes, fringed by thick lashes, snare me with the sincerity, the earnestness there. Still holding her chin, I stroke the powder-fine texture of her jaw. Confusion wrinkles her expression for a second before she pulls away from my touch.

"Um…maybe." She runs her hands over her face and slumps

her shoulders. Tugging out the pencils anchoring her hair, she tosses them on the table. Sable waves fall over her shoulders and across her chest. I can't look away. Don't want to. She's usually so pulled together. Seeing her literally let her hair down is a privilege I've only had a few times this semester.

"Well, at least today showed him I can do something right," she says sardonically, laughing without much humor. "In spite of my ovaries."

"What happened today?"

"Oh, I forgot to tell you." A smile lights her face. "I got the Bagley internship."

"No way." I shake my head, genuinely impressed. "I didn't know you were still in the running. I got knocked out in round two."

"It's not a big deal." That faint flush rises over her cheeks, and she waves her hand. "I just didn't want to jinx it. I honestly thought I had no chance. I figured Prescott had it on lock."

Hearing Banner say that asshole's name, I go still. Has he ever approached her with the kind of crazy shit he proposed to me tonight? I'd break him in half.

"Prescott?" I reach for a water from the neat rows of bottles she always keeps at hand when we study. "I didn't think you even knew him."

"I don't." She shrugs. "But I found out his dad is best friends or fraternity brothers or something with Cal Bagley. I assumed it was Prescott's to lose. I know he did, too."

Damn. All the pieces fall into place, and I understand why he wanted to humiliate her. Payback is a whiny, entitled, selfish bitch named William Prescott.

"Wow," I say even while the wheels keep turning in my head. "Congratulations. That's amazing."

"It is," she says, her grin wide and proud. "They decided late, though, so now I'm scrambling to find a place in New York and to get my schedule adjusted for next semester."

She stands and heads out to the main room, where a load just finished drying.

New York.

I clench my fists on my knees, absorbing the information. She's transferring a load from the dryer to a plastic basket when I venture back out there.

"So, New York, huh?" I ask, digging into the stack of white T-shirts and starting to fold.

"You don't have to do that." She aims a frown at the diminishing pile of laundry we're plowing our way through. I quirk a challenging brow, and she rolls her eyes. "Thanks." She resumes folding. "Yeah, remember it's a practicum, so my advisor wanted to talk through adjustments for my last semester and me working in New York."

Dammit.

I'm happy for her. It's the most prestigious internship in our department. Bagley & Associates is a powerhouse sports agency and landing a job with it post-graduation would catapult anyone's career. But New York? We take our exams in just a few days and then go home for holiday break. I thought I'd have all of next semester to win Banner over.

I may only have tonight.

And right then I come to a decision. Darwin. Maslow. Tomato. Tomah-toe. I've been taking the scenic route instead of the shortest path from me to what I want. That shit's about to end.

"Congrats again," I say, placing the last of the T-shirts into the basket. "Like I said, you're good at everything."

"Thank you, but I think we already established I don't do everything well."

"Yeah, so you tell bad jokes. Big deal." I pause, taking the reins of this conversation carefully in hand. "What about kissing? Are you a good kisser?"

Her hands are suspended, frozen midair over the warm laundry. Wide eyes collide with mine, and her mouth drops open.

Oh, yeah. Keep your mouth open like that, Banner. I have just the thing to put between those lips.

"What did you say?" she asks on a startled breath.

"I said are you a good kisser?" I cross my arms over my chest and wait for her to breathe deeply enough to answer me.

"Um, I guess." She bends her head and reaches to scoop up all that glorious hair back into whatever knot she had it imprisoned in before. I stop her, taking her wrist in my hand. I wait for her to look at me, to really, maybe for the first time all semester, see me.

"If you're a good kisser," I say softly, not releasing her eyes and leaning one last time on our professor, "convince me."

CHAPTER 3
BANNER

"Convince me."

The challenge lands at my feet like a gauntlet. Jared and I consider each other, unblinking. Confidence and questions darken his eyes to blackest-blue. What is even happening right now? Did he… Is he asking me to… Does he want…

Nooooooo.

Guys like Jared Foster don't proposition girls like me in laundromats. Don't get me wrong, I think he likes me. A lot. We laugh every time we're together. Our conversations are stimulating. No one challenges me more in a debate. He's the smartest guy I know, but he also looks like a handsome ski instructor who traded in the slopes for an Ivy League campus.

As for how I feel…it's more how I've *been* feeling for the last three years, ever since freshman orientation when Jared asked to borrow a pencil. That day his hair, now a sun-colored buzz, hung to the angled line of his jaw, the darker and brighter blond strands twisting into shampoo-commercial perfection. He was beautiful then, but he was barely out of high school. He's filled out the last four years. His features have hardened, the sharp incline of bone at his cheeks rising under taut, tanned skin. I could barely concentrate during orientation because he was so close, and many a night here in the laundromat I've read the same page five times trying not to stare.

It was an added bonus when his brain proved to be as alluring as his face. And I've never laughed as much as I have studying with him this semester. Knowing he was out of my league, I've been forcibly content as just friends, and the possibility that he wants more leaves me thoroughly thrilled and confused.

"I'm sorry," I finally say, barely hearing my voice over the heartbeat pounding in my ears. "I don't know what you mean."

He tilts his head, the tuft of blond hair capturing the harsh fluorescent lights overhead. He quirks that wide mouth. Jared can say more with the corner of his mouth than most people do with a hundred words. Turned down, canted up, twisted. Humor, disdain, skepticism. Those lips say it all without uttering a sound, but I have no idea what they are saying now.

"I said convince me you're a good kisser," he speaks slowly, like I might have a processing disorder, which could be the case because… *huh?*

Dark blond brows elevate over a simmering stare while he waits.

"And how would I convince you?" I ask, my words coming out on thin air. The longer he looks at me like this, like I'm a meal and he hasn't eaten, the breathier I sound.

He steps forward, eliminating the sanity-giving space between us. He's so close I have to tip my head back to keep our eyes connected.

"You could kiss me," he offers, so close now his breath feathers over my skin. Steamy yet minty. So close the rumble of his deep voice reverberates in my own chest.

"You mean kiss you?" I ask. "Or like *kiss you kiss you?*"

He chuckles and lifts the hair off my shoulder, tucking a chunk of it behind my ear.

"I'm pretty sure the second one," he says, piercing me with another heated glance. "Is that the one with tongue?"

My brain, temporarily atrophied though usually agile, reaches for the nearest excuse.

"I–I don't kiss guys who have girlfriends." I arrange my face into polite apology and hope to end this perplexing conversation.

"Ahhh." He nods, his expression reflective. "I figured you'd say that."

"Yeah, so we should probably—"

"That's why I don't have a girlfriend anymore."

The breath stalls in my throat. My heart pummels me from the inside out, rattling against the cage of my ribs.

"You mean Cindy?" I ask.

"Yeah, no more Cindy."

"You wha-wha…huh?"

"You wha-wha," he mocks me, his full lips spreading into a blinding grin. "You heard me. I don't have a girlfriend anymore. Cindy and I broke up."

"But I'm not your type," I blurt.

"And yet I broke up with her so *you*," he says, laying the tip of one long finger on my breastbone, "would kiss *me*."

I glance from the finger resting between my breasts to the sculpted lines of Jared's face. Does he feel my heartbeat *tom tom*–ing through my sweatshirt, hope and doubt trading thumps in my chest? I've imagined kissing him, not just how he would taste or how his lips would feel but him wanting it as much as I did. Imagined how it would feel to be wanted *back*. Now that he says he does, it seems too good to be true.

"I think I'm getting, um," I say, licking my lips, "mixed signals."

His eyes trace the slide of my tongue, making me self-conscious. I tuck my lips in, hiding them from the singeing heat of his glance.

"Really?" he asks with a husky chuckle. "You're too smart to be confused by something so simple."

His other hand cups the nape of my neck, subtly pulling me closer.

"No mixed signals, Banner." He lowers his head to breathe the next words over my lips. "Just this one."

From doing laundry the last few years, I have come to understand static electricity—the charge produced when things rub against each other. I didn't even realize we'd been rubbing against each other all semester in some form or fashion; the clash of our wills, the meeting of our minds, and now our lips rub together. Our tongues move in tandem. We cling.

He possesses my mouth. There's no other way to say it. As much a command as it is a kiss. I've never been kissed this way. His thumb presses my chin so my lips open wider, and he storms in. It doesn't feel like a first kiss. There's nothing uncertain or tentative about the way he fits his lips over mine. He kisses me like he's rehearsed it a thousand times.

And God help me, after a startled gasp, I kiss him back. The heat between our mouths burns through my shock like a flame eating through wax, and he quickly reaches the wick—the very end of my hesitation. He flattens his hand between my breasts while we kiss, and though he's nowhere near my nipples, they peak. Tight and hard and sensitive, anticipating the possibility of his touch. His other hand angles my head back, and he plumbs the depths of my mouth, licking inside, stroking my tongue with his. He traps my hair in his fist and pulls, growling into the kiss.

What the actual fuck?

It's so intense. It's deeper and hotter and on the edge of what I can handle. His hunger grabs me, holds me so tight for a moment I can't breathe.

"Jared," I mumble against his mouth, pull back, and touch my throbbing lips. "Slow down. I… It's a lot."

His forehead crashes against mine, his hand still at my neck and his fingers wedged into my hair.

"Shit," he breathes. "Sorry. I've just been thinking about this for a long time. It's hard to go slow."

I'm struggling to keep up. This golden boy from the upper reaches of Kerrington's social stratosphere, whom I've been secretly crushing on—for not one year, not two years, but *three*, even while I was dating the last jerk—has been thinking about kissing me for a long time? For so long that it's hard to go slow?

"Sorry," I say dazedly. "This feels like *The Twilight Zone*."

"*The Twilight Zone*?"

"Yeah, it was this show that—"

"Banner, I know what *The Twilight Zone* is, but why does it feel that way to you? Is it because we've known each other all semester and I'm just now making a move? The first day we met in Albright's class—"

"We didn't first meet in Albright's class," I cut in. "We met four years ago."

"What?" He frowns. "No, I would have remembered."

No, he wouldn't.

"Obviously, you *don't*." My laugh is soft, self-conscious. "We met at freshman orientation. All the girls were squealing about you and Benton Carter. *I want the blond one. I'll take the one with dark hair.*"

I drop my eyes to the floor.

"I sat right beside you," I tell him. "And you asked to borrow a pencil."

"I don't remember any of this, but I do remember the first day I noticed you in Albright's class."

He looks at me, a dark-blue direct assault.

"And I've been noticing you ever since," he adds. "I thought we'd have more time, but when you said you'd be in New York next semester, I realized this might be our last night here together, and I couldn't wait anymore."

"For me? You couldn't wait for *me*?" Despite the wondrous words coming out of his mouth, I still have to ask. To be sure. "I'm sorry, but I'm so confused."

"Still?" Something close to irritation mixes with the humor in his eyes.

He slides wide palms down my arms, gently squeezing the muscles through the heavy cotton of my sweatshirt.

"Then let me make it abundantly clear," he says, his voice husky and sure. "I like you, Banner."

Guys like him, not only this good-looking but also brilliant, have that one girl in college they date for the sake of her brain. It assures them they aren't entirely superficial. When that girl is a CEO, cures cancer, or is the first woman on Mars, they can say I knew her when. I dated her...*nay, I fucked her*...when.

I was that girl to my last boyfriend, Byron. He dated me while he needed help getting through his Econ class, but that wore off. He cheated on me before the ink was dry on his final exam. I grew up with a father who never looked at another woman besides my mother and made faithfulness look good. Look possible, normal. So I have a zero-tolerance cheat policy. When I discovered Byron's infidelity and dumped him, he felt insulted that I, who should have been grateful he'd deigned to date me, ended it.

I could barely breathe when she was on top.

Everything jiggled when I fucked her.

Those are his cruel words I overheard. He said worse things that I didn't hear for myself but got back to me and still haunt my thoughts. Still nick my confidence.

"You like me, huh?" I finally ask, training my glance on his chin, avoiding his eyes. "You mean in an 'I think you're smart and have a great personality' way?"

A muscle along his jawline flexes, and his lips tighten. He pulls me in to him, and he's big and hard through his jeans.

"No, I mean in an 'I want to fuck you' kind of way," he says sharply. "Any other questions?"

My heart stops beating for a microsecond and then rushes out of the blocks, sprinting so far ahead my brain can't catch up.

"Tonight?" I press my hand to my chest, hoping to soothe the rapid rate.

"Yeah, tonight, if you want." He links his fingers with mine and presses his hand to my chest. "Your heart is racing."

Embarrassment burns under my skin and spreads over my cheeks in a flush, confessing my self-consciousness. Another way this body has betrayed me. The freshman fifteen. Sophomore seven. Junior jelly belly. Senior cellulite. With each year at Kerrington, I accomplished my goals and my confidence grew, but so did my waistline. My confidence has never been dictated by the number on the tag in my jeans. I know what I am and I know what I'm not, and I've made my peace with that. But these things Jared's saying...they confuse me. They mix things up again and reignite the futile hopes of that chubby girl sitting beside the most beautiful guy at freshman orientation. The guy who probably remembered the pencil I gave him more than he remembered me.

So yeah. This is strange, and I don't trust it. When Jared and I started studying together this semester, I put my crush in time-out. I disciplined it. I locked it in its room with no dinner.

I starved it.

Now he's feeding it with impossible words and heated looks and urgent touches. He brings my hand to his chest. His heart beneath my palm thuds fast and heavy.

"Feel," he says, twisting our fingers together over the tight muscles and ungiving bone. "My heart's racing, too."

His heart *is* racing.

And his breath is short, panting.

His eyelids are at half-mast over the desire smoking in his eyes.

His body is giving me clues, but I'm still having trouble putting it all together.

"This could be our last night together, Banner," he says softly.

Since elementary school I've been focused. Perfect attendance from kindergarten until high school graduation. Charity work, skipped grades, extracurricular activities, and always the highest GPA. I've dated very little and ended any relationship as soon as it started distracting me.

The guy I've crushed on since freshman year wants me. I have no idea why or how, but he does. His racing heart beneath my hand attests to it. What if tonight, for one damn night, I do what I want to do instead of what is required? I don't know how all the pieces fit together, but I *do* know I've denied myself many things over the years while pursuing my goals. I want this. I want *him*, and for once, I'm going to indulge.

"Okay," I say, my answer clearer than my thoughts.

Surprise and relief skitter across his expression, and he isn't the guy always outfitted in assurance, surrounded by campus elites well beyond my social reach. It's just us, Jared and Banner. When I say yes, he looks at me like this is too good, like *I'm* too good to be true, too. He recovers quickly, resuming control, coasting his hands down my back.

"Then you owe me a kiss." Jared's words slide over me, and every cell in my body seems to lift in his direction, straining for another syllable from those lips.

"I do?" I force myself to meet his hooded stare. "I kissed you."

"No, *I* kissed *you*. Your turn."

I'm not short, but at six three, Jared's still taller. If he doesn't bend, I have to tip up on my toes to reach him.

He doesn't bend.

Drawing in a steadying breath that does no good because I remain unsteady, I lift on the balls of my feet and take his bottom lip between both of mine. I'm not as confident as he was. I suck softly, tentatively, and his chest lifts, breath drawn sharply through his nostrils. He squeezes me tighter but otherwise gives no indication that I'm affecting him.

But I am.

Suddenly, his body is giving *him* away, telling me how much he wants this. How much he wants me, and every part of him—his dick like stone pressing into me, his hands clenching, the measured breaths—tells me he wants this badly.

I loop my arms around his neck and press my breasts to him,

slipping my fingers into the smooth fair pelt of hair. I hold his head exactly where I want it and dive into his mouth, sucking his tongue the way he did mine, licking at the interior. I said we aren't animals, but I'm like a savage with my first taste of blood. I'm straining up, biting, grunting at the tangy taste of him. At the perfect firm and soft of his mouth. The kiss turns wet and hot and feral.

"Shit," he mutters, dragging his open mouth over my jaw. "Yeah. Give me all of that."

He walks us backward in slow steps while his hands cup my breasts.

"Great tits, Ban," he breathes into my ear. Even through my sweatshirt, my nipples bud under the fingers rubbing and twisting and tweaking.

We've reached the back room, and he pauses at the entrance, pressing me into the doorjamb. The wood digs into my back, the discomfort counterpoint to all the pleasure at my front. Jared rests against me, the hardened length of him nudging between my legs. He unfastens the button and zip of my jeans, slips his hand past my panties to spread my lips and rub my clit. It's sudden and electric and aggressive—the most shocking pleasure I've ever experienced. I full-body quiver, and my head bangs against the wood behind me as I grind helplessly into his hand.

"I want in here," he says, breath heaving. "But I want you to come first. Have you ever come standing up?"

I comb through the sensual fog of my memories for the times I've come. The few boyfriends I've had weren't skilled lovers, or at least they didn't waste their skills on me. Eyes closed, I shake my head.

"Well, you're about to." One thick finger penetrates me.

"Ahhh." My knees tremble.

His thumb strokes my clit, and he adds another finger and then a third. I whimper, biting my lip to stop the moans. In the quiet, I hear the sounds of my wetness as he strokes and rubs and his fingers possess me. He bends to bite my breast, the pleasure-pain sharp even through my clothes, and I burst. I wail, and it echoes in the laundromat, blending with the swish and tumble of clothes in the machines. My backbone melts. The only thing keeping me upright is his hand between my legs.

"God, yes, Banner," he says. "Touch me."

"Touch you where?" I'm slurring like a drunk woman, intoxicated by his fingers and his mouth and his heart racing for me.

"Where do you think?" He laughs, his eyes lit with humor and passion. He drags my hand to his dick. I squeeze without thinking, and he drops his head so our temples kiss. He's long and thick and hard in my hand through the denim. He spears his fingers into my hair.

"Pull on it," he gasps. "Stroke me. Roll my balls."

"Um…are you always this bossy?"

He angles his head until our glances collide and lock.

"Fuck me and find out."

I couldn't say no with a gun to my head, I want it so much, but for a moment I freeze. Wanting something badly, secretly, for so long then it suddenly drops into your lap is disconcerting.

"Banner, don't…" He squeezes his eyes shut, and his fingers twist tighter in my hair. "Stop *thinking* and just say yes."

He's right. Indulge.

"Yes."

My whispered consent drifts between us like a feather, but Jared doesn't wait for it to hit the floor before he pounces, capturing my mouth and touching me everywhere.

He kicks the door closed, blocking out the spin cycle of my last load for the night. I'm in a cloud, a daze, my body barely solvent as he walks me backward, one hand on my hip, guiding me, the other at my neck, holding me steady while he ravages my mouth. The backs of my knees hit the couch, and I fall onto the lumpy cushions. How many nights have we studied here? Talked here? Laughed?

And I never knew this was brewing inside him. I never suspected he wanted me as much as I wanted him.

He stares down at me and raises his arms, pulls the hoodie over his head. The T-shirt beneath strains across his chest. He tugs again, and the T-shirt is gone.

Ave Maria and good God in heaven.

I've never seen a chest and abs and arms like this in real life, this close in the flesh, not on a screen. Sculpted and carved and chiseled and all the words that call to mind cut and molded into a work of art. Unselfconscious, comfortable in his flawless skin, Jared slides his jeans down over lean hips and muscular legs. My eyes scroll over every inch of him. I'm covetous and awed.

"Wow." I don't mean to say it aloud.

He pauses, hand at his briefs, and cocks a brow. "Did you say wow?"

I forgot about this part. The brain-numbing pleasure dimmed my rational thought. I didn't consider that sex typically happens, for the most part, naked. And though Jared Foster is a work of art, I am not.

Everything jiggled when I fucked her.

Like tiny stilettos, Byron's words boomerang from the past, leaving a million rips in my self-esteem as they pass through. That passion, that deep desire in Jared's eyes, will it die? Will it disappear when he sees me? My jiggly parts? My un-sculpted body? I've had it less than an hour, that look in his eyes, the anticipation of wanting me. No way I can keep it, sustain it if he sees me. I just want to hold on to it a bit longer.

"Let's turn out the lights."

CHAPTER 4
JARED

"LET'S TURN OUT THE LIGHTS."

Her whispered request deflates the moment. I'm so close to having Banner Morales for the first time, and she thinks we'll turn out the lights? No way we're fucking in the dark.

"Hell no."

Disappointment scurries across her pretty face at my refusal.

God, she has such a pretty face.

I hate that someone made her doubt herself, the only person out of hundreds to answer our asshole professor in Russian from the very back of a crowded lecture hall. Who challenged and stretched the greatest minds at Kerrington with her curiosity and keen intellect. I've never seen her anything but badass until tonight. I've wanted Banner for a long time, and with the New York internship looming, I will have her. I'll make her want me so much, it won't matter how many states separate us next semester.

"Then it's a no." She bites her lip and glances at my mouth one more time like she'll miss it. If she feels regret, she clears her throat and chases it away, standing from the couch. "We should probably hit the books anyway."

She moves to step around me, but I catch her wrist and pull her flush against my bare chest. She looks up at me, our wills clashing, both determined to get our way. Our eyes gridlock, neither of us yielding, but underneath her resolve, a shadow of something else lurks.

Fear? Insecurity? As much time as we've spent together this semester, I don't really know her well enough to be sure. And I want to know Banner. Badly.

Fuck a fat girl.

Prescott's harsh words from earlier return to mock me. For a moment, guilt assails me. He ordered me to have sex with Banner for admission to the Pride, and this same night I'm doing just that. But not for him, not for that. I've walked away from the Pride.

Has she heard things like that before? Maybe not to her face. Maybe subtly been made to feel like she's not sexy as hell. But to me, she is. I honestly don't know what's under all those layers Banner wears, but those aren't the layers I care about. I want to peel back her surface and study her soul.

Study her soul? What the hell? I don't recognize myself. Who is this guy? And who gave his balls to Banner Morales?

I have to admit I *am* different with Banner because she's different. I'm not great boyfriend material. Just ask Cindy. I'm not very attentive, but when I'm with Banner, it's hard to focus on anything else. I lose interest quickly, but I find myself thinking about things Banner said, about her opinions, days later. She fascinates me without even really trying. I want to know her as intimately as possible.

Her beautiful same-size lips settle into an immovable line. We stand here like she's waiting for my decision, but she holds all the power. The ball is still in her court because she's willing to walk away from this, to go back to our books and act like this never happened, but I'm not. I've had sex with a lot of girls. The most gorgeous girls on campus and beyond, but I've never had Banner, and right now I want her more than everything. More than all the Cindys combined. Important rule of negotiation: Know what you're willing to give up before you start. One thing I know for sure: I'm not willing to give up on this.

I stretch my arm toward the wall and turn out the lights.

With the light snuffed out, my other senses rise, hunting for her in the dark. The smell of her hair and her quick, shallow breaths. My sight adjusts until the heavy black curtain completely obscuring her fades to gray. Light from the outer room spills under the door, revealing just the shape, the outline of her, but still camouflaging details. I cup her cheek, taking a moment to appreciate the softness of her skin, the silky hair brushing my knuckles. I'm not an idiot. She wants the lights out because she's self-conscious, but from my perspective, she has nothing to be ashamed of.

"I think you're beautiful, Ban."

"You do?" she asks, her voice hushed.

My words surprise me as much as they seem to surprise her because I don't say shit like that to girls. The prettiest ones usually seem to already know, which makes any admiration I'd express redundant. But Banner... She's so beautiful, and I'm not sure she knows.

"I do." I push the hair away from her face.

"Uh...thank you." Her laugh isn't much more than a breath. "The lights are out, so I'm not sure that compliment counts."

"I know your face by heart. You have seven freckles here." I swipe a finger over the straight bridge of her nose and drift down to caress her full lips and the tiny dent in her cheek her smile displays. "And a dimple right here."

I explore the smooth skin of her nape, under a heavy fall of hair.

"Now I want to know your body, too," I say softly. "Take off your clothes for me, Banner."

After a sharply indrawn breath, she raises her arms. The rustle of her clothes—the sweatshirt, jeans, socks, shoes—being discarded whisper in the dark. I approximate her by touch, reaching for her arms and closing my fingers around the softness, the velvety skin. I lower my head and run my nose along her neck, discovering.

"You always smell so good." I've wanted to tell her that since the first night we studied here.

"Pretty Pastel," she replies, her laugh low, nervous.

"What?" I pause.

"The smell. It's my dryer sheets. The scent is Pretty Pastel."

"I like it." I resume my exploration, running a palm over her shoulder, her collarbone, until I find the soft, full weight of her breasts, testing them in my hands, cupping them, holding them, brushing the nipples with my thumbs until they pebble and her breaths come harshly.

"You like that?" I ask.

I see her head nod in the semi-darkness. "Yeah. It feels good."

Her touch startles me in the best way, her hand finding my face, traveling over my mouth, eyes, and hair. I sense her approach, feel tiny pants of breath on my lips, and anticipation has me panting, too, shortens my breath and sharpens my senses. Her mouth seeks mine, eager and sweet when she kisses me. Her pleasure, her excitement matches, answers, fans mine.

I guide her back down to the couch and, with a hand at her shoulder, urge her to stretch out. I'd shave points off my GPA for a glimpse of her, but she doesn't want that. I get it, so I settle for a taste.

At first I just rub my lips over her nipples, back and forth until they tighten and lift under my mouth, and then I wrap my lips around the tip, stretch open to encompass the full swell. Suck, lick, rub. Suck, lick, rub. Suck, lick, rub. I set a sensual rhythm that incites us both.

"Oh." Every sound she makes is a mating call.

I walk my hands down her sides, over her waist, and roll the pads of my fingers through the short hairs sheltering her pussy. I find the nub crowning her slit and caress it, varying the pace from swift and urgent to agonizingly slow. Her restraint, her tenuous control is palpable, and I want to shatter it. I scoot to the other end of the couch and carefully slide one of her legs off the cushion, cracking her open. I fit my shoulders between her thighs and lower my head. For a moment, I just blow over her wet flesh, and while I'm breathing out, I'm breathing her in.

Sometimes a dish carries a scent so rich you taste it before it hits your tongue. Your olfactory sense preludes your taste buds. That's Banner's pussy, so sweet and musky it's as much flavor as scent, and I taste her before even taking my first bite, my first sip. Before my tongue swipes through the soaked silky folds. I spread her and for a few seconds content myself by simply rubbing my lips between hers, gathering her wetness and licking it away.

"*Hěn hào chī,*" I say softly, a wicked grin she can't see to appreciate stamped on my face.

Very delicious.

"Oh my God." A laugh swallows her gasp. Her knees jerk against my head, but I press them open wider, determined that she may have denied me sight, but I'll taste; I'll eat as much as I want. I feast between her legs, sloppily, roughly, famished. My face is wet, and my tongue aches by the time I'm done. She's making these little sobbing sounds that have me so close to spilling. Her hands rifle through my hair, scraping my scalp while she grinds her pussy in my face.

"*Chinga,*" she whispers.

"What'd you say?" I demand, lifting my head.

A silence follows before she answers.

"Nothing," she replies hastily. "It's nothing."

"It's Spanish?" I persist. "What does it mean?"

"Jared," she groans. "Don't."

"Tell me or I leave you just like this."

It's an empty threat because leaving her "just like this" means leaving me "just like this," and there's no way *this* ends any way other than me inside her.

"What's *chinga* mean, Ban?"

"It means…" There are resignation and reluctance in her sigh. "Fuck. It means fuck, okay?"

"Ahhh, like, fuck," I say, lowering my head and closing my mouth over her clit again. "That feels good?"

"Oh, God," she pants. "Yeah."

"Like, fuck"—I drag my tongue from her asshole to the top of her slit—"don't stop?"

"Please," she begs, her fingers twisting in my hair. "Please don't stop."

I fumble around on the floor until I find my jeans and reach into the pocket for my wallet. This I've done in the dark. I could put on a condom in a coma.

The narrowness of the sofa makes it awkward, so I sit on the couch, find her in the dark, and tug her to her knees. And the same way I felt her pleasure, I feel her freeze and then pull back, away.

"Uh, no." She clears her throat. "You get on top."

Whatever. On top. Underneath. On the side. *In* is all I care about right now. Back on my knees at the end of the couch, I bring her legs over my shoulders. I touch her again, and she's still dripping wet, slick, hot. I poise myself at her entrance, and though we can't see each other, I look to where I know her eyes should be, and I sense her looking where mine should be. And even in the dark, I think we see each other. There's an intimacy to the darkness. I see less of her, but I somehow feel this more deeply. Every smell, every sound, every texture becomes a clue to her pleasure. I plunge in, and we both gasp. She clamps around me. Is she a virgin? I didn't even think to ask. I should have.

"You okay, Ban? You've…uh, done this before, right?"

"Yes, it's just…just been a while. Is everything okay?"

Okay? Is nirvana okay? Is utopia *okay*? Because that is what Banner's tight pussy feels like around my hungry cock. Like someone tossed paradise and heaven into a blender to make this moment.

"Yeah, it's good," I say.

Understatement. No need to reveal that her pussy sent me into an existential crisis.

I withdraw only for a second and to the very tip, but it feels like torture until I push back in. She surrounds me. The smell of her invading my nostrils, the taste of her lingering on my tongue, the feel of her gripping not just my cock but my whole body.

Banner Morales has a hold on me.

"*Chinga,*" I whisper in her ear with my next thrust.

"God, Jared." She tightens around me.

"*Chinga,*" I say again, plunging in as far as her body will allow. I want to reach the bottom, to mark and claim her from the inside out.

"*Sí, sí,*" she pants, her English disintegrating. "*Por favor.*"

The sound of her begging in her first language, knowing we've stripped away not just the layers of lumpy sweatshirt and baggy pants but the layers we hide behind and use to protect ourselves, undoes me. Her body contracts around me, and I empty into her with a roar that reiterates what I told her earlier tonight. Darwin. Maslow. Who cares. In the end, we *are* just animals. Primitives driven by urges we barely understand but, with the right person, find ourselves slave to.

Banner's the right person.

I don't care if her internship is on the moon, there's no way this was the last time. We'll do it again, the sooner the better. And I guarantee the next time I have her, there will be light.

CHAPTER 5
BANNER

AFTERSHOCK.

How the earth tremors following a seismic disruption. A result of great upheaval at the core.

That so perfectly describes what I'm feeling. A disruption. I'm not sure if it started *at* my core or shook me *to* it.

But I know at the epicenter lies Jared Foster.

We're facing each other on the narrow couch, my bare leg slotted between his and my head tucked under his chin. He strokes my back, my hair, my shoulders. He can't seem to stop touching me, and for a few moments, I don't care about my lumps or dimples or rolls. It just feels good to be touched this way—with passion and care. Byron was the last guy I shared any kind of intimacy with, and every touch was a lie. There's always been a frankness, an honesty between Jared and me. It translates to physical intimacy, and I want to hold on to it as long as my logical brain will allow. I want to stop asking *why me* and just enjoy *him*, us together.

He smells like yesterday's bodywash and clean sweat. And… him. Whatever "he" is naturally, I detect it under everything else. For whatever reason, I have a temporary brain lapse and dart my tongue out to taste the shallow well at the base of his throat. Salty and smooth. Maybe he won't notice that bit of stalkerism.

"Did you just lick me?"

Ugh.

"No." *Deny, deny, deny.*

"You did." He dips his head, his chuckle feathering over my lips. "You licked me."

"I just wanted to—"

"No need to apologize. You can lick me anywhere." He tips my chin. "As long as I can lick you back."

His tongue passes over my neck, and I shudder. Another aftershock. My skin prickles. I shift my legs between his, and my thigh grazes his dick.

"Oh. I'm sorry. I—"

"You keep apologizing for things that feel good."

I see the outline of his head moving toward me. He's going to kiss me. Even with time to prepare, to brace myself, I'm still not ready for the possessive fit of his mouth over mine, the slow, lazy stroke of his tongue, the thrust of his hips mimicking the motions of our mouths. His hand slips between my legs, separating the lips of my pussy and sliding up and down the wet slit, soothing the sore tissues. He did not hold back and took me hard. It was rough and thorough and the best thing that has happened to my vagina.

Like, ever.

He shifts his weight so he's hovering over me, his elbows digging into the cushions on either side of my head. When he settles between my thighs, I reflexively wrap my legs around his waist.

"Why, Ms. Morales," he laughs into my hair. "I do believe you want to be fucked again."

"Oh, I… I just…"

"Let's go back to your place." His breath is warm against my face. He kisses the sensitive spot behind my ear. "There's no way we're doing it again on this couch. The next time it'll be in a bed."

His hands roam over my thighs clenched around him, and he grips my butt, locking us tighter.

My wide, fleshy butt. God, he casts some kind of sensual spell on me. With every kiss and touch, he makes me feel like the most beautiful woman in the world long enough to forget the rolls and dimples Byron made sure to tell his friends about. Maybe somehow I'm the one who cast a spell on Jared, and as soon as the lights come on, that spell will break.

"Maybe I should go." I drop my legs and push lightly against his chest.

"Okay, we can do it again on the couch, if that's what you want," he says quickly. "Just stay."

"Jared!" I giggle and shake my head.

"At least promise I'll see you tomorrow. We don't have much time before you leave for New York."

"Why is that so significant to you?" I ask, frowning even though he can't see my face. "I mean, I admit that was…the sex was amazing, but this is all kind of sudden."

"Not to me." He clears his throat and brushes my hair back, cupping the back of my head. "I've been wanting this all semester, Ban."

I snort, unable to keep my earlier disbelief completely at bay.

"You honestly expect me to believe you've been dating Cindy all year, who I'm pretty sure is Miss Iowa, and you've been secretly longing to be with me?"

"Miss Idaho," he corrects. "But, yeah, pretty much."

He runs a hand over my leg and wraps me around him again. Now all I can think of is how thick my thighs are. How my stomach probably feels all soft and squishy under that sheet of muscled abs. Self-consciousness rushes back in, and I shove a little harder, dislodging him enough to slide off the couch.

"Like I said, I need to go." I feel around on the floor, searching for my sweatshirt. I'm determined to at least put that on before I turn on the lights. The sex was off the charts. Cloaked in darkness, I fooled myself that I was a sensual creature who was Jared's match. A small voice inside protests that it wasn't the dark that made me feel beautiful. It was Jared.

What does that voice know?

I've found my sweatshirt and am about to put it on when the door bangs open and the lights come on.

In my shock, I don't move for a second, and I'm standing completely naked in front of not only Jared, who has the wide-angle view of my ass from behind, but William Prescott, Benton Carter, and several other guys I don't know but vaguely recognize from campus. All their eyes crawl over the roll around my middle, the dimples in my thighs, the tiny tufts under my arms because I skip shaves in winter, and the dark triangle of hair I keep neatly trimmed between my legs.

"Oh my God." I squint against the sudden brightness of light after being in the dark for so long and instinctively fold my arms across my breasts.

"What the hell!" Jared yells from behind me.

His voice galvanizes me, and I grab the panties tangled up with my tennis shoes and fumble to get the sweatshirt on. I can't find the holes for the arms, though, and it's turned inside out. *I'm* turned inside out. My thoughts are so scrambled I can't even run for cover. My hands are shaking too badly to execute even this basic motor function.

Jared takes the sweatshirt from my trembling fingers and jerks it over my head, pushing my arms through. He turns me so his broad shoulders block out the rest of the room, a brick wall between me and all those greedy, curious eyes. He presses his forehead to mine, his fingers gripping the nape of my neck through layers of hair. I look at him for the first time since he turned off the lights. I've never seen this look on his face. Desperate, almost afraid.

"Ban," he says urgently, still clutching my neck. "You have to let me explain."

"Explain what?" I ask, confounded by him, by them, by tonight. I'm on another planet, floating because the law of gravity doesn't apply here.

"You actually did it," Prescott says.

I peer around Jared to meet the mocking malice of William Prescott. Why is he here? How are they here?

"I didn't think you had the balls, Foster," he says, running his eyes over my bare legs disparagingly. "Or the stomach for it. But you did it. You've earned it. You're in."

Jared wheels around, fist raised, and lunges for Prescott, but Bent steps between them.

"You don't want to do that, Foster," Bent says, his voice pitched low but still reaching my ears. "I know this is fucked up. I'm only here to keep you both out of jail."

"You son of a bitch," Jared growls over Bent's shoulder, straining against his hold. "I'll kill you for this."

"Now, is that any way to speak to your new brother?" Prescott asks, a wide grin spreading over his face. "I told you to fuck the fat girl, and you did, so you're in. I'll excuse all this drama. I understand you're trying to protect her feelings. I wouldn't have come and made this awkward, but you realize we had to verify you completed the last rite of passage."

Fuck the fat girl.

Rite of passage.

The words sledgehammer my head, muddling my thoughts. But one thing is clear. Jared's in? He had to fuck the fat girl, *me*, to get into the stupid fraternity he's been chasing all semester? I press one hand to my swimming head and one to my heaving stomach.

"I'm gonna be..." I focus on swallowing my nausea and not further humiliating myself.

"You're gonna be sick?" Prescott asks, his glance falling over the length of my body. "Maybe it was something you *ate*."

The cruel barb punctures the balloon of humiliation and shame that has been swelling inside ever since they barged in. And with a *pop*, my fury explodes.

All the high pressure and hot air whoosh from my mouth in

one gush. I've had about enough of these animals who think they're better than I am because they have dicks and I don't. My mother may not have known what to do with a little girl asking about the theory of relativity or been able to teach me Russian, but one thing she did instill in me was her take-no-crap fight, and it claws its way past my embarrassment. My advisor wants killer instinct? Well, here the hell you go.

I'm standing in a roomful of frat boys, wearing a sweatshirt that barely clears the tops of my thighs. They might see my panties, and my knees are shaking. My palms practically drip sweat. Every doubt and insecurity about my body crowds in on me, but I force those aside. I shove past Jared and my humiliation and fear until I'm standing directly in front of Prescott. He's several inches taller, and I have to look up at him. I'm at eye level with his huge Adam's apple that threatens to poke through his skinny neck with one big gulp.

"This is about the internship, right?" I demand, stepping so close I smell his repugnant aftershave. "You're pissed that I beat you out for the Bagley? Well, tough luck, you sorry, entitled, Ichabod Crane–looking motherfucker. I beat you with something you wouldn't recognize if it hit you. Hard work. If it wasn't for your daddy's gener-ous donations, you wouldn't even *be* on this campus."

I poke his chest, and he stumbles back a step, disconcerted that the wounded animal is fighting back.

"So you told the hottest guy on campus to fuck me for your little fraternity or whatever you boys have created to compensate for the fact that you'll barely make it in the real world." I force a laugh that's the absolute opposite of how my heart is banging and break-ing. "That's your revenge? You repay me in orgasms? Feel free to take your resentment out on me anytime, Prescott."

I step another inch closer and go up on my toes until we are practically nose to nose, until I can fire-breathe the words over his lips.

"As you know, I'll be off campus in New York next semester for our department's most coveted internship, but for the last few days I have left here, stay out of my way," I grit out, shaking my hair back and widening my eyes for good measure like the crazy Latina shrew he probably stereotyped me as. "Where I'm from, we eat little boys like you for breakfast, and I have no doubt, if pressed, I *can* kick your narrow ass."

I curl my lip and glare.

"Despite your daddy's money and all your connections and this little post-pubescent posse at your back, when it comes down to it, you're just a pathetic boy with nothing to show for *himself.*"

I grab my jeans from the pile, along with my shoes and socks. In complete awkward silence, I pull my jeans on, looking each one of those cowards in the eye while I do it. Even when I have to wiggle and wiggle to get my jeans over my hips and buttoned. I don't know how much longer my bravado will hold. It's straining and about to break. I rush past them all to leave the back room, determined to get out of here before the dam bursts and tears give away just how shattered I am. I'm scooping up my backpack and on my way out the door when a gentle hand stops me. I look over my shoulder and cannot believe the audacity of Jared Foster.

"Banner, wait." That desperation brightens his eyes to azure. It *looks* like desperation. But he's really good at making things look like what they're not. He made me think he liked me, that he *wanted* me. Mama didn't raise no fool, but tonight that's exactly what he made me. And over what? A sculpted body, blond hair, and blue eyes. I did it again, fell for a man's lies and the flattery of his touch. Am I that desperate? That pathetic?

"You better let me go right now," I snarl, my eyes tracing a jagged line from his grip on my arm to that damn handsome face.

"No, you will listen." Frustration sketches lines around his mouth and between his brows.

My hand flies up and slams into his cheek. I've never slapped anyone before. Despite my hubris with Prescott, I abhor violence of any kind, but I don't regret the bright-red handprint blooming over his cheekbone. Anger flares in the stare we hold, his bouncing off mine.

"Oh shit," someone says from the back room.

I glance over his shoulder to find all the guys gathered at the door, watching our exchange. Prescott's smirk and a few snickers are last straws. Hot tears prick my eyes, and I jerk away, walking as swiftly as I can toward the door. On the sidewalk, I can't hold back the torrent of emotions any longer. A sob erupts from that place I've been guarding ever since those lights came on. The indignity, the humiliation, the cruelty of the situation press against me on all sides, closing in and trying to crush me. I don't even know how I make it home through the blur of tears, but as soon as I am on the other side of my apartment door, I slide my back down the wall until my butt hits the floor.

And the tears won't stop. I'm shaking, trembling at the shocking cruelty of those guys.

Aftershock.

How the earth tremors following a seismic disruption. A result of great upheaval at the core. And at the epicenter lies Jared Foster.

I hate him.

I hate them all.

I hate the wretched, pitiful sound of my own tears. I hate the sting of shame piercing my heart like a thorn. I hate my stupidity, my naivete believing Jared Foster wanted someone like me instead of someone like Cindy. I hate the way my thighs spread, stretching the denim of my jeans. The way my legs rub together when I walk. I hate this roll of fat hanging over my waistband.

This body is an inadequate shell that doesn't reflect the powerful, confident person I am inside. And yet there's a part of me that knows it shouldn't matter. That knows whether I'm a size 2 or 22, I'm still smart and ambitious and kind and generous. And, yes, speak Italian, Russian, and a little Chinese.

It shouldn't matter, but I have to be honest with myself as I weep uncontrollably and admit that it does. Right now, it does.

"Banner, open the door."

Jared's voice bellows from the hall.

Could this night get any worse?

"I'm not leaving." He gives the door four successive bangs. "You left your coat and your clients' laundry. You have to get those, so you'll have to open the door."

I cup my hand over my mouth to catch the sobs that won't stay down. He won't hear me crying for his fine sorry ass. I can imagine how glamorous I look with my just-fucked hair all over the place, puffy eyes, and blotchy cheeks. When I cry this hard, the blood vessels around my eyes always burst. Technical term: facial petechiae. Layman's term: hot mess.

"Okay. You want to do this." I hear a sliding sound on the other side of the door and assume he sits on the floor, mirroring my position. "We can do this. I'll stay out here until you open the door. I swear I had nothing to do with this. Prescott is a liar."

I sniff, hope pushing through like a tiny bud in a storm somehow preserved from the wind and the rain, but I keep my voice hard and sure. I've seen what he does with my vulnerability. I focus on my anger to dry up my tears.

"So you had nothing to do with it? He's lying? Did Prescott ask you to"—I clear my throat and close my eyes but force myself to say the words—"fuck the fat girl—me in case we're confused about that. Yes or no?"

There are a few seconds of guilty silence through the door before he speaks.

"It wasn't like—"

"Yes. Or. No."

"Yes, he did tell me that if I wanted to get into the Pride, I had to fuck...you, but I—"

"The Pride?" I run through the various fraternities on campus and cannot place that one. "What the hell is the Pride? Like lions?"

"It's a secret society that I'm not allowed to talk about. I've signed papers that I won't, even though I told them tonight I'm not joining. Not after they asked... Not after what Prescott wanted me to do."

"So let me get this straight. You've been running around like a fool all semester to get into this secret society of privileged spoiled brats, and you've done everything they asked. Tonight they crossed the line when they asked you to fuck the fat girl."

"Banner, stop saying that," he cuts in harshly.

"I'm sorry it's *so* hard on you hearing that I'm fat," I say, every word sardonic.

"That's not what I meant."

"And you," I continue without acknowledging his denial, "were so *outraged* by Prescott's heinous suggestion that you told them you don't want to play his little games anymore."

"It's not... Yeah. I told them to fuck off."

"Oh, I just bet you did. Then you come to me, and all of a sudden, when you've shown no indication of being attracted to me, you just *happen* to decide we should fuck." I get on my knees and face the door, glaring at him with X-ray vision through the cheap faux wood. "Am I getting this right, Jared?"

"No, it's not right," he yells back, frustration reaching through the flimsy door. "I told you I've liked you all semester."

"And Cindy? Why did you stay with her if you were *pining* for me?"

"I don't... Shit, I don't know. Habit? Someone convenient to fuck? What do you want me to say? I've never pretended to be anyone but who I am, Ban. I'm not gonna lie to you now."

"Maybe you were curious," I offer, fresh tears burning my eyes. "How it would be with someone..."

Fat.

"Like me," I finish aloud, biting the insides of my cheeks to control the tears. "Maybe you didn't want anyone to know. Were ashamed and needed someone like Cindy for show."

"That's bullshit." Something slams into the door, startling me because I'm so close to it. "None of that is true, Banner. I promise you it isn't. God, just open the door and give me a chance."

"Why?" I ask, forcing a hollow laugh through my tears. "Let's just call it a one-night stand and move on. I'm sure this won't be your first time doing that."

"It was more than that, and you know it." He pauses. "It was more to me, Banner."

I hate him. I hate the way he makes lies sound true and makes me melt inside when I should be hardening myself against him.

"Look, one night in four years is not some grand passion," I tell him.

"But how do we know what it *could* be if you don't give me a chance?"

"You had your chance, Foster, if you even wanted it."

"I wanted it," he growls through the door. "Don't tell me what I wanted. You wanted it, too."

"When I thought it was real, yeah."

"It was fucking real. Just..." His voice trails off into the silence of the hall. "Believe me. Just please believe me, Banner."

All the parts that felt beautiful with the lights off war with all the parts that felt hideous under the bright glare, under their cruel stares. I've never felt the way I did tonight with Jared, but how can I know what really happened? Is it worth risking this kind of pain again if he's lying to me?

No. I have dreams, ambitions, goals that will require all my focus. There is an uphill climb ahead of me, and I won't make it if I'm broken.

"I don't believe you," I finally reply. "And I want you to leave me alone. Here's what's gonna happen. We'll take our final. We'll go our separate ways. I'm moving to New York, and you can go wherever the hell you want."

"Banner, don't do this."

"Go."

"I'm not leaving."

"Yeah, you are, buddy," someone says from the hall. Sounds like my neighbor, Mr. Harden. "He bothering you, Banner?"

"No, I'm her…" Jared sighs heavily enough for me to hear it. "Please, sir, just stay out of this."

"Banner, you want him to leave?"

Yes.

No.

I don't know.

"Yes," I answer, hoping I sound more sure than I am. "I need him to leave me alone."

"That's it," Mr. Harden says. "I'm calling the cops."

"Come on, man," Jared says. "We're just talking. Banner, tell him."

"Call the cops, Mr. Harden." I sound steady, but hot tears squiggle streaks over my cheeks.

"Banner," Jared growls.

"Just go before the cops get here." I press my forehead to the door. "And we can forget this night ever happened."

"You want to forget tonight?" Jared asks softly.

Forget the best sex of my life? Forget intimacy, closeness I didn't think was possible? Set aside what I thought was true friendship between Jared and me? Dismiss the possibility of what this *could* have been had it been real?

"Yes." My tone is final, cutting him out for good. "Leave my coat and my clients' laundry. Mr. Harden, those are my things. Don't let him take them."

"Really, Banner?" Jared asks, doing an Oscar-worthy job of sounding not only angry but hurt.

"Really, Jared."

"You can't just erase a whole semester. At least not our friendship. You can't just spit on it."

"Why not? You did." The words slide out, coating my tongue with bitterness.

"So that's it?" he asks after a brief pause. "You're just gonna let Prescott win?"

"Prescott won't win." I seize any vestiges of pride I have left. "I will."

CHAPTER 6
BANNER

I'M NOT FROM A SMALL TOWN BY ANY MEANS. I GREW UP IN SAN Diego, where my mother moved from Mexico when she was a child. The city sprawls and covers a lot of ground, but it can't be bothered to bustle. The small college town in Maryland where Kerrington is situated doesn't bustle either. New York bustles. It *hustles*. It truly never sleeps and is ever-grinding. It took a while to get used to the noise and the pace and the smell of urgency in the air.

Okay, I'm still not used to it, but I love it. There's an obstinacy to this place. A grit and determination that hover over the city like dense fog. I may not have ever lived in a city this large, but I've always been obstinate, always been driven. There's no doubt in my mind I'm in the right place.

"Daydreaming?"

I glance up from my laptop to find Mitch Sanderson, a fellow intern, standing at my desk.

"Uh, no." I close my laptop because he's always in my business and looking over my shoulder. "Just pulling together some analysis for Cal."

Cal Bagley is Bagley & Associates' founding partner. He's also the best friend of Prescott's father. Or maybe he's in that Pride thing Jared was joining.

Ugh. I promised myself I wouldn't think about Jared Foster, but that doesn't always work. When I'm awake, I can tame my thoughts. When I'm asleep? A different matter entirely. My brain and my heart believe he's disgusting and cruel and a phony. My body, though? Ain't buying it. More than once I've awakened from dreams of that night, of how he made me feel. Not just the incredible sex but the closeness. And not just of that night but that entire semester. We were genuinely friends, or so I thought.

"You can't tell me you aren't daydreaming," Mitch says, "and then zone out in the middle of our conversation."

"Sorry." I laugh and open my laptop. "I should get back to work."

"What're you working on?"

"Not so much working as catching up on this Quinn Barrow story."

"The runner who lost her leg?" Mitch rubs his chin, his mark of concentration I've come to learn. "It was a freak thing, right?"

"Yeah," I say, swallowing the emotion that scalds my throat every time I read her story. "She dislocated her knee, and it cut an artery. No blood to the leg for hours, and they had to amputate."

I glance at the side-by-side pictures accompanying the article. In the first photo, Quinn is running, chest pushed forward, smile blazing white, auburn hair whipping behind her like a fiery pennant as she crashes through the finish line. The second photo is of a ghost with no smile, lines of beginning bitterness settling around her mouth. A solemn figure staring vacantly into the camera from a hospital bed.

"You do know we're in the business of signing performing athletes, right?" Mitch asks. "Not has-beens."

I should be surprised by his harshness, but I'm not. Not anymore. Most agents see these athletes as commodities. So do the teams they play for. And I get it. Sports is a business, and if I've chosen this as my career, I gotta play the game.

In the two months I've been here, I've learned a few things. Darwin wasn't all wrong, and neither was my advisor. This industry *is* survival of the fittest. It's a fast machine with nonstop gears that can grind your soul to dust. It's not for the faint of heart. I've seen ruthlessness at its finest here. The competition for talent is fierce and requires constant vigilance in scouting, recruiting, pursuing, signing. Elite athletes have earning potential most people can't even wrap their minds around. When you find extraordinary talent, convincing them you will represent them best is crucial. Every other agent thinks the same thing, so distinguishing yourself often and early is the name of the game.

I don't just want to be at the top of the food chain, though. Achieving has always been a driving force for me, but so has contributing and being a part of something bigger than myself.

Killer with a heart.

I hate that Jared's words, his encouragement, give me perspective as I figure out my place in this jungle. Was that part of his *fuck the fat girl* act? The things he said and did that night? I don't know what was real, what I can trust, but his words keep coming back to me.

"She's not a has-been," I finally reply, deliberately turning my attention back to the screen, hoping Mitch will read it as the dismissal it is. "Maybe she just needs some help getting back on her feet."

"Don't you mean 'foot'?"

I cut a disgusted glance up at him. Men are essentially *boys*. Just boys whose penises kept growing…some more than others. That's what I've come to realize being the only girl in the room most of the time. Their sophomoric humor and crude jokes turn racist or sexist as soon as they forget a Hispanic woman is in their midst. Add in the fact that I'm overweight, and I'm basically a piece of furniture to them within five minutes.

But this sofa still has ears and a heart, which is more than I can say for guys like Mitch.

"I'm sorry," he mumbles when I stare at him with silent censure. "That was in bad taste."

"I should be used to it by now," I say, hoping I didn't disguise the insult in the words so well that he doesn't feel it. "But you guys continue to surprise me with your insensitivity."

"Sensitivity won't get you paid," Mitch returns flatly. "Go ahead and waste your time crying over an amputee who wouldn't clock one commission. I'm going after a fish I can actually fry."

"Which fish?" I stuff down my outrage and school my face into fewer fucks.

"Alonzo Vidale." Mitch preens. "Cal's meeting with him today."

Alonzo Vidale is one of the most promising international players poised for this summer's NBA Draft. A definite first-rounder.

"And you think Cal will bring you into the meeting?" I ask. "A lowly intern?"

"He hasn't said it in so many words," Mitch says, wearing a smug expression, "but I'm becoming pretty much indispensable around here."

"In your two months of fetching coffee and making copies? Yeah, where would we be without you?"

His smile dissolves into a sneer.

"At least Bagley knows I'm alive."

"Just because my lips aren't permanently puckered to kiss his ass doesn't mean my good work goes overlooked."

I hope.

It's no secret Cal Bagley has a group of guys he takes under his wing. "Under his wing" means drinks after work, "special parties" fully stocked with strippers, and any manner of "dick tricks" in which I have no interest. Mitch is definitely in that group. Come to think of it, I'm pretty sure Mitch's father is one of Cal's best friends, too. Probably another Pride connection.

"A little pucker goes a long way." He tilts his head, and his eyes wander from my face and over my body in the shapeless dress I put on this morning. "You know, Morales, with a little effort, you might not be half bad."

"And with a little effort, you might evolve into a Homo sapien."

"Jokes." A tight smile plays around his weak mouth. "Keep making them when I land Vidale or someone else from this next crop."

"You know you can't actually sign anyone," I remind him. "We technically don't have our degrees yet and haven't taken the agent's exam."

"We're only months away from graduation, and that exam'll be a breeze." Mitch picks invisible lint from the shoulder of his suit. "It's open book, and you get to take in notes. How hard can it be?"

"Maybe, but I'm still studying my ass off. I need to make sure I'm up to speed on the intricacies of the collective bargaining agreement."

"Yeah, okay. You do that." Mitch rolls his eyes and picks up the photo of my family from my cubicle desk and replaces it quickly. "Meanwhile I get to meet Vidale."

"I'm kind of surprised he's ready for this process already."

"Why do you say that?"

"Um, because his entire family was just killed in a car accident last month?"

I swear these guys have their feelings surgically removed before they enter this field.

"Ahhh, yeah." Mitch nods, scrunching his face into what he probably thinks passes for sympathy. "Real men move on. He knows he's gotta strike while the iron is hot. With the draft coming up, he needs to get his shit settled. Sign with an agent who can start scoping endorsements and talking to executives, getting him workouts with teams. The whole nine."

"We *need* to scope a good grief counselor," I mumble, looking under my desk for the Tupperware containing my lunch. I'm so hungry it's hard to focus on what Mitch is saying.

As if that struggle wasn't real enough already.

I've been doing much better without the demands of a heavy college course load. Eating more regularly and paying attention to what I eat, down five pounds. I'm still tuning out the drone of Mitch's voice and looking for string cheese in the oversized bag under my desk when Cal's booming voice startles me.

I jerk up, banging my head on the desk above. I slide out, rubbing the sore spot and blinking back tears.

"You okay?" Cal demands, his gaze zeroing in on my tears.

"Yeah. Just, um, hit my head."

Out of habit, I go to push hair behind my ear, forgetting that it's up today. I have no idea what to do with my hands right now, so they just hang in the air for a few seconds before I drop them.

I'm such a goober, and by the look Cal is giving me, he knows it.

"Yeah, well, I need you," he says brusquely and starts walking away. "Conference room. Now, Morales."

Mitch and I exchange wide-eyed looks.

"What'd you do to piss him off?" Mitch asks, barely suppressed glee shining in his eyes.

"I have no idea." I scurry after Cal, mentally running through my latest assignments. I thought I'd thoroughly completed every task.

Cal, wearing an impatient look, stands in front of the closed conference room door.

"You speak a lot of languages, right?" he asks abruptly.

"Uh, not a lot. Just Spanish, Russian, some Italian and Mandarin Chinese." A nervous laugh trips and falls from my mouth. "Oh, and English. I speak English."

"I need your Spanish." He looks over his shoulder at the closed conference room door. "Got Alonzo Vidale in there."

"Oh." My stomach turns over at the prospect of helping with such a huge potential client.

"Apparently he doesn't speak much English."

"Really?" I pinch my brows together. "From what I recall, his family was from Argentina's middle class. It would be somewhat unusual for him not to speak any English."

"No idea," Cal says with a shrug. "But he says he needs someone to translate for him."

"Of course." I tug at the neckline of my dress. I wish I'd worn something nicer today.

The first thing I think when I see Alonzo Vidale is that photos don't do him justice. His dark hair is scooped back from his face in a tight ponytail at the base of his neck, but a few silky strands escape and fall over dark, soulful eyes.

The second thing I notice is an ill-disguised sorrow that he wears like ashes on his head. There's a droop to his broad shoulders, and the wide, full lips look like they've never known a smile. I think of my family—Mama, Papa, my sister Camilla and her daughter Anna. The devastation I would feel if I lost them all in one day, it's unimaginable, but that's what this man endured just a month ago.

He has the long, sensitive fingers of a musician. His hands look more like he plays the piano than basketball, and I scour my memory for details of his background. He hasn't been playing basketball long by American standards. Most of our ballers started on playgrounds, rose through AAU ranks, played in college at least the obligatory year, and then after pouring years of their lives into the sport, only a fraction make it to the NBA. From what I recall, Alonzo discovered his talent much later. He came on America's radar when he played for Argentina's team in the last Olympics. As one of the few possible stars emerging from Argentina, everyone has been calling him the next Manu Ginóbili.

Alonzo glances up from the conference room table, looking from Cal to me, eyes narrowed. I'm surprised he is alone, no handlers or anyone accompanying him, but usually at this stage before an agent is selected, an athlete only has family. The magnitude of his loss weighs on me again, and even though I know when he stands he'll be six six, he looks incredibly vulnerable seated at the huge conference room table alone.

"Uh, this is Banner Morales," Cal says, pulling out a chair at the table for me to sit. "She will be…"

He flounders, uncustomary for Cal, and looks to me for help.

"I have no idea how much he understands," he finishes with a shrug.

"I'm guessing enough to realize we're discussing him while he's in the room," I say, offering an apologetic smile to Alonzo. "*Hola. Buenos días. ¿Cómo estás?*"

His eyes crinkle slightly at the corners when I offer the greeting.

"*Hola*, Señorita Morales," he replies, dipping his head in my direction.

I look to Cal for cues of what he wants me to say.

"Um, tell him that we first want to say we've been impressed by the footage we've seen of him," Cal says. "Including his performance in the Olympics and his workouts."

I hesitate, torn between translating to the letter and at least priming the pump a little.

"We first want to say," I start in Spanish, but falter when I meet the shadows in those dark eyes.

His brows lift, inquiring, waiting.

"We first want to say," I begin again, "that we are so very sorry for your recent loss."

He flicks a speculative glance from me to Cal and back to me.

"I cannot imagine what you've experienced over the last month," I press forward in a rush. "And you have our deepest sympathy."

A breath of silence follows my statement before he responds. "*Gracias.*"

I dive in before Cal questions why I'm still going and convey the initial words he asked me to say.

It's not perfect, and a word or two may have been lost here and there, but Cal trots out all the reasons Bagley is the firm to represent him, and I translate. Alonzo asks pointed, intelligent questions. He may be alone, but he's not naive. After half an hour of the back-and-forth, with Alonzo asking questions through me and Cal offering the right answers through me, I'm not sure if we're any closer to signing.

"I need to ask you a question," Alonzo says, still in Spanish, leveling his probing dark stare on me.

I turn to Cal to interpret.

"He wants to ask—"

"No, Señorita Morale," Alonzo interrupts. "You. I want to ask *you* a question."

I slide a careful glance to Cal, whose eyes are fixed on my lips, waiting for the English equivalent of whatever Alonzo is saying.

"Okay," I answer still in Spanish. "Of course. What is your question?"

"What's he saying?" Cal demands.

"This man, he talks the good *talk*," Alonzo says. "But is he a good *man*? You tell me the truth."

I have no idea what makes him think I would give anything other than an answer that paints Cal in a great light. I prepare my response, but it dissolves on the tip of my tongue when I meet Alonzo's solemn stare. This man has been through so much already. I read that he never left the hospital but stayed there hoping for even one surviving family member. And one by one, they all died. I can't imagine that the transition into America, into a complex ecosystem like the NBA, will be easy.

Survival of the fittest.

Do what you have to do to be the last one standing.

If Mitch were sitting in this seat, he'd already have answered. He'd have already told Alonzo unequivocally that Cal is a good man. I barely know Cal, but I'm pretty sure he's a member of the Pride, and from my experience, I wouldn't trust anyone in that secret society. Maybe my advisor *is* right. Maybe I don't have the ruthless streak to survive this game because when faced with the moment of truth, I cannot tell a lie.

"I honestly don't know, Alonzo," I say. "There are few men I trust with my life and money, which is what you are doing. So is he a good man? I'm not sure, but will he make good deals? Absolutely."

The quiet builds in the room while Cal and I wait for Alonzo's response.

"That was an awful lot," Cal says suspiciously. "What did you say to him?"

Before I can answer, Alonzo responds.

"I will sign with Bagley," he says in Spanish.

"Oh my God!" I turn a wide smile to Cal. "He says he will sign with Bagley."

"Yes." Cal rubs his hands together. "We just need you to—"

"*Con una condición*," Alonzo interrupts.

"Um, on one condition," I say.

"I'll sign with Bagley," he repeats.

"He'll sign with Bagley," I translate.

"If Banner Morales is my agent."

"If Banner Morales..." My eyes saucer, and my mouth drops open. "Oh, shit."

Alonzo grins, and for the first time, the clouds break in his somber eyes.

"Oh, shit," he replies in heavily accented English, chuckling and sitting back in his chair. "That I understand."

"What is it?" Cal asks sharply. "Did I hear your name?"

"Um, yeah." I lick my lips nervously and force myself to face Cal's curious demand head-on. "He says he'll sign with Bagley on the condition that I'm his agent."

"What the hell?" Cal leans toward me, anger in the lines of his face and his taut body. "What did you say to him, Morales?"

"Just what you said," I fib. I did take a few liberties in the beginning, and I was honest when by all rights I should have lied, but that's all.

"Tell him that you are a fucking *intern*." Cal squashes the word like gum under his shoe. "Who has not taken the agent test and isn't qualified to represent a professional athlete. Tell him that you know nothing about this business and he would deeply regret trusting a wet-behind-the-ears novice with a future as promising and complex as his."

I bite my lip, preparing myself to tell Alonzo what Cal said verbatim, no matter how ridiculous it makes me look.

"That is my condition. No Banner, no deal," Alonzo responds before I can...in English!

Cal and I gape at his perfect, if heavily accented, English words. When neither of us have managed a response, Alonzo stands and starts for the door.

"Okay, okay," Cal says to Alonzo's back. "She'll be your agent."

Alonzo slowly turns and leans against the door, his eyes fairly twinkling at me.

"But she won't have her degree for a few months," Cal offers, his voice grudging. "And she has to pass the agent test. You need to be with an agency soon to take advantage of this window before the draft in June. Nike, Reebok, Gatorade—all of them will be sniffing around before the draft, and you need some representation in the meantime."

Out of habit, I begin translating.

"I understood him," Alonzo interrupts softly. Of course he did, since I guess he magically learned English in the last five minutes. "But surely I can sign a provisional contract ensuring that as soon as Banner is eligible and available, she will represent me. You will guide her, yes?"

Cal slants me a side-eye and blows out a weary breath.

"Yes."

And just like that, I went from lowly intern to agent for one of the biggest fish who has walked through the doors of Bagley & Associates in years. And all, I *guess*, because I showed some basic human decency and told the truth.

Let them have their Pride of lions and their alpha male cliques and the parties and connections they don't want me privy to. I'll do this my way. Represent clients my way. Lead my way. Fight my way. Survival of the fittest, my ass. Who needs the Pride?

PART II

"There will be men who fall in love with your skin and others who drown themselves in everything that lies beneath."

—*Cindy Cherie, poetess*

CHAPTER 7
JARED

"Look at me, Uncle Jared!"

I squint through the glare of sunlight in the direction of the high-pitched voice. A splash follows the tiny projectile human into the pool.

"Great cannonball, Sarai!" I yell back to my niece. "Make sure to tuck your knees in."

I slip off my short boots and socks, roll up the pants of my suit, and sit on the edge of the pool, lowering my legs into the cool water.

"Now this is the life." I glance at my brother, August, seated beside me in his trunks. "I'd say this is an upgrade from your apartment."

"Yeah, we needed the bigger place." He looks past the pool in his backyard to the electric-blue sprawl of the Pacific Ocean just beyond. "Much better view, and it's close to Sarai's school. Not too much of a commute for Iris to the Elevation office either."

"How's she adjusting to the new setup?" I scoop a handful of water and splash Sarai, who's swimming toward us.

August's initial reluctance to relocate our sports agency headquarters to LA from San Diego, where his team, the Waves, plays, centered around his wife. Iris works in marketing with us but wanted to stay with August in San Diego.

"You're her boss," August says. "Shouldn't you know?"

"You're her husband. Shouldn't *you*?"

We share a grin because we both know Iris wouldn't choose to be anywhere my brother wasn't.

"Dude," I say, loosening my tie and tossing it over my shoulder. "You are married with kids. What the hell?"

August's smile is wide and satisfied.

"One kid for now," he says. "But hopefully more soon. Isn't life grand?"

"As much as I love Iris and Sarai, you can have that life." I lean back, arms straight and palms pressed to the concrete. "I'm not ready to settle down with just one woman."

"You're in your thirties, bruh. You must at least think about it."

"I *do* think about it," I agree. "And break out in hives."

We both laugh, but I'm serious.

"Two reasons marriage is not even on my radar," I continue. "One, I have a low tolerance for people."

"That's ridiculous."

August can't relate to my view because he's one of those "*people people.*" We couldn't be more different. Not just that I'm blond and blue-eyed and that his darker skin and thick curls proclaim his biracial heritage, but we're different inside.

"No, it's true," I say. "People have hidden agendas. They lie, and they bore me."

"All of them?"

"No, just most of them, but I don't care enough to find the exceptions. I'm definitely not taking the time right now to find one I could tolerate forever."

"You said two reasons," August reminds me. "What's the other one?"

"Oh, simple." I waggle my brows suggestively. "I like pussy in assorted flavors."

August's laugh booms across the placid backyard. I've loved making him laugh since we were kids, stepbrothers who had no clue about the other but pretty sure almost from day one that we could be best friends.

And even though I'm a few years older, we always have been.

"So *is* Iris okay with the new setup?" I ask, directing us back to the previous topic of discussion.

"She's fine." August shrugs broad, bare shoulders. "Probably wondering if all the best action is happening there in LA while she's in the San Diego office."

August pauses, shooting me a searching glance before going on.

"Once the season is over, I might lease something in LA so she could work out of that office this summer. I'm sure we can find a good preschool for Sarai. I want Iris to have that experience. That okay with you?"

"Sure. You *are* a partner, albeit silent. Elevation is just as much yours as it is mine, Gus."

"Just making sure." August stands, hauling Sarai out of the water. "Come on, princess."

She giggles when he tickles her while toweling her off. She is precious. I wouldn't mind having a beautiful little girl if she didn't come permanently attached to a woman.

"One day I'll get to focus more on it," August says, bundling Sarai against his chest. "For now, ball is life."

"Which is exactly what it needs to be," I remind him. "Our strategy is working. Athletes see one of the NBA's brightest rising stars signed with Elevation, they feel confident we'll take care of them, too."

"You were right to relocate headquarters to LA."

"It's the smart move considering how many of our clients want to transition into acting, producing, entertainment in general. Getting to know the wizards behind the curtain can only help."

"Yeah, especially with Cal Bagley setting up shop in LA," August says, kissing Sarai's hair. "And he sent his big guns out to run the office, right? Didn't Banner Morales leave New York to come out here?"

"Yeah." I lock my teeth around the reply. "Banner's running their LA office."

I've never talked to August about Banner and what happened senior year. Even after ten years, something still pinches in my chest when I hear her name. Not my heart. I traded that useless organ in long ago to get where I am now. It's in the vicinity, though, of where my heart *used* to be. And that pisses me off.

She pisses me off.

At least it's mutual. It's a small industry, sports management, when you get down to it. Sure, there are lots of professional athletes, but they comprise such a small percentage of the general population. The number of agents who make it to the level I have, owning an agency and representing the caliber of talent we do, is fractional. Even with sports management, specifically the NBA, being such a small world, I don't see Banner often.

Early on, our paths crossed infrequently. She was at Bagley & Associates in New York, and I was at Richter Sports in Chicago. I saw her for the first time at a convention in Philly. When we spotted each other, she turned and walked the other way. I followed. I *may* have cornered her and tried to talk about that night again.

Okay. I *did* corner her and try to talk about that night again.

She threatened to blow her rape whistle if I didn't leave her alone. Seeing how she called the cops on me before, I didn't want to chance it. After a few more thwarted attempts, I gave up. She made it abundantly clear she wanted to put that night and me behind her. As badly as I wanted another night, and another one and another one, that wasn't meant to be.

What did it matter anyway? Banner was a soft spot, and the further up the ladder I climbed, the less I could afford those. Especially when we were pursuing the same clients. It's a dog-eat-dog and spit him—or her—out game.

Survival of the fittest.

Banner can be the killer with the heart.

I'm just the killer. It has served me well.

"You think we could ever tempt her to work for Elevation?" August asks as we walk back into the house.

"Who?" I snap my head around to look at him.

"Banner." He walks up the stairs with Sarai in his arms, her head on his shoulder.

"Banner Morales?" Iris asks from the top of the stairs and reaches to take Sarai from August. "I love her."

Of course she does.

"Is she gonna come work for us?" Iris's eyes light up like a Christmas tree.

"No," I say decisively.

"Maybe," August replies at the same time. "You don't think she would even be interested? Cal Bagley's a jerk."

"So's Jared," Iris says with a straight face because it's true. "I want to go on record that I approve of recruiting Banner to come work at Elevation."

"And I want to go on record that your opinion is completely irrelevant," I say, only half-jokingly. Iris is still young to the game and is working her way up from the bottom. I don't afford her preferential treatment just because she's married to my brother. She doesn't expect it.

"You don't like her?" Iris rolls her eyes. "Men are always intimidated by her."

"Hell if I am." I huff a disparaging breath. "I could negotiate Banner Morales under the table. Gimme a fucking break."

"Her clients love her," August says, a sly look in his eye that tells me he's trying to get under my skin. He should know by now I don't have skin to get under anymore. Just an exoskeleton to ward off provocation and bullshit.

"I guess so," I say with a shrug. "She matronizes them enough."

"She does not *matronize* them," Iris shoots back. "She takes care of them."

"My clients know representation doesn't come with ass-wiping, hand-holding, and cuddles, not that my guys need it," I reply. "If Banner wants children, she should give birth."

"Whoa." Iris shifts Sarai to her other hip, brows sky-high. "I know Bagley's a rival firm, but wow, Jared. Harsh."

"Yeah, she represents Kenan," August offers. "And you know Glad doesn't cuddle with anyone but his kid."

Kenan "Gladiator" Ross, August's teammate on the San Diego Waves, is about as un-cuddly as a man could be. I wanted to sign him, but Banner beat me to it. That loss hurt and actually came up in one of my last performance reviews at Richter before I struck out on my own to start Elevation. By then, Banner and I had bumped heads enough professionally and avoided each other enough personally to extinguish any "tender feelings."

Still…

There is that occasional inexplicable pinch when I hear her name.

"We may see her at tonight's game," Iris says. "Since both her clients are playing."

"Yeah, I'm on Vidale tonight." August shakes his head. "One of the toughest guys in the league to guard."

"Are Sarai and I still riding with you, Jared?" Iris asks, walking backward slowly toward Sarai's room.

"Yeah. I'll work outside by the pool 'til it's time to go."

She closes the door to Sarai's room, leaving August and me on the landing alone.

"Dude, everybody in the locker room was talking about this thing with Banner and her favorite client," August says, giving me a pointed look. "If you know what I mean."

"No, I don't know what you mean."

"Apparently, it's been going on for a while," he says as we head back down the stairs and out to the pool. "But it's just now getting out. Or maybe they're letting it out now."

"What the hell are you talking about?" I gather my boots and socks and head over to the umbrella-covered table where I left my laptop.

"Banner and Zo Vidale," August says. "You hadn't heard?"

"Dammit, Gus. Heard what?"

"They're dating."

Pinch.

CHAPTER 8
BANNER

"Quinn, can I get your autograph?"

My client smiles wide in response to the request. That smile sells cereal, lipstick, and sports bras like nobody's business.

I make sure of that.

Turns out Quinn Barrow, the "has-been" Mitch was so quick to dismiss all those years ago, had a lot more to do and give. She wouldn't see me the first five times I visited her in the hospital. After her second suicide attempt, I got through, and everything changed. Not overnight. There were times during her rehab and the painful process of learning to live with a prosthetic that Quinn wanted to give up and so did I. The whole country was pulling for her, though, a fact I shamelessly leveraged when it was time to negotiate her first endorsement deal.

"I don't think I'll ever get used to that," Quinn murmurs as the kid walks off with an autographed nachos tray. "Being recognized and randomly approached. It's surreal that people know me, much less want me to sign stuff."

"You're America's Titanium Sweetheart." I chuckle at the grimace on Quinn's face. "Hey. It tested well. It stuck. We're using it."

There's a point when an athlete, any public figure really, has to distinguish between their public self and their private self.

Between the product and the person. Quinn still struggles with that sometimes. She balked at contract clauses requiring her to wear the titanium prosthetic so many times in public each month.

"Sometimes it just feels slimy." Quinn takes a sip of her beer. "Like this thing I thought had ruined my life, that almost *ended* my life, now I make my living from it?"

"No, you make a living from your hard work and ingenuity." I give her a firm look. "No different from models who trade on their beauty or athletes who get paid to play ball. You had to learn to walk again, Quinn. To drive, to live. You'd already honed that body all your life as a runner. Now you help other people hone theirs. Just because you've monetized the experience doesn't mean you've cheapened it."

"You always know what to say to every client, huh?" Quinn dips her hand into the carton of buttered popcorn.

"It's my job. Speaking of, we need to meet with the Netflix people to discuss that collaboration with Chef Paddy."

Several networks have approached us before about television specials, reality shows and the like. This *Biggest Loser*–esque concept encompassing nutrition, fitness, and meditation is the first to truly pique Quinn's interest.

"Oh, yeah." A smile lights Quinn's delicate features. She recently cropped her auburn hair to a cap of loose curls. Her green eyes sparkle with excitement as we wait for the Waves versus Titans game to begin.

"Want some popcorn?" Quinn offers her carton to me. She's the most disciplined woman I know, and every line and curve of her body is honed to perfection, but she's never one to deny herself the occasional indulgence.

"Nope." I extract a string cheese packet from my purse and sip from my bottled water. "I don't have enough points left for buttered popcorn. And damn you for tempting me."

"How are you liking Weight Watchers?" Quinn asks, licking fingers shiny with butter.

"I think it's my favorite program so far. It feels measurable to me."

"You look great, Banner." Quinn's smile gentles. "I'm proud of you."

I got serious the last few years about my outside reflecting the confident, powerful woman I was on the inside. Quinn has been instrumental in my weight loss journey and helping me get to the bottom of the emotional and hormonal barriers keeping me from being fit. "Eating your feelings" was a way of life for me, and I didn't realize that in times of high stress, I ate too much and anything I wanted. All four years of college were high stress, and so were the first few years at Bagley. Now I manage it better.

"And are you taking your meds?" Quinn probes, slipping into trainer and motivator mode as easily as she slipped into the tight jeans that turned more than one head tonight.

"Every day, Mom," I say with an eye roll.

I also discovered I had polycystic ovary syndrome, or PCOS, a hormonal condition that can affect metabolism, fertility, and other reproductive dynamics. Taking the right medication, carefully monitoring what I eat, and working out regularly have made a tremendous difference.

"Loving this look, by the way," Quinn says, eyeing ripped boyfriend jeans, fitted T-shirt, blazer, and stilettos.

"Thanks."

"I bet Zo will like it, too," Quinn says innocently with naughty eyes.

I reach to push my hair behind my ear only to find it all scooped up in a topknot. Damn habit. One thing I've never grown out of.

"We'll see," I offer with a stiff smile. "I'm still getting used to being...public."

"Well, you've been private for six months," Quinn reminds me. "It's a miracle you managed to keep it under wraps as long as you did."

"Not a miracle." I bite into my string cheese. "I was very careful. I still don't know how to feel about it."

"The fact that people know or the fact that you're dating Zo?"

"All of it." I fiddle with the oversize gold hoop earrings Zo gave me for my thirtieth birthday. "What if this goes wrong? I could lose my biggest client and my best friend in one fell swoop. That's why it took me so long to cave and go out with him. Now that it's leaking, I just hope things stay as good as they've been."

"You guys are great together," Quinn reassures.

"We'll see this summer, won't we?" I take a deep breath. "He's staying with me once the season is over. With the Titans being in Vancouver, we so rarely get real time together."

Alonzo has a few business interests here in LA, but I know this will be a test drive for us seeing how it feels to be in the same place longer than a night or two every few weeks. I've been trying to ignore the unease that creeps in every time I think of us living together. Our friendship has always been so *right*. The thought of things going *wrong* with Zo because we're dating scares me a little.

"You guys will be fine. Just focus on what's real. All this," Quinn says, waving her hand at the crowded arena packed with television cameras and fans, "goes away when the game is over. You have a real relationship with a real man. Not the image you help create."

Image.

I actually hate how much I have to think about it, especially now that I live in LA. It was one thing living in New York, but the image consciousness goes up another level out here. I'm a double-digit chick in a single-digit town. I've accepted that. I've shopped with Quinn in exclusive boutiques where the salesperson immediately offered to show me their shoes or jewelry, assuming that was all that would fit. I'm over it. I've stopped trying to keep up and have just determined I'll be the best Banner I can be. That doesn't mean I'm immune to other people talking about my image.

Hey, Hollywood, a highly successful blog, seems to have taken a special interest in my relationship with Zo. The commentary has been some of the most vicious.

"You know Hannah from *Hey, Hollywood* called me Sponge Banner Square Pants last week?"

Quinn spits a little of her beer out.

"Oh my God, what?" Her eyes widen first with humor and then shock and then morph to narrow angry slits.

"Yeah, and I quote, 'Is it just me? Or does Zo Vidale's agent-slash-girlfriend have a squarer than normal ass? Let's call her Sponge Banner Square Pants.' End quote."

"That little bitch," Quinn says hotly. "Criticizing every detail of other people's appearance. Meanwhile we've never seen what that little twat looks like. And you can betcha bottom dollar it's nothing like the avatar she hides behind."

"Whatever." I shrug, pretending the barb doesn't still burn where it landed.

"Not whatever." Quinn grabs my hand and forces me to look her in the eyes the same way I've done over the years. "You're beautiful, Banner. And your body is beautiful. You've worked hard. You're disciplined and healthy, and heredity and squats have given you a great ass that is not abnormally square."

"Hey, what more can a girl ask for than a 'within normal range' square ass?" I quip sarcastically.

"Maybe Hannah's just pissed because she doesn't have a fine, rich boyfriend." Quinn's eyes crinkle at the corners, and a saucy smile spills over her mouth. "Ohhh, but boyfriend or not, you gotta appreciate premium man-flesh. Incoming. Check out fine and rich, if that Tom Ford suit is anything to go by, at two o'clock."

"Where?" I turn my head slightly to the right.

"Don't look," she says hastily. "He'll know we're interested."

"*We* aren't interested. You are, so I'm looking. Also that wasn't two o'clock. That was ten o'clock. Did you fail driver's ed or what?"

"Driver's ed?" Consternation crinkles Quinn's smooth expression.

"Ten and two?" I demonstrate the hand positions on an imaginary steering wheel.

"Good grief." Quinn laughs and gives an exasperated shake of her head. "Just look. But guard your ovaries. He's got a kid. He was fine in the first place. Add his adorable little girl and no ovaries are safe."

I glance over my shoulder, and everything inside me jerks. There was a time I deliberately avoided news of Jared Foster. Over the years, I haven't had to avoid news. There just wasn't much of it. Not personal anyway. I know he started his own agency a couple of years ago, Elevation, formerly based in San Diego—now headquartered mere blocks from the LA office of Bagley & Associates I'm managing.

The same way he was the golden boy of Kerrington College, he has become the golden boy of sports management. Not even thirty-five years old and owns one of the fastest-growing agencies in the business. Cal hates him. I suspect Cal was so determined to set up shop on the West Coast because Jared was out here. And I suspect Jared set up an office in LA because Cal did. I don't want to be caught in the middle of their turf war, but if it happens, I won't back down. I've cultivated the killer as much as the heart and know which to deploy in any given situation. Jared Foster would definitely qualify as a "situation."

I don't think of him or that night…if I can help it. Humiliation. Hurt. Confusion. Anger. That's all I remember.

Oh. And the best sex of my life. Jared Foster remains the best thing that ever happened to my vagina despite how horrendously left that night went. So, yeah, I didn't want to hear any personal details about him. I couldn't have missed that he had gotten married, but I guess I *did* miss that he has a daughter.

I swallow around some strange hot lump in my throat as I watch her dark head touching the silky fair strands I threaded my fingers through for one night. He's carrying her like she's the most precious thing in the world. They're laughing, and her skinny arms loop around his neck. A petite dark-haired woman walks up behind them carrying hot dogs and beer. Her face is a replica of the little angel in Jared's arms.

She *would* be petite. She *would* be perfect. At least she's not a Cindy.

I turn away, hopefully before he noticed me gaping at him and his family.

"Hot, right?" Quinn asks, hush-voiced. "And the kid takes him to lava level."

"Hmm," I offer noncommittally around a bite of string cheese and a sip of water.

"Oh God," Quinn sotto-squeals. "He's coming over here."

I choke on my cheese, and a light sweat sprouts across the surface of my entire body. I will not let him reduce me to this again. To this naive, nervous…*girl* who starts breathing heavily every time he's within a two-yard radius. If I was facing him across a negotiating table, it would be an even playing field. I can hold my own with the best of them. But this isn't a boardroom. It's a basketball game. My current lover just ran onto the court. My one-night lover is headed this way. And even knowing I'm long over Jared, my stupid heart does that thing it does sometimes when I think about him.

Jerk.

CHAPTER 9
JARED

"Where are we sitting?" Iris asks from slightly behind me.

"I want nachos," Sarai whines, frowning at the hot dogs her mother carries.

"Sarai, you said hot dogs," Iris returns firmly. "And I got hot dogs. I'm not going all the way back to get nachos now."

"But, Mommy, I—"

"I'll get the nachos," I cut in. "Once we get settled and find our seats, I'll go back."

"Thank you, Uncle Jared," Sarai says sweetly, blinking those mile-long lashes at me.

They start so young.

How does August live with this? Not gonna lie. It's a lot of estrogen right now. After a hard day, I'd much rather be in my LA apartment with the city sprawled beneath my balcony and a glass of that overpriced whiskey Bent sent me for Christmas. Instead, I'm at a basketball game refereeing the two beautiful girls in August's life. Don't get me wrong, on my short list of people I can tolerate for more than a day, Iris and Sarai are near the top.

But damn.

We're approaching the section of seats where I recognize several Waves team friends and family when I see her. Beside our three empty seats are Banner Morales and Quinn Barrow, one of her clients. As always, Banner's beautiful. It really bothers me that she is always gorgeous. It would be much more convenient if she didn't glow. If those silky hairs weren't escaping that knot on top of her head and skimming her cheeks and the nape of her neck. If those wide same-size lips weren't curved in a genuine smile. Her features aren't delicate. They're bold, each one daring you to look away.

Fuck my life.

And hearing that she's dating Zo Vidale doesn't help. Not that I still have feelings for her. I don't. Not the soft, gooey ones I nurtured in college. But the hard ones? The ones poking behind my zipper? They *might* still be around, especially when Banner is roaming out in public looking like this.

"Oh gosh," Iris says, her voice tinged with excitement. "Are those our seats right beside Banner?"

"Yup. Looks like."

"Oh, this is perfect." Iris beams up at me. "You know how much I—"

"Love her," I interrupt with a grimace. "Yeah. You mentioned. Look, if you can check your inner fangirl, that'd be great. Banner may be your Wonder Woman caped crusader in this business, but she's also the managing partner for a rival agency that just set up shop a few blocks from Elevation."

"Okay." Iris nods and gives me a rueful smile. "But I do really like her."

"Most people do." I roll my eyes. "Just remember you work for *me*, and she and I vie for the same clients."

"Have you ever blocked her shot?" Iris asks softly, probably because we're closer to our seats now. And Banner.

A cocky grin takes over my mouth. I'm known for the block shot. Like in basketball, when one opponent deflects a field goal attempt as the ball is on its way to the hole, I love nothing more than to let another agent think he has a client on lock. Meanwhile, I knock on back doors and meet in back rooms to convince the client

I'm the better option. I block their shit just when they think they're about to score.

"No, I've never blocked Banner's shot," I reply, but level a frank warning look at Iris. "But I wouldn't hesitate. Results trump feelings."

"Jeesh. Glad I'm not an agent," Iris says. "I'll stick to marketing. Less blood."

That's what she thinks. If I was in marketing, there would be blood.

Banner is studying her phone when we reach the seats, but her client Quinn isn't. She's smiling up at me like I'm an ice cream cone in the Mojave Desert.

I get that a lot and use it with no shame.

"Hi," I say, meeting Quinn's eyes with a smile of my own. "I think these are our seats."

Banner's head pops up, and her eyes narrow before she pulls her professional mask in place.

"Banner Morales, wow," I drawl, setting Sarai down at the seat between Iris and me. "Long time no see."

Her expression says *not long enough*, and her polite smile barely disguises it.

"Jared, great to see you again." She looks over at Iris and Sarai. "Introduce me to your family."

Pause.

Does she think I've...*procreated*?

"This is Iris *West*," I say pointedly. "My sister-in-law, and my niece, Sarai. Iris, this is Banner Morales."

"Nice to meet you." Banner shakes Iris's hand and offers a wide, natural smile for Sarai. "Hi, Sarai. Aren't you the prettiest thing?"

Sarai burrows her head into the pant leg of my suit and peeka-boo smiles at Banner, who tweaks her nose and chuckles.

"I bet you're not shy at all," Banner continues, her whole focus on my niece. Sarai giggles and shakes her head. "She's beautiful, Iris."

"Thank you," my sister-in-law replies, sliding me a cautious glance before going on. "I'm really looking forward to hearing you speak at the convention next week."

"In Denver?" Banner asks, her expression showing surprise. "You're an agent?"

"No, sports marketing," Iris says.

"Well, I look forward to seeing you there." Banner glances at me. "I'm just putting it all together now. Sister-in-law, so you're married to August?"

"Yes." Iris beams, and only the most hardened cynic would doubt she's with my famous brother for any reason but love.

"Now I recognize you," Banner says. "You haven't been married long, right? Congratulations."

"Thank you."

"Oh." Banner sends her friend an apologetic look. "Sorry! This is my friend Quinn Barrow."

"I love your app. I was lucky enough to get in the beta group," Iris says, accepting Quinn's outstretched hand. "This morning it told me to put my wide ride in gear."

Is this a good thing? My confusion must show because Banner chuckles and explains.

"Quinn developed a fitness app called Girl, You Better. It's still in beta," she says, pride shining from every pore. "It gives you messages like a Garmin would, but sassier."

"It's affectionately known as the ghetto Garmin," Quinn pipes in with a laugh.

She, Iris, and Banner are chatting more about the app and Quinn's line of workout gear when I leave to get the nachos.

Quinn really is a beautiful woman. Beyond her red hair and creamy skin, there are a strength and power on the inside. They come across. She has talked more than once about how Banner pursued her when she was depressed, suicidal in the hospital after she lost her leg. She wouldn't be a multimillion-dollar empire if Banner hadn't seen her potential.

Good for you, Banner.

She's not like the rest of us. I knew she wouldn't be, but I'm not allowing myself *feelings*. Elevation is at a crucial place in our development. If you're not with us, you're against us. And Banner is definitely not with us.

When I return with Sarai's nachos, Iris is screaming at the refs as usual. August may have found a girl who loves basketball as much as he does. I sit…finally. Damn, I'm exhausted and still have to drive back to LA tonight. If I hadn't promised August I'd stay with the girls until the game is over, I'd leave early. I'm also not used to being this close to Banner for any amount of time.

She's fully engaged with the game when I return to our seats with Sarai's nachos—or doing a great imitation of it and just ignoring me.

Probably that last one.

"How are you liking LA, Jared?" Quinn leans forward to ask. "Iris was just telling us you've only been there a few months."

"Yeah. I'm getting settled." I'll stick to the personal stuff since Banner and my business should not mix. "Whole Foods and Starbucks are the marks of any great civilization. Long as I have those, I can figure out the rest. I'm looking for a gym, if you know of a good one."

"Come to my gym!" Quinn clasps her hands under her chin. "It's called Titanium."

Banner almost imperceptibly shakes her head, widening her eyes at Quinn, a subtle signal to shut the hell up.

"Oh, I've heard of that," I say, injecting my voice with more enthusiasm just to bother Banner. "I'd *love* to come."

"I have guest passes," Quinn says absently, squinting at Banner like she's trying to decode the message her friend is sending. "I can leave them up front in your name."

"Excellent." I catch Banner's eye and wink. "Then it's settled."

Exasperation skids across her face before she smooths it over.

"You'll love it," she says neutrally. "Seems like you'll be everywhere I turn. My city. My gym."

"It'll be like old times," I murmur, allowing just enough suggestiveness in my voice to maybe make her blush. Laundromat Banner's cheeks would be flushed pink by now. This new Banner doesn't even blink but stares at me like she's waiting for me to come harder.

Come harder? I need to check my thoughts because *coming harder* shouldn't be in the same zip code as this woman.

We retreat to our corners for the next three quarters, her talking and laughing with Quinn, me answering Sarai's one million and one questions and helping Iris keep her entertained. How could someone so small be so much work? By the fourth quarter, I'm convinced August deserves a gold medal. Even though we don't exchange two words, I'm acutely aware of Banner beside me. I surreptitiously take in the changes she's undergone. I never really paid attention to Banner's weight before, ironic since that was ultimately what sabotaged whatever we might have had, but even I can tell she's lost a significant amount. I glimpse flashes of toned thighs in the fashionably holey jeans. She's wearing makeup, which conceals the seven freckles I know march across her nose.

At a break in her conversation with Quinn and mine with Iris, I lean toward her.

"So who you got?" I ask.

She does a double take, like she had forgotten I was even here.

Flattering.

"Oh, sorry." She spares me a quick glance before turning her attention back to the court. "What did you say?"

"Who are you pulling for?"

"My client," she replies cagily, full lips quirking.

Of course, she has a client on each team. Kenan on the Waves and Zo on the Vancouver Titans.

"So you and Vidale, huh?"

I didn't mean to ask that question. I usually exercise more control over the space between what I think and what I say.

"Excuse me?" Her voice is imperiously chilly when she turns to look me in the eye.

"I heard you were dating your client," I say, hoping it makes her uncomfortable because what the hell? I thought she was smarter than that. "I thought you were smarter than that."

So much for controlling what comes out of my mouth.

"And I thought you were better at minding your own damn business," she snaps, eyes pinched at the corners. "There is nothing unethical about my relationship, business or personal, with Zo."

"Then why are you defensive?"

"Why are you prying?"

"I'm not," I say, my own tone icing over. "The question isn't is it ethical. The better question may be is it wise?"

"And maybe an even better question is why do you care?"

"Hey." I twist my lips and shrug. "Just trying to help a friend."

"I've seen your idea of 'friendship,' Jared," she says stiffly. "I'll take my chances."

Before I can address those fighting words, Mitch Sanderson approaches with a tall young man in tow. Sanderson is such a waste of space. He's an awful negotiator and a shit agent. He wouldn't know a good deal if it sucked his dick under the table. How he's still at Bagley I have no idea. Actually, I do know how. The Pride. The same way he got there in the first place.

"Banner, I want you to meet someone," he says, stopping in front of Banner and Quinn. "This is Lamont Christopher."

"Very nice to meet you, Lamont," Banner says, smiling warmly and shaking the kid's hand. "I hope Mitch is taking good care of you."

"Yes, ma'am," he answers with a hint of a Southern drawl.

"Enjoying the game?" Banner asks.

"We have been," Sanderson replies before Lamont can. "But we're gonna head out to beat the traffic."

You gotta be kidding me. Banner is letting Sanderson handle the presumptive overall number one draft pick? I assumed she was handling discussions with Christopher since she is known around the league as the Rookie Whisperer. Setting up rookies to succeed in their finances, performance, and general well-being is her MO. Her rookies are notorious for keeping clean noses and full bank accounts even post-ball.

She basically babies them into stellar careers.

But if she's trusting such a prize to Sanderson's ineptitude, blocking this shot will be like taking candy from a baby.

"Good to see you again, Lamont," I interject since neither Banner nor Sanderson seems inclined to introduce him to the "enemy." Smart. Well, Banner's smart. I won't make assumptions about Sanderson.

"Mr. Foster." Lamont's eyes light with recognition. "Good to see you, too."

I visited a few of his college games, but he got into some trouble near the end of his freshman year. His on-court abilities make him a hot commodity, but his off-court antics make him a possible liability. I had decided he wasn't worth the trouble, but now that I know Bagley's after him, I may change my mind. If I'm recalling correctly, he likes strip clubs. Of course he does. Pigs love slop. It's self-evident. He's a red-blooded male. It's tits, ass, and lots of cash floating around—an unholy trinity few men can resist.

Sanderson and Lamont exit the arena, and Banner resumes conversation with Quinn, studiously ignoring me for the rest of the game and not revisiting our budding argument from before, which disappoints me. There are few things more arousing than Banner on a warpath.

She stands as the final buzzer sounds and would probably leave without another word to me if not for Quinn's manners.

"It was nice meeting you, Jared," Quinn says, her friendly smile determinedly in place, even though her friend's glare must be burning a hole in the side of her face. "Don't forget, I'll leave the guest pass at the Titanium front desk for you."

"Thanks. That's really sweet," I say and mean it. Quinn seems like a genuinely kind person, an endangered species in LA.

"It was great meeting you, too, Iris," Banner says, reaching around me to touch my sister-in-law's shoulder and brush a hand over a sleeping Sarai's curls.

"Same," Iris near-gushes. "I'll see you next week in Denver."

"Sure thing." Finally, reluctantly, Banner's eyes land on me, and she speaks grudgingly. "Good to see you again, Foster."

"I'm sure we'll see more of each other now that we're both in LA," I remind her. "Maybe at the gym tomorrow."

She grimaces but salvages it into a grin at the last moment.

"One can only hope." She turns to Quinn. "You ready? I need to find Zo."

"Finally a night together," Quinn says, her tone teasing and salacious.

Banner flashes a quick self-conscious look my way but doesn't answer. She just takes Quinn's hand and drags her in the direction of the opposing team's players' tunnel.

So he's staying with Banner instead of flying back with the team. Makes sense. If Banner was my girl, I'd stay back and fuck her, too.

If Banner was my girl.

The phrase boings around my head on a pogo stick for a few minutes while I escort Iris and Sarai to the opposite players' tunnel where August will be. As soon as they are safely with him, I head for my car to start the trip from San Diego to LA. I pull up the Bluetooth for a phone call before I even make it out of the lot. It's late to call my assistant, but she knows how I operate.

All the time.

"Seriously?" Chyna sounds like she was asleep. It's not that late. "This is way after hours, Jared. What do you need?"

"Now don't go drawing personal boundaries," I tell her, letting her hear the rare affection I hold for her and so few others. "It's too late for that shit. You've spoiled me all these years."

Her heavy sigh is followed by a long-suffering chuckle.

"One day you're gonna meet the woman you can't charm."

Already did, my friend. Just left her.

"So what we got?" she asks. "Now that I'm up?"

"You remember the guy we met who owns the new strip club downtown?"

"Yeah. You said he reminded you of a lizard in snakeskin."

"That's the one." I laugh, pushing the button to lower the top on my convertible. It's a glorious night for a drive. "Call him. I need a favor."

CHAPTER 10
BANNER

"*Girl, you better get you some.*"

In the early morning quiet of my bathroom, I *shhh* Quinn's app like it understands me. It's five o'clock, and I'm recording my food and workout from yesterday because I forgot last night. In addition to tracking nutrition, fitness, and water intake, it also logs sexual activity and menstrual cycle. Considering my PCOS diagnosis, I need to monitor this closely. Zo spent the night with me instead of at the hotel with the team. He's in the bedroom asleep, and I don't want to wake him up.

We had sex. That's not unusual in a healthy relationship between two consenting adults, but we've been best friends since he coerced Cal Bagley into making me his agent nearly ten years ago. At that point in his life, Zo needed a friend more than he needed sharp negotiation skills and experience. I was that friend. I walked with him through that first year following his family's deaths. In interviews, he always says he probably wouldn't have gotten through the pressures of his rookie year and all the grief he had to process without me. It went both ways. I needed a friend just as badly. I got tossed into a pool of sharks, sink or swim. It was the rookie year for us both, and he was there for me, too.

Only in the last year did he express that he wanted more than friendship. Initially, I was a hard no. Why ruin a good thing? And frankly, as fine as Zo is, I'd never thought of him that way. I told him as much, but he kept asking. Eventually, I caved, and we went out on one date. And then another. And then a third. I'm not going to say lightning struck. It didn't, but it was nice to have someone as attractive as Zo want me. It was nice having someone to cuddle with while watching a movie. Nice to be holding someone's hand when walking on the beach.

The first time we made love, I cried into my pillow after. Not because it was awful. It was good. It was sweet and tender and...good. But I couldn't shake the feeling that I had just ruined something precious. That I jumped off a building and was just waiting for the splat. But there has been no splat. Just falling. I guess this is falling in love? It's a shame that at thirty-two years old, I've never been in love, but who's had time? The occasional hookup. Drinks here and there. Dinner. I'd made myself vulnerable to two men in college, and both were disastrous. I may still be falling for Zo, but I know I can trust him, and he knows he can trust me. That must be a huge part of love.

"Girl, you better get your butt in gear."

My workout times are also scheduled into the app, so "she" knows I haven't left the house and should already be on my way to Titanium.

"I'm going," I grumble.

Before I leave, I perform my everyday ritual of looking at myself naked in the mirror. There was a time I couldn't do it. I couldn't stand naked in front of a mirror and just stare at myself, take in my imperfections without flinching. Without hearing the criticisms from culture, of men on the street, of my exes.

From myself, the harshest critic of all.

And looking at myself naked each morning, I may see a little extra flesh around the middle. Or one day—not yet, thank God—some boob droop. Or, God forbid, a square-er ass, but I make the choice every day to accept the girl who stares back at me. To offer her the same unconditional love she offers the people she cares about, her family and friends. I would never judge those closest to me, never say the things to them that I used to say to myself. If there are things I see that I want to change, I develop a plan to work on them. If there are things I cannot change, I work to accept them.

I will never be petite. I'm just not made that way. Some of it's just genetic. My hips, my ass, my very bones are too big for that. I'm not interested in being tiny. I want to be strong and healthy and feel good in my clothes, and now I do.

My relationship with food is more complicated than any relationship I've had with a man. My feelings drive me into binges or starvation. In counseling, I sorted out what food should be to me. It's for nutrition. Not to make me feel better. It's not comfort. It's not a companion to make me feel less lonely. It is not a friend I celebrate special occasions with. It is fuel. It oils my engine so I can live my best life. So I can pursue my dreams. So I can make this world a better place.

Once I've braved my daily look in the mirror, I tame my hair into two long braids, brush my teeth, and splash water on my face. I'll shower at the gym, but I'm wearing no makeup. I look about sixteen. Not exactly my tough-chick face. I grab pieces from Quinn's Titanium workout gear collection out of my laundry basket. Even a year ago, I never would have worn something this revealing, though it's modest by most standards. The cutoff T-shirt reads "The Future Is Latina" and shows my midriff, consequently leaving my hips, ass, and thighs exposed in the capri workout pants.

I can't resist. I turn my back to the mirror and stare at my ass. Accepting myself as I am doesn't mean I won't work to improve and be the best version of myself inside and out.

"Sponge Banner Square Pants, huh?" I say aloud. "Extra squats for you today."

I tiptoe through the bedroom, making sure the drapes are drawn tight to keep out light until Zo is ready to wake up. I peer down at him, picking out his striking features in the shadows. He's a beautiful man, inside and out. He's won citizen awards for his humanitarian work and is generally held as the kindest guy in the NBA. You'd be hard-pressed to find anyone who doesn't love Zo. I drop a light kiss on his unruly mop of dark curls. I'm a very lucky girl.

I climb into my ivory Range Rover with butterscotch hand-stitched leather seats, a special treat to myself, and keep counting blessings on my way to the gym. I try to start every day with grati-tude. Zo is at the top of that list, along with my family and friends like Quinn.

Every time I walk through Titanium's doors, I feel a spark of pride. Quinn, that broken girl with bandages covering fresh slits on her wrists, the one who did nothing but glare all day at the space where her leg used to be… She made this. She wept on my shoulder after each rehab session, not because learning to walk with only one leg hurt so much but because she wanted her other leg back so badly. That girl did this. I believed in her so much that I even invested seed money into this gym. Best investment I ever made.

I fob in at the front desk and head up to the studio where Quinn trains me three times a week. I would have referred to the girl she's chatting with in front of the barre as a "Cindy" at one point. She's the grown-up version with tasteful highlights in her blond hair and gorgeous implants and a perfectly toned body. And Tanya's also one of the sweetest people I know.

I've never been able to shake the image of the types of girls Jared dated when we were in college. It only heightened my embarrass-ment, realizing how gullible I was to think he actually wanted me that night. I hope it was worth it, being a part of the Pride. He told me he didn't join, but I've seen photos of him with Bent on yachts, at galas, ski trips. They remain close, and Bent stood with that group of jackals who taunted me. I know August West is involved with Elevation, probably funding much of it, but you don't end up owning an agency like Elevation at Jared's age without a lot of favors. And nobody does favors like the Pride.

"Morning, ladies," I greet Quinn and Tanya, who teaches Titanium's pole-dancing classes.

"Hey, love." Tanya pulls me into a Chanel-scented hug. Even at six in the morning, she smells of her signature scent. "You look amazing, Banner. I've been meaning to tell you."

"Thank you," I reply, returning Tanya's squeeze. "You look beautiful as usual. Best calves in the business."

"Stripper heels and stripper poles, honey!" She tosses a swath of blond hair and looks me up and down. "I'd love to get you in one of my classes. Hell, I'd love to get you in one of my *clubs*, Banner. Men love tits and ass, and you've got both, m'dear."

My face heats. I'm used to being complimented on my intelligence and things that have little to do with the outside. I always said it didn't matter, but that was another lie I fed myself. The gulf between the truth and the lies we tell ourselves is filled with misery. It's not bad to enjoy praise about the physical. That doesn't make me shallow. I can be as proud of losing more than fifty pounds as I am of negotiating an eight-figure deal for one of my clients. I'm not the smart girl. Or the pretty one. Or the *whatever* label people want to assign to me. I can be all those things at once.

"The class, maybe," I say. "The club, never."

"My last date appreciated my time on the pole," Quinn interjects with a roguish grin. "If you know what I mean."

"My virgin ears!" I cover my ears and laugh.

"I doubt there is anything 'virgin' left on you," Quinn says. "Not after last night with Zo. It's been weeks since you saw each other, right? I'll take it easy on you today, since I'm sure he didn't last night."

I chuckle right along with my friends, neither confirming nor denying, and quickly change the subject.

"Speaking of the pole," I say to Tanya, "you still do those parties here in the city?"

"As long as there are horny men looking to get shit-faced," Tanya says wryly, "I'm doing parties. But those are separate from the clubs. All private, high-end affairs."

"Yeah, I know." I look at her frankly. "I have an awkward favor."

"Anything for you, Banner. You know that."

"I have a couple of guys who, if they sneeze too hard, could be out on their asses. The league is watching them like a hawk. Think you and your girls could keep an eye out?"

"What exactly are we watching out for?" Tanya asks, her precisely plucked brows lifting.

"Not just being at a party. They can have their fun. I mean drugs or something that could get them in real trouble. I don't want it on Instagram or TMZ if we can help it."

"It wouldn't be exactly professional," Tanya says, a glint in her eye. "And I can't make any promises, but tell me who I'm looking for."

"Oh, I got a list."

The three of us laugh. Many of my duties representing clients, especially young players in the NBA, which has become somewhat of a specialty of mine, are written in invisible fine print.

"Between tail, weed, and fights in the club," I add as our laughter dies off, "I need all the help I can get keeping these guys in line and under contracts."

"We'll be on the lookout." Tanya grabs her tote from the floor and heads toward the exit. "In the meantime, try to make one of my pole-dancing classes."

I nod and laugh, starting to stretch before Quinn tells me to.

"Is that the new model AesThetic sent?" I ask, nodding to the prosthetic lower leg I haven't seen her wear before.

"Yeah." Quinn extends it for me to see. "Pretty cool, actually."

"Cool enough for you to put your name behind it?" I lean into an abductor stretch. AesThetic has been after her for a year to endorse its line of prosthetics.

"We'll see." She puts on her drill sergeant face. "I'm more

concerned about *your* legs than theirs right now. Come on, gimme some squats. Ass to grass, lady."

We're both incredibly focused people, so we go through the motions of my workout with almost no chatter for the first twenty minutes, other than the orders she barks to guide me. We're starting battle ropes before she delves into her juicy gossip phase.

"So about last night," she says, lips pressed into a sneaky grin.

I pause to look at her warily, a rope in each hand.

"What about last night?"

"I just thought I picked up on something..." She pretends to search for a word, but I know how calculating my friend is when she "senses" a tidbit. She probably practiced this conversation in the mirror this morning. "Interesting."

"Oh?" I start the workout, snapping the ropes, alternating left and right. "What was so interesting?"

"You and Jared Foster."

One rope slips from my hand, throwing the rhythm off. I ignore her raised brows and pick up the fallen rope. Our two names even linked casually stands the hair up on my neck. I don't have feelings for him anymore, but I would never presume to be safe around Jared. The man is his own danger zone.

"There *is* no me and Jared Foster." I fix all my concentration on the forceful undulation of the ropes in my hands.

"Really?" Quinn takes a sip of her berry-infused water. "Then what was that my Spidey senses picked up between you two?"

"Disdain? Revulsion? Nausea?" I ask with false pleasantness. "I think you got your webs crossed, Spidey."

"You forget I can sniff out sexual tension like a bloodhound."

"I didn't forget. I never knew." I drop the ropes and walk away to grab a towel and wipe my face.

"Well, I can," she asserts, hands on slim hips. "And there was *something* there. 'Fess up."

"There's nothing to 'fess."

"I won't judge, you know," she says softly. "I mean, if you're worried about Zo or whatever."

I freeze with a bottle of water midway to my mouth and glance Quinn's way. Her expression is the patience of a saint and the obstinacy of the devil.

"Okay, so we have a history," I admit. "We went to college together."

"Oh my God." She clutches her imaginary pearls dramatically. "To see that man in his prime."

"I'm pretty sure he's *in* his prime now," I say, remembering how Jared looked last night. "This was pre-prime, and he was still kind of prime-ish."

"So did you guys"—she makes a hole with two fingers and thrusts another finger in and out—"do the nasty?"

I heave a breath and close my eyes, not wanting the flood of curiosity and questions I know my answer could unleash.

"One night. We had a one-night stand my senior year, but it ended badly."

Fuck the fat girl.

"Really badly," I reiterate, focusing on the high shine of the studio floor. "And we haven't been around each other much over the last decade. When we are, our interactions range from polite to awkward, but I suspect we have the potential for downright hostile."

"So in college it was hate fucking?" Quinn whispers hopefully. "'Cause that shit is intense."

If there was a chair in here, she'd pull one right up.

"No, in college we were…" All the nights we laughed and studied and challenged each other in that laundromat invade my memory: Jared helping fold my clients' clothes and teasing me about my bad knock-knock jokes. "We were friends."

"Maybe you can be friends again," Quinn says. "He seemed pretty cool last night."

"I think it's best to just leave it alone." I grab a yoga mat for poses to end the workout. "We're at rival firms, and if there's one thing I know has not changed about Jared, he's still ruthless. More now than ever."

"And I had to go and give him guest passes." Quinn adjusts my body in Ustrasana pose.

"Yeah, thanks for that." I laugh at her chagrined expression. "It's okay. Hopefully we can avoid each other."

"And how was it last night after not seeing Zo for so long?" Her knowing look seeks to know more. "You guys fuck like savages?"

Never.

I chastise myself for the thought. We've been together six months, and I keep hoping for wild chandelier sex, but that hasn't happened. It sounds crazy, but sex has never been as important to me as all the other things that make a relationship work, that make it rich.

"It was really good to be with him again for sure," I say, neatly sidestepping her question.

The timer on her watch goes off, indicating that our session is over.

"When is he moving in?" she asks.

"The Titans will make the playoffs." I grab my water bottle and bag from the corner of the studio. "I don't anticipate them going too far, though. Not this year. He'll come here after his last playoff game and plans to stay until he has to report for preseason workouts."

"Wow. That sounds serious." Quinn smiles warmly. "He's a good man."

"The best." I deftly shift topics. "I'm loving the Girl, You Better app, by the way."

We chat about the app and how it might be improved until we reach the front desk. As soon as employees spot her, Quinn is pulled in several different directions.

"I gotta go." She kisses my cheek. "Make sure to log your points."

"All right, Sarge," I joke. "I will."

I'm leaving, focused on logging my workout into my phone, when I bump into someone entering the building as I exit. We somehow end up trapped together in a partition of the revolving door.

"I'm so sorry! I…"

Him.

"Imagine seeing you here," Jared drawls, standing still so I can't move forward either. His closely cropped hair glints golden in the bright morning sun.

"It *is* my gym," I answer caustically.

"*Your* gym," Jared says, arms folded across his chest. "*Your* city. I don't remember you being this possessive."

"I'm surprised you remember me at all."

One dark-blond brow ascends, and that wide mouth tips at one corner.

"Pretty Pastel," he murmurs, his deep voice and his damn seductive scent suffusing the tight glass-encased space, making it a hothouse.

"What?" My mind blanks because he couldn't be saying…

"You still use the same dryer sheets." He leans forward and sniffs my shoulder.

"Stop that." I bat him away, conscious of the fact I didn't take the shower I had planned.

"Are they or are they not called Pretty Pastel?" he asks.

His self-satisfied look darkens and intensifies the longer we stand transfixed in this glass box of boiling air.

"You don't want to know all the things I remember, Ban," he says, his laugh husky. "Or maybe you do."

"I do not." Our words, our breath, whatever is condensing in this partition between us, is literally fogging the glass. "Let me out."

A woman enters on the other side, bewildered that the revolving door isn't revolving, that we aren't moving. Jared flashes her one of those smiles, and she blushes and bats her damn eyelashes. We can only get out of this if he steps forward and I step back. Even for just the few seconds it takes to free us, it feels like he's advancing on me.

"I'll be seeing you, Banner," he calls from inside as I walk to the parking lot.

"Not if I see you first," I mutter.

I click my car open and climb in, slamming the door with unnecessary roughness. I don't even make it to the interstate before the phone rings in my car, my mother's name displaying on the screen.

"*Hola*, Mama."

"*Hola*, Bannini."

When Mama's family first moved here from Mexico, she spoke no English. One teacher in the overcrowded San Diego public school took extra time and care to make sure Mama learned English and helped her adjust to her new circumstances, her new country. That teacher was Ms. Banner Johnson. My namesake, but my family calls me Bannini. How that started, no one remembers, but it stuck.

"How are you?" I continue in Spanish. "How's Papa?"

"Eh. We are fine. Always fine."

"Papa's taking his medication?"

Considering what Mama cooks every day, diabetes was practically an inevitability. I'm constantly after Mama to adjust their diets. Between what he eats and how hard he works running the construction business he built from the ground up, I have reason to worry.

"Yes, yes," Mama replies with a touch of impatience. "How are you? Are you eating? You were wasting away last time I saw you."

Only my mother would accuse me of wasting away at a size ten.

"I'm eating. Promise, Mama."

"How is my boy?" Mama's voice goes soft and sweet with the question, and there's no doubt who she's asking about.

"Zo is fine." I laugh and take the exit to my house. "He's at my place. Still sleeping when I left."

"Tell him I'm mad he was in San Diego and I didn't get to see him," Mama says. She's actually chastising *me* for not bringing Zo to the house.

"Scheduling was tight," I say by way of apology. "I'll make sure you get to see him soon."

"He's coming to Anna's quinceañera, yeah?"

My niece, Anna, turns fifteen this year. The quinceañera is like our blowout sweet sixteen party…but at fifteen. Our bat mitzvah. Our rite of passage making the transition from girl to woman and the perfect excuse to throw a massive party.

"That's months away, Mama, but, yes, Zo is planning to be there."

"Good. He's family."

Even before we started dating, Zo was considered family. That first Christmas after his family died, I invited him to spend it with us. He's been adopted into my family and spends every holiday with us. They dropped hints about a romantic relationship between us years before Zo expressed interest. Once they found out he wanted more, the teasing, the pressure only intensified. It was just a matter of time. We've only been dating six months, but talk of a wedding and little *bebés* for Mama to spoil has already begun.

"Camilla knows I'm paying for the venue, right?" I ask. My sister is a single mother, doing so much on her own and always refusing my help.

"She didn't like it," Mama admits, "but she has agreed."

"Why is it so hard for her to let me help, Mama? We are sisters."

"She is your *older* sister, Bannini," Mama says softly. "All the things you both dreamed about, you've actually done. Your sister made different choices. She wouldn't trade Anna for the world, but hers was a different path. She's been slowed down. Maybe sometimes it's hard for her to see you running so far ahead."

That renders me speechless. It never occurred to me that Camilla, gorgeous, perfectly formed Camilla, could ever envy me. My sister does not have a weight problem. Never has. She's beautiful, and with that beauty came many temptations. While I was studying and wondering why no one else wanted to spend their weekends learning Italian, she yielded to every temptation, the greatest of which was Anna's father, who is now nowhere to be found. I suck my teeth and shake my head, exasperated.

"Well, this is Anna's big day, and I will help make it as special as it can possibly be," I say. "Like Camilla and I had."

My quinceañera wasn't in a beautiful villa like the one I'm reserving for Anna. It was in a small *salon* near the church where Mass was held. My aunts all prepared the food and the entire family was involved. My *damas* and I worked for months on the carefully choreographed dance. I bonded with all fourteen girls and did the same for them when it was their turn.

"I still have my first heels I received that night," I tell Mama, smiling, reminiscing.

"Your Uncle Javier picked those out, believe it or not," Mama says, her deep chuckle making me miss her smile.

"Yes, but he could barely stand up to help put them on when the time came," I say, my words touched with affection for one of my favorite godparents.

"Yes, well, Javier loves his tequila almost as much as he loves you."

We laugh together as I pull into the short, pebbled driveway of my pride and joy, the midcentury-modern post-and-beam house I purchased when I relocated. Though it has only three bedrooms and two baths, the tongue-and-groove ceilings, clerestory windows, walls of glass, and cool concrete floors create an open, airy tone that I appreciate after apartment living in New York for years. And the view through all that glass offers me the Hollywood Hills on nature's platter.

I let myself into the house through the garage, still listening to Mama, and smile at Zo over his bare, muscled chest and bowl of cereal.

"Mama, let's talk later," I say. "There's someone here who wants to speak to you."

I hand the phone to Zo.

"*Hola*, Mama," he says, trying to pull me onto his lap. I avoid his hands and laugh over my shoulder, leaving him and my mother chatting in rapid Spanish and laughing like the old friends they are. Probably plotting our engagement. I leave them to it so I can shower and get to work.

I'm drying off when the bathroom door opens, letting steam out and my boyfriend in. Irrationally self-conscious, I grip the towel tighter around my breasts. Silly. He's seen me naked many times during our relationship, but I'm not used to sharing my space and my privacy. His big hands grip me by the hips as he pulls me close and kisses me thoroughly. I'm breathless and reassured by the time he's done. This can work. This *should* and *will* work. There's no reason it shouldn't.

"How was the gym?" he asks, stepping away to shuck off his boxers, revealing his beautiful, well-conditioned athlete's body.

"It was great." I go into my walk-in closet, pulling out a summer pantsuit to put on once I'm done with my hair and makeup. "Quinn had no mercy, as usual."

"I wish I'd gotten to spend more time with her." He raises his voice over the shower. "I wish I had more time with you, for that matter."

"I know. This trip was much too quick," I yell back. "And next week I'm in Denver for that convention."

I head back into the bathroom to grab my hair dryer. There's a snow globe on the counter beside it. It's heavy when I pick it up. The base is marble with *Vancouver, British Columbia* etched into the stone. A winter sunset fills the glass arch, a gold-and-scarlet sky vivid against the snowy ground and the drift of powdery flakes when I shake it.

I walk over to the shower, globe in hand, delighted grin on my face.

"And what is this?" I ask.

A pleased smile creases Zo's handsome face. "Just a little something I picked up for you."

"It's beautiful." I lean my head in to kiss him lightly on the lips, but his soapy hands slide down my arms and bring me under the spray.

"Zo!" I laugh and grab at the towel slipping from my breasts and the globe slipping from my hand.

"Thank me properly," he says, his voice husky, his eyes hot on my wet, bare skin.

I tip up on my toes to kiss him, taking his tongue into my mouth and allowing the towel to fall. I press my body into his and slide my fingers into the thick, wet curls at his neck. He groans, cups my ass, and pushes into the V of my naked thighs.

"I can't. I'm already late." I giggle into the watery kiss, pick up the now-sodden towel, and step out of the shower. "But consider yourself properly thanked."

His laughter follows me to the linen closet, where I find a fresh towel to dry off and wrap around myself again.

"You got a full day?" Zo asks, his voice still slightly raised over the shower.

"Very." I run a hand through the hair hanging past my shoulders and pick up the dryer. "Isn't every day?"

"When do you meet with Lowell?"

Even with my back turned, I know Zo well enough to hear concern in his voice.

Lowell, the Titans' president of basketball operations, is a tough customer. He'll play hardball because Zo's numbers are down, and it's bad timing. Right at the end of the regular season, going into post, his performance started suffering, but Zo has almost a decade of outstanding performance in this league. He's eligible for a supermax contract, the designated veteran player extension, which can be up to 35 percent of a team's cap space but can only be given by the team that drafted the player. He's earned it, and I plan to get it for him.

"Hey." I put my dryer on the counter and turn to face the shower, propping my butt against the counter and meeting the concern I anticipated in his eyes. "You know I got you."

"*En las buenas*," he says, our private message of loyalty through the years.

Through thick.

"*En las malas*," I reply.

Through thin.

I'm reassured by the warm feeling of contentment his smile brings. The trepidation I haven't been able to shake, my fear that our relationship will somehow ruin our friendship is unfounded. We've been too close for too long.

En las buenas y en las malas.

What could possibly come between us?

CHAPTER 11
JARED

"Do not live someone else's life and someone else's idea of what womanhood is. Womanhood is you."
　　　　　　　　　—Viola Davis, Oscar-winning actress

I DON'T BELIEVE IN FATE.

"The universe" is not some omnipotent force moving us around like chess pieces, manipulating us or protecting us or colliding us. Work hard, good things happen.

Or not.

It's life. A cosmic crapshoot in which odds don't mean shit. I'm more fatalism, less fate. With that said, I do believe circumstances happen in a certain order at a certain time. And for a certain reason. That does sound suspiciously like fate, but I dwell less on the why things happen and more on how I should respond when they do.

I sense storms coming, things shifting in the air. That helps me plan. It's helped me in every area of my life, especially the market. I have my own money, nothing compared to Bent's generational coffers. His mother traces her roots back to the Mayflower. Several times Bent has tipped me off, gotten me in on the ground floor of something big, but it's my gut that tells me when to play. An intuition. I just know.

I've seen Banner Morales more in the last two weeks than I have in the last ten years, and I "just know" something's shifting. When we literally ran into each other at the gym, the scent of those dryer sheets transported me back to late nights in Sudz. Before we worked for rival firms. Before Prescott's stupid prank broke the fragile connection between us. Back to a time of discovery. Deciding what I felt for her. Figuring out how she felt about me when all I had to go on were the shifting winds.

Something's shifting.

I stand outside the ballroom where Banner's doing her talk on women in sports management. I finished my presentation for this convention in Denver a little early and found my feet bringing me here. I'm not a woman in sports management. I could lie to myself and say I'm coming to meet Iris. We'd arranged to connect after our respective sessions. She's in here. Knowing her hero worship for Banner, she's in the front row capturing every word as soon as it leaves Banner's mouth.

I may be a ruthless son of a bitch, but I don't lie. Especially not to myself.

I'm not here for Iris. I'm here for Banner.

I push the door open, hoping I can, even as the only male in the room—and six three to boot—go unnoticed. I stand at the very back, pressed into a corner. At some point there was probably standing room only in here, but they've all sat down in seats and on the floor. There's a growing number of women in sports management, and they all seem to be squeezed into Banner's session.

"I'm not here to talk to you about sports," Banner says from the small stage. "We all specialize in various sports or fields. Some are agents. Some are in sports broadcasting. Some marketing. We could be here all day talking about the ways we're different in our focus."

She takes a sip from a nearby water bottle and spreads a smile around the room.

"I'm here to talk about how we are the same. Our common challenges and possibilities," Banner says. "For example, women only make eighty cents on the dollar to what men make. That's white women. Black women, not so fast. You're only at sixty-three cents on the dollar. And my Latina sisters, *lo siento*. We average only fifty-four percent of every dollar men make."

Banner pauses, giving the discouraging numbers space to sink in. I haven't seen her hair down much in the past, but it's loose around her shoulders today, thick and dark and shiny. She wears a narrow black leather skirt and a red silk blouse. The front view shows a breakneck curve from waist to hip. She turns to the side, and I see the diabolical dip from back to ass. Her only accessories are simple gold earrings and her confidence, which drapes her from head to toe.

Damn, she looks good. Like the girl I knew, the one I *saw* even back then. The girl I saw *inside* has taken over the outside, too. Banner slowly scans the crowd from left to right. It feels like she's meeting every eye even though that's impossible. Dr. Albright taught us that trick in our Debate & Public Speaking class.

Convince me.

Our old professor's mantra pops into my head, and inevitably, I recall the night I asked Banner to convince me she was a good kisser. It was too much at first, that kiss. *I* was too much. Too hungry and deprived after a semester of wanting something I knew would be devastatingly sweet.

And it was. Sweeter, better than I thought it would be. She was better. She was sweeter. I literally stole her breath with that kiss.

She stole mine, too.

"The truth is in the numbers," Banner continues. "We make less than men do, but the *future* isn't in the numbers. What's true today won't be in a hundred years. In ten years. It was held as *fact* that the Earth was flat until it was proven otherwise. It was *true* that women couldn't vote a hundred years ago. But the Earth is round, and now we vote. Now we speak and are heard. We remade truth. We reshaped fact."

Banner is lit from the inside by her passion, and her convictions stand her up straight and proud.

"Our field is male-dominated," she says. "We are a minority, some of us a few times over, but we have a voice. You have your talent. You have determination. I was doubted in every boardroom I walked into, but I never doubted myself because I knew what I was capable of. Do you know what you're capable of? Because if you don't, they'll never know either. *You* are your greatest natural resource and don't let anyone strip you of that or tell you it's not enough. We are making the future, defying the odds just being in this room right now."

Banner swings a look over the crowd.

"I don't give a damn about odds," she says. "Odds don't tell me what I can't do. Odds just tell me how hard I'll have to work to get what I want. Don't allow anyone to make you feel less."

A wry smile quirks the mouth that so captivated me ten years ago.

"Let me get even more personal for a minute." She swallows, glances at the floor and then back up to meet the crowd's attentiveness head-on. "I've always struggled with my weight. For most of my life, I compared myself to my sister, who was naturally slim. I compared myself to women in magazines, who looked nothing like me. I let men determine how I felt about my body based on how *they* saw me. I allowed those things to make me feel smaller than I was. Not on the outside, on the inside. On the inside I was a highly intelligent woman who spoke several languages, was the first in my family to go to college, and won full scholarships to the schools of my choice, but I hid that girl under bulky clothes."

Banner disabuses me of the notion that I've gone undetected when she looks directly at me, finds me in the very back.

"I hid her in the dark," she says more softly, holding my stare for a few seconds before moving past me, but even when she looks away, I feel seared. Like in one glance and with a few words she's burned years away. She takes us back to a darkened laundromat. The bright swirl of whites flashing in the washing machine. The toss and slap of darks in the dryer. The *thump-thump* of my heart while I waited to kiss her again.

"I don't hide anymore," Banner continues. "Not in the dark. Not under bulky clothes. Not even behind my intelligence, which I sometimes used as a shield to keep people out. Whether I'm five pounds up or ten pounds down, I'm done hiding. I am done letting my waistline and other people define me."

She shares her husky laugh with the crowd.

"Culture twists what it is to even be a feminist, tries to sort us into categories and force us to choose between being a good mother and being a successful businesswoman. I unabashedly want to rule every boardroom meeting I step into, and I unashamedly want at least four kids."

She smiles and shrugs.

"What can I say? I'm Catholic."

She pauses for her audience to laugh, wearing a small grin while she waits.

"What I'm saying is be unafraid to want it all and be disciplined enough to work hard to get it." Her smile fades, replaced by a steely determination that radiates from her inside and glows out. "We can be fierce and feminine. Tenderhearted and tough as nails. Life is seldom binary. And I've talked a lot about patriarchy and living, working in a male-dominated culture, but men are not our enemies. Any force that would diminish us, pigeonhole us, would make us one thing instead of all that we are, that's the enemy...even if it's inside *you*.

"There are some real jerks out there, especially in the locker rooms and boardrooms we frequent, but there are good men, too. I have good men in my life. My father, who's been faithful to my mother for forty years. My boyfriend is a good man. Sometimes they feel more like exceptions than the rule, but they're out there."

Her expression softens, and her smile grows wide.

"If there is one thing I can leave with you, it's this: We work in a jungle and are surrounded by alpha males and apex predators. Everyone's looking to be the last one standing, to be at the top of the food chain, and they sometimes don't care who gets hurt in the process. Don't lose your heart. Don't lose your soul. Don't lose your compass, and that doesn't mean don't win. Win. Fight. *Conquer*. You have just as much right to success as anyone who works for it. It may be a jungle, and they may be lions…"

She pauses, her eyes finding mine again, holding mine.

"But the daughter of a lion is still a lion, and this is your domain."

"You got everything?" I ask Iris, rolling her suitcase out to the front of the hotel and peering up the street for the car taking her to the airport.

"Yeah," she answers absently, checking her phone. "I'm sure Sarai is fine. It's just lice, but August figuring out lice?"

"Yeah," I agree with a wry grin. "Get home as fast as you can."

We both laugh at that.

"I just want to make sure it's handled thoroughly." She pokes out her bottom lip. "I do hate to leave early, but I've gone to all the sessions I wanted to attend."

"Good. I'll debrief with the team next week to hear takeaways, things we learned. That kind of thing."

"I, uh, saw you." Iris glances up from her phone, assessing me and chewing the corner of her bottom lip. "In Banner's session. In the back."

"Oh yeah?"

And, Iris? And?

"Iris, I think this is your guy in the black Tahoe. Oh, nope."

"Was it just a matter of checking out the enemy, or…" Her expression asks me to fill in a blank I have no intention of filling in.

"Bagley's a rival firm." I keep my voice even, neutral. "But Banner's not my enemy. I was just curious. Don't read too much into it."

"What would I read into it?" Her eyes are wide and innocent, but I know better. Iris has survived a lot, been through things that sharpen your senses and intuition.

"Just checking on an old"—I search for the right word—"friend. Banner and I went to college together."

"I had no idea." A grin spreads on her face. "Did you two date or something?"

I look past her shoulder to the black SUV pulling up.

"Not exactly. Drop it, okay? Your car's here."

After a searching glance, she shrugs. "Consider it dropped."

We greet the driver, and I haul her bag into the back.

"What are you doing tonight?" she asks, one foot on the running board, one foot on the ground.

"There's a thing at the bar. I'll show my face. Or I may skip it and go crash. I'm exhausted."

She climbs in and leans out the window. "Thank you for the opportunity to come and experience this."

"Guess I don't have to ask which session was your favorite. Banner, right?"

"You looked like you were enjoying her..." Mischief sparks behind her eyes. "I mean, *the talk*, too."

"What happened to consider it dropped?" I lightly tap the hood, signaling it's time to head out. "Go exterminate my niece's hair."

As soon as I enter the hotel lobby, Mitch and a few other agents accost me.

"Foster," Mitch slurs, already halfway to falling down. "Join us at the bar."

Why the hell not? Alone in my room, I'll only rehearse what I heard today, the things Banner said that have been looping through my head. The last thing I need to be thinking about is Banner. She works for a rival firm. She's dating a man widely considered the NBA's patron saint. And the main reason I shouldn't be thinking about Banner? She hates me.

All day I've walked around with this...*emotion* I can't quite name agitating my insides, seething under my skin. Of all the things Banner said in her session today, the least impactful thing has impacted me the most. The one I can't stop rehearing.

My boyfriend is a good man.

Zo Vidale digs wells in Africa, feeds hungry kids in India, and probably helps old ladies cross the street. Every Good Samaritan and citizen award there is, he has won. He *is* a good man, and I, along with the rest of the known world, admire him. I respect him.

So why the hell does it bother me to hear Banner call him a good man?

"So, Foster," one of the agents—maybe Jimmy, I think is his name—says, "I heard you went to college with Banner Morales. That right?"

Is the world conspiring against my peace of mind?

"Yeah," I one-word it, prop my elbows on the bar, and motion to the bartender. "Jameson, please."

"I heard her session was packed."

"Yeah," I answer automatically.

"You were in there?" Mitch perks up to demand. "I thought it was just for chicks."

"I needed my sister-in-law," I lie. "So I poked my head in to find her."

"What I want to know," Maybe Jimmy asks, leaning forward conspiratorially, "did she look that good in college?"

Frumpy sweater. Baggy sweatpants. Hair scraped back. No makeup. Seven freckles.

"Yeah," I reply, staring into my drink. "She did."

"Did not," Mitch counters with a sneer. "I interned with her at Bagley. She didn't look anything like that, but I guess it didn't matter to Vidale."

"What's that mean?" Maybe Jimmy asks, practically smacking his lips for some juicy gossip.

"*I* was supposed to meet with Vidale." Mitch leans forward, glancing around to make sure he's not being overheard...or more likely to make sure he *is* overheard. "Last minute, Cal grabs Morales for the meeting. She goes into the conference room. Next thing I know, wham, bam! She's Vidale's agent. Hadn't even graduated or taken the exam yet. How's that happen?"

Mitch's "theory" of how that happened is scrawled all over his face.

"Whoa," Maybe Jimmy says, eyes wide. "Are you saying she fucked Vidale to get the job?"

My muscles tighten, straining with the effort not to slam Mitch's head into the bar. Everyone knows how good Banner is. These assholes don't commission a third of what she makes. Jealousy is an ugly emotion that makes you do and say petty things. A defense for her burns the tip of my tongue, but I say nothing. I swallow my Jameson, my frustration, and that same nameless emotion clawing at my insides.

"At least now they aren't trying to hide it anymore," Mitch says. "I'm surprised Cal hasn't put a stop to it. If their relationship goes south, Bagley could lose our best baller."

"What if he knows it won't go south?" Maybe Jimmy asks. "If this has been going on for years, they might be getting married or something."

My boyfriend is a good man.

"Even marriage is no guarantee," I hear myself saying. "And if Banner is stupid enough to fuck her client now, she has to know people will think that's how she landed him in the first place."

As soon as I say the harsh words I want to take them back, but it's too late. Mitch looks past my shoulder, and his eyes widen. His mouth drops open.

"B-Banner," he stutters. "Uh... We were just... Pull up a chair. Have a drink."

I close my eyes, praying to the whiskey gods that Banner didn't hear my last comment. When I turn on my barstool, there is no doubt in my mind that she heard every word.

"Let me get this straight," she says through tight lips, ignoring Mitch's pitiful cover-up attempt. "I got where I am by fucking Zo. Do I have it right?"

"Banner," I start.

"Fuck you, Jared." She doesn't even look at me when she says it. She glares at Maybe Jimmy. "*You* haven't signed a new client in two years, and the few you have left are jumping like you're the *Titanic* because you've managed their careers into the toilet."

She points to Mitch. "Cal Bagley would have fired *you* years ago if your father wasn't his best friend. I spend half my time cleaning up your shit and the other half taking up your slack."

Her eyes, when they shift to me, are obsidian. Hard. Dark. Cold. Even when she's been furious with me in the past, irritated with me, she's never looked at me this way.

"And how dare you intimate that anyone would assume I'm successful because I fuck my clients?" She hurls the question at me.

"I didn't say—"

"When you wouldn't even own your agency," she cuts in over me, "if your brother hadn't *bought* it for you. So is your success because of nepotism?"

The hell?

I stand up fast and step so close I smell her shampoo. After all these years, it's the same scent. Something fresh and clean and distinctly hers. I step so close her head falls back so she can maintain her glare, but *she* doesn't fall back. I'm so close the sight of her in this black dress hugging her curves, with her hair piled high on her head like a crown, swallows up my peripheral vision and Banner is all I see.

"You should get your facts straight before you speak," I say so low only she can hear me, though I'm sure Mitch and Maybe Jimmy strain to catch it.

"And you should be careful before you insult me," she returns, her words a challenge, a pistol drawn. "Or my boyfriend."

I don't allow myself many regrets. I don't say I'm sorry often simply because I'm usually not. I say what I mean, I mean what I say, and I stand behind it. If it hurts someone, as long as it was true I'm not sorry. But I regret saying that about Banner to these two idiots. I *don't* think it's a good idea for agents to date clients, and I expressed as much to Banner at the game, but saying it to Mitch and Maybe Jimmy felt wrong. Tearing Banner down feels wrong.

I bend until we're eye level, stare to unflinching stare.

"I'm sorry, Ban," I whisper. "I shouldn't have said it."

She blinks like my apology startled her and steps back, inserting space between us. She spares a quick glance at Mitch and Maybe Jimmy before looking back up at me.

"You're not sorry, Jared," she says softly, glaring at me. "But you will be."

That's her parting shot. She turns on her high heels and leaves the bar, dignity in the set of her shoulders and indignation in the rigid line of her back.

It's only when I'm still at the bar long after Mitch and Maybe Jimmy have left, nursing my fourth Jameson, that I process what's happened. For once I allowed emotion to get the best of me and I said something I should never have said in front of people who should never have heard me say it.

Ironically, it's only when I'm almost too drunk to stand that I gain perfect clarity. Only when the room starts spinning am I still enough to understand.

My boyfriend is a good man.

You should be careful before you insult me or my boyfriend.

Banner praising Zo. Banner protecting Zo. Banner *being* with Zo.

That emotion that has been choking me since I heard Banner speak today—hell, maybe since August told me about Banner dating Zo—that emotion is the one that makes you do and say petty things. That emotion has a name.

It's jealousy.

CHAPTER 12
JARED

"So you survived your first lice infestation, huh?" I ask August. He's on speakerphone, and I'm on my laptop checking the market, half my attention on my brother, the other half on the numbers.

"Barely and only because Iris came home early," he replies from the other end. "She loved the conference, by the way."

"Yeah, she told me." I squint at the upward-pointing arrow on the last investment Bent told me about. Maybe time to buy more shares.

"She especially enjoyed Banner Morales," August says.

My fingers pause over the keyboard at the mention of Banner. I've been back three days, and the burn in my belly hasn't gone away. It's like a half-lit stick of dynamite, a sizzle waiting to blow. I don't know if I'm waiting for her to make a move or to make mine. Either way, something will happen.

"Yeah, she told me Banner's session was great," I say after a few moments.

"She said you were *in* the session," August continues, a question in his voice.

"Sounds like Iris said a lot. Glad she enjoyed it."

"Are you seriously considering recruiting Banner to Elevation? Because I think it's a great idea. I'd love to have Kenan represented through us instead of Bagley."

"Not that I'm saying I'd try for Banner," I say neutrally, "but you think Kenan would leave Bagley and follow her?"

"Pffft. In a second. Kenan will never leave Banner. He trusts her, and you know how hard it is for Kenan to trust anyone."

"Yeah, with good reason after the number his ex did on him."

"Not ex yet. She's still giving him a hard time on the divorce."

"You gotta be shitting me. She cheats with one of his teammates and has the audacity to pitch a fit?"

"She's frustrated because Banner made sure his prenup was ironclad. Banner worked with his lawyer to build in special protections. Apparently, Banner didn't trust her from the beginning."

"Yeah. Banner has good instincts."

"Which brings me back to my question," August says, persistent son of a bitch. "Think she'd come to Elevation?"

Not as long as I'm here.

"Who knows?" I say aloud, completing the transaction to buy more shares. "We can revisit the Banner thing later, though I don't hold out much hope that she would leave Bagley when he just gave her the LA office to manage."

"Just wondering. I like her. She's smart and honest."

"True on both counts," I agree. "But I *will* have some good news about Lamont Christopher the next time we talk."

"*Going number one in the draft* Lamont Christopher?" Surprise colors August's voice. "Damn, bruh. That would be quite the coup. I thought it was all but a done deal with Mitch Sanderson."

"It's never a done deal with Sanderson because Sanderson couldn't 'do' a deal if his mother's life depended on it. It's still developing. I'll keep you posted."

"Do that."

"And enjoy the Bahamas," I say, remembering the trip they have planned. "You and the fam deserve a little postseason vacay."

"I'd rather be in the playoffs," August says solemnly.

"The Waves are an expansion team," I remind him unnecessarily.

"One you chose to stay with when you had the chance to play for a championship squad."

Even though it turned out well, it still grates that one of the best deals I ever negotiated got left on the table when August walked away from it.

"Is this really the best time for an I-told-you-so conversation?" August asks, irritation clear in his tone.

"It is when I told you so." I laugh at the heavy sigh he releases on speakerphone. "Soon, Brother. It takes time. And with you and Kenan on the same team, it's only a *matter* of time."

"We *do* work well together," he admits. "Which reminds me, we have a charity project we wanna collab on. I need to talk it through with you. Sponsors and details and stuff."

"Sure." I glance up when Chyna walks in, an I-got-a-secret smirk plastered on her face. "Hey, let's talk later, Gus. Some developments with that Christopher kid I need to handle."

"Nice. All right, Brother. Later."

I disconnect and lean back in my chair, hands linked over my stomach while Chyna plops down into the seat on the other side of my desk.

"Whatcha got?" I ask, returning her eager smile.

"Lamont and his cousin Eric enjoyed their night on the town," she purrs, flicking one dreadlock over her shoulder and sinking deeper into the leather seat.

"Good." I grimace remembering that night. "They went hard. I could barely keep up."

"Well, we did provide a bottomless stack of singles in LA's hottest strip club," Chyna says wryly. "So going hard was the point."

"Any fruit from our labor?" My voice is casual, but inside I'm anything but laid-back. I've never liked or respected Mitch Sanderson, but after the things he said about Banner, blocking his shot feels personal. My inner tiger wants off the leash.

The daughter of a lion is still a lion.

She thinks I'm in the Pride, which means she still thinks that night was about some stupid rite of passage. Over the years, as the gulf between us widened, it seemed less important that she believe me. She had her life, her career in New York, and I had mine in Chicago. Now that we're in the same city, moving in the same circles, I have to admit I want *something* with Banner again. She's dating Vidale, so I keep telling myself I'd settle for friendship. That's the right thing to do, but the right thing doesn't always come naturally to me.

"Are you even hearing me?" Chyna demands, ripping me out of my own thoughts.

"Sorry, yeah." I refocus my attention on her face. "What'd you say again?"

"Man, I hope your head is in the game for this meeting," Chyna says sharply. "We've invested a lot into this deal. Eric says Lamont is ready to sign."

"Shit." I did zone out. "Where? When?"

"His hotel in under an hour." Chyna taps her phone. "Just sent you the address. Get over there and close the deal."

"Contract already sent over?" I ask, adjusting the cuffs on my shirt and slipping into my suit jacket.

"Yup." Chyna nods and also stands, heading back to her desk in the outer office. "Emailed you the standard contract, already modified."

I'm on my way to the elevator but circle back to her desk. I drop a kiss on her cheek and walk backward to the elevator while pointing at her. "Now don't you go falling in love with me."

Chyna laughs, sitting down at her desk and shaking her head but looking pleased. "I've seen girls after you're done with them. No, thank you. I like my heart in one piece."

So do I. The closest I've ever come to a broken heart was Banner, and she didn't even know it. Still doesn't realize how real it was, what I felt for her. I haven't allowed myself to think of what could have happened, how things might have gone if Prescott hadn't ruined that night. With Banner back in my orbit, my mind keeps drifting back to those possibilities. As I make the fifteen-minute drive to Lamont's hotel, that's what I think about instead of what it will take to seal the deal with this year's number one draft pick.

"Get your shit together, Foster," I reprimand myself when I pull up in front of the hotel. I hand the keys to the valet, enter the hotel, and head up to the suite Chyna texted me. I'm rounding the corner when Banner emerges from a room just ahead. She's dressed in all black. Wide-legged cuffed pants and a fitted black turtleneck, punctuated with a red belt tied at the waist. Red lips, shiny stilettos, hair a sleek, dark curtain hanging loose past her shoulders.

"Banner, fancy meeting you here." I glance at the room number above her head. Lamont's room.

"Very fancy," she replies, stepping around me. She takes a few steps and then snaps her fingers, turning to find me still watching her. "Oh. I almost forgot. Knock, knock."

I'm piecing this together, and I'm not sure how one of her infamous knock-knock jokes fits in, but it's a blast from the past I've been mentally revisiting all day.

"Huh?" I ask.

"Knock. Knock." She quirks her mouth so that damn dimple dents one cheek. "Humor me."

"Okay. Who's there?"

All signs of humor fall off her face.

"Lamont Christopher's new agent." A few quick steps bring her back immediately in front of me, and she pokes her sharp little nail into my chest. "Block *that*, motherfucker."

She blocked my shot.

I knew what it meant seeing her leave Lamont's room, but it's only when she voices it that I truly appreciate what a masterful move this is.

"Karma's a bitch, huh?" she asks, satisfaction stretching her mouth into a wide smile.

"Apparently, she's not the only one," I reply admiringly.

Her smile holds, but her eyes narrow and frost over.

"Remember this *bitch* next time you and your pride of lions think about insulting me," she spits, lightning in her eyes, thunder in her voice. "Or assuming I got where I am any way other than hard work. Remember this moment when I handed you your ass, Foster."

Her anger, her indignation hit me with a blast of heat that burns through all my reasons and rationale and excuses to cover up what I have known deep down since senior year.

This woman is my match.

She is bright and good. And I can be dark, bad when I have to be. Sometimes when I *don't* have to be but just want to be. She is day, and I am night. When day and night are absolutely equal, it's equinox. Banner is my equinox. My equal. The revelation rattles around inside me, but my face, my surface remains smooth.

The game we're playing just changed, and she doesn't even know it. Banner is smarter than I am, but my gut is better. My instincts are sharper. I'm a weather vane. I feel shifts in the air, sense coming storms before she does. That sentience is my greatest advantage.

"So how'd you do it?" I ask easily, not missing a beat and giving nothing away.

"Effortlessly." She angles a look up at me that is both withering and full of pity. "While you were entertaining Cousin It at strip clubs, I was talking to Lamont's mother."

I lean back against the closed door to listen. I really don't care how she did it. I just want her to stay a few minutes longer so I can take my time appreciating every magnificent inch of her.

"Ahhh." I nod and turn down the corners of my mouth. "His mother back in Atlanta."

"I flew there straight from Denver, actually. Even attended a Sunday service and donated to help pay for the church's new roof."

"Wow." *I don't care about the church's roof.* "You pulled out all the stops."

"They really *do* need that new roof."

She smirks and turns to leave, but I cuff her wrist with my hand to stop her. Her surprised glance collides with mine over her shoulder. I subtly tighten around the delicate bones of her wrist, push away from the door, and step into her comfort zone, close enough for our scents to mingle and our breaths to mix in the tiny bit of space I'm allowing. I'm crowding her, but I don't care. Every minute that passes, I care less about Lamont Christopher and his cousin and his mama and their church and its roof.

And Alonzo Vidale. I care least about him and his committed relationship with my equinox.

"You really showed me," I say, pitching my voice low and dipping my head until our foreheads almost touch, intimacy cocooning us in the open, in the hallway. Her pulse sputters through the warm skin under my fingers. Her breath catches, and her eyelashes flutter in rapid blinks. She swallows, the muscles of her throat working under the velvety skin. I'd love to sink my teeth into that tendon, to mark the slim column of her neck. I want her to wear me and carry my scent everywhere she goes. She's the only one who has ever stirred anything primal in me.

Her eyes shift from my hand encompassing her wrist to my face, a mask I've smoothed free of all the urges and feelings and *things* roiling under the surface. She tugs at her wrist, but I don't relent.

"Let me go." Her voice is husky but calm.

"Of course," I say politely, releasing her.

With one last searching glance, the one trying to figure out what's changed, what's going on, she turns and leaves.

I'll let you go, Banner.

For now.

CHAPTER 13
BANNER

"IF YOU TRY TO SHUT US DOWN, WE'LL SHOW YOU JUST HOW WE GET DOWN." The opening lines of "Girl Gang" blast through the Echo by my bed, tearing me from a nightmare. A sensual nightmare starring none other than Jared Foster. The dream started with him gripping my wrist the way he did in the hall. An innocent enough beginning, but then he sucked my neck, untied the red belt at my waist, pushed his head under my turtleneck, and bit my breast. Thank God Alexa put a stop to that horror show before it went any further.

The song still blasts from the Echo, and I'm buried under my pillow. I moan, rubbing my legs together like a horny cricket.

"Alexa, shut the hell up," I say impatiently.

The music stops abruptly, but the voice from Quinn's app triggered by the five a.m. workout on my schedule takes up where Alexa left off.

"Girl, you better get that ass up and out the door."

"What the hell?" Zo asks from behind me, his voice sleepy and confused. "All these alarms and bells and shit. How do you ever sleep in?"

"I don't." I toss the covers back and throw my legs over the side, talking myself into standing up when a muscled arm reaches around my waist and drags me backward. "Zo, I have to get up."

"No, you don't." He presses me back into the pillows and settles between my legs. "Sleep in with me."

He dots kisses along my neck and squeezes my breast. My nipple lifts involuntarily under the persistence of his thumb. He slips a hand into my pajama bottoms, and I know what he'll find. Dread twists inside my belly.

"*Dios*," Zo says, sliding his mouth down my chest, taking my nipple through the silk pajama top. "*Tan mojado.*"

So wet.

Guilt clogs my throat. I can't do this. Not with him after dreaming about damn Jared Foster. I hate this. I'm so disciplined in every waking moment of my life, but I have no control over my unfaithful subconscious and its contrary longings.

"I really need to get up, Zo," I whisper, biting my lip and training my eyes on the ceiling instead of looking at him.

His large palm cups my bottom, pulling me into his erection, into his eager thrust. My body doesn't care that I was dreaming about Jared. Doesn't care how disrespectful it would be to sleep with Zo right now, that it would feel like a betrayal. It just wants to be filled. It just wants to fuck.

And so I do.

I flip through the pages of the preliminary contract, a frown puckering my brows. Sutton Lowell, Vancouver Titans' president of basketball operations, sits across the conference room table, waiting. When I reach the last page, I look around the room, ostensibly searching, and then under the table. I half-stand from my seat and peer out into the reception area just beyond the glass wall separating us from his staff in their cubicles.

"What are you looking for?" he asks.

"Another zero." I shove the contract across the table to him. "I think you're missing one."

"Banner, come on." He leans forward, looking me directly in the eyes. If he's searching for softness, I can tell him right now he won't find it. Not on this.

"You need to max Zo out, and you know it."

"You really think you have the leverage for a maximum contract? You know his numbers were down."

"At the end of the season, yes," I concede. "Not *all* season and not his entire career."

"We need that cap space to do some rebuilding with younger players."

"I'm well aware." I slide my iPad into its leather sleeve. "But I fail to see how that affects my client. If he doesn't get a max contract now, then when?"

"You need to back down on this," he says, voice quiet but stern like he's lecturing a recalcitrant child. "The owners—"

"The owners can kiss my ass, Lowell." I stand and stare him down. "If you don't appreciate the rare talent that Zo is and has proven to be *for a decade,* I've already heard from several teams who will."

"You can't meet with other teams," he says, eyes widening in outrage.

"Funny." I touch my chin, fake contemplating. "I negotiated Zo's contract myself, and I don't remember seeing that stipulation anywhere."

"I thought it was understood. A gentlemen's agreement."

"Ohhh. A *gentlemen's* agreement. So it's a *man* thing. About time being a woman worked to my advantage."

"Banner, you know what I mean. If you even think about talking to other teams—"

"I'm not thinking about it," I say, brandishing the words like a knife. "I *am* talking to other teams because I knew you'd pull this shit when his numbers were down at the end of the season. Any excuse not to pay him what he's worth."

I press the heel of my hand into the conference room table and lean forward.

"I don't want your balls, Lowell, but I *will* take them."

Frustration settles between his brows and around his mouth, but he doesn't offer anything else. I head for the door and toss a warning over my shoulder.

"I don't care where you get it, but you better find my zero."

What a day. Despite all my bravado in Lowell's office, I feel less certain about Zo's contract than I ever have in an off-season. His numbers *are* down. I don't know why. It's the first time in ten years he finished down. I'm thinking about taking care of one client when another calls. I answer with Bluetooth, negotiating the back roads to my house from downtown.

"Kenan, hey," I answer, smiling. Kenan makes me smile. He's so big and serious and daunting but has one of the best hearts around underneath all the bluster. He and Zo remind me of each other, and I've known Kenan almost as long.

"Hey, Banner." His deep voice comes quietly, and he sounds weary.

"Everything okay?" I ask, on alert.

"Yeah. Just more drama with Bridget." He clears his throat. "Nothing I can't handle."

"Is she trying to make it harder to see Simone?"

"I got it," he replies more sharply than I anticipated. Probably more sharply than he meant to. "I'm sorry. Didn't mean to be short. It's just... I don't want to talk about Bridget. I didn't call to talk about her."

"Okay." I put aside my ass-kicking reflex. Any woman who would cheat on Kenan, and with a teammate, deserves an ass kicking, but he won't let me at her. "So what do you need?"

"August and I want to do a charity golf tournament," he says. "The homeless situation in San Diego is at a record high, and we want to help with funding."

"You're right." I pull into my driveway and open the garage but don't get out of the car quite yet. "My family still lives there, and it's worse every time I visit. What do you need from me?"

"Work on sponsors."

"Of course."

"I assume you'll start with the brands I already endorse."

"Yeah. I think we can count on them, but depending on the scale, we may need a few more."

"We want to have significant impact." He sucks his teeth, a rueful sound. "Well, as significant an impact as you can have on something this huge and unfixable."

"Right. True." I switch from my car's Bluetooth and bring my phone to my ear. "I'll knock on some doors starting tomorrow."

I mentally shift a few things around so I can devote an hour or so to finding possible sponsors.

"Great, and you'll have help," Kenan says. "So don't think this is all on you. I know how much you have on your plate."

"Help?" I get out of the car, lock up, and let down the garage door. "How so?"

"Jared Foster will be coordinating with you," Kenan says. "From Elevation. You know him, right? August's agent? His brother?"

I cross around the front of the car but, at the mention of Jared's name, lean against the passenger-side door and release an extended breath.

Seriously?

I go ten years and barely see the man, and now he's behind every bush and around every corner. I do not need this. It's bad enough I dreamed about him and had to guilt-fuck my boyfriend after. It's bad enough I see him at my gym and at conferences and it just feels like everywhere lately. Now I'm expected to work with him and remain civil?

Remain faithful?

It's a whisper, a warning from my subconscious. The same place harboring hot, dirty dreams about the man I should hate. The same place that quivers when he's too close.

"I need distance," I mumble.

"Huh?" Kenan's confusion reaches me over the phone. "What'd you say? You still there, Banner?"

"Uh, yeah." I push off the car door and enter the house through the garage. "Just getting home. I'll coordinate with Foster."

"Good. Let me know what you need from me."

"And, Kenan?" I place my bag on the marble counter and give him my full attention for the last few seconds. "Don't worry about Bridget, okay?"

The silence on the other end is thick with his discomfort. A fiercely private man. A proud man whose name was dragged through the mud by a whore.

Yes, whore.

She cheated on this amazing, kind, marvelous man with his teammate, and the whole world pulled up a seat to watch his humiliation with 3D glasses and popcorn.

Whore.

From the moment I met Bridget, I was waiting for the other shoe to drop. I knew she was an opportunist. I questioned her character immediately. I come from a family where fidelity and loyalty are as important as love. Maybe even more. I'm not sure my father always loved my mother, but I know he never cheated on her.

"She's not getting all your money," I say firmly. "And she's not getting sole custody. I have ideas. Let me work with your lawyers."

Let me at her.

"Okay." He releases a resigned sigh. "I'll tell my lawyers they'll hear from you."

My clients know my integrity is unmatched, but right and wrong are the only boundaries I draw around my actions. I'll do whatever it takes for them.

Killer with a heart.

Jared again. It's like the universe keeps bumping me into him, even inside my own head.

"*Hola.*" Zo hugs me from behind just as Kenan and I disconnect.

"Hey, you."

I lean back into the warm, comforting length of him. We've been best friends a lot longer than we've been lovers. Whatever this is percolating with Jared, I can't let it come between Zo and me. I've always had Zo. We literally started in this business together. He launched us the day he chose a green, untried intern as his agent.

"Long day?" He brushes my hair aside and kisses behind my ear.

"Yeah." I cross my fingers that he won't ask about the meeting with Lowell. I know I can get him the max contract he deserves, but it will take time, and it won't be pretty. I need him to leave me alone and let me do my job without the pressure.

In the silence that follows my one-word response, I can almost hear him asking the question in his mind and then thinking better of it. After a moment, he briefly tightens his hands at my waist before letting go. He reaches into my bag and lifts my phone.

"See this?" He holds it in the air. "It's off for the rest of the night."

He powers it down and grabs my hand, leading me back to my bedroom.

Please don't want sex.

He peels my blouse off, unhooks my bra, bending to kiss each nipple. He looks up, and I smile but keep my expression only vaguely interested.

"You're tired." He kisses my cheek. "Shower. I already have steaks on the grill."

I go limp with relief. It's ridiculous. Zo is one of the country's most eligible bachelors. A humanitarian. Handsome. Wealthy. The kindest man I know. And I'm relieved over a sex pardon?

I shower and pull my wet hair into a loose knot on my head, slip on my fave "at home" dress. It's like a hooded sweatshirt but with cutoff sleeves and hangs almost to my knees. Barefoot, I pad out to the patio, lured by the smell of grilled meat.

Zo already has salads on the table so we're just waiting for the steaks, when the doorbell rings.

"I'll get it." He presses my shoulder until my butt hits the seat. "You sit."

As soon as he's gone, I want wine. He's done everything else. I can at least do that. I walk back into the kitchen, distracted by the rumble of two distinct deep voices. I assumed it was a package being delivered or something, but my curiosity gets the best of me. I walk toward the voices in the front room and stop in my tracks.

My nemesis is in my house.

Jared Foster is everywhere. In my dreams. In my conversations. In my thoughts. And now in my damn house.

"Why are you here?"

The words barge out, rude and rushed, before I remember my manners.

Both men turn to me, and I'm struck by the contrast and by the sameness. Both beautiful men. Both oozing confidence. Zo is a couple of inches taller. Physically, he's dark, and Jared, in the late-evening sun framing him in the arch of my front door, is gilded. Breathtakingly bronzed and beautiful. But beneath their skin, he is the darker of the two. There's a barely beating black heart under that Tom Ford suit. He and Zo know each other by sight, reputation, and not much else. Zo heard someone ask me about attending Kerrington with Jared Foster once. That's all he knows about our connection. The three of us stand trapped in an awkward silence for a few moments. Awkward for me at least, but a pleasant smile curves Jared's lips.

"Sorry to show up unannounced," Jared says, darting an apologetic look—that I don't buy—at Zo. "I tried to call."

"I turned her phone off," Zo says, eyes steady on Jared's face. "It's after hours, and she needs to rest."

"I get it." Again the false apology of a smile. "I'm exhausted, too."

Lies. He practically vibrates with energy even at the end of the day. The man's a damn robot with no off button.

"But we have a meeting tomorrow," Jared says, shifting to me. "And when I couldn't reach you, I thought I'd come by and make sure you're prepared."

"What meeting?" I walk deeper into the room, conscious of my bare legs and feet and face. Of the hair piled messily on my head. I'm always armored when I see Jared. I need to be, and I feel strangely vulnerable having him in my house. Even with Zo standing between us, it feels too intimate.

"Did Kenan talk to you?" Jared asks. "About the golf tournament?"

The smell of the steaks seems stronger all of a sudden. Zo must notice, too.

"Excuse me," he says, watching Jared watching me. "I'll check on the grill. Good seeing you again, Foster."

They offer each other civil smiles. Zo drops a quick branding kiss on my lips while cupping my neck with one hand, the other hand at my waist, uncharacteristically possessive. He doesn't need to know I slept with Jared to recognize a male threat. I feel threatened, too—but by the dream that held me hostage this morning.

"*Rápido, mi amor*," Zo mutters by my ear and heads back to the patio.

Jared watches his departure with a wry smile. It's our first time alone since the confrontation at the hotel. Since I blocked his shot. It feels weird to just dive right into discussing the golf tournament without at least addressing what happened.

"Look, if this is really about Lamont," I say, slipping my hands into the front pocket of the dress, "you deserved that. I'm not sorry, and you know he'll do better with me anyway."

"Ah, yes." A sardonic press of sinfully full lips. "The Rookie Whisperer."

"Whatever." I shrug faux carelessly. "Lamont will be under intense scrutiny, and we both know he has some issues that could derail him. I'll take care of him."

"You're right. I don't play babysitter to grown men making

millions of dollars," he says. "I agree he's better suited to you. I thought he was signing with Mitch, in which case I would have been doing him a favor."

"He was, actually. I intervened after hearing Mitch's choice words about me at the bar that night."

Jared grimaces, as close to contrite as I can expect from him.

"I *am* sorry for what I said, Banner. I was…" He searches my face, but seems to be searching for words, too. "Wrong. I was wrong."

It's just words, probably empty ones, but his admission soothes a sting I didn't realize I still carried.

"Apology accepted." I clear my throat and, I hope, the air. "Since we have to work together for our clients, let's put it behind us."

"Right," he says briskly, donning a businesslike expression like he would put on one of his silk ties. "We have an appointment tomorrow."

"How do we have an appointment tomorrow? You didn't consult my schedule. I don't know whom we're meeting with or what we're meeting about."

"Should we sit?" he gestures to the sofa.

No way I'm sitting on a sofa with Jared Foster and Zo just outside. I wouldn't straddle the man but don't trust my subconscious. Look what it made of an argument in the hall. There's no telling what it will concoct even from these few minutes together.

"No need to sit," I reply. "Just tell me how you have commandeered my schedule and I can get back to my dinner and my boyfriend."

Knowing he disapproves of my relationship with a client, I don't miss the chance for a dig.

"Okay." He exasperates me by stubbornly remaining unoffended and suppressing a smile. "We're having lunch with a huge potential sponsor. It's all but done."

"I know you're not used to playing well with others, but this is pretty high-handed even for you."

"I called your office, and your assistant said you were free for lunch."

"Why would Maali give you that information?" I can't believe my usually lips-are-sealed assistant would be that forthcoming.

"Don't blame her. I can be pretty persuasive." He chuckles when I roll my eyes. "So lunch tomorrow with Kip Carter."

"Wait." I frown and rack my brain. "That name sounds familiar."

Jared rubs the back of his neck, wearing reluctance like a red flag. "He's Benton's father."

I'm momentarily too mad to speak, but that doesn't last.

"Are you kidding me?" My words bounce between us like a medicine ball. "Benton who saw me naked and laughed? That Benton?"

"He did not laugh." A muscle bunches along his jaw. "He felt like an ass about that night, and we didn't speak for years. I know you don't believe me, but I didn't join the Pride."

"I'm not revisiting this," I snap. "Stick to business."

"You're the one willing to compromise business because you can't let go of what you *think* happened a decade ago."

"What I think…" I swallow my anger and the words that would only extend my time in his presence. "Whatever. When and where?"

"I'll pick you up around eleven."

"I can meet you. That won't be necessary."

"It'll be easier," he says before I can protest more. "He's sending his helicopter for us. We're having lunch with him on Catalina Island."

"Isn't that a bit extra?" I frown and reach up to tighten the slipping knot of my hair. The motion of raising my arms lifts my dress, exposing a few more inches of my thighs. Jared scrolls a leisurely glance over the length of my legs, landing and lingering on my toes. I keep my face expressionless though it's burning with a blush.

"Not for the people we deal with," he says. "Kobe Bryant took the helicopter to every home game his last few seasons with the Lakers to avoid traffic. It's only a fifteen-minute ride, and it's either water or air since Catalina regulates cars so strictly."

"All right, then." I blow out a resigned breath. "I could still meet you. I don't want anyone from my office seeing you pick me up."

I pause for effect.

"They abhor you," I say with deliberate glee.

To my dismay, he barks out a laugh, looking pleased with himself.

"Good. Means I'm doing my job." He turns to leave. "We are rivals after all, right?"

"Very right." I follow him to the door, eager to shut it behind him.

At the last second, he turns before he reaches the door, and barely an inch separates us.

"You know," he breathes the words, "tonight it's easy to forget we're supposed to be enemies when you look like my friend from college. The one I used to study with in the laundromat."

It's one thing for him to bring up Bent, for us to argue about what he did or did not intend to happen that night. I'm not sure I'll ever really know. It's another thing for him to bring up our friendship. What I *believed* to be our friendship. That's not fair.

"Goodbye, Jared," I say, my tone sharpened to a fine point, eyes on my bare feet.

"You look the same," he continues. I feel his eyes on my face but refuse to look up.

"I hope not." I cross one foot over the other. "That dumpy girl had no clue."

I laugh, some of my old self-consciousness rushing back, and glance up at him. I'm not prepared for the intensity on his face. It's watchful. It's frustrated. It's something I can't translate and in a language I don't speak.

"I liked her," he says, his voice a heated rasp. "She was smart and funny and honest and principled. She was...*you were*...one of the few people on that campus I could tolerate for more than an hour without wanting to saw my arm off."

Then why?

The question rips through my defenses. Yes, it hurt to think he set me up with the Pride, that he would sleep with me as part of some prank or rite of passage I never understood. What hurt most was the uncertainty of what had been true, what had been real. If I'd misjudged every moment of our friendship. And if I hadn't, then how could he do that to me?

"I'll see you tomorrow," I say woodenly.

"Ban, if you would just—"

"Eleven you said?" I cut in and school my face to look at him.

He runs a hand through his hair, disrupting it into a silky mess I remember too well. The way the strands clung to my fingers.

"We *will* have this out one day, Banner," he says, his voice rough and impatient.

"Not today we won't," I lob back at him. "I don't need a walk down memory lane, Jared. We have a job to do, and we'll do it. No need to talk about the past. It's dead and gone."

"The past isn't all gone," he says, his voice suddenly softer. I'm unprepared for him to eliminate the protective space between us, for him to touch my face. He runs a finger over my nose. I jerk back, startled. "You still have the freckles."

"What?" I rub my nose, wiping away his touch.

"You had seven freckles on your nose then," he says, one side of his mouth canted up. "You still do."

That's the last mystifying thing he says before turning and walking up my short drive to the convertible sports car at the curb. I lean against the closed door for a minute, maybe more, reassembling my splintered composure. I don't know what's happening between us. My greatest defense against Jared has been my anger and bitterness over his treatment that night. When he denies it, when he makes me think it could have been real…that the fiery connection, the perfect give and take of our bodies, the closeness we shared before the sex and even more so after may have been real, my defenses flag. I can't allow that to happen. If my armor slips, I'm exposed. I don't want to think of all the ways Jared could ruin my life.

CHAPTER 14
BANNER

THE THING ABOUT FLYING IN A HELICOPTER IS I'VE NEVER FLOWN in one. I was so preoccupied with Jared's unexpected visit and all the ways I could maintain some distance, I forgot that I would probably be scared to death. I'm faced with that reality once we approach the helicopter, a giant bug-eyed insect with rapidly rotating wings. The helipad sits on top of a thirty-story building downtown, overlooking LA's flat-topped Lego-like skyline. The Staples Center lies in one direction, the Sheraton in another. Those are the only buildings I distinguish. The rest are just a blur of glass and stone as I drag my feet toward the bull's-eye where the helicopter waits.

"Are those shoes slowing you down?" Jared yells over the noise of the spinning propellers.

"No," I yell back, speeding up my steps in the black Balenciaga pumps I splurged on last year. "I'm fine."

"Agreed," Jared says, giving my appearance an appreciative quick scan.

I chose the paper-thin leather jacket and form-fitting black pencil dress carefully, knowing Kip Carter, Bent's dad, is a big deal. I may be thicker than a lot of the girls in the circles I move in, but I know this dress highlights the toned curves I've literally worked my ass off for. Some of my hair is pulled into a half-up top knot, and the rest spills in loose waves down my back. For better or worse, image is a lot in this town, and I want to put my best foot forward meeting such an influential man.

Even if his son is an asshole I hope to never see again. Fingers crossed Bent won't be around at all. Last I heard, he lives in Boston, tearing his way through a string of women unfortunate enough to be fooled by his gorgeous face.

My heart pounds harder the closer we get to the helicopter with *Carter* emblazoned on the side. I'm not short of breath trying to keep pace with Jared's long-legged stride. I'm short of breath because I may hyperventilate before this is all over.

"You've been in one of these before, yeah?" Jared asks offhandedly.

"Uh, no. I haven't, actually."

"What'd you say?" Jared yells, stopping at the two steps leading up into the helicopter.

"No!" I scream, less for volume sake and more because of my rising hysteria.

"Oh." He searches my face, and I'm sure he doesn't miss the signs of strain. "Sorry. Come on."

Hand at the small of my back, he helps me up into the helicopter. The red-leather seat wraps around my body and gives me a reassuring squeeze. Jared greets the pilot with familiarity and takes two headsets from him, offering one to me. I slip mine on and buckle up, mimicking Jared's actions. I jump when his voice comes in my ear.

"We can talk using this." He taps the headset microphone at his mouth. "It's only about fifteen minutes to the house."

My stomach roils when we lift off, and I grip the armrests tightly. Riding in a helicopter is nothing like flying on an airplane. That's probably self-evident. It's not a smooth gradual ascent but a more immediate lift. More exhilarating, rawer, without the insulation of thick steel separating you from the air and the ground growing smaller below you. It's loud, and the machine sounds like it's working hard to overcome the laws that would chain us to the ground. I'm more conscious of what a miracle flight is, more aware that we are defying gravity with every mile we travel and every foot we rise.

"You okay?" Jared asks, pulling me from my thoughts and my senses absorbing the experience.

"Getting there," I say wryly.

"Well, we have a little time to review your changes to the proposal I sent. You have it, right?"

"Yeah."

We both pull out our iPads to discuss the proposal he drew up.

I knew Jared must be thorough to have accomplished all that he has, but I haven't seen this side of him. Haven't actually done business with him. The proposal came over just before midnight. Zo had gone to bed, exhausted from off-season demands with sponsors and charities and probably just postseason weariness. I stayed up and made notes and suggestions, which I sent over before I went to sleep.

I tap my screen, identifying the areas I had questions about. When I look up, Jared wears black-rimmed glasses and frowns down at his screen.

"So you finally did it," I say into the headset microphone.

"Did what?" He glances up, one brow raised. It's all very sexy professor.

"You got glasses." I laugh lightly, disguising how yet another memory from that night penetrates the protective bubble I've encased myself in. "I told you so."

His deep-throated chuckle reaches through the headset and strokes my skin. Thankfully the leather jacket hides the gooseflesh sprouting on my arms.

"Only for reading." He takes them off and hands them to me.

I hold them up, looking through the lenses, and he's right. There doesn't seem to be much medicine. I slip them onto the bridge of my nose, peering at him over the rims.

"Believe it or not, I used to want glasses so badly I asked Mama to get them for me."

"Why?" he asks with a narrow smile.

"I wanted to look smart."

He snorts and shakes his head.

"Well, how do I look?" I lift my nose in the air and touch the corners of the frames. "Smart?"

He relaxes into the supple leather like a king considering his consort, scouring me from the pointed tips of my pumps up the length of my legs, where the fitted dress interrupts the bare skin at my knees. His eyes trace the curve of my hips and waist, caress my breasts, lingering so long my nipples tighten under the stretchy fabric. I pull my leather jacket closer around me, hiding the effect of his sensual perusal.

"How do you look?" he finally repeats. "Sexy as fuck."

What the hell?

Not addressing his comment or that hungry look, I hastily hand his glasses back, making sure our fingers don't touch.

"Um…I had a question on page three." I drag my finger down the screen until I reach the spot. "Can we talk about the incentives for sponsors again at the platinum level?"

When I glance up, he holds my stare for a second longer, suspending the tension between us. Finally he laughs, and I redirect the conversation back to the proposal.

"We're almost there," he says a few minutes later, turning toward the window overlooking the jeweled Pacific coastline, a shimmering sheet of emerald and sapphire butted against semiprecious sand.

From here, it appears infinite, stretching as far as my eyes can see in any direction. The hills rising up from the coastline are studded with terra-cotta-topped houses dangled precipitously over the almost painfully vibrant water. It's breathtaking. I've survived my first helicopter ride. After the initial rush of fear, Jared and I had been so consumed preparing for the meeting that my fears fell to the side.

"Thanks for distracting me," I say, realizing that's exactly what he did and why he did it.

"I threw up my first time flying out here to see Kip," he confides with a wry smile. "So don't feel bad about a few jitters."

"Careful, or I'll stop believing you're the asshole everyone thinks you are," I tease.

"Oh, I'm an asshole." He tips his head back to rest against the seat and watches me, eyes heavy-lidded. "Just not to you."

Jared admitting weakness, alleviating my fears, singling me out for kindness feels strange. This whole sequence of events feels strange, as though beneath the surface and in the air something is changing. Invisible but affecting our every interaction. I have to keep reminding myself I don't like him because the very fabric of our relationship is morphing so quickly I'm no longer sure what it's made of.

Kip Carter's helicopter lands on a carpet of lush grass in front of a Mediterranean-style mansion. He personally greets us at the front door. I'm taken aback by the warmth between him and Jared. Not the cool handshake of a business acquaintance but an extended hug, inside jokes, and the kind of familiarity usually reserved for family.

Managing millionaires has earned me my own millions, and I've grown accustomed to decadence and luxury I never imagined growing up in our modest San Diego neighborhood. This ocean-side estate is beyond anything I've personally experienced. With its high ceilings, cool marble floors, and priceless art tucked into alcoves everywhere I turn, the house smacks of opulence, just like its owners.

Kip and Karen Carter are exactly what I would expect of an LA couple with more money than they know what to do with. His clothes are tailored. There's an ascot at his neck and a wildly expensive boat moored in his landing. Her face is lightly Botoxed, and the years are marked by sparkles on her fingers and throat. All the trappings of a celluloid life leap out at me, but the truth may lie in the subtle details. The way they hold hands and touch every chance they get. The kindness and genuine affection between them and the staff who keep their mammoth home running smoothly. The wistfulness in their voices when they speak of their children over a chilled lunch. It's a Hollywood life, yes, but it's real. Somehow for them, it's still real.

"*Gracias*, Luciana," Karen murmurs when a dark-haired young woman clears the delicious salads and fruit we had for lunch from the table. I notice Karen speaks fluent Spanish with her staff, a point for her in my book.

"You have a lovely home, Karen," I say, taking in the spectacular view of the Pacific from the terrace where we're eating. I sip the spring water I'd requested. I don't drink my calories when I don't have to.

"Thank you." She touches the beautifully casual stones at her throat. "Should we leave the men to talk business and I could show you more? The west terrace offers the best view of the ocean."

"I'm afraid she needs to stay for the business," Jared says before I have to explain. "She's an agent like I am, Karen. Sorry. I thought I mentioned that."

"Oh." Surprise registers on Karen's still-pretty face. "I thought you two were…you know. Together."

"Oh, no." I laugh lightly. "Just business. I'm not his type."

"Well, if Jared doesn't like smart, beautiful women," Karen replies, offering me a wink, "then he doesn't know what he's missing."

"Oh, I know exactly what I'm missing," Jared says, taking a sip of Perrier and studying me over the rim of his glass. "I miss it more every day."

Kip and Karen chuckle into the pool of awkward silence rippling around us, but neither Jared nor I laugh. We don't smile. We stare at each other, assessing, plotting our next moves. Mine is to withdraw. By the determined set of Jared's lips and the hard gleam in his eyes, I'm afraid his next move will be to charge. I'm just not sure when.

"This looks good," Kip says, considering the proposal once Karen has excused herself. He may have greeted Jared like a son, but he grilled him like a stranger. He's a shrewd businessman, and Jared's assertion that the deal was "all but done" may have overstated the matter. Kip might have intended to sponsor the tournament from the beginning, but he made me believe he needed to be convinced. And if there's one thing I learned from Professor Albright's debate class, it's how to persuade, so I add my input every chance I get.

"This will be great," Kip says, flipping to the last page of the proposal. "The homeless situation in San Diego and in LA is abominable."

"My client, Kenan, and Jared's client, August... We have the same concerns," I say. "We couldn't stay on the sidelines, so to speak."

"I'm hoping you have some friends who will be as concerned as you are, Kip." Jared's expression is expectant and assured.

"I do, of course," Kip replies, smiling. "Could the two of you make it up to the house in Santa Barbara next weekend? We're having a little barbecue, and many of my concerned friends will be there, wallets open."

"Wouldn't miss it for the world," I reply, returning Kip's warm smile.

"This one's sharp," he tells Jared, his eyes resting on my face with what appears to be respect. "Since you're not smart enough to snap her up, maybe Bent would be."

"Matchmaking again, Dad?"

The deep voice comes from behind me, but I know it right away, though I haven't heard it in almost a decade. I look around to find Bent Carter at the entryway to the terrace. He was always the flipside of Jared's coin. Lighthearted while Jared was intense. Dark where Jared was fair. Entitled when Jared was ambitious. But that awful night, I saw no difference between the two of them. They were the same as Prescott and his hyenas laughing at all my chubby, naked and exposed flesh. Fresh humiliation chokes me with the visual reminder of Bent standing there, an all-too-familiar smile on his face. The smile dies when his eyes meet mine.

"Banner." He sobers, his surprise fading. "Mom said Jared had a woman with him, and I just had to see for myself."

"You make it sound like I don't like girls,"Jared says easily, dividing a careful glance between his friend and me. "Not the case since apparently I have a type."

His words draw my attention and irritation, as he knew they would. If he's trying to distract me from the memory of what he and those assholes did—Bent included—it won't work. I endure Bent's presence while he greets his father and then mother when she returns to the terrace. My body is stiff as if tensed for a blow the whole time. My teeth grind together. It's bad enough Jared is still friends with this cretin and only convinces me further that he lied when he said he didn't join the Pride after all. My nerves are drawn tight like the strings of a violin, but there is no music. Just the sound of their laughter from that night. The sound of my tears. The sound of Jared's lies.

"I'm so sorry, but I really do need to get back," I interrupt as soon as there's a natural opening. I turn a genuinely grateful smile on Karen. I can't blame her for her son's despicable behavior. "It was so nice meeting you, and thank you for lunch."

I stand and take one last look at the gorgeous scenery, letting the beauty of it cool my anger.

"Please come again soon, Banner." Karen loops her elbow through mine.

"I'd like that very much."

Jared studies us over his shoulder from up ahead before returning to the conversation with Kip and Bent. Karen kisses both my cheeks with promises of more time together at the barbecue next weekend. Jared wraps up his conversation, and quick, long strides take him across the vast yard to the waiting helicopter. I'm close behind when a gentle tug stops me halfway there. I look up from the long fingers gripping my elbow to Bent's handsome face. He bends to speak in my ear over the noise of the helicopter.

"There wasn't time before," he says loudly. "But I wanted to apologize for…"

He stares at the well-manicured grass under our feet for a few seconds before speaking again.

"For what happened senior year, Banner." He runs an impatient hand through the dark waves all the girls gushed over at Kerrington. "I'm ashamed for going along with it."

"It was years ago," I say, tugging on my elbow, but he doesn't let go.

"It was years ago, which makes it even worse that I'm only now apologizing," he says. "I gave in to the pressure because I wanted to get in. I *needed* to. I'm a legacy."

"I have no idea what you're talking about." I steal a look at the helicopter. Jared wears a heavy frown and stands at the door, hands jammed into his pockets. "I should go."

"He had nothing to do with it." Bent dips his head to capture and hold my gaze. "He was furious that night when Prescott told him to—"

"Fuck the fat girl," I finish for him, my words stiff.

"Yeah," Bent admits with a heavy sigh.

"And yet he still reaped the benefits," I say scornfully.

"What benefits?" Bent asks, a frown gathered over the confusion in his eyes.

"Of the Pride. I've seen him with you and your friends at events and vacations and…I'm not stupid. Obviously he's in."

"You see him with me and my friends and family because we *are* friends. My parents see Jared as a second son. It took two years for him to speak to me again, and only then because my mother begged him to."

I take in the new information but can't make sense of everything.

"So he's really not in the Pride?" I ask, searching the rugged lines of his face for deceit.

"Look, I can't talk about this with you," Bent says. "It's a secret society, which means *secret*. Even what I've told you could get me tossed out, and unlike Jared, I need the connections. I will tell you that not only is he not a member, but he's banned for life."

"For life? Why?"

Humor twitches the corners of Bent's mouth.

"For assaulting a legacy," Bent says with a chuckle. "He came back that night and knocked two of Prescott's teeth out."

A startled laugh pops from my mouth.

"Why would he do that?"

The humor drains from Bent's face, and he takes my hands between his, squeezing.

"He was crazy about you, Banner."

Shock and disbelief wrestle inside me. My heart beats louder in my ears than the propellers of the waiting helicopter chopping through the air.

"No, he—"

"Yes," Bent cuts in, his stare unwavering. "He was. I promise you."

I brave a glance at Jared, still waiting, hair blown into an unruly mess by the propellers. He slides a questioning look from me to Bent and then cocks his head toward the helicopter, indicating that we need to go.

"Um, thanks for telling me, Bent," I say, turning to go. He catches my elbow again.

"Apology accepted?" he asks with a half smile.

"Of course." I manage a smile back, but I'm still stunned by his revelation. Could it have been true? Real? Could that night have been real to Jared? It's dangerous to think so.

I jog the rest of the way to the helicopter, and Jared helps me up the two steps and inside. I've barely settled in and buckled my seat belt when Jared hands me a headset.

"Put it on," he says. I can barely hear him but can read his lips and slip the headset on. "What did Bent say to you?"

"It was a private conversation," I say, stalling. I turn to the window, not even seeing the jewel-toned waters or the majestic cliffs.

"I'll just ask him," he says over the headset.

No response from me.

"He'll tell me," Jared continues. He reaches around to grasp my chin gently and turns my face to his. "But I'd rather hear it from you."

His thumb is rough against my face, but the caress, his touch, brushing back and forth over my skin, is soft.

"He said you weren't in on what happened that night," I say haltingly, tugging my chin free. "He said you weren't a member of the Pride."

"I told you that."

"I didn't believe you."

His grin is crooked. "I can't blame you for that."

"Right."

"But you believe me now? You believe Bent?"

"He says you aren't in the Pride," I say without answering definitively. "That you never were."

"I never was," he confirms, not looking away. Not allowing me to. "I withdrew as soon as Prescott told me what he wanted me to do."

I nod jerkily, twisting my fingers in my lap.

"That's what he said." I look up, pressing my lips against an irrepressible smile. "He said you're banned for life because you knocked out two of Prescott's teeth."

His husky laugh rumbles in my ears through the headset. "He could afford the dental work."

I allow myself a grin but look down at my hands.

"Is that all he said?" Jared asks, humor and curiosity still apparent in his expression.

He was crazy about you, Banner.

I can't consider the possibility that Jared actually felt even a fraction of what I felt for him back then. Can't allow myself to think about the what-ifs and what-could-have-beens. Even speculating about those could jeopardize all I have now with Zo.

"Yeah." I turn back to the gorgeous view, not really seeing it. "That was all he said."

CHAPTER 15
JARED

I PARK AT THE CURB IN FRONT OF BANNER'S HOUSE AND WALK UP the cobblestone path to the door. I hesitate and don't ring the doorbell right away. She knows I'm coming. We agreed on the time I'd pick her up for Kip's party, but I assume Zo is here since he's living with Banner for the summer. Not a pleasant thought. I only know him by reputation. He's beloved in the league and beyond. He's also sharp. I'd know immediately if someone wanted my girl, and I could be wrong but I think Zo is sharp enough to at least suspect I want his. Only I don't think of Banner as *his*. Banner was taken from me. If not for Prescott's stupid stunt, who knows what would have happened for us. I always wondered.

Soon I'll know.

She's been avoiding me all week. Ever since the helicopter ride and her conversation with Bent, she's made sure to be busy every time I called. Admittedly, I *did* use trumped-up excuses to call, but I wanted to build on the ground I'd gained. Instead, the last few days have given Banner time to retreat and regroup. She hasn't had to deal with me and the connection I know she feels. She's been able to focus on Zo, who's living with her.

Dammit.

I won't pretend to feel remorse for what I'm going to do. I won't fake regret. I will take her from him, little by little, day by day, until he doesn't even cross her mind. In business and in life, I always take the shortest route between me and what I want. In this case, the shortest route to Banner just happens to run right over Alonzo Vidale. It's a shame, really, but there are other girls for him. Dozens of girls he could live with, love, whatever. Banner is the only one I can tolerate.

Okay. More than tolerate. Crave. I kind of crave her company.

Being around her again reminded me how much I *like* her. The way she challenges me and makes me laugh. She's the only one I enjoy being with and the only one I've ever felt I could be myself with. That she'd accept my good, bad, and ugly. Good, the little there is of it. Bad, my wealth of bad. And ugly. I'm not an ugly guy. I know that without conceit. Conceit is such a waste of time and energy. I've always known that, though Banner was attracted to me, for her it wasn't about how I looked. Not really. Just like it wasn't about that for me either. I would have fallen for Banner blindfolded. You can camouflage flaws and fool a man with implants and the right trappings, but you can't fake a brilliant mind like Banner's. Or feign her obstinate belief in people, her desire to help them. Or all the other qualities that make her distinct from every other woman I've ever met.

The door opens, and she's standing there, a curious look on her face.

"You've been at my door for five minutes," she says, hands on those curvy hips. "Are we leaving or what?"

"Oh. Yeah. I was thinking." I look back at my car and then return to her, hoping she buys my lame excuse. "You ready?"

"Yes." She steps out, offering me a wry glance, and locks the door behind her. "Five minutes ago."

She looks down at herself.

"I should have asked what to wear," she says, frowning. "Is this okay?"

I don't know how to talk about Banner's body without offending her. I've never thought she was fat, but she didn't believe me. Now

she's even *less* fat, toned with curves for days, most notably a spectacular ass. She's tight, but there's a seductive swell to her hips and butt
and thighs. I love that she's more brick house than stick thin, but I'd
probably step in it if I say any of that, so I'll play it safe.

"You look fine," I reply neutrally.

"You sure it's not too casual?" she asks, pinching the skirt of her
dress.

The halter ties behind her neck, leaving her shoulders bare. The
dress is red with black accents at the pockets and hem, which hits
just below her knees. It falls loosely, hinting at the full curve of her
hips and butt. Her breasts sit high and proud and full. I remember
those breasts in my hands, between my lips. The sweet nipples—

"Jared." Banner snaps her fingers in my face. "Did you hear me?"

"Yeah." *No idea what she's talking about. I'm stuck on sweet nipples.*
"I agree."

"You agree?" She looks at me like I'm not all there, which I'm
not. "You agree that it's too casual or—"

"Oh. That. No. It looks fine. You look great."

I touch the small of her back, just above the swell of her ass—so
close and yet so far—guiding her down the short flight of steps
toward my car. She walks a little ahead, pulling away from my hand.

Oh, it's like that.

She reaches for the door, but I hit the clicker to lock the car,
hanging back so she's tugging on the handle uselessly. She turns to
face me, leaning on the car.

"Unlock the door," she says, a slight smile tilting the corners of
those *Pretty Woman* lips.

"I'm a gentleman," I remind her. "I'm supposed to open the door
for you."

"I can open my own doors. Have been for a long time."

"You're too liberated for simple good manners? To accept
kindness?"

"When was the last time you were kind?" she huffs with a laugh.

"You got me there," I admit with a chuckle.

"I thought so."

"You look beautiful," I tell her, dropping all pretense of banter, meeting her eyes frankly. I step closer, sandwiching her between my body and the car, reaching behind her for the handle so my arm brushes her bare skin. I smell her hair and her perfume and *her*. My gaze trickles over her, savors her in centimeters, starting at the hair caught up, soft tendrils escaping and curling around her hairline and at her neck, taking in all the dips and swells on the way to her feet in red open-toed high-heeled sandals.

I reach up to toy with her gold hoop earrings. "I like these."

"Thank you. My boyfriend gave them to me," she says pointedly.

I bite back a grin. That's so cute. She thinks I give a fuck about her boyfriend. She thinks she can put me off by pulling away from my touch, reminding me about what's-his-name. She doesn't realize yet that I don't care. She'll soon see. Maybe even tonight.

I click the door unlocked and step back so she can get in. At the wheel, I check the mirrors and hover my finger over the button to peel the roof back.

"Roof up or down?"

"My hair." She pats the dark strands held perfectly in place. "Up going. Down on the way back."

"Up it is." I take over and fiddle with the system. "Driver is DJ."

"No." She groans and flops her head back. "How long is this drive again?"

"I have great taste in music." I spare an offended glance from the road. "We'll every other it, but I go first."

"Of course you will," she mutters under her breath. "Always do."

"What was that?" I ask, enjoying myself.

"Nothing." She creases her face with a quick fake grin. "You're the driver."

"That's what I thought you said." I cue up my first song: "Get Lucky" by Daft Punk and Pharrell.

Her head bops, and she pats her thighs.

"So you like it?" I ask. "'Jared, you have great taste in music' will suffice in lieu of a formal apology."

"One song does not great taste make." She laughs, searching Spotify on my phone for the next song. "Oooh. I've got a good one."

"I'll be the judge of that."

"I think we should each get one judgment-free song."

"What? You can choose a crap song and I don't get to laugh at you?" I shake my head. "I would never miss an opportunity to demean your choices."

"I'm well aware," she says wryly. "But it also means you get a judgment-free song."

"I don't like crap music, so I don't need a bye."

"Everyone needs a freebie sometimes. We should all get one shitty choice."

"I never would have thought that *you'd* want a shitty choice."

"I'm not perfect, Jared."

Pretty close.

I don't say it because her knowing how much I'm into her works against my endgame. If she heard a warning shot like that, she'd run in the other direction. I need her off guard, taken aback. Unprepared. By the time she realizes I'm pursuing her, I want her begging to be caught.

It's her turn, and she chooses one of my favorite songs of all time. I don't give any indication that I love "Crazy" by Gnarls Barkley.

"Oh, come on, Foster." She points at me, laughing and shaking her head. "I know you love this song."

"It's all right," I deadpan. Shrug.

"Hmm." She folds her arms over her chest, pushing her breasts up and almost distracting me from the road, but...discipline. "This was the top song on your study playlist senior year."

Ah, now we're getting somewhere. She remembers my details, too.

"Was it?" I feign ignorance like the great feigner I am. "I don't even remember that. How would *you* remember that?"

"I don't know." She shrugs smooth bare shoulders and scrolls through the phone for her next choice. "Just popped in my head for whatever reason."

"Ahhh. The way I remembered your dryer sheets?" I ask innocently. "Just popped in my head, too."

Silence. She sits back to enjoy the Pacific bordering the road. I opted to take PCH, which is a little longer drive, but Banner in the car for more time is no hardship. Gives her something to look at while she regroups. We go back and forth on songs for the couple of hours in the car. I deliberately avoid shop talk, not wanting to remind her that I'm supposed to be the opposition.

"Okay, here's my judgment-free pick," she says after a while, giving me wide eyes and twitching lips. "Don't hate on my jam."

"You calling it 'your jam' already has my Hatorade out."

"And you using the word 'Hatorade' has mine out."

We both laugh, and I wait to hear just how bad her song sucks. *It's pretty bad.*

"Seriously?" There's a slowdown up ahead, so I can look at her fully while we idle. "One Direction?"

She turns up the volume so "What Makes You Beautiful" soaks the interior of my car. I'll have to hose it down later, but watching her dance beside me, the most carefree I've seen her since our laundromat days, is worth enduring a British boy band that is *not* the Beatles.

"Okay." She hands me the phone. "Now you choose your craptastic song so I don't feel so bad."

"I told you I don't listen to shit music," I remind her.

"Oh, come on. You've got one. Everybody does."

I mentally flip through the songs I listen to, struggling to find something that isn't great.

And then I have it.

One eye on the road, one eye on my phone, I search until I find it. Never have I looked so forward to a ball-busting as when the soft, melodic strains of Shaggy's "It Wasn't Me" fill the air.

"Oh my God!" Banner doubles over in her seat, head pressed to her knees, shoulders shaking. "No way you get to judge me. This is...awful."

I don't mind never getting to live this down. It's worth it to hear Banner's full-throated laugh. I haven't heard her laugh like that since college. Completely uninhibited and honest and free. And because of me.

"I guess we should at least talk about our strategy for recruiting sponsors at this party," she says when we're about thirty minutes from Kip and Karen's Santa Barbara home.

"Right." *I couldn't care less.* "Very important."

Half these potential sponsors have already committed from an email Kip sent the day we had lunch, but she doesn't need to know that one detail. She might not have come.

"I say we divide and conquer." Banner pulls down the visor mirror to check her makeup and add more red to her lips.

"Divide" sounds like it might defeat my purpose, which is to spend as much time with Banner as possible.

"Maybe we should stick together," I suggest.

"I've memorized the list of potential sponsors you sent."

Of course you have.

"And pulled up photos," she continues blithely.

Overachiever...but we knew that already.

"So I think I have faces and names matched and will be fine on my own," she says. "If that's what you're worried about."

It's not.

"Okay," I say, resigned. We turn down the long private drive leading to the Carter estate. "Divide and conquer it is."

"How lovely," Banner says with a gasp when the house comes into view.

I consider the Carters' Cape Dutch estate with fresh eyes. I've been coming here since freshman year. In the beginning, of course, I'd visit with Bent, but especially now that I live on the West Coast and Bent is in Boston, I come here without him all the time. I was dumbstruck the first time I drove up, too. On one side, moss-colored mountains overlook the vast estate. Aquamarine waters border the other side. Truly the best of both worlds.

I can tell Banner thinks the interior is as impressive by the way she peers up at the cathedral ceilings and reverently approaches the priceless paintings dotting the walls.

"This home is as lovely as your other one," she tells Karen after a quick hug. "So warm and beautiful."

"I could say the same of you," Kip says, turning on Old World charm like he originally hails from Italy, though he grew up in Detroit. He grabs both Banner's hands, kisses both cheeks.

"Thank you." She smiles sweetly and accepts his elbow.

"I have several people for you to meet." He leads her out to the sprawling oceanside backyard already packed with about a hundred guests.

"Kip likes your friend," Karen says, taking my arm and following at a discreet distance. "He was very impressed by her."

"You mean at lunch?" I ask wryly. "Or afterward when he dug up information about her?"

She chuckles, slanting me a knowing glance. "Mostly what he dug up after. He loves ambition and drive and intelligence. She has all three."

"That she does," I say, hoping I do a good job hiding the touch of pride I feel about the woman Banner has become. She's far exceeded even what I thought she would be when I knew her in college.

"I can tell you like her, too," Karen says slyly, catching and holding my eyes. "A lot."

"I'm that obvious, am I?" I affect a frown. "Need to work on that."

"I know you well. You've never brought a woman around before."

"She's a colleague, Karen," I deflect. "She's around because we have business that intersects with Kip's interests."

"Oh, tell me another one," Karen scoffs, smiling at her guests in that way she's perfected: *I'm glad you're here. Thank you for coming. I'll deal with you later and can't you tell I'm in the middle of something.* "I see the way you look at that girl."

"How?" I ask, certain that I've disguised my hunger for Banner.

"It's rude to stare at a woman's ass like that."

My shout of laughter startles us both. Apparently, I haven't done a good job after all.

"And you don't usually laugh this way," she adds. "I like how you are with her. Where'd you find her, and does she have a sister we could trick into marrying Bent?"

"No one said anything about marriage." I give her a quelling frown. "I can really like her and want to…well, you know."

Fuck her…again…and again…and again…and repeat.

The look Karen returns tells me she *does* know all too well.

"I can want *that* without wanting marriage," I say. "I don't know how I feel about that institution. Everyone isn't as lucky as you and Kip or as my dad and stepmother."

"Hard to be faithful to one woman?" she asks.

In ten years, no one has measured up to Banner in the dark. Banner on a narrow couch, rushed, hurried. Frantic and perfect. I'd trade every woman I've had since for one more night like that with Banner.

"I think I could be faithful." I grab a glass of the champagne lemonade Karen's parties are so famous for from a passing tray. "Though I haven't ever met a woman I wanted to test that theory with."

"Until Banner, you mean?" Karen wears that pleased grin my stepmother sports whenever she mistakenly thinks I'm going to "settle down" with one of the nice girls she introduces me to. Who wants a nice girl when I could have Banner painfully extracting a pound of my flesh every night?

I search the crowded yard for Banner's bright dress. A splash of scarlet by the pool gives her away. She's chatting with a man Kip simply calls Baron, a German businessman whom I've never even seen smile. He's talking animatedly with Banner, probably *in* German, a besotted grin hanging between his two oversized ears. Everyone falls for Banner. Whether they see her as the daughter they never had, as Karen likely does, or think she's the best thing that ever happened to their business, like that blowhard Cal Bagley. Or that she's the only girl for them, like Zo does. Too bad about Zo because she's actually the only girl for *me*. He'll find someone else. I have faith in him.

I go through the motions of our divide-and-conquer strategy, basically confirming with the sponsors who've already signed on that they'll hear from me this week, and stay close enough to Banner so that when the dancing starts, which Kip and Karen always have at these things, I'll be within striking distance.

When the band gets in place on the small stage set up with the ocean as its backdrop, I make my move. Banner's talking with a guy from San Jose who developed an app that made him a millionaire several times over in less than a year. He's on his way to a billion and has already signed on to sponsor the golf tournament.

"So the app tracks my diet, nutrition, exercise," she's telling San Jose when I walk up.

"That's fascinating," he says, eyes dropping to her breasts every other word.

"It is," Banner agrees enthusiastically, clueless that his next move will be to touch her in a nonthreatening way and get her somewhere alone.

"And your client Quinn developed it?" he asks, taking her arm and steering her slightly away from the cluster of people surrounding them. "Could we step over to the terrace? I feel like we're having to yell, and this app is so—"

"Fascinating," I cut in. "You mentioned that."

They both turn surprised eyes to me. Banner smiles, but San Jose, rightfully sensing a threat, frowns.

"Jared, hey," Banner says, her heavy-lidded look telling me she's had enough of the champagne lemonade to make her relaxed but not enough to make her careless. "I was just chatting with... Oh, gosh. I didn't catch your name."

"Miller," he grits out, clearly disappointed she doesn't already know him or isn't enraptured by his net worth. "Kyle Miller."

"That's right." Banner taps his shoulder. "You were going to tell me about *your* app. Maybe you could collaborate with Quinn to work out some of the kinks in Girl, You Better?"

She blinks long lashes at him over her champagne lemonade, full lips wrapped around the rim of the glass as she takes a sip. A droplet trails down her throat and into her cleavage.

"Oops. Spilled a little." She giggles.

Banner never giggles. And where'd she learn that? When did she start *doing* that?

She catches the wayward droplet, shrewdly watching Kyle tracing the path her finger takes as she scoops the lemonade from between her breasts and sucks it from her finger. By the time he looks back, she's blinking her lashes and smiling again.

"Uh, yeah," he says eagerly. "I could do that."

"Oh great." Banner pulls her phone from her pocket. "Could you AirDrop your number?" Another flurry of blinks. "Please?"

They exchange contacts, and the music starts up.

"They're clearing the floor for dancing," Kyle says. "Maybe we could—"

"I don't think so," I interrupt, to his dismay.

"But she and I were about to—"

"I know," I say, trying for a rueful look and probably failing. "Maybe next time."

"But we—"

"Could you go now?" I'm over this and missing the beginning of the dance I've plotted all night for.

Banner's throaty chuckle draws both of our attention.

"I'll call you Monday, Kyle," Banner says, slipping the phone back into her pocket. "It was great chatting with you."

He takes her polite dismissal much better than mine, nodding and walking off.

"That was rude." She sips her lemonade and blinks hard and fast like she did with Kyle. "And I was just getting started."

"I think," I say, plucking the champagne flute from her fingers and setting it on a nearby ledge, "we should retire those batting eyelashes for the night. They got what they came for."

"Yes, they did," she agrees. "Quinn's been calling Kyle's office for weeks asking for help with her app. When I saw his name on the guest list, I saw opportunity knocking. I answered."

My equinox, indeed.

"Well, there's music," I point out. "And dancing."

"Yes, everybody's doing it, apparently," she intones, glancing around at the partygoers coupling off on the makeshift dance floor.

"A shame if we don't."

"I *do* like to dance." She angles a mischievous glance up at me. "Though I don't typically fraternize with the enemy."

I glide my hand down her back until it rests at the dip of her waist and steer her to the floor.

"Oh, I'm the enemy, am I?" I pull her into my arms, and her hands rest on my shoulders.

"I've always thought so," she says, glancing down at our feet and swaying to the music.

"No, you haven't," I remind her softly. "Not always."

It's the golden hour. The sun is in flux, not quite down and not high. It's a breath before sunset, and the whole sky explodes with a final burst of color like fireworks over the ocean. The same blush washing the horizon rises on Banner's cheeks.

"No, not always," she agrees, eyes still trained on the ground, none of the coquettish blinking and drop-gathering she treated Kyle to for me.

Thank God.

"You know I'm not the enemy, right, Ban?" I press her closer until there's no space between our bodies and my mouth is at her ear. "We're on different teams, but not really enemies. Would that be an accurate assessment?"

A slight shudder ripples through her body at my breath in her hair, at her ear. She nods slowly.

"I'm seeing that. Bent confirming that you weren't in on"—she looks up at me, her eyes guarded but showing more than she probably wants to—"that you weren't in on what Prescott did has made me see things differently. Clearly."

"Good." My hands venture subtle inches from the dip of her waist to the rounded curve of her hips. "I've wanted to sort that out for years, but I guess we both had other things going on."

"Yes, living in different cities."

"Working at different firms," I add.

"Separate paths," she whispers, eyes locked with mine.

I twirl us in a half circle, sliding my thigh between hers, and the only thing separating us is the linen of my pants and the cotton of her dress. Her warmth seeps through the thin layers, and I want nothing more than to push under her dress and squeeze that lush ass.

Thong? Bikini? Shit. What if Banner isn't wearing *any panties at all?*

I insert a small space between us so she won't feel how hard I am imagining her bare pussy under that red dress.

"But now our paths seem to keep crossing," I tell her. "So it feels like time to repair things. To pick up where we left off."

"You're right." She smiles, the dimple denting her smooth cheek. Her makeup conceals the seven freckles, but I could tell you exactly where each of them rests on her nose. "I think reviving our friendship is a good thing."

Friendship? That's a start.

"I love this song," she says, tilting her head to pick the song out from the noise of the crowd.

"Kiss Me" by Sixpence None The Richer.

"So do I." I twirl her again and gather our joined hands against my chest.

"Oh, we finally agree on something," she says with a laugh.

"Don't get used to it," I tease back.

When the song ends, Banner pulls her phone out and grimaces.

"I should get going," she says.

"Zo's waiting at home for you?" I force myself to ask.

It sounds so domestic and permanent and settled. I glue my smile in place, though the thought of her still sleeping with Vidale makes me want to vomit my champagne lemonade on his head.

"Uh, no." She licks her lips and slides her glance to the side. "He's traveling. He's actually in Argentina for a few weeks working with an orphanage down there."

Because he's a saint.

"But I have an early-morning workout," she says. "I'm tired, and we've done what we came to do."

Speak for yourself, Banner. I came to chip away at that wall around you, and I'm not sure how much progress I've made. We say our goodbyes to Kip and Karen, thanking them for a great evening, and zip back down the drive.

"Top down?" I ask, glancing at the carefully coiffed hair she wanted to preserve on the ride here.

"Top down," she confirms, tugging at the pins until her hair tumbles around her shoulders and whips behind her in the wind. She glances over at me, her wide smile bright in the moonlight. "This feels fantastic."

Me and Banner finally alone.

"Yup," I agree. "Fantastic."

CHAPTER 16
BANNER

I HAVE TO BE CAREFUL.

I've done a good job concealing how Jared affects me. He's a shark, and he's been circling me all night. Any sign of weakness would be like blood in the water. He'd devour me whole.

But ever since Bent told me the truth, confirmed what Jared said years ago, two tiny insidious words keep worming through my brain.

What if…

What if Prescott hadn't pulled his trick? What if he and his pride of lions had never interrupted us? What if I hadn't called the cops? What if I'd *believed* Jared? We were young and ambitious and had things we wanted to do. Who knows if a relationship between us could have survived the distance, our immaturity? My insecurities. His ruthless single-mindedness. Things happen the way they do for a reason. Things probably happened exactly as they should have, but sitting beside the man whom I've always had trouble resisting, those two words taunt me.

What if…the most dangerous words in the English language. Hell, in every language I speak.

On the ride home, I'm quiet, resisting his every attempt to talk. I'm contemplating the shadows of mountains and the shimmer of water in the dark. The cool air lifts my hair away from my neck. I fight the intoxicating effects of champagne lemonade traveling through my blood. I need to be alert. On guard. I'm so absorbed in ignoring the pull of Jared beside me that at first I don't notice we've pulled off the main road.

"Where are we going?" I ask, looking at him for the first time since we left the Carter estate.

"So you do remember I'm here," he says lightly, sarcasm in his voice.

"Of course. I was…" I take in our surroundings, the road we're traveling down. "Where are we going?"

He pulls onto a sprawling yard with a few cars parked here and there. A huge screen looms over the patch of grass.

"A drive-in?" I ask, panic stealing all my cool points.

Words like "necking" and "making out" come to mind as soon as I think "drive-in." He kills the engine and faces me, illuminated by the moon and the screen.

"It's not that late. You'll have plenty of time to sleep."

"No, I won't, and we don't know what's playing," I say. "We may not even want to see this movie."

"It's the experience that counts," he says, his expression, the tone of his voice, everything about him persuading, urging. "What can it hurt?"

I'm formulating my argument to convince him, since that seems to be the only thing he understands, when a girl—maybe seventeen years old—strolls up to the car, and Jared pays admission.

"Evening. I'm Sally," she says and fishes a notepad from her pocket and a pencil from behind her ear. "What can I get you tonight?"

"We're not staying," I say at the same time Jared says, "Popcorn."

She darts a confused look between us. "You want butter on that popcorn?"

"Yeah," Jared answers, paying in cash. "And two Vanilla Cokes."

She walks away, and I batten down my hatches, preparing for the fight ahead.

"This whole thing is incredibly presumptuous," I say, irritation coloring my words. "Bringing me here without my permission. Ordering Vanilla Coke, which I've never had—"

"You'll love it."

"And buttered popcorn, which I don't have enough points left for."

"Points?" Dark-blond brows collide. "What do you mean, 'points'?"

Growing up overweight, struggling with it for so many years, I didn't realize how much shame I held around food. In public, I'd imagine the chiding conversations thin people were having about what I'd ordered. I'd conjure up their secret dismay that I'd selected the burger when there was a perfectly good garden salad on the menu. I was self-conscious about my portions, always concerned I'd gotten so much people would say, "Ah, *that's* why." I didn't want people to think about food and me in the same sentence because then they would "remember" I was overweight. To talk about dieting with someone draws attention to "my problem." To talk about it with Jared, considering our unique, humiliating past, would have been nearly impossible.

But that was then. This is now. This is me now.

"Weight Watchers," I say. "We assign points to food, and I'm allowed only so many points each day. I don't think I have enough for buttered popcorn."

"Oh. I get that." His expression doesn't change, but he drapes an arm along the back of my seat. "You look great, Banner."

Before I can awkwardly thank him, he goes on.

"But you've always looked great to me," he says, mesmerizing me with the forthright admiration in his eyes. "I can tell *you're* happier now with how you look, so that's important, but you've always been beautiful to me. I hope you know that."

A lump forms in my throat, hot and huge. God, why does he have to *be* this way? How does he look at me with the same...intent now as he did that night? Like I'm the same person? When most guys didn't even bother to look twice then, he looked at me like *this*. Like he's looking at me tonight and doesn't even notice that now I actually have a waistline. I'm on the verge of completely humiliating myself when Sally walks back up.

Jared takes the popcorn and drinks. "Thanks. What's the movie, by the way?"

"*An Affair to Remember*," Sally says. "It's Oldie but Goodie night. Not many folks here. Sorry. I have no idea what it's about."

I at least know the plot. Cary Grant. Deborah Kerr. Both in relationships with other people, but they fall for each other. The universe hates me.

"I've never seen this," Jared says. "Have you?"

"No." I discipline my lips into a firm line. "But I'm not watching this movie, and I'm not eating that popcorn or drinking Vanilla Coke. Take me home, Jared."

He considers me in silence for a moment and then plops the popcorn between us and sips his drink.

"No."

Why does he challenge me and torture me at every turn?

"You could have any girl sitting here eating popcorn and drinking dessert soda with you while you watch this movie," I say hotly. "Take me home and find one of them."

"No." His expression hardens into implacability. "Eat the popcorn, drink the Coke, or don't. I don't care. Just turn around and watch the damn movie."

"Why?" I demand, my voice ascending in volume. "I don't want to see this movie, and I could be home in an hour."

"Exactly. I don't want to *take* you home," he says, matching my volume, the fierceness of my glare. "To be a damn genius, you are so obtuse. I don't care if it's *Godzilla* or *Frankenstein* or fucking *Teenage Mutant Ninja Turtles*. It doesn't matter what's on the screen, Banner. I just don't want you to leave."

Dread and delight wrangle inside me. He's on the verge of saying things that could take me down a dark path, one I would never consider following. A path that breaks all my rules and violates all my codes. One that could break my best friend's heart.

"But, Jared—"

"Eat your popcorn," he says irritably. "The movie's starting."

I sit back and fold my arms, a physical barricade between my heart and the man eating popcorn beside me. Yes, I've had my reservations about the relationship with Zo, but I'm still *with* him. I can't allow this thing seething between Jared and me, this thing that took up where it left off one cold December night a decade ago, to compromise my future.

My body has been reacting to Jared all day, as though once I knew that night was as real to him as it was to me, all my defenses fell and I'm left with this dangerous vulnerability that could wreck my relationship, destroy my friendship. Hell, set back my career. If Zo, one of our biggest clients, walked away from Bagley because I cheated on him, Cal would have legitimate grounds to dismiss me or at the very least hand the LA office over to someone else.

This calls for popcorn. I have a history of dealing with my emotions through food, but I can control it. I'm measuring it out and then stopping. I'll eat a handful of this piping-hot, buttery goodness. Just one taste.

Speaking of hands, mine brushes up against Jared's in the tub of popcorn, and a shiver skitters over my spine. I pull back, but he captures my fingers, not releasing me. I tug uselessly. He's not simply holding my fingers hostage. He's holding my whole life in his hands and he doesn't even know it. Or maybe he does but doesn't care.

"Jared..." I'm breathless, helpless.

"Watch the movie, Banner," he says, eyes fixed on Cary and Deborah. His right hand occupied with my left, he reaches into the tub with his left and keeps eating. I stare at the screen, eyes unseeing, ears unhearing. My full attention centers on the searing point of contact between our fingertips. Foolishly, I will myself to relax. I actually follow the storyline for the next few minutes, and I'm getting invested, wanting Cary and Deborah to figure it out, when Jared's thumb ghosts over the thin skin of my wrist. It feels like he's caressed the nerves beneath. It feels like he's stroked my pulse because now my heart bangs like a mallet. My breath catches, hitches, stalls as he traces my palm. My mouth waters. Why is that even happening? Like my taste buds have been warned that soon I'll taste him again. I give another half-hearted tug, but he doesn't release my hand.

I don't want him to.

"Fuck this," he mutters, turning away from the movie. He cups my cheek and presses his forehead to mine, the smell of fresh popcorn wafting up between us. "I'm going to kiss you."

"No," I protest but don't pull away. I'm paralyzed. I could physically move, but I'm held by the scent of him and the warmth of him and the promise of him. The taste of him so close.

"Yes, I am, Banner, because we both want it," he says flatly. "And there's no reason for us not to have it."

"There *is* a reason. I have…" I pause and try to gather my scattered wits. "Jared, you know I have a boyfriend."

"And if you haven't figured it out by now, I don't give a fuck." He pushes his fingers into my hair, angles his mouth over mine, and licks my bottom lip once, sending a current of electricity over my skin. I squeeze my eyes shut, like that will somehow block the sensations quaking through every cell of my body.

His tongue laps at the corners of my mouth. He groans and captures my bottom lip between his, sucking at me, alternating force and gentleness, leaving me unsure which I want more. I clench my right fist on my thigh, the only sign of resistance I can muster, but it's not enough. Not when he pushes the popcorn away and grips my waist and brings me incrementally closer until we're pressed together and our hearts bang on each other's chests, one demanding entrance from the other.

"Your heart's racing," he says, an echo from years ago. He drags our linked hands to his chest. "So is mine."

"Jared, we can't."

"I am."

He tilts my chin just so, tugs my mouth open, and kisses me. With his dominant nature, I expect an invasion. Maybe I could have resisted that, could have prepared for that, but his mouth tenderly begs, and our tongues desperately tangle. This propulsive force has *me* leaning into him, has *my* hand clawed in his hair. Has me fucking *his* mouth. And I can't stop. I'd forgotten how he tastes, but this moment under a star-spangled sky, this moon hurls me into retrograde. Backward so many years to our first kiss when he exploded across my senses and detonated any coherent thought with one stroke of his tongue.

Air cools my legs when he lifts my skirt, his hand lighting up the sensitive skin of my inner thigh on the inevitable journey to my pussy. He barely brushes me through my panties, and my muscles clench, anticipating his touch. I can't even manage to feel embarrassed that my panties are already soaked.

"I want to finger you," he rasps over my lips. "Can I, Ban?"

Dios mío, ayúdame.

God, help me.

But there's no help. No salvation. Only the sin of this moment, of my dreams. I want to wake up. When this happened in my dreams, I woke up, and I was beside Zo. He was sleeping peacefully, blissfully unaware that I was wet-dreaming about a man from my past. A man from my present. But Zo's not here, and I can't remember why I should deny myself what I know Jared will give me. What I've been aching for ever since he reentered my life. I nod my permission quickly before I change my mind, widening my thighs to make it easy for him. He slips his thumb beneath the wet silk and runs it over my clit.

"Jesus." I jerk, and his mouth is at my shoulder, his tongue soothing the burning, naked skin. With his free hand, he tugs one string of my halter until they both flop down over my breasts. His eyes never leaving mine, he strokes my clit again and slowly slides his middle finger inside. The erotic contact between our eyes is as potent as that one finger finding passage inside of me, over and over. With every unblinking stroke, I'm closer to giving Jared the surrender I promised Zo only he would have.

"Jared, we have to…"

Stop.

The word won't leave my mouth. It's trapped behind my teeth. Anything that would stop this, would stem this, even my fear of getting caught, being seen, freezes and everything else runs hot. Goes green. Begs him to floor it. With the strings untied, he nudges my dress down with his lips, and cool air kisses my nipples. He stares at them, swallowing so hard I see his throat move in the dimmest moonlight.

"God, Banner," he says hoarsely, lifting his eyes to penetrate mine. "How could you not see how beautiful you are?"

His words undo what's left of my resistance, and I pull him down to my breast, needing to give myself to this man who has always *seen* me. He opens his mouth completely over my nipple, pulling on me in a steady rhythm. Biting my breast, rubbing my clit, pumping his middle fuck-you finger into the hungry hole between my legs. My hips roll into him, seeking him, urging him to do his worst. He shifts to my other breast and adds another finger.

"Come on my hand," he says, his voice confident and pleading. "Show me how you look when you come. I've never seen it."

In the dark. We made love in the dark before, and we're in the dark now, but there's just enough light for me to see his beautiful face and just enough light for him to see mine.

So I show him.

"Ah," I cry out, heedless of the few cars parked around us while my body dissolves for him. I bite my bottom lip and frantically ride his hand, pleasure spilling from my body onto his fingers.

"Say my name," he demands. "Who's doing this for you, Banner?"

"It's you." Helpless tears slip over my cheeks, tears of passion and regret and shame and joy. "God, Jared, I know it's you."

CHAPTER 17
JARED

BANNER IS AVOIDING ME AGAIN. SENDING MY CALLS TO VOICEMAIL, ignoring my emails, not replying to text messages. Saturday night should have been a step forward, but we backslid like a wayward believer, and I don't know how to move us in the right direction.

Right direction may not be accurate. There is nothing right about systematically plotting to take another man's woman. I won't call it the *right* direction. It's *my* direction, and I know it's ultimately where Banner belongs. And after what happened at the drive-in, I have no doubt it's where she wants to be.

Here's the thing about falling for a good girl: they have all these *rules*. And *qualms*. And the worst? *Guilt*. She has all this integrity that gets in the way of what she wants, which is me. But I won't allow it to get in the way of what *I* want, which is her. So we're at an impasse where she avoids me, slinks back into her comfort zone with Alonzo.

Fuck that shit. If she thinks I'm letting this go, letting her go again, she's delusional. I know, I'm the one who *sounds* crazy, but that is not the case. What's crazy is denying yourself something this special. I'm living proof that ruthless people who don't give a fuck want special things, too. And I'm taking mine.

As soon as I get her to talk to me.

I've been camped out here at the Seven Grand for an hour,

nursing this same Jameson and Coke. I don't do this. I don't sit around thinking about women. I don't let them disrupt my rhythm. They are generally the solution to a problem, which is that I like to fuck. And when I don't fuck, I get agitated and lose focus, which ultimately costs me money. This is a problem since the only girl I want to sleep with won't return my calls. Won't leave her damn boyfriend. Won't *yield*. And I've determined that sleeping with Banner isn't enough. Leaving Zo isn't enough. I want her to *yield*. I want her as preoccupied with me as I am with her. As fixated on me as I am on her. Anything less than her feeling as obsessed as I do just doesn't seem fair.

I check my phone one more time in case she deigned to actually respond. Nothing from her, but a text message from Tanya asking me to call. She runs a strip club I take prospects to all the time. I ran into her at Titanium. I had no idea she taught Quinn's pole-dancing classes at the gym. She keeps her eyes peeled for ballers and gives me tips on where they are, what they like, shit they do that might come in handy. When her recon pans out, I grease her palm.

"What's up, Tan?" I ask, using my handsfree and knocking back the last of my drink, giving the table a good slam with the glass.

"I wondered if you got my message," Tanya says. "Took you long enough to call."

"What's up?" I repeat. No time for bullshit. Get to the point. My patience is ice-thin tonight.

"I got something."

It's the first time in days my heart rate has increased.

"Whatta you got?" I signal for the bartender to bring my tab.

"That guy who's leaving Dallas. What's his name, Lim or Lyn or—"

"Link," I cut in, dropping some cash and standing. "Link Pullen. He recently became an unrestricted free agent. Biggest name available in free agency season."

Also on the outs with his current agent. Opportunity, meet need. Supply, say hello to demand.

"He's here," she whispers. "Everybody's here tonight. Biggest party of the summer."

"Where is *here?*"

"I'll text the address."

"Will I have trouble getting in?" I know so many players, that's rarely an issue, but some parties are more exclusive than others.

"You'll be fine," Tanya replies. "Some of your guys are here, too."

Not surprising.

"Headed over now."

I'm nearly at the door when someone calls my name. I turn, irritated to find Cal Bagley wearing his permanent cocksure grin and a pathetic suit. He should know better. I mean, the guy's making millions. You can't buy *one* decent suit? And what's he even doing on my coast? He's supposed to be in New York.

"Cal, good to see you." *Lie.* "How are you?" *Don't care.*

"I'm good," he replies, shooting me a speculative glance. "I'll be even better if you keep your hands to yourself."

"Excuse me? No idea what you're talking about."

"Banner Morales," he says, his lips tightening.

Visions of Banner's bare breasts in the moonlight and me finger-fucking her in the front seat run through my mind.

"Uh, maybe you could be more specific, Cal."

"I know you're working together on the charity golf tournament. I had some friends at Kip's party Saturday. Said the two of you looked like a team. You can't have her. She's the best I've ever had."

Funny. She's the best I've ever had, too.

Ohhh. He means in business.

Cal is Pride, like Kip and Bent, for that matter. Some well-meaning "brother" probably gave him a full report when they saw me with Banner.

"Your prize mare is safe for now," I tell him, forcing a grin. "But it's true we'd take better care of her at Elevation."

"Don't even think about it," Cal says harshly, all signs of the phony smile disappearing. "If there's one thing Banner is, it's loyal. We gave her a job straight out of college."

"First of all, Banner is many things, not one, and don't make it sound like you did her any favors. I heard Alonzo only signed because of Banner, and you know damn well half your clients would leave if she did."

"So you admit it? You *are* trying to entice her to leave?"

I'm trying to fuck her. To have her. To keep her, but none of that is any of his concern. He's playing checkers at a chess match. Clueless about what the game actually is.

"Go have a drink, Cal." I pat his shoulder. "It'll do wonders."

I relish the undisguised look of frustration on his face the entire drive to the party.

Could I take Banner from not just Zo but Cal, too? What a coup that would be. August and Iris would be ecstatic. No question all her clients would jump Cal's ship and follow her to Elevation. What I want is Banner, in my bed and wherever that leads us, but stealing Banner from that asshole would be an amazing bonus.

When I pull up to the ultra-modern Hollywood Hills home, cars spill from the drive and overflow the curbs. Loud music blares through the walls and permeates the air. Once I'm inside, topless girls walk around unselfconsciously. An open-door ménage à trois is going on up in one of the bedrooms. Last season's defensive player of the year has his dick in some girl's mouth. She has some guy's dick in her ass. I can't tell what's going on with door number three, but their sexual game of Twister is so commonplace at parties like this, no one even gapes, and they don't bother to close the door. If Link is in a situation like that, it would be rude to interrupt, and I wouldn't want to join in. I'd show myself out and corner him some other time. It's a testament to how focused I am on Banner that I'm not even tempted by the abundance of naked flesh being flashed around the large house.

When I reach the landing for the next floor, a man, probably a baller based on his height, drunkenly yells at a woman I can't see because his large frame blocks her, has her trapped against the wall.

"Clothes," he slurs. "What's a stripper doing with clothes on? I wanna see them tits. And that fat ass. Take 'em off."

"I told you I'm not a damn stripper," a strident female voice fires back. "Now get your hands off me or I'll kick *and* sue your drunk ass."

That voice…it couldn't be. It better not be. Not here in this den of iniquity.

The woman steps away from the wall, buttoning her blouse and muttering under her breath in something other than English.

The hell.

"Banner?"

CHAPTER 18
BANNER

"JARED?"

I utter his name, shocked to come face-to-face with the handsome devil I've been avoiding all week.

"What are you doing here?" I ask, stalling and hoping to distract him from the fact that *I'm* here.

Needless to say, it doesn't work.

"You're asking why *I'm* here?" he demands, confusion and disapproval settling onto his face. "I belong here. I'm in places like this, parties like this all the time doing business."

"Well, so am I," I say, willing my hands to stop shaking after the confrontation with the drunken giant. "I have business here, too."

I step around him, hoping to get away, but no such luck. He grabs my arm and drags me into the nearest bedroom, slamming the door behind us. I can't believe it's empty. Seems like every corner of this house is occupied by rutting athletes and willing strippers, but he finds the first available in seconds.

"Who's here with you?" he asks.

"No one. Why would someone be with me?"

"Why are you *here*, Banner?" He looks back at the door and then back to me, storm clouds darkening the vibrant blue of his eyes. "Was he bothering you? Did that guy touch you?"

Groped is more like it, but I'm not telling Jared with his face looking like that. I wouldn't put it past him to go after the guy, and I know Jared used to ball and can handle himself, but let's not risk it with a guy nearly seven feet tall.

"I'm fine." I push past him. "I need to go."

"Yeah, home." He catches my elbow again.

I glance down to his hand on my arm.

"You really have to stop doing that."

"What?" he asks, the clouds in his eyes shifting from stormy to cumulus. "Touching you?"

His grip gentles, and he cups both my elbows, drawing me into the hard heat emanating through his well-tailored suit.

"You liked it when I touched you at the movie, right?" His low-voiced words steam the small space around us.

How many times have I relived those scorching moments with Jared over the last week? Asleep, awake, working out, while reviewing a contract. The memory of those electric, erotic moments assails me without warning and has given me no rest. I woke up wet again this morning. I'd come in my sleep. Thank God Zo is traveling. I may have been making noises while I slept or said Jared's name. I have no idea, but it would have been awkward and hurtful, and I refuse to hurt Zo any more than I have to.

What I've already done is more than enough. My heart aches every time I think about the conversation we need to have. I'll have to tell him what happened with Jared, but I can't even imagine how that would feel telling him another man touched me that way when I was supposed to be faithful to him. Telling him another man has overtaken my thoughts, my dreams. I'm not a cheat. I keep reassuring myself it was an indiscretion, but nothing we couldn't get past.

But do I want to get past it? Get past Jared? Stay with Zo? I know I have to deal with it, but I can't right now. It's free agency season. Several of my clients, including Zo, are in the thick of it. That means constant contact with teams, meetings with GMs, negotiations with lawyers, phone calls with clients vacationing in time zones all over the world. I don't have time to be preoccupied with a personal life, much less one as complicated as Jared Foster is making mine.

"Banner, you did like it, right?" Jared's still touching me, his hands sure, his words confident, but uncertainty lies just behind his eyes. "Why have you been ignoring me?"

"Jared, you know why. It's complicated." I sigh heavily and pull away, walking over to open the door. "I'm working, and I can't do this with you right now."

"Working how?" His question comes from behind me, and his hand slams the door closed again. He's at my back. I've been outmaneuvered. I wanted to keep my distance, but there's no distance between my back and his front. Between my body and the long, hard length of him. "Was he bothering you?" Jared asks, his lips at my ear, his breath in my hair. There's genuine concern in his voice, and I hate that this man everyone assumes would sell his grandmother to make the right deal cares about me. Always has. It complicates things even more.

"I'm fine, Jared." I rest my forehead against the door, refusing to relax against him, though every cell in my body urges me to do just that.

"You were buttoning your blouse," he says, voice tight. "If he bothered you, then—"

"Then what?" I turn around to face him and lean against the door.

Big mistake. I'm confronted with eyes the dark blue of a midnight sky and the face carved from my fantasies with a lust-tipped chisel. He's wearing a three-piece suit. The powerful width of his chest stretches beneath a navy-blue jacket and vest, a shirt the color of pink champagne, no tie. His hand still rests against the closed door, and his arm crowds me in.

"I hate it when you ignore me," he says unexpectedly.

My eyes snap to his, and that's a mistake, too. Looking into his eyes. The intensity there is mesmerizing.

"Not just this week," he says. "But when we first graduated, right after all that shit went down with the Pride. We were at a few of the same conferences. Every time I tried to talk to you, you froze me out. Once you even threatened to blow your—"

"Rape whistle," I finish for him, chuckling. I was so desperate to keep him out of my life. I understood the danger then of giving myself to him, and even when I wasn't sure what his role had been in what happened, when I didn't believe I could trust him, I knew I couldn't trust myself. I knew it then, and I know it now. "I need to go," I say abruptly, turning back around and pulling on the handle. Under the weight of his hand, the door remains closed. "Jared, my client needs me."

It's true. It's why I came here when Tanya texted me that one of my rookies might be in trouble, but it's also my get-out-of-this-room card. I'm relieved when his hand falls from the door, but that's short-lived because his hands grip my hips from behind, and he presses himself into me.

"Banner, I know you have things you're working through." A short laugh rustles the hair at my neck. "Hell, if your free agency season is anything like mine, you're busy every second of the day."

I nod, holding my body tense to create even an inch between our bodies.

"But I can't stop thinking about Saturday," he whispers across my neck, his words followed closely behind by his lips feathering light kisses across my skin. I shiver, and he pushes into me, his thick length wedged into the cheeks of my ass. "About your pussy clenching around my fingers."

"Oh, God." I drop my forehead to the door again, my breath coming heavier. "Stop."

"Your nipples," he continues, his breath thinning out, his palms spreading at my waist until he can brush the underside of my breasts. "I want them in my mouth again. Ban, please."

"Don't ask me to…" I swallow my words, but my fear won't go down. "I cannot hurt him like this, Jared."

"I don't want you to hurt him. I want you to choose me." He squeezes my waist, a warning. "But if you don't choose me, you *will* hurt him because this… *We* are going to happen."

"I have to go." I step back into him only long enough to wrench the door open. "I need to find my guy before he destroys his career."

I've been distracted by Jared long enough. I need to handle what I came here to do and get out before I allow Jared to wreak any more havoc on my life.

"Which guy?" he asks from right behind me. "You can't wander around this house looking for your client, Banner."

He takes my arm…again…and stops me in the hall.

"Do you know what kind of party this is?" His face hardens above me. "Anything goes, and half these guys are so high out of their minds, they wouldn't even notice if you said no. So *the hell* I'm letting you run all over this house looking for your client."

"Letting me?" Feminist indignation has me raising both brows. "Since when do you think you *let* me do anything? You're not my father or my boyfriend, and even they don't *let* me do things. I just do them. I'm a grown-ass woman, not some little girl who requires an escort at a fucking party."

"Oh, the grown-ass woman who was being accosted when I found her?" he demands, anger sparking in his eyes. "That was going well."

"I have a job to do."

"Well, you're not doing it without me in this house at this party, and I don't care if you like it or not. Try to shake me."

Our wills war as we exchange glares, neither backing down.

"Tell me who you're trying to find," he says, softening his hands on me, his eyes on mine. "And I'll help you, but I'm not letting you out of my sight in this house."

A weary sigh forces its way past my lips. I've been here for an hour already and haven't found my baller yet. There's no telling how much trouble he's gotten into since Tanya texted me.

"Hakeem Okafor." I look up and see recognition and realization on his face. "Yeah, the one who was suspended for weed twice this season. He's here, and it's a lot worse than weed. Tanya saw him over a line of coke. He hadn't done anything then, but I need to intervene before it gets out. One post to Instagram, one tweet, one peep about this, and he could be out of the league for good."

"A line of coke." A muscle knots under the sculpted line of Jared's jaw. "Let me get this straight. You're at what is essentially an orgy to 'rescue' a seven-foot man who's probably high on cocaine, from himself? Have I missed anything? Some detail that would make this a good idea?"

My concern gives way to anger.

"I told you why I'm here."

"And I'm telling you it's not wise." He places his hand at the small of my back and urges me toward the stairs. "Where are you parked?"

I dig in the heels of my Stuart Weitzmans and whip around, shoving him back.

"I need to find Hakeem first, Jared."

"You're his agent, not his mother, *Banner*," he returns with heat.

"Right. I'm not his mother," I snap, slicing one hand through the air for emphasis. "His *mother* fled a war-torn country with four children and nothing but the clothes on her back. His *mother* worked three jobs to support them by herself in a new place where she knew no one and had to restart their life from scratch."

"Ban—"

"His *mother* is the one I looked dead in the face and promised if she sent her son to the NBA, I would do everything in my power to help him. To protect him." I swallow an anxious lump, recalling that conversation at her tiny kitchen table on the south side of Chicago. "She's the one who, for the first time in her life, isn't worried about how her kids will eat or how they'll go to college. How her family will make it, and that's because her son is making eight figures playing basketball."

I push past him and start toward the set of stairs that takes me to the next floor.

"I need to find him so he can keep playing basketball and I can keep my promise to her."

"Killer with a heart," he says softly behind me.

I freeze, one foot on the next stair, and look at him over my shoulder. The years fall away, and I'm not the high-powered agent wearing six-hundred-dollar shoes, and he's not the ruthless man with a fleet of well-tailored suits and the fastest-growing agency around. We're just two barely adults dreaming about our futures and wondering who we will ultimately become. I'm happy with the path I chose, and I know he's happy with the road he's taken. Our paths diverged, but for whatever reason, lately we keep coming back to this.

"Are you gonna help me or what?" I ask, offering a wry grudging smile.

He rolls his eyes and steps around me to lead the way up the next flight of stairs.

"Ten minutes," he says sternly. "We look for ten minutes, and then you're leaving with or without him."

So he thinks. If I haven't found Hakeem in ten minutes, we'll renegotiate.

But we do. On the next floor in a room with a few guys and, thankfully, no phones out taking pictures or recording it. And, yes, with cocaine everywhere.

"Please let me handle this," I ask Jared in the hall outside the room. "You helped me, and I appreciate it, but this is my guy. You'll be right here if I need you."

For a second he looks like he'll protest, but he finally nods and leans against the wall.

"If you're not out in five minutes…"

He leaves a trail of unspoken consequences in the wake of that sentence. I nod my agreement and head in, closing the door behind me.

"What the hell are you doing, Hakeem?" I ask without preamble.

He glances up, his eyes droopy and dazed from the drugs.

"Huh?" He blinks a few times like I'm a hallucination. "Banner?"

"Yes, Banner." I stand over him, pointing to the drugs and bottles of liquor on the table. "You already had two suspensions for weed. What do you think they'll do to you for this shit?"

"Nobody would tell—"

"Somebody did," I cut in, slit-eyed and furious. "And they called me."

"It's a private party." Dismay and panic clear some of his haze.

"Nothing is private. I told you that on day one. Maybe once your little coke party pops up on Instagram you'll believe me."

He glances around the room, probably seeing the faces around him with new eyes. Some he knows, and some he doesn't. I pray he's realizing how foolhardy it is to do drugs at all, much less with guys he doesn't know and can't be sure he can trust.

I step closer and bend to speak so low only he will hear me.

"Think of Adeago," I whisper his sister's name to him. "She wants to go to Northwestern, right? She doesn't have a scholarship. She's depending on you, Hakeem. So are Kambili and Ekeema." I pull back and touch his shoulder. "So is your mother. You know this."

He glances from the table littered with coke and weed and destruction and then back to me and nods solemnly. He's a good kid, barely a man, who went from having nothing one day to having riches and resources beyond his wildest imagination the next. It's a lot. It's a trap if you don't have the right people surrounding you. I don't recognize half the men here. They're not the right people. Not ballers but hangers-on. Opportunists. Some of them predators. By now, I've had enough predators assume I was prey that I know how to spot them.

"Let's get out of here." I reach for his arm, but someone reaches for mine.

"You do lap dances?" the huge man attached to the arm asks me, staring at my ass.

I was out, for once, having dinner with Quinn when Tanya texted me, so I'm dressed well. Black harem pants that snap tight at the ankles and a silk blouse longer in the front and cut higher in the back, exposing my lower back and butt.

"Hands off. I'm not a stripper," I say for the third time tonight.

I mean, really? Do strippers dress this well?

"I like this fat ass," he says, smacking the derriere in question.

Oh, hell no.

"I said hands off, *hijo de puta*," I snap, slipping into the language that always seems to best convey my strongest emotions.

"Uh, I don't know what you called me," he says, amusement lighting his drug-hazed eyes, "but my dick got hard."

"You want that dick shoved down your throat," Jared says from the open door with a calm I recognize as false, "touch her ass again."

His eyes are burning the spot where the man holds my arm. I jerk free and touch Hakeem's shoulder. "Let's go."

Hakeem stands and stumbles. I catch his arm, but his weight buckles my knees, and we both almost fall. Jared rushes over and slips under Hakeem's arm, supporting him.

"Sorry," Hakeem slurs. "That Grey Goose got me like…"

"And that Molly got you, too," the ass-slapper says. "You gon' feel that, bruh."

"You took Molly, too, Hakeem?" I ask.

"I guess." Hakeem slumps into me, all seven feet of him, and I grunt under his weight.

"I got him," Jared says, irritation barbing his voice. "Man, try to walk."

Hakeem is practically deadweight, but we get him to the hall. I start dragging him toward the stairs we came up, but Jared stops short.

"There's a back staircase," he says. "Let's take him that way."

"Good idea." I shift Hakeem on my shoulder and follow Jared's lead.

It's difficult getting his bulk down the steps, and I almost lose my footing several times. Hakeem alternates between drunken snickers and tearful apologies. He can't decide what kind of drunk he wants to be, but he's getting on my damn nerves. He steps on Jared's foot more than once, and based on the muttered curses coming from the other side, Hakeem has gotten on Jared's nerves, too.

"I think he broke my toe," Jared complains when we get outside.

It's been a long night, and we narrowly averted disaster. Only time will tell if some damning photo surfaces to wreck Hakeem's career. For now, though, we saved the day, and I'm so relieved that when I see Jared's almost-sullen face, my lips twitch in the closest thing to a smile I can manage under the circumstances.

I step away and leave Hakeem leaning on Jared while I search for my car. I was in such a hurry to get here, I don't even remember where I parked. I turn to tell Jared I found it and catch him staring at my ass.

"Are you looking at my butt?" I ask, waffling between flattered and offended.

"Of course," Jared replies as if I'm crazy for asking. "I actually wish you'd stop talking because I was literally committing your ass in those pants to memory, and you're breaking my concentration."

I try my best to scold him with a look, which is hard to do when my lips are twitching.

"What?" He shrugs as best he can with Hakeem leaning on him. "I mean, it's right there. What do you expect? At least I'm honest."

"The guy who slapped my ass was honest, too," I remind him. "So maybe there's a balance you could find between honest and lecher."

"If I find it, you'll be the first to know."

I shake my head, still fighting twitching lips. I'm not doing this. I refuse to *enjoy* him.

"If you can just help me get him to the car," I say over my shoulder. "We'll be on our way."

"What car?"

I stop and turn, looking at him like *he's* crazy now.

"My car."

"And you're taking him where?" Jared demands. "Do you know where he's staying?"

"No." Hakeem doesn't live in LA. He's here strictly to party, I guess. I have no idea where he's staying, and he's in no condition to tell me. "I'll take him to my house."

"The hell you will." Jared jerks his brows together. "Isn't Zo out of town?"

"Yeah."

"You are not taking Hakeem back to your place, not like this. He's drunk, high, and twice your size. No way."

Hakeem makes mild sounds of protest but looks like he could float away any minute.

"Well, what do you suggest?" I ask, irritated with his logic and frustrated by my lack of forethought.

"Oh, now that I broke my back *and* a toe dragging around a three-hundred-pound seven-footer, you're open to suggestions?" Jared shifts Hakeem into a more comfortable position. "Fucking figures."

The twitch of my lips is just the beginning. He looks so put out, like a little boy not getting his way, that a laugh escapes me before I can catch it. And once it's out, it won't stop.

"Your toe," I gasp, pointing to the foot Hakeem kept smashing as we descended the stairs. "I'm so sorry."

"Apologies usually seem more sincere if you're not laughing when you deliver them," he says dryly. "You must have missed that in *How to Win Friends and Influence People*."

"Oh, shut it." After I get my borderline-hysterical laughter under control, he's staring at me, a small smile teasing his lips.

"What?" I ask, smiling back involuntarily.

"Your laugh," he says. "I want to make you laugh like that every day."

The comment blindsides me. We were working so well together, it was easy to forget how dangerous being around him is.

I walk the few steps to my car, unlock it. "We need to get him out of here."

"So that's how you're going to play this? You'll just keep ignoring it?"

I don't answer, but that's what I do. Ignore him.

"What should we do about Hakeem?" I ask, risking a glance at him over my shoulder.

Jared stares at me for long seconds before sighing and nodding toward my car. "I'll follow you and sleep on your couch. I'm parked over there."

"There's no need for you to stay," I rush to assure him. "To sleep on my couch, I mean."

"Banner, it's late," he says wearily. "I've been up since four this morning. He's not coming back to my place. He's not staying at yours if you're there alone. This is as much of a compromise as you're getting."

I reluctantly nod and help him load Hakeem, who has gone quiet—asleep but breathing evenly—into the car. He's buckled into the back seat while we ride to my house. The whole way, I recite all the reasons it's a bad idea to have Jared in my house with Zo not there. I pep talk myself into believing that everything will be okay. That I will emerge from this night unscathed and still faithful.

But as soon as Hakeem is tucked peacefully into my guest bedroom with the door closed and Jared and I are alone, my confidence wavers. He hangs his jacket on the back of a stool at my kitchen bar. The muscles in his arms strain against the expensive material of his shirt. He rolls the cuffs back, eyes fixed on me.

"Would you like some water before we go to bed?" I hear how

that sounds. "Uh, sleep. Before we go to *sleep*. Me in my room, you on the couch."

He cocks one brow and folds his arms across the width of his chest and watches me sputter.

"Or...food?" I march over to the wood-panel refrigerator and pull it open, studying the contents. "Let's see. We have some grilled chicken. Or there's..."

I trail off when I feel him at my back, the heat from his body contrasting with the cool air from the fridge.

"Some cheese or..." I can't think when his hands span my waist, his thumbs seeking out the tense muscles in my back. "Leftover Indian."

I lick dry lips and try to control my breathing that's growing more erratic with every probe of his fingers.

"Thai," I squeak, my voice high-pitched when he lifts my hair away and kisses the curve of my neck. "Ummm...or Viet-Vietnamese."

His hands slide under my shirt from behind and come around to cup my breasts, stroking the nipples barely but insistently.

"Oh, God," I gasp and drop my head back against him. "Jared, I can't do this. I'm not a cheat."

"Then let him go," he whispers in my ear and slips his fingers under the lace cups of my bra to squeeze my breasts. "He doesn't have to be caught in the middle of this. He doesn't have to get hurt."

"But he *will* get hurt." The thought of Zo hurt by my betrayal, by me choosing someone else, fortifies me enough to pull away from Jared's hands. I face him, breasts still heaving. I'm aching, throbbing between my legs, and my body is a live wire, humming with the electricity of his touch. "You have to respect my relationship."

"No, I don't." Jared runs an agitated hand through his hair. "It's your relationship, so you can respect it, but I don't. You're not married to him."

"That would make a difference?"

He clutches the back of his neck, head lowered and eyes narrowed, as he considers the question.

"I honestly don't know." He shrugs, his face as open and honest as I've ever seen it. "I've never wanted anyone the way I want you, so I can't say for sure that a ring would stop me."

This is worse than I thought, and I thought it was awful.

"Don't you feel bad, though?" I ask, pressing the back of my hand to my forehead like I might have a fever.

"If you're serious about not cheating on him, one of us has to care, and it's not me," he says flatly. "I'm not made that way."

"Not made to care?"

"I'm not made to deny myself something I want." He drops his eyes to the tight buds of my nipples still poking through the silk of my blouse. "Especially when I know it wants me back."

"Don't." I cross my arms over my breasts.

"Don't what? Tell the truth? You want me to lie to myself? I'm not made like that either."

"You're going to wreck my life, Jared," I tell him, fear and longing muddled in the words, mixing inside me.

"Only if you want me to," he says softly. "Do you want me to?"

"I don't know what you mean."

"Is that what this is about?" He flattens the fullness of his lips into a hardened ridge. "You want me to keep pressing you, keep cornering you until you give in so I'm the bad guy? The one who made you fall?"

"No," I choke out, hating the picture he's painting.

"You want me to relieve you of the responsibility? 'Cause I'll do it. I don't mind being the villain, but between you and me, we'll know that you want it as badly as I do. I'm just the one with the balls to make it happen."

"It's not like that." Tears burn my throat. "I'm confused."

"No, you're not." He shakes his head decisively. "You're not confused about the fact that you want me in a way you don't want him. I know you, Banner. If you loved Zo, really loved him, there's no way I could tempt you."

God, he's right. I hate that he's right. I watch him in silence, sure that he's not done.

"You're not confused," he continues. "You're conflicted because you don't want to hurt him, but you don't want to tell him the truth. I, however, am not confused, and I'm not conflicted."

He moves suddenly, breaching the imaginary fortress I erected to buy myself thinking room. He cups my face in his big hands, rubbing his thumbs over my cheeks.

"I know exactly what I want." He bends and leaves featherlight kisses on my lips. "I want another chance with you, Banner. The chance that was taken from us. I want to make love to you with the lights on."

He kisses my chin, caresses my throat. I close my eyes against what I see in his eyes. It's so much more than the need to fuck, than the base urge of one alpha male compelled to take a woman from another of his species. It's tender and sincere and all the things I've told myself all these years he wasn't capable of.

"I saw you first," he whispers, kissing the bridge of my nose where my freckles are.

"I had you first." He kisses my face where the dimple dents my cheek when I smile.

"I want you back," he declares, meeting my eyes and taking my mouth in a deep kiss, never looking away. He sucks my tongue into his mouth with eyes wide open, and the intimacy of it overwhelms me.

I can't close my eyes, can't look away even when the kiss turns more aggressive, possessive. When he coaxes my lips open wider and goes deeper, taking and giving with every stroke. He skids his hands down my waist and cups my ass, kneading the muscles until finally my eyes drift closed and I slump against him, bliss stealing the last of my pitiful resistance. I groan, and my hands creep up over his shoulders and around his neck, my fingers stealing into the cool, silky hair. He presses me into the refrigerator door, hooks my leg on his hip, and opens me up, grinds his erection into the divide of my pussy.

"Jared, oh, God." My head drops back as he pushes against my clit through our clothes. The pleasure swells with each forceful thrust, arrowing from between my legs and up through my chest, coiling at the base of my throat and then breaking free on a silent scream.

"Does he make you feel this way?" he asks, a tightness to his voice that makes me look at him even in the midst of this unimaginable pleasure. "Has he seen you when you come? Seen how beautiful you are when you fall apart? Or do you make him fuck you in the dark, too?"

I squirm free, dropping my leg and pushing away, stumbling over to the counter and leaning there, head dropped forward so my hair hides my heated cheeks.

"Don't talk about him." I turn a serious stare on him, ignoring my body's unfulfilled needs. "You may have seen me first and had me first, but Zo's been my best friend for a long time. That means something to me. He's like family, and as much as I want you, and I admit I do, I don't want to hurt him."

He walks over, and I flinch when he touches my face because I know how frail my guard is. I could go up in flames again if he wants me to. With just one touch.

"Then you have some tough decisions to make, and you should make them soon." He bends to drop a soft kiss on my nose. "Because I won't give up until you're completely mine, Banner, and I won't wait much longer."

CHAPTER 19
BANNER

"*GIRL, YOU BETTER EAT. ALL WORK AND NO FOOD DOES THE BODY no good.*"

Quinn designed the app to alert if no food has been recorded at certain preprogrammed intervals. Now that I understand my body better than I did before, I usually eat several small meals instead of three large ones. Or, worse, skipping breakfast and loading up only twice a day. I work out hard and need to fuel and burn all day. Sometimes I simply forget to record what I eat, but today, the app is right. I haven't left this laptop in hours. I reach across the desk to buzz my assistant.

"Maali, could you grab me a salad from that place up the street?"

Instead of answering, she appears in my doorway. Her inky-black hair swishes at her chin in a bob, and her dark eyes mirror concern.

"Sure." She approaches my desk. "It's almost quitting time. I'll go grab the food before I go. The usual?"

"Yeah," I answer distractedly, scanning the first draft of Zo's new contract. "Dammit. Lowell is not making this easy."

"Still holding out?" She props one hip against my desk.

"I think he considers this meeting me halfway, but he's in for a rude awakening." I close my laptop with a snap. "Max or we walk."

"And does Zo have other options?" Hesitation shadows her delicate features. "He did seem to drop off there at the end."

I shoot her a sharp glance, and she rushes to fix it.

"I'm just saying he was doing so well all season and then seemed out of gas at the end."

"That happens to lots of guys," I remind her, trying to keep my voice free of defensiveness. "Zo is in season number ten, not two, so maybe it was typical wear and tear. I have every confidence that he'll be back to his usual level of performance when the new season starts. He's an elite athlete, one of the best we've seen, and he deserves supermax."

I open my laptop and start an email to politely but firmly tell the Titans front office where they can insert their underwhelming offer.

"Of course," Maali says, not looking as sure as I am. "I'll be back with your salad."

She walks out, only to pop her head back in a few seconds later.

"Oh, and Cal's in the building." With a glance, she commiserates with me. "Don't shoot the messenger."

"You're safe," I say with half a smile before returning my attention to the email. "Thanks for the heads-up."

Through the years, Cal and I have brokered an understanding. He stays out of my way and doesn't expect me to behave like the rest of the assholes who work for him, and I bring him clients. Lots of clients. Lots of business. Lots of money. He gave me the LA office to manage because he's afraid I'll branch off and start my own agency. One day I will, but that is a massive undertaking I don't want right now. I'm settling into a new city. I have more clients than any other agent at Bagley, and they're as loyal to me as I am to them. When I do leave, I know they'll follow me out the door. Cal knows that, too, and usually bends over backward to keep me happy but still feels the need to reassert himself as my "boss" every once in a while, remind me whose name is on the letterhead. He's been in LA for a week making sure things are going well with the new branch, which they are. If he's in the building, that means at some point he'll be in my office.

I'm making progress on a marketing plan for Lamont Christopher, the rookie I "blocked" from Jared, when my cell rings. I'm so tempted not to answer, but a glance at the screen shows me it's Zo. He's in another time zone, and with our busy schedules, it's been hard to really connect. Guilt knots my stomach, and my palms actually start sweating. When he comes back, I have to tell him about what has happened with Jared. We haven't had sex, but what we have done is unacceptable. I pray he forgives me, but I'm still not sure we need to continue forward as we have been, irrespective of Jared.

"*Hola*," I answer, forcing a smile into my voice.

"*Hola*, Bannini," he says, using the name reserved for family. "*Te echo de menos.*"

"I miss you, too," I reply in Spanish, as we conduct most of our private conversations. "How are things at the orphanage?"

He recounts all the amazing things that have been done since I visited the orphanage in San Nicolas with him last summer. Zo does more than simply write checks. He's hands-on as much as he can be, especially during the summer and in his home country.

"You sound tired," I say, scribbling on an old draft of a shoe contract.

"I am." His weary sigh makes me frown. He's legendary for his boundless energy and rarely admits to fatigue.

"Come home," I urge him, tossing the pen on my desk and leaning back in my seat. "Rest."

"Tomorrow." I know him so well I can envision how the smile in his voice looks on his face.

My heart thuds heavily. I want him to come home and rest, but that means I have to deal with the situation…that he doesn't even realize is a situation yet.

"Tomorrow?" I ask weakly.

"Yes. A quick trip. Only a day in LA and then I fly to Vancouver for some standard team stuff," he replies. "But I miss you too much. I have to see you, even if it's only for a day."

"Oh." I smile and inject enthusiasm into my voice. I do want to see him. I've missed him, too, but the conversation I didn't want to have will happen sooner than I thought. "Can't wait."

"You have no idea, baby." His voice is husky, eager. "Be naked when I get there."

It hurts to swallow. It's hard to breathe. It feels wrong to even converse intimately with him when I've come on Jared's fingers. When last night I dreamed about Jared making love to me with the lights on. We haven't spoken since yesterday morning, when he carted a chagrined and hungover Hakeem to his hotel. With Hakeem watching, we kept things professional, but the look Jared gave me on his way out burned through my clothes.

"It'll be good to have you home, if only for a day," I deflect, making no promises of nudity, and hope Zo doesn't notice.

No such luck. The silence on the other end swells for a few seconds.

"You're okay?" I hate the uncertainty in his voice. "You sound...I don't know. Off somehow."

The trouble with dating your best friend...

"No, just a lot of work," I lie. Only I can't lie to Zo, thus the conversation we need to have tomorrow. "That's not entirely true. We need to talk when you get home."

"You can tell me anything, Bannini. You know this, yes?"

Tears burn my eyes, and my chest aches with the pain I'm going to cause him, with the knowledge that things won't be the same between us after we talk. I don't know exactly what that means or how we'll look, but it will be different. And the "same," the constancy, is what we've always needed and gotten from each other. But maybe that's the problem. Too much of the same.

"Banner?" Zo asks when I don't answer. "I said you know this, right?"

"Yeah." I clear my throat. "Yeah, I know. There's so much going on with free agency and work and...we just need to talk."

There's a small break, a silence in which the man who knows me so well tries to figure out what the hell is going on.

"Whatever this is," he says, "I love you."

A runaway tear skates over my cheek, and I swipe at it impatiently. No time for tears or weakness.

"I know, Zo. I—"

Movement at my office door momentarily distracts me. I press my lips into a stiff smile of welcome for Cal Bagley.

"Zo, Cal's here," I say in English for my boss's sake. "I need to go."

"Of course. We'll talk tomorrow when I get home."

I place my phone on the desk and gesture for Cal to take the seat across from me. My spine stiffens at the calculating gleam in his eye and the plastic smile on his face.

"Good old Zo," Cal says to start the conversation.

"Not that old," I return with a small smile.

"Do the Titans agree? Lowell says there's still no deal."

I lean back so my ergonomic chair tilts.

"Checking up on me, Cal?" I ask casually. Too casually. He knows I'm the last shoulder he needs to look over.

"No, I happened to run into Lowell." Cal crosses one ankle over his knee. "But I have heard some things that I wanted to address before we have any..."

He squints and waves his hand in the air.

"Any issues," he finishes.

"Issues?" I cross my legs, too. "Uh-huh. Go on."

"I know you and Jared Foster are working on a project together."

"Yes, Kenan and August, one of Jared's clients obviously, are doing a fundraiser together."

"The golf tournament, yes."

That gives me pause. He and I haven't spoken about the specifics of the project. Why would we? He hasn't interfered in my business for years. If he and I haven't spoken about the project, he's obviously spoken to *someone* about it. And I have to wonder why.

"What's going on, Cal?" I lean forward and set my elbows on the desk and rest my chin on folded hands.

"Now, you know I trust you, Banner."

"I thought I knew," I reply, deliberately keeping my voice light.

"I do trust you," Cal assures hastily. "It's that damn Foster I don't trust."

"Jared?" My heartbeat stills and starts again. "Why? I mean, I know he's at another firm, but we're coordinating sponsors for our clients' fundraiser, not swapping company secrets."

"Nothing like that. I think he means to lure you over to Elevation." I laugh because it's ridiculous.

"You're mistaken." I shake my head, relieved that this is all. "He doesn't."

"He definitely has an interest in you."

I won't stop until you're completely mine.

An interest. That's one way to put it. I bite into an involuntary smile and suppress a shiver. As complicated as Jared has made things with Zo, I haven't felt so alive in ages. Anticipating the next time I'll see him. The intimacy of his kisses, the fire in his touch, how he stimulates my body and my mind. I shift in my seat and uncross my legs.

"Don't worry, Cal," I tell him with a wry smile. "Jared's no threat."

"Really?" Cal looks anything but sure. "He told me himself that my prize mare, as he put it, was safe but that he could take better care of you at Elevation."

All the gooey residual feelings congeal and thicken, settling like a lump at the bottom of my belly.

"Prize mare?" I ask numbly. "He said that?"

"Word for word," Cal says, watching my face closely. "He all but warned me. You'd tell me if he made any offers, right? At least give me a chance to match whatever he presents, Banner."

"Uh…he hasn't made any offers," I say absently.

Of the professional variety anyway, but maybe that was his endgame. Even though Bent told me Jared wasn't in on Prescott's cruel joke, doubt floods me again. It's like a habit, doubting myself. From the outside, no one would suspect, but there's a crack in every wall. I'm no exception. I've lost a lot of weight. I'm in the best shape of my life, but I'm not nor will I ever be a Quinn. A Tanya. A Cindy.

I'm a Banner, and Jared made me believe—again—that's what he wanted. Legitimately, desperately wanted that from the way he looks at me, the things he's said. Did I misjudge the situation?

You've always been beautiful to me. I hope you know that.

Jared is a master strategist. He'll do anything to get what he wants, but I thought he wanted me. The me I thought he had *seen*. Really seen. Not the agent who could bring in hefty commissions.

"Just be sure I get to counter whatever he offers," Cal says, standing and tapping my desk. "We've invested too much over the last decade to lose you to some upstart."

"Of course." I clear my throat and try to clear my head. I stand to walk him to the elevator. "How much longer are you in town? When do you fly back to New York?"

"In the morning." He squeezes my arm. "You're doing a great job out here, Banner, in case I hadn't told you."

"Thanks." I smile, bending my lips into a waxy curve that doesn't reflect the turmoil and uncertainty this conversation caused.

The elevator doors open, and Maali gets off as Cal gets on. I thank her, take the salad, and head back to my office.

"You okay?" she asks, a frown pleating her expression. "You look…I don't know. Did Cal upset you?"

"No." I dig into my salad and pull up my email to the Titans, avoiding Maali's probing stare. "That look is probably hunger."

She keeps watching me, like she needs convincing, so I look up and give her a confident smile. I'm good at convincing.

"I have some Titan ass to kick for Zo," I say easily. "Could you close the door behind you?"

Assured, she smiles back and leaves.

Yeah. I'm great at convincing, but Jared is even better.

CHAPTER 20
JARED

I'm a reasonable man. Most people who know me would agree. Two days with no word from Banner and I'm not feeling particularly reasonable. I've given her space. I know this situation is difficult for her and that she genuinely cares about Zo. I haven't badgered her with messages, but I hoped she'd call me.

Is this how women feel when men don't call? When we go dark and they don't hear from us? Do they wonder if we're with someone else? Only I don't have to wonder. I know that when Zo comes home from his trip, he comes home to Banner. To her house and her bed.

And I cannot *fucking* take it. The thought of him inside her even one more time is an itch in my veins, coursing through my imagination. My very blood is agitated when I think of them together. I'm not a jealous person by nature. You have to actually care about things to feel that way, and I care about my family and the few people I count as true friends. Expending that kind of energy and emotion on a girl I may not even remember in a month? Nah. But Banner? She's like an image burn, that impression left on your screen long after the photo is gone. Her outline is seared into my memory.

I told myself I wouldn't call, and I haven't, but I'm sitting outside her office at seven o'clock, and her car is still in the parking lot. I've never been to the Bagley offices, but of course I know where they're located. Know your enemy. The reasonable thing would be to keep driving.

I dial.

"Hello?" she answers on the first ring.

Good sign.

"Hey." I search for something neutral to discuss before diving into the decision she needs to make. "How are things?"

"You mean how are things at work?" Banner asks, her tone cooler than it's been in weeks. "Why? Are you still deciding if this prize mare is worth the investment?"

Prize mare?

"What are you talking…"

Cal Bagley. Son of a bitch.

"So how is good ol' Cal?" I don't pretend ignorance.

"Concerned that you'll lure me away." Her laugh is made of tinfoil. "I assured him nothing could tempt me to work with you."

The whip in her voice lashes my ears.

"Something wrong, Ban?"

"No, everything is very right." I hear the dismissal before she voices it. "Thanks for calling. Let me know if we need to do anything for the sponsors. Otherwise…"

Otherwise I can fuck off.

I kill the engine and head for the building.

"So that's it?" I ask, checking the list of offices in the lobby to find Bagley. "You won't tell me what I've done so wrong that we're back at square one?"

"We never really left square one. I just needed reminding." She sighs impatiently. "Look, I'm swamped. I need to go. Goodbye."

On the elevator, anger percolates under my skin and throbs at my temples. Does she actually think I can be dismissed so summarily? Like I'm some puppy she can get rid of with one good kick? I will myself to calm down on the walk from the elevator to her office. Surprisingly, the door isn't locked yet, and I walk right in. Note to self: She needs to fix that. The LA office is small, with most of Bagley's agents still operating from New York. And it's empty because everyone else has a life and has gone home. I find Banner's office easily, and the knob turns, the door opening right away. She's at the window, watching the city skyline start to glitter. She whips around as I catch her unaware.

I lock the door behind me.

The vulnerability and disappointment on her face before the indifferent mask locks in place make me want to choke Cal Bagley.

"What do you want?" The ice in her eyes freezes me out, but I know how to warm her, how to warm us both.

"I thought I was very clear about what I wanted," I say, walking over to stand beside her at the window. "I want you."

She snorts, scorn distorting the sweet symmetry of her lips. She moves over to her desk and starts straightening papers and packing her bag.

"You want me?" she asks, not looking up from her task. "I already have a job, so you can stop recruiting."

I move swiftly to the desk and put my hands over hers on top of the laptop she was about to pack.

"You know I don't give a damn about that, Banner." I dip my head to catch her eyes.

"No, I don't know," she says softly. "For years I believed you had ulterior motives that night when we…"

"Made love?" I offer. "But you said you believed Bent when he told you I had nothing to do with Prescott's scheme."

"Yeah. I… Well, I did. It still all seems sudden and strange." She pulls her hands from under mine and slides them into the pockets of the narrow black skirt hugging her ass like a lover. "I'm not your usual type, you must admit."

She laughs, a rueful grin tipping one side of her mouth.

"I'm no Cindy."

"Who the hell is Cindy?" I ask, perplexed.

"Seriously?" Incredulity is all over her face. "Miss Iowa from senior year?"

"Oh, hell, Banner. I forgot her before graduation day. Not really, but pretty damn close. That isn't what this is about, is it?"

She lifts her lashes, but the gate is slammed shut over her dark eyes. "I don't know what you mean."

I capture her wrist, sit on the edge of the desk, and draw her between my legs.

"If I'm the asshole who pretends I want to be with you so you'll come work for me," I say, linking our fingers and sliding my other hand around her waist, "then I can't be the guy who has always seen you, has always wanted you, and is willing to blow up your life, as you put it, to have you. If I'm lying, then this thing between us can't be real and you won't have to deal with it."

I lift our linked hands to my lips, connecting our eyes and not relinquishing her.

"You wouldn't have to deal with me."

"No, that isn't—"

"Shut up, Ban," I cut in softly. "I'm not giving you that out. Tonight you face the truth."

"Which is what?" she asks.

"Do you have any idea how many women I've been with?" I ask instead of answering her question directly.

"No, I—"

"Neither do I. I literally don't remember some of them. Just a blur of hair and faces. I got some of their names wrong the night they were in my bed."

I grasp her stubborn chin, lift it.

"But you? I remember exactly how tight you were. How wet. I still hear the sounds you made in the dark, and I know how we smell together. I have perfect recall of every second I was inside you. That's the truth."

Her pupils dilate, and she draws a stuttering breath.

"Banner, you're my match."

Finally saying the words out loud, declaring it, feels right.

"I'm not your match," she says, one imperious brow ascending. "I'm too good for you."

"True," I grin, tightening my hand at her waist. "But I'm going to have you anyway."

"It was a one-night stand, Jared," she says lamely.

"Now who's lying? It wasn't a one-night stand. It was one *night*, and I never intended that to be the end. You let that prick mother-fucker take away all the nights we should have had."

I dip to nuzzle her neck, nudge aside the collar of her blouse to kiss the soft skin beneath.

"I want them back, Ban. I want you back."

"It doesn't work that way," she says breathlessly, still fighting it. "You can't just have me back as if the last ten years never happened. I'm in a committed relationship, and you can't ignore that."

I stare at her, waiting for her to remember that my moral compass spins. There is no true north. There's only what I want and what stands in my way. I cup her neck and sift the fingers of one hand into her hair and grab her ass with the other.

"What I can't do," I say, "what I won't do any longer is wait. I tried to give you space, but you only use that space to make more excuses. So that ends tonight."

And without warning, I kiss her the way I've wanted to since I walked in.

CHAPTER 21
BANNER

IT'S LIKE THAT FIRST TIME HE KISSED ME, AND IT'S LIKE NO KISS I've ever had before.

When Jared first kissed me in Sudz senior year, the zeal, the fervor of it snatched my breath. Yes, it was deep and hard and demanding, but what startled me was that all that intensity was turned on *me*. Watching Jared, crushing on him for years, and then kissing him was like seeing a cyclone from land—marveling at its power and dark, twisting beauty only to find yourself suddenly, improbably, at its center. Standing still in my office, I'm at the spinning center of a kiss that will demolish my life. I know it, but I can't stop.

I want it too much.

I crave the deliberate seduction, the methodical, plunging, sweeping stroke of his tongue over mine. He angles me, fits his lips over mine, controlling the pace and depth of the kiss, standing and flipping our positions. He hoists me by my waist onto the cluttered desk surface and, inch by inch, urges my skirt higher and higher until the hem collects at my waist. With a glance down at the triangle of black silk between my thighs, he groans, falls to his knees, raining kisses on my stomach through my blouse. The hot, wet suction of his mouth at my breast penetrates the flimsy layers of silk.

I can't form the words that would stop him. Maybe I could have before he slid down my belly and buried his nose in my panties. I like to think I could have before he dragged the black silk down my thighs and past my stilettos. But I'll never be sure. Because he did those things and then he pressed me open wider and separated the lips of my pussy and sucked my clit.

"Ahhh." A rumbling starts at my center, like the warning tremors of Mt. Vesuvius. A premonition of ruin. "Jared... Oh, God."

His mouth never leaves me, but he presses one big hand between my breasts until my back hits the desk and my legs dangle over its side. Then he opens me like a flower, peeling back the petals and flattening his tongue against me, his mouth hungry, thirsty, needy, and my body surrendering every response he demands. His is unrelenting worship, and I'm his altar. I stretch my arms down, knotting my fingers in his hair and caressing the rugged beauty of his face. His jaw flexes under my fingers with the ardor, the wondrous labor of his mouth between my legs.

"Don't stop. Don't stop. Don't stop."

It's an order. It's a plea. It's a breathless incantation tumbling past my lips in cadence with my hips thrusting into his face. I'm at the precipice, peering over the edge into an unlit well—a mystery my body begs to solve. Jared adds his finger, a thumb inside me, while his mouth lavishes that bud of nerves that has become the center of my existence.

And I tip over.

I fall headlong into a wave of unmitigated pleasure that shakes my body. Entirely. Not a cell, an atom, a molecule is left intact when the orgasm touches down on my body like a tornado. Bones, flesh, muscle, sinew, blood. Insecurities, fears, reservations—everything I'm composed of dissolves. I squeeze his head between my knees. I twist his hair in my hands. My body is wholly selfish, consumed by and taking the pleasure he promised.

"God, Banner." Jared laps at the wetness inside my left thigh and grips my legs. "Better than I remembered."

He rises from kneeling. Looms over me, pinning me to the desk with one hand and one look. The supplicant becomes the master, but I've marked him, wreaked the same havoc on him that he wreaked on me. I've twisted his hair into gilded chaos. I've poured myself over his lips and left them wet, shiny. I've never felt so possessive of anything in my life as I do when I see myself all over Jared Foster, but the hard set of his lips, the storm in his stare tells me it's his turn.

Our eyes remain locked while he undoes his pants, the belt buckle jangling and the zip hissing in the deserted office. There is no way back, and as much as I know guilt, condemnation, shame await me on the other side, I can't turn around. I want to rush ahead with him. He jerks me by my thighs to the edge of the desk.

"You have to say it." The rough timbre of his voice calls the hairs on my arms to attention. "Tell me yes."

Ragged breath. Feral gaze. Dick like a brick against my thigh. He is the picture of primitive male, demanding entrance, but still offers me one last chance to escape. I know I should. I'll regret this. I close my eyes and see Zo's dear face, hear his voice saying he loves me, but it's not enough. It's never been enough, and my only sin was not telling him, not facing the truth that I don't love him that way. That was my only sin.

Until now. Now I add another.

"Yes."

The whisper barely clears my lips before Jared's inside me. I'm translated from one state—empty, yearning—to another. Completely full. My walls strain to accommodate the girth of his passion. He's big and aggressive. He does me like he does all things, ruthlessly, mercilessly. He pushes his hand under my blouse, traverses my belly, captures my breast and squeezes hard, his thumb scraping the nipple again and again in harmony with each thrust.

"Shit." My startled curse is accompanied by my body contracting around him.

Loose papers rustle beneath me on the desk every time he pounds into me. He grabs my knees to anchor us, to hold me still while he plunders with no end in sight. Long, languorous strokes turn short, frantic the longer he goes. Jared tips his head back, the strong column of his throat working as he loses himself in the pleasure of these treasonous moments.

I want to touch him. I have to kiss him. I sit up, our bodies still joined, an unbroken line of carnality, and slide my fingers into the cool, shorn curls at his nape. He immediately takes my mouth captive. The kiss tastes desperate. Urgency tinges his touch along my thigh, climbing my torso and squeezing my face.

"Don't regret this, Banner," he says fiercely. "You don't get to regret this."

I drop my forehead to his, already crying even as another orgasm builds from the center of my body and fans out over every limb and extremity.

"I can't promise I won't regret it." Tears slip over my cheeks and between our lips, sealing our kiss. "Only that right now, I have to have it. I have to have you."

Our gazes hold. Mine, passion and apology. His, disappointment, determination. In a flash, we both know where the other stands. Then his head falls back, and he growls.

"Fuck, I'm coming."

Liquid heat rushes inside me, and I link my ankles at his back, fitting our bodies together like lost puzzles pieces. A jigsaw joining that moves the desk with the force of his climactic thrusts. Papers fly, picture frames fall, my laptop slips over the edge and crashes to the floor. Everything topples around me. Everything inside shatters. My promises, my integrity, my relationship—my world falls apart. I've destroyed everything, and I can't even care. With Jared's body possessing mine, heart to heart and clinging to each other, I can't even care. I can't feel anything but this man's name burning my lips.

CHAPTER 22
JARED

"Never do anything you can't live with
or walk away from the person you can't live without."
—Pee Wee Kirkland, basketball legend

"We didn't use a condom."

I say it, adding to the growing list of my transgressions. It's the only one I care about, though. I don't care that I made love to Banner because she is mine. It's jungle-level, my understanding that Banner is my mate. Fit for me, fashioned for me. It's not civilized or rational. It doesn't acknowledge Zo or what other people would view as infidelity. To them, what we did here was wrong. To me, it was the most natural expression of the truth, even if it's truth at its most vascular. In my blood, in my veins.

I hesitate to say heart. I don't know Banner's heart. I easily read her body, all the signs that signal she wants me. That she likes me even though she may not always want to. I've never handed my heart over to anyone, and I'm not sure I should start with a woman who regrets me. Who sees the most earth-shattering sex of my life as a mistake.

"Yeah, I know." Banner bends to retrieve her laptop from the floor. "I… I'm covered and, uh, clean."

She glances up at me, silently asking the question.

"Me, too," I answer. "I'm clean, of course. I've never... I always use protection. This time I..."

Forgot. Failed. Spiraled out of control.

I don't have to say those things. She felt them. We felt them together. Neither of us cared or considered it. The only thing I paused for was her consent. I had to close that escape route. Not that she would say I took her by force, but that she didn't want it as badly as I did. Her *yes* yanked the pin on a grenade. Everything from there was as instinctual as breathing. My brain took a back seat to my body.

"I get it," she says, her voice low, subdued.

She stands, appearing as unraveled as I am. Her skirt looks like a stretched accordion from being shoved up around her waist. Her blouse is half tucked in and missing a few buttons. Red lipstick smears her jaw. Dark, silky hair tangles around her shoulders. The office doesn't look much better. Papers litter the floor. A vase of flowers lies on its side in a puddle of spilled water. Picture frames face down on the desk. I could at least help.

I start setting the desk to rights and flip over a photo that arrests my attention. It's a shot from the holidays. Banner's family poses in front of a Christmas tree, all smiling. And there, sandwiched between Banner and a woman I assume is her mother, stands Zo, seamlessly integrated into the family like thread in a tapestry.

"Christmas two years ago," Banner says, taking the photo and setting it on the corner of her desk.

"Zo spent Christmas with your family?" I ask carefully, practically feeling the shaky ground under my feet.

"He's spent every Christmas with us the last ten years." She swallows convulsively and brushes tears from her cheek. "Ever since his family died."

For a moment, the weight of what I'm up against is crushing. I've known Banner longer, but he's had the last ten years with her. I had, what? A semester? One night? I can appreciate the sheer audacity of me barging into her life and dismembering a relationship, a decade-long friendship. It's a hard road ahead of us, but I'm willing to walk it if she is.

I hope she is. I don't feel remorse, but Banner feels enough for us both. It's written in every line of her body. Stamped on her face. It's beyond remorse. It's sorrow—a union of grief and shame.

Because of me.

That does sting. I hate seeing Banner hurt. Always have. Even knowing I'm the source of it, I'm compelled to comfort her. She's shuffling the papers littering her desk into neat stacks. I put my hands over hers, stopping her and pulling her in to me. She looks up, tears standing in her eyes.

"We shouldn't have, Jared," she whispers. "We—"

"You can't unfuck what's been fucked, Ban. I'd do it again right now if you'd let me." My voice is husky but certain. "I don't regret it. That you regret me is…"

I'm not sure how to express what her response does to me. How it makes me ache and itch and want to flee, but I can't leave her. You'd have to drag me out of this room right now, away from her.

"Not…*you*." She lifts a hand to cup my face, meeting my eyes squarely and with honesty. "It was amazing. You know that, but that doesn't make it right."

I press deeper into her hand, turn to kiss the palm.

"Right is relative."

"For you it is. Not for me." She clenches her eyes closed, and tears trickle under her long lashes. "I can't believe I did this to Zo. He won't forgive me. I've lost my best friend, and I…"

Sobs shake her body, and she's an earthquake in my arms, ripping apart at the fault line. Her head falls to my shoulder, and my shirt is instantly wet with her tears. Some feeling claws through my belly. It's the closest to remorse I can come. Not because of what we did, but because she's hurting.

"I'm sorry," I whisper into her hair. I inhale her scent, the freshness, the cleanness of her, and I know I'm not worthy of this woman. She's right. She *is* too good for me, but it's the fact that I'm *not* good that will secure her as mine. Another man would allow his scruples, his values, his *fucking conscience* to give her up. To cede the field to the better man, but in the end that man wouldn't have Banner.

And I will.

CHAPTER 23
BANNER

I'VE DREADED THIS SOUND ALL DAY.

The sound of the front door opening. Of approaching footsteps. The sound of pending devastation, Zo's and mine.

I didn't go to work today. For the first time in years, I called in sick. It's not a lie. I've been nauseous since I woke up this morning. Nauseous and heartsick. Guilt pools like battery acid, corrosive in my stomach, and dread coils like barbwire in my throat. It hurts to swallow, and I can barely breathe.

The worst part is that in my dreams, I still couldn't shake Jared. I want to hate him. To forget him. To ignore him, but nothing works. He's embedded in my head, insinuated himself under my skin. Sunk into my bones. I still feel him, a phantom moving inside me. I want to compartmentalize. To consign Jared to a corner while I address this disaster with Zo, but it doesn't work that way. Memories of him, of us together, saturate every moment. Even the ones while I wait for Zo to come home.

"*Hola.*" Zo drops his bag and walks over to the couch where I'm seated, legs tucked under me.

"*Hola.*" Genuine pleasure makes me smile. Despite what's about to happen, I'm glad to see him.

"I missed you." He pulls me up from the couch, muscular arms wrapping around my waist. His lips descend, but I turn my head at the last moment so his kiss lands on my cheek. I can't. Not with this secret, this unspeakable betrayal between us.

"Banner?" He draws back, his expression puzzled, concerned. "*¿Qué pasa?*"

"Nothing," I answer out of habit, so used to things being right. So used to being fine and able to handle whatever problem I'm facing. But I created this problem, and there's no fixing it. "That's not true."

His frown deepens, concern in his touch. I relish it because I know it won't last.

"Sit." I gesture to the couch. After the briefest of hesitations, he does, and I join him. "I have to tell you something."

"Okay." He touches my knee. "Just tell me, Bannini."

The words wait in my throat, a lit match suspended over gasoline. I think that's the only way I'll get them out, if they burn through my skin and singe the air.

"I…" I lick my lips, shallow breathing through this moment charged with anxiety and shame. "Zo, I…"

A sob combusts in my chest and into the tension of the room.

"Baby, what?" Zo cups my face, pushing my hair back with one hand. "What the hell? Did someone hurt you? Are you—"

"I slept with someone else."

He goes completely still, and the only sound in the room is the tortured hiccup of my breathing as I struggle to contain the sobs. I want to withdraw and lick my self-inflicted wounds, but that cowardice isn't an option. Not with Zo staring at me, stunned. His hands tighten around my face, and for a moment I think all that strength will be used to crush my bones. Maybe he feels that violent urge because he drops his hands from my face like I've burned him, like he's afraid of what he'll do if he keeps touching me. He walks to stand by the mantel over my fireplace, turned away. In the silence after his hands leave me, one word slithers into my ears and under my skin.

Whore.

That's what I called Kenan's cheating wife. So easy to say, to stand in judgment when you think you're immune. I've always resisted every temptation, but nothing prepared me for Jared.

I hazard a glance up to where Zo still stands, elbows propped on the mantel between keepsakes and photos of my family. His head rests in his hands. The snow globe he brought from Vancouver, a winter sunset ending a fairy-tale day, mocks me from its prized position.

"Please, say something," I beg softly, breaking the taut silence.

His shoulders stiffen, and for a second, I think all he'll give me is the proud line of his back, but then he looks at me, his face an ice sculpture carved in sharp, cold lines. My tears have always been his weakness, but the hot tears pouring from my eyes won't melt the frozen terrain of his face. It's a tundra. Desolate.

"*¿Cómo pudiste hacerme esto?*" he asks, his voice hoarsened with emotion. "*¿A nosotros?*"

How could you do this to me? To us?

"Zo, *¡lo siento mucho!*"

I'm so sorry.

"Sorry?" His harsh laugh mangles the air. "You're *sorry?*"

His face twists into a mask of his fury. With a roar, he grabs the snow globe and hurls it across the room. The heavy marble base dents the wall, and the dome shatters, an explosion of glass and liquid and snow splattering the surface. I flinch and draw in a sharp, shocked breath. I know Zo won't hurt me, but it's an act of violence, killing the tenderness that has existed between us for a decade.

No, Zo didn't kill it. I did. With my selfishness. With my weakness.

"You fuck someone else," he rasps, breathing heavily as though his rage is wearing him out. "And you offer me an *apology?* You share your body, share your..."

His words falter, and there's a question in his voice. In the tortured lines of his face. "Share your heart? Do you…you love this man, Banner?"

"No." I say it even as my heart asks if I'm sure. Is love more powerful than the pull between Jared and me? The one that endured for years? Is it more real than what I feel when he's near? When he's inside me? Have I ever felt a more powerful emotion? "It was just once. A mistake… I knew it was wrong. It just happened."

God, everything coming out of my mouth is a platitude, the pat phrases people reach for to excuse the inexcusable.

"It just *happened*?" he asks, his expression lit with outrage. "Do you know how much *coño* I turn down? How the guys tease me for being faithful to one woman when I could have four every night? In every city? But I didn't. I wouldn't ever do that to you. To my best friend. To the woman I…"

He cuts himself off, biting back the word he's said to me so many times.

"So do not tell me this just happens, Banner. It never happened to me."

"I kn-know," I stutter, eyes so blurred with tears I can barely see him. "I promise I have never done anything like this before. I wouldn't. You know that. You know me. I would never…"

Only I did. My voice trails away with that realization. There are no words I can say to make this better, to make it right. My inadequacy and shame meet his fury and disappointment head-on, across the room. The only thing that could make this right, could make it better, is if it had never happened.

But it did.

"*¿Con quién?*" Zo's demand is a growl, his narrow-eyed stare promising retribution.

I was a fool not to have anticipated this, that he would want to know who. Of course he does. They always do. I would want to know, but I can't tell him. He and Jared move in the same circles. It will only make things more awkward. Worse.

"I... It's not important who," I say lamely, fixing my puffy-eyed stare on the hands twisting in my lap. "It was...someone from my past."

"From your past?" A heavy frown hangs between his thick, dark brows. "What? From college? From business? I know all your friends. I know everything about you."

A scowl and cynical twist of his lips mock me.

"At least I thought I did," he says. "I didn't know you were a cheat who could not be trusted."

I don't reply but take every word like a lash on my back, a verbal flogging tearing at my dignity and my pride.

"Fuck, Banner!" He detonates the expletive. Frustration tenses the powerful lines of his huge body. "You've ruined everything. My entire life is intertwined with yours."

"I know." I sniff and swipe at the tears leaking from the corners of my eyes.

"Your family is my family. Your career is my career."

The emotion hardens like cement on his face.

"If I can't trust you to keep your legs closed," he says, deliberately coarse in a way he has never been with me, "I certainly can't trust you with my career."

I anticipated that, of course, but to hear him voice it...the dissolution of a yearslong partnership breaks my heart. Not because I'll lose his business, but because no one else will take better care of his career than I will. He won't be in better hands. He can't be. No one else will care about not just the player or the bottom line but about the man the way I do.

He strides back to the door, grabs the bag he dropped what seems like hours ago but was only a few minutes, and turns to give me one more disparaging look.

"I'll send for my things," he spits. "And start looking for a new agent."

"But your contract," I protest. "I'm so close to getting you the supermax deal you deserve. If you'd let me—"

"You think I care about that when you've…" He shakes his head and adjusts the bag on his shoulder. "Once I put my career in the hands of an inexperienced girl who knew next to nothing, and I've made millions. I thought it was because you were special, but you're not. So I'm sure someone else can do just as good."

I nod, biting my lip to choke back another sob. Losing my best friend, the man who has been with me—and I have been with him—through ten years of triumph and pain and success and failure feels like I'm losing a part of me.

"Zo, you have to know I'm so very ashamed of myself," I tell him, not bothering to dry the tears coursing down my cheeks.

He doesn't look back when he jerks the door open but tosses his final words over his shoulder.

"*Yo también.*"

So am I.

CHAPTER 24
BANNER

I'VE BEEN SITTING HERE IN THE DARK, PICKLING IN MY OWN TEARS and staring at Gino's take-out menu. Only fifteen minutes away lies the best pepperoni pizza I've ever tasted. Usually I pick off the pepperoni, blot most of the grease away with a paper towel, peel off the doughy crust, and restrict myself to one slice. If I'm splurging, maybe two.

But tonight, with Zo's disappointment heavy on my shoulders and his shouted recriminations trapped in my walls, echoing in my mind even after he's gone, I want to eat the whole pizza. I imagine how good it would feel to tear my teeth into something soft and carby, not crunchy salads or strips of lean meat. Something puffy as a marshmallow. Something gooey that feels like a pillow in my mouth.

Comforting.

I'm reminding myself of all the things I learned in counseling, but it wouldn't kill me to eat pizza. My body wouldn't balloon overnight. I indulge every once in a while. It would be *why* I'm eating it: the fact that there's a deep crater in my chest hollowed out by how I've let myself down and let Zo down, how I've hurt the kindest man I've ever met. I want to stuff food in that hole, and I want to believe, even if it's only as long as it takes me to finish the meal, that pepperoni makes it better. Giving in to that feels like tossing a sobriety coin in a wishing well and hoping for the best. But right now I don't care *how* I feel better. I just need to.

Fuck it.

I pick up my cell to select Gino's contact when the phone rings in my hand. And, of course, it's Quinn. For two rings, I consider not picking up, but I know she'll just keep calling. I canceled our workout this morning. I haven't been answering my phone. If she tried the office, Maali will have told her I called in sick. If I don't answer, she'll be at my door.

That's what I would do for her.

"Hey." I lovingly caress the take-out menu and try to sound normal. "What's up, *chica?*"

"What's up?" Quinn asks, her voice tight. "What's up is you blowing off this morning's workout, calling in sick, and missing our appointment tonight."

"Appointment?" I sit up straight on my couch, suddenly alert. "What appointment?"

"Remember we had the AesThetics pitch tonight?"

I'm sinking through my living room floor with embarrassment.

"Shit," I mutter and cover my face with one hand. "I can't believe I... Maali would have—"

"Called?" Quinn interjects. "Yeah, she did. A few times, but you weren't answering."

I close my eyes and push the hair, tangled from the abuse my fingers have given it all day, out of my face.

"I'm so sorry." I swallow fresh tears. Not only have I ruined things with Zo, but I may have jeopardized an opportunity I've been cultivating for Quinn for months. "I'll call them and reschedule."

"Oh, I still met with them." A smile enters her voice. "You'd already sent the ideas you wanted to discuss, and you and I had gone over them. It was easy to listen to what they had to say and tell them what we were thinking."

"And?" I ask hopefully.

"Well, I didn't *do* anything." Quinn offers a teasing laugh. "You have to earn your keep. I told them you'd follow up tomorrow since you were sick tonight."

A pause redolent with questions.

"*Are* you sick?" Quinn asks. "None of this is like you. All us mere mortals take a day or so to play hooky, but you never have. So what's going on?"

And I can't even say. Shame, hurt, and frustration roll into a gag shoved in my mouth. They stop the words for how royally I've messed up. My best friend hurt and gone. One of my firm's biggest clients leaving. Not to mention the censure I will inevitably receive from my family. Mama would be hard-pressed to choose between her natural daughter and Alonzo Vidale. How many rosaries have there been for his big games or when he was injured? I can already see her glaring at the empty seat where he should be this Christmas.

"Banner?" Quinn prompts.

And the crying starts again. Not the racking sobs of the last few hours, but a trickle of hurt and disappointment that I'm too tired to wipe away. Just sniffling and my helpless silence.

"Oh, God," Quinn says, her voice sinking to a horrified whisper. "Is it Zo? Did he cheat? Some ho on the road? Because I have just the thing for when a guy cheats."

"What do you have for when a girl does?" I ask, hush-voiced.

Shock waves blast me from the other end.

"I'm on my way."

Thirty minutes later, I haven't moved from my spot on the couch, still reviewing how things got so messed up. One glance at my phone confirms that Maali left several voicemails, as did Quinn. I don't have the kind of life you can just drop out of for a day. My life is a train at full speed. Try just "hopping" off for a minute without a scheduled stop, and things get run over.

One person I don't have any missed calls from is Jared. Something burns in my chest. Hurt or disappointment. I feel like

Buffy after Angel finally got into her pants and then became a cool aloof demon who never called and then tried to kill her. Of course, that's extreme. For one, Jared has been a devil all along. I knew that. Two, I don't think he'll come after my heart with a stake. He'd be more subtle than that. I could be reading too much into it. Before we so fucktastically wrecked my desk…and my life…he was giving me space. Maybe this is more space while I sort through things with Zo. Or maybe he's done? I should be grateful, but I think I feel bereft.

I know exactly how I feel about what I've done to Zo. I know how I feel about the violent betrayal of my own code of values and principles. But I don't know how to feel about Jared giving up on me. And I should. I should know this. Moral clarity, based on what I embrace as true for my life, has always been my guide. Right now I feel murkier than ever, stuck in this morass. Unsure.

The door opening shakes me from my philosophical musings on the couch. Quinn has a key. She appears, still dressed from her AesThetics meeting, I assume, because she's very smartly turned out. In contrast, I look…

"You look like shit," she confirms what was heretofore only a suspicion.

"I figured as much." I touch my swollen eyelids and cheeks still hot from crying.

"I brought reinforcements." She holds up a plastic bag. "Vodka popsicles. Only a hundred calories, and it's like alcohol *and* ice cream!"

I smile for the first time in what feels like years.

"That's better than the pepperoni pizza I was contemplating." I hold up the Gino's menu.

She looks from my blotchy, swollen face to the menu.

"Some days call for pizza, honey." She snatches the menu from me. "Don't overthink it and don't overdo it. Tomorrow's a new day."

She dials the number on the menu.

"Yes, do you have personal size? How many slices?" She beams at me. "We'll take one of those."

One hour and four miniature slices of pepperoni pizza later, two for each of us, she's drawn the whole gory tale out of me, fully loaded with additional tears and self-recriminations. I hope I'd be as compassionate as she is listening to me. There's no judgment in her kind eyes.

"I can't believe I did this," I gasp, fighting back more tears. "And all this damn crying. I don't cry like this. I'm sorry."

I blink back tears and stare at my hands tremoring in my lap.

"I hurt him so badly, Quinn. If you could have seen, have heard how crushed he was. Zo, the sweetest man on the planet, and I do this to him. I'm such a—"

"Ah, ah, ah…" Quinn slices in with a wagging finger. "Watch what you say about the woman who literally saved my life."

"Don't be ridiculous." I shake my head and shake off the praise.

"I'm not." Quinn puts her hands over mine. "I had one leg and a death wish when you came for me, lady. I'd already tried to kill myself twice, if you remember."

Quinn's normally cheery gaze goes solemn with the memories.

"You saw something in me no one else did, Banner," she says softly. "And you wouldn't stop, you stubborn bitch, until I saw it, too. And it made me want to live again."

She blinks back tears of her own.

"Do you realize how many people you've done that for?" she asks. "How many guys are still in the NBA because of how you fight for them? Protect them? Smacked them on the head when they needed it? Everyone's not like you. The way you care for people, how you fight for them, it's extraordinary. Your loyalty is extraordinary."

A humorless laugh huffs past my lips.

"I think Zo would probably question my loyalty right about now," I say, glancing back down at my lap.

"You're a good person who did something out of character. You can't beat yourself up forever. Banging your head against the wall burns a hundred and fifty calories, but is that good for you?"

"What?" I laugh, even though I'm not sure when I'll be rid of this guilt. "Oh my God."

"I'm just saying I know it will take time, but you'll have to forgive yourself," she says, sharing a smile with me. "And the connection you describe with Jared, what I saw for myself between the two of you, it's hard to ignore—to walk away from—especially if your relationship is…"

Quinn squints, searching for the right word.

"Unsatisfying," she settles on. "You probably knew before Jared even came back into your life that things were not quite what they should be with Zo. It's painful now, but maybe in the long run…"

I process that, not sure I'm ready to let myself off the hook that easily.

"And Jared Foster?" Quinn asks tentatively. "May I ask a highly inappropriate and insensitive question?"

My lips quirk into another smile. "Those are your specialty, aren't they?"

Her eyes are avid, and she's practically licking her lips. "Was it good?"

Good would be an understatement. I'm forming words for what sex with Jared was like when the doorbell rings. I glance down at my grimy appearance and grimace.

"Yeah, I'll get it," Quinn says, standing and patting my shoulder reassuringly on her way to the door. "And get rid of whoever it is. Have one of those Popsicles!"

I'm giving the frozen alcoholic treat a nice long lick when she reappears, eyes bright and cheeks rosy. Or what I like to call the Jared Foster effect. He walks in right behind her.

God, why does he have to look like that?

Jared's appeal has never been wholly physical. I've seen lots of beautiful men in my line of work. True specimens of manhood. There's more to my connection with Jared than how gorgeous he is.

But it certainly doesn't hurt.

"Hey," he says, filling the arched entrance to my living room. His hands are shoved into dark-wash jeans, and a white Kerrington T-shirt stretches across the width of his chest. His hair is wildly tousled like he's been running his fingers through it.

Or like I have.

"Hey." I look at Quinn and then at the Popsicle in my hand. Anywhere but at him. It's the first time we've been in the same room since what I've come to term as Deskageddon, where the world as I knew it ended.

An awkward silence encircles the three of us, and I'm not sure how to break it. Quinn knows what we did. Jared probably suspects I told her. Meanwhile I'm wrestling with a cacophony of emotions and sensations, ranging from guilt to turned on. I've never been an oversexed person. I enjoy sex but can always back-burner it. It was one of the reasons a long-distance relationship worked so well for me and Zo. But Jared unleashes something wild inside me. Something I'm not sure how to tame.

"Um, I should go," Quinn says after a few seconds. She grabs her purse and clears her throat. "Good seeing you again, Jared."

Peripherally I see him nod, but I feel him looking at me unwaveringly.

"We'll touch base tomorrow then, Banner." Quinn sounds unnaturally bright. I look up, and she widens her eyes meaningfully—her sign for *OMG*.

"Okay," I say, rediscovering my vocal cords. "I'll call AesThetics first thing in the morning. Thanks for coming by."

The soft click of her leaving through the front door doesn't mobilize me. I stare at the liquored ice in my hand, heedless of it melting and dripping between my fingers. I'm not sure what should happen next. My principles, my convictions, have always anchored me, made me certain of every step. They *prescribed* every step. Now that I've violated them so egregiously, I'm in a minefield, and any step I take could cause an explosion under my feet.

"You're making a mess," Jared says, walking over to take what's left of the Popsicle and tossing it into the trash.

He takes my hand and slowly licks the icy flavored vodka from my fingers. His tongue is like warm velvet making love to the delicate webbing between each digit. All the muscles below the belt clench. I'll never see that tongue again without remembering how he lapped at what my body poured out for him. In the moment, it felt like perfection. But confessing it to Zo, it felt like sin. I snatch my hand away and finally look up at him. Concern crinkles the smooth lines of his face.

"What have you done to yourself?" He traces around my puffy eyes. "You've burst the blood vessels."

I should have known. That happens whenever I cry too hard, but I haven't cried this hard in a very long time. Maybe since the last time I cried over him. I pull back from his touch, and he drops his hand to his side. His concerned expression hardens like cement.

"So you told him?" he asks. "What happened?"

I walk away, needing space, and sit in the sleek leather recliner closest to the fireplace. I avoid the couch where I've perched all day because when Jared sits down, I don't want it to be next to me. The man should come with a highly flammable tag, preferably near his cock.

"I told him, yeah." I fiddle with the drawstring at the waist of my lounge pants.

He doesn't respond, and I glance up to see his attention fixed on the wall, dented, decorated with fake snowflakes, a pool of glass on the floor.

"He was upset," I offer by way of explanation.

Jared frowns, his brows jerking together.

"He didn't…touch you, hurt you?"

"Of course not," I answer immediately. "He took his anger out on the wall, not on me."

"I imagine he'd like to take it out on me, too," Jared says, a rueful tilt to his mouth.

"I, uh…didn't tell him who."

A heartbeat of silence in which he continues to look at me and I studiously avoid his stare.

"Why not?" he asks.

"You move in the same circles." I shrug. "I didn't think it was necessary, though he did want to know."

"You should have told him. He'll figure it out eventually."

"Why do you say that?" I lift puzzled eyes and find him still fixed on me.

"Because it's going to happen again," he says huskily, casually, as though it should be self-evident. "And I want everyone to know."

Breath rises from my chest in a slow push. I'm not sure if it's anger, frustration.

Or worse, relief.

"I wasn't sure if…" My fingers find their way back to the drawstring. "You didn't call, so I thought maybe…"

"Jesus, Ban," he says softly but with intensity. "I call and text every day and you ignore me, so I give you space. I lie back as long as I can stand it so you can sort this shit out with Zo, and you assume I don't want you? What the hell?"

Welcome to the female mind. Hope you enjoy your stay.

He crosses over to the recliner where I'm seated and takes my hand.

"Do you know why I came here tonight?" he asks, stroking the lifeline on my palm with the pad of his thumb.

"No," I whisper and look up to find an emotion so naked on Jared's face I almost don't recognize him. "Why'd you come?"

"To make sure he didn't forgive you."

CHAPTER 25
JARED

It's a shitty thing to say. I know that, but I'm being honest. All day I wrestled with the thought that maybe Zo would find it in that famously magnanimous heart to forgive Banner, and then she would feel compelled to stay with him. And I'd just have to break it up all over again.

Messy.

"What?" Banner touches her chest like my words wound her. They probably did. "How could you say that, Jared? If you knew what this is doing to me, that I've hurt him and ruined our friendship, you wouldn't say that."

She attributes more empathy to me than she should.

"If the shoe were on the other foot," she says, blinking her puffy eyes at me, "how would you feel? How would you respond?"

She should be glad this is purely hypothetical. I'm not as civilized and kind as Zo, but I think we've established that.

"I would deal with him first." I tug on her hands until she's standing in front of me, close enough to feel each other's heat. "I would beat him to just short of dying because we both know I'm much too pretty for prison."

She cracks the smallest smile as I hoped she would.

"And then," I say, my voice dropping to a rough vibration in my chest, "I would deal with you."

I trace my thumb over her lips, squeeze her chin so her mouth opens the smallest bit and I can see her sweet pink tongue. My thumb fits neatly inside, and I push her jaw closed, watching, waiting for her to suck down. When she does, my dick twitches. I draw a sharp breath through my nose and caress the lining of her jaw and the sharp edges of her teeth.

"You, I would fuck clean." I bend until our foreheads press together. "I would fuck you until you felt like a virgin. Like I was your first. I'd stay inside you until your body couldn't remember how he ever felt. How anyone else ever felt."

She blinks quickly and pants around my thumb in her mouth. I pull out and track a wet trail down her neck and over her collarbone.

"But I plan to do that anyway."

Her lashes drift closed and sweep over the splintered veins fanning out from her eyes and across her cheeks where she has cried so much.

Over him.

I knew this would happen. That I would have to watch her *grieve* this way for him, but it still upsets me. Angers and frustrates me. I want her to be able to discard him and move on, focused only on me, on us, and not give him a second thought. Ironically, she wouldn't be the woman I want if she did that. I can be so heartless in so many ways, and I love that she is good. Not like me at all. It's sometimes inconvenient and more trouble than it's probably worth, but it's what makes her glimmer. I want all that shine for myself and will endure her crying for another man to keep it.

She steps away from my touch and shakes her head as if clearing away the thoughts and feelings my words stirred in her.

"I kind of flaked today," she says abruptly. "Skipped my workout, didn't go to the office, missed a meeting. I need an early start tomorrow."

"Okay," I say, waiting for her to try to kick me out.

"So"—she looks off to the side and bites her lip—"so I'm gonna turn in."

"Great idea." I toe my shoes off and fake a yawn. "I'm beat myself."

Her mouth gapes open with shock.

"You aren't spending the night." She folds her arms around her midriff, protecting herself. "We can't… Jared, I can't…"

"We won't." I tip up her chin and make sure she sees I mean it. "But I am staying. I don't like the state you're in right now."

"Surely you don't think I'll hurt myself."

"I think you'll condemn yourself," I correct. "The way you've been condemning yourself in this room all alone in the dark all day."

Her seven freckles are lost in the capillaries dotting the skin around her eyes. I'm fully prepared to argue if she protests any more, but her shoulders slump, and her head falls to my chest, and she sighs heavily. Exhausted.

I gently turn her toward the hall, link my arms around her middle, my front to her back, and walk us to the rear of her house. I have no idea which room is hers. She turns us to the right and into a spacious room, darkened. I have a vague impression of a large headboard and bed, a side table, and a bench of some sort at the foot of her bed, but it's all shapes. I want to turn on the light because I've had enough of touching her in the dark, but I don't. I slip my thumbs in the waistband of her pants and push down. She goes completely still as they slide over her thighs.

"Jared, I told you—"

"I know. We won't."

I peel the T-shirt over her head and unsnap the bra at her back, tensing as her breasts spill free.

"Is there something you want to sleep in?" I ask, looking around for her closet or a dresser.

And surprising me, as Banner always manages to do, she tugs my T-shirt over my head, works silently at my belt and zipper for a few seconds, head bent, slides my jeans down, before looking back up at me.

"Yes," she whispers, sadness and hope knotted in that one word. "I want to sleep in your arms."

CHAPTER 26
BANNER

LIKE I HAVE SO MANY MORNINGS BEFORE, I WAKE UP FEELING guilty. Guilty that I dreamed of Jared with Zo warm and solid at my back. Then in the gray predawn light before all the alarms clamor to kick me out of bed, my senses pick out the subtle differences. The arm around me grips tighter, higher with a large palm cupping my breast. The torso at my back is smoother to the touch, a fine line of hair arrowing down the middle instead of the thicker hair on Zo's chest. And the scent. I smell him and see a deserted laundromat and hear the *thump-thump* of a spin cycle.

Pleasure sets guilt aside long enough for me to breathe Jared in, and then shame shoves its way through as the memory of yesterday's catastrophe with Zo reminds me that all is not well. That although being in Jared's arms feels so right, in my world now nothing is.

"You're awake," he sleep-slurs into my hair, giving my breast a gentle squeeze and sliding his hand down to my waist.

After all these years and in spite of all the pounds I've shed, I still tense when he touches my stomach under his Kerrington T-shirt, which I put on at some point during the night. The rolls of fat I worked so hard to rid myself of are back. At least in my mind and at least for an instant.

Everything jiggled when I fucked her.

It's amazing, the power of words, cruel or kind, even from

someone you don't respect. How they stay with you, healing or haunting. Growing up a good Catholic, I heard tales of God creating the universe with nothing more than His words and His intentions.

Let there be light.

And there was light.

Life and death in the power of the tongue.

And we are made in His image, with the same life-giving, life-stealing power nestled between the rows of our teeth. So many times that power has been used against me. My imperfect body was the ammunition others needed to put me in my place when I was too smart, talked too much, soared too high. Oh, they knew how to clip my wings. They aimed for my Achilles' heel, the only weakness they could find, and their aim was sure.

"Ban?" Jared asks, his hands tightening at my waist. "You're awake?"

I shake off those old foes, my insecurities, and turn over to face him.

"If I wasn't," I say with a voice graveled by sleep, "I would be by now."

A strip of white flashes in the gray light, his smile chasing the last of my self-doubt away. I watch the shape of his hand approaching, feel it warm against my face. Sense him drawing closer until his lips curl in a smile he buries into the curve of my neck.

"We slept together," he murmurs, sounding so pleased I want to reach over and turn on the lamp to see his face.

This man, this *guy* practically cuddling isn't the Jared Foster I've come to expect over the years. He's made his hunger, his desire clear the last few weeks, but there's something…else. Something that harkens back to our days at the laundromat when we were first friends. When I looked forward to him loping through Sudz's door with his backpack and a bag of dirty laundry. Those two people, those *kids*, lived a hundred years ago. Things felt so complicated that night when Prescott pulled his prank, but now, with Jared in a bed

I'm used to sharing with my ex-boyfriend, with my career imperiled because of our recklessness, that night feels like what it was.

Child's play.

"That first time," he continues, toying with the curling hairs at my temple, "was so quick and in the dark. And the second time was rushed and on your desk."

He traces the bones of my face, lingering on my lips.

"When can I make love to you slowly, Banner?"

My body screams *NOW* while he kisses my nose.

"In a bed?" he asks.

A trail of kisses blaze my jawline.

"With the lights on?" he whispers.

He threads his fingers into my hair and licks into my mouth, and I forget that my breath may not be the freshest and that I'd probably look a fright if he turned the light on. He moves over me, his strong forearms framing my face on the pillow, lean hips cradled between my thighs. His erection is insistent, already demanding. He moves, and the tips of my breasts brush through the T-shirt against his chest. Our breaths mingle in a gasp at the feel of each other under the sheets.

"Can I make love to you?" He sprinkles kisses down my neck. "Can we turn on the light?"

When I turn my head to find the lamp with my eyes, my face presses into the pillowcase. These sheets are clean, but the faint traces of Zo's cologne freeze me.

"I can't, Jared." Tears gather in my throat. "Not here. Not now. Not this bed. The sheets smell like him."

He stills over me. The lighthearted, almost boyish pleasure I sensed in him from the time I woke withers. I feel it die in the air.

"What the hell did you say?" Now he sounds like the man I'm used to. Irreverent and hard. "The sheets?"

He fists a handful of Egyptian cotton.

"These sheets?"

"They've been washed," I say hastily. "It's just a trace of his cologne, and I can't."

He rolls out of bed, reaches back, drags me out. I land unceremoniously on my rear while he strips the sheets from the bed and strides, surefooted in the near-dark, out of the bedroom with them bundled in his arms.

"Jared." I scramble to my feet. "What are you doing?"

I check the laundry room, but he's not there. I hear rustling under my sink, and by the time I reach the kitchen, he's stuffing a thousand dollars' worth of bedding into a garbage bag. I lean one shoulder on the doorjamb.

"You just tossed a small fortune in sheets in the trash," I say calmly.

"I'll buy you new sheets."

He strides over, grabs my jaw, and kisses me hard, pressing my teeth against my lips. I deliberately soften under him, open my mouth to his, hoping to soothe him with my compliance. At first I'm not sure it will, that I can. Brutal hunger drives him into my mouth, chasing and capturing my tongue. I whimper, reaching up and tangling my fingers in the soft hair curling at his ears and neck, and he changes. He shifts, and his hands gentle on my face. He presses his forehead to mine, never breaking contact with my lips.

"I'm sorry," he mumbles into the thawing kiss. "I know I'm being ridiculous."

"Hmm," I agree, kissing under his chin. "Zo is the only one entitled to outrage in this situation."

I pull back and peer up at him in the growing sunlight breaking through my kitchen window.

"We're in the wrong."

"Are you telling me," he says, sliding his hands down to the small of my back, "that it felt wrong when I was inside you?"

"No, I—"

"Have you ever felt anything like that before?" He lifts his brows, waiting in my surprised silence for a second or two before going on. "Because I haven't. Not with anyone else."

His unexpected confession knocks my answer right out of me, and I blink at him owlishly. He dips to push my unruly bedhead hair back.

"How did it feel for you?" His eyes never leave my face.

Perfect. Right. Finally.

Those are the words that leap to mind when I recall Jared inside me, moving with the certainty of a thousand times when it was only our first, then only our second. As if in some time hole, behind a secret door in the cosmos, we had been making love to one another since time began.

"It was good," I say instead, avoiding the probe of his eyes.

"Banner, give me this." He's as close to pleading as I've ever heard him. "Tell me the truth."

No one has ever pushed me the way Jared does, demanded my surrender at every turn. I *am* the resistance, and yet I can't resist this man.

I drop my forehead to rest against his chin. "God, it was so good, Jared. It was like nothing I've felt. You know that."

"I *don't* know. I hoped." His words melt into the curve between my neck and shoulder. "I want you so bad right now."

Pressing my breasts into his firm chest is an involuntary response to the desperate need, to the passion roughening his voice. I angle my head to kiss his neck, sucking at the warm skin. He tilts his head, offering as much of him as I want.

I'm losing myself in the taste of him, of his saltiness on my tongue, when "Girl Gang" blasts on the nearby counter. We both jump and then laugh, startled by the loud music shattering the early-morning serenity.

"What the hell?" Jared walks over and picks up the device, turning it in his hand and looking for the off button.

"Alexa, stop," I say, mixing humor in my command.

Alexa rewards me with her abrupt, obedient silence, but Quinn's app immediately follows, charging in with reinforcements.

"Girl, you better rise and grind," shouts from the living room.

"Is this every morning?" Jared asks, folding muscle-corded arms over his bare chest.

"Pretty much." I walk toward the living room to catch the app before it digs out a follow-up phrase to make sure I'm out of bed.

I'm inputting the pizza from last night, trying not to think about my points overage, when Jared comes behind me, rests his chin on my shoulder, and hugs me from behind. At first I hold myself stiffly in the circle of warm muscle, but he runs his nose along the line of my neck, smells my hair like he's absorbing me. I sink back into him and drop my head against him.

"That's it," he whispers in my ear. "That's all I want."

His erection twitches against my ass, and I turn my head to look at him with one lifted brow.

"Okay, not *all*," he admits, laughing and rocking me from side to side in his arms. "Is this the app your lashes were working overtime to get Kyle's help with?"

"He actually did help Quinn a lot." I chuckle and tuck my head deeper into him behind me. "And, yes. This is the Girl, You Better app."

"Lemme see." He plucks the phone from my hand and walks away to explore the app's functions. After a few seconds, I realize my whole life is logged in there. What I eat, how much I exercise, when I—

"You log sex?" he asks, his voice deceptively mild.

"Uh, yeah." I reach for the phone, but he holds it above his head where I can't reach it. "Jared, give it to me."

"Wait." He walks a few feet away, still sliding his finger over the screen. He leans against the mantelpiece over my fireplace. "I'm not in here."

"What?"

"We had sex two days ago. I see your activity from yesterday, but I'm not in here."

Stunned silence drifts into discomfort as we stare at one another across the gulf of my living room.

"I… Well, I didn't have time." I bite my lip and know that isn't entirely true.

"Ahhh." Jared nods and holds the phone up to read. "Seven a.m. Yoga. Morning salutation."

I close my eyes and swallow any protest. I know where he's going, and he'll see right through any denial I make.

"Nine o'clock. Three boiled egg whites. Zero points." He glances up at me. "Well, that's good, huh? Who knew egg whites are free foods? Three slices of turkey bacon, three points."

"Okay, Jared. I—"

"Lunch," he continues. "Three points. Not bad."

"You can stop now. I know—"

"Wow, when I look back, I can even see you had a four-point salad after fucking me," he says, looking confused. "But somehow there's no record in here of us actually fucking."

"You're being ridiculous." I brush a hand over my eyes.

"Let's see about good ol' Zo." He scrolls, eyebrows lifting. "Oh, look. Excellent records here. Fucked. Fucked. Fucked. Fucked."

He offers me a wry false grin.

"He's had a good summer."

I walk out. This is an exercise in futility in which I won't participate. In my spacious closet, I jerk open a drawer, blindly sifting through all the items I have from Quinn's line. I need to do something with my hands that does not involve throttling the nearly naked man in my living room. I grab a sports bra, capri workout pants, and a tank. I turn, only to slam into Jared's chest.

"Should I record this for you, too?" he asks. "What are we doing? Yoga? Pilates? You're so meticulous in all your records, other than what pertains to me, of course."

"I'm not doing this with you," I mutter.

I try to step around him, but he grabs me, and we struggle until both my wrists are cuffed in his one hand behind my back. It's not uncomfortable, but I'm completely immobile. His handsome face is sketched in lines of grim frustration.

"Am I your bye?" he demands.

"My bye?" I shake my head, clueless. "What does that even mean?"

"On the way to the Carters' for that party, you said we should all get at least one bye song. A no-judgment freebie," he says, a muscle flexing in his jaw. "We should all get one shitty choice. Am I your shitty choice, Banner? The mistake you don't want sullying your perfect record?"

"I'm not perfect."

"I know you're not," he says sharply. "And I'm fine with you not being perfect, but apparently, it's a problem for you."

"Jared, this isn't about me." I shake my head, feeling helpless. "You can throw the sheets in the garbage, and I'm sure if you messed with the app long enough, you could figure out how to delete all the records of me having sex with Zo, but you can't toss him out of my life. You can't delete him like he never happened."

"I'm not trying to delete him," Jared snaps, his frown dark and heavy. "I'm trying to add me. I mean, did I happen? Am I happening?"

He bends until our gazes are level and locked, the whole universe narrowing down to this fulcrum hinging on this handful of seconds.

"Are *we* happening, Ban?" he asks softly.

I'm at a loss. Beneath the anger, the sheer force of his frustration, lies some strain of vulnerability I'm not accustomed to in him.

"If you want me to say that us having sex while I was still in a relationship with Zo was right," I say, looking at him as directly as I can, "I won't ever say that. It wasn't right, and I'll always feel awful that I hurt him that way."

"Yeah," he says and clears his throat, loosening his grip on my wrists. "I get that."

"But," I say quickly before he lets me go completely, "that doesn't mean I…"

How do I say this without sounding like a hypocrite? A hussy?

How do I convey to him what is still not completely clear to me? That my despair over hurting Zo sits right beside the pleasure I've found with Jared, the irrational sense of rightness.

"Doesn't mean you what?" he asks, eyes guarded. He's protecting himself from me, as if I could hurt him. I never suspected I had that power, but I read it in the cautious way he's watching me and in the hands that still haven't let me go.

I lean up and into his body held taut and offer the words to give him the reassurance I never thought he would need.

"We are definitely happening," I whisper.

And then I kiss him. Not wildly or with urgency like I did two nights ago. This kiss recalls the first tentative press of my lips into his in the laundromat years ago. Like that night, I'm not sure about where this kiss will take us or what it will prove. I'm not even sure what he wants from me beyond the obvious because with Jared, it's never merely the obvious.

At first, his lips remain set in an unyielding line, and I'm kissing a brick wall. After a few unresponsive seconds, I pull back, ready to give up and possibly put this behind us, but he tightens his hands on my wrists and twists into the kiss, pushing me deeper into the closet until my back is at the wall. He commandeers my mouth, taking control and groaning into the kiss. I tug at his hold on me until he frees my hands to explore his chest and the sleek muscles of his back until I find his hands and link our fingers between us.

"I don't want to be your shitty choice," he says harshly, brows drawn together.

"You're not." I bite my lip. "I mean, of course I wish Zo hadn't been caught in the middle of everything. Hurting him has been awful, and it will take time to get over it."

"Over it?" he asks, eyes never leaving my face. "Or over him?"

"Not like that." I run my fingers through my hair, still at a loss. "I knew that it was a mistake to start dating Zo, not because I was his agent but because I was his friend "

I bite back a sob and blink at the inevitable tears.

"I was lonely and looking for companionship," I continue. "And wanted someone to… God, what if I used him, Jared? That, I can't live with."

He dips until he hovers over me and drops kisses on my nose, my cheek, and finally my lips.

"I forget you're Catholic," he murmurs, humor making its way back into his voice.

I punch his chest and find myself laughing along with him. "What's that supposed to mean?"

"You guys should patent that brand of guilt." He settles his hands at my hips, and most of the humor flees as fast as it came. "I know we process right and wrong differently, but I refuse to believe what happened between us was wrong, and I don't think you staying in a relationship that might never be what Zo wanted would have been right. I think we do things and we live with the consequences. We make the best decisions we can with what we have, with what we feel and know, and live through the fallout if it comes."

"That's how you get through"—the word *mistakes* stalls in my mouth—"decisions that hurt other people?"

"I live through those things by caring less," he says. "And I know that isn't an option for you."

A humorless chuckle strangles in my throat. "Um…no. That isn't likely for me."

"But it's one of the things I like about you most."

Surprise gives me pause and has me staring at him like he has two heads.

"We're often drawn to our opposite, right?" He lowers his head to nip my earlobe, sending a shudder skittering over my spine. "Saying I'm drawn to you would be putting it mildly."

It pleases me how easily he tells me he wants me. His frank appreciation after years of self-doubt in varying shapes and forms feels good. Not that Zo wasn't up front about how attracted he was to me or that I haven't been with other men who told me they liked my ass or my breasts or my brain or my drive or...whatever. I feel in this moment when Jared looks down at me that he sees all of me at a glance. He takes in all my disparate parts, synthesizes them, and is pleased with the whole. I've always felt seen with him, understood and accepted in a way that almost frightens me.

"I have an idea," he says after a few seconds of us standing in the circle of each other's arms, quietly, contentedly.

"This sounds dangerous." I lift my head from his shoulder and peer up at him.

"I have to go to the Virgin Islands on a recruiting trip," he says. "You should come with me."

"Oh, so you need my help signing a new client?" I joke. "Cal wouldn't be very happy about me working for the enemy."

He slides my hand down between us and presses it to an impressive erection.

"This is the only thing I need your help with," he says. "Let me know when you're ready to do me a solid."

My face burns, but I laugh and slowly—maybe slower than necessary—pull my hand away.

"You wouldn't happen to be visiting Richard Tillman, would you?" I ask to shift the conversation to less flammable ground.

Tillman is a guaranteed first-rounder next year.

"Maybe," he says slyly. "He might be the best thing coming from the Islands since Tim Duncan. Maybe once I'm done working, we could play a little."

My teasing grin wilts around the edges. It's fast. I was practically catatonic on my couch, depressed about Zo yesterday, and already Jared has spent the night and wants us to go on a romantic getaway.

"I don't know." I step away and turn my back to sort the workout clothes I set into chaos. "I have a lot of work to do."

"You always have work to do." He presses his hand over mine, staying the unnecessary task. "We both do. I can't even remember my last vacation, Ban. Can you?"

I don't answer. It *has* been a long time, and my body is aching for some rest. The biggest contract in my off-season cut me loose last night in more ways than one. Everything else feels manageable. I could afford a few days.

"How long are you thinking?"

And as if reading my mind, he says, "A few days, maybe a week, and you can have your own room if you want."

We stare at one another, and the heat, the clawing hunger that possessed us in my office, rears and roars long enough to remind me my best intentions tend to run amok where this man is concerned. But I've already hurt Zo, driven him out of the agency. Things may have been painful, but they've gotten simpler. I want Jared, and he wants me. It's worth exploring, and now I can.

"My own room sounds great," I finally agree.

"Your own room sounds redundant." He laughs and shoots me a knowing look. "But we'll cross that burning bridge when we get to it."

CHAPTER 27
JARED

I JUST SIGNED ONE OF NEXT SEASON'S COLOSSAL TALENTS. HIS potential in the NBA has no ceiling. LeBron kind of impact. Signing this kid to Elevation may be the greatest coup in our young company's history. I'd typically be crowing to August and already on the phone priming the endorsement pump with Nike and Gatorade. Those things can wait.

How often do you get a second chance at something truly great? Something you couldn't fully appreciate at the time because you hadn't yet experienced what the world had to offer and found it lacking? Hadn't been with countless women only to always find your mind drifting back to that one who got away?

Now that the one who got away is sunbathing by the pool of a borrowed St. John villa, what do I do with her? I'm not screwing this up. I have to be patient and give her time to adjust to this Zo thing. Give her time to get over how things ended between them and time to forgive herself. Hell, maybe forgive me. I made no secret of the fact that I didn't care about her relationship, didn't acknowledge or respect it. Does that make me bad? Maybe, but I wanted Banner back, and I have her. No one will convince me I shouldn't have pursued her. I want her too much. I always have. Never more than right now.

If I finally have a week with Banner Morales, it won't be in some hotel where I have to act civilized for other people. One of my fellow prospects from the Pride, who actually made it in, owns this villa in the Virgin Islands. Private. Secluded. I may not have joined the Pride, but I did make a few lifelong friends who come in handy regularly. He and Bent were two of the good apples in a barrel full of rotten ones.

Banner has scooped all her hair up, and she's lying by the pool. Topless.

Yes, topless.

I can't see much because she is stretched out on her stomach. The ties of the white bikini lie loose on the ground beside her while she reads. Her olive-toned skin glows with health and sunscreen. She adjusts the oversized sunglasses and turns the page of her book.

"Whatcha reading?" I ask once I'm within pouncing distance.

She jumps and almost loses her top. Unfortunately, she catches and carefully reties it before flipping over.

"You don't have to do that for my benefit." I gesture to the straps holding the top in place. "Wouldn't want you to have tan lines."

"Very thoughtful of you, but I'm fine," she says with a wry twist of her lips. "I was heading in soon anyway. I don't want to burn."

She slips a thin cover-up over her head. The words "cover up" in relation to Banner should be outlawed. Struck from the English language. Hiding that beautiful body she works so hard for is criminal. There's a glimpse of swelling breasts and full ass and hips before the offending cloth covers her.

There are two books on the ground: *Hunger* by Roxane Gay and another opened pages down, the one she was so engrossed in before I came. I angle my head to read the cover.

"*All the Single Ladies: Unmarried Women and the Rise of an Independent Nation.*" I serve up some sarcasm with my grin. "Just some light beach reading, huh? No half-naked man on the cover of a romance novel for you?"

"Oh, I have those, too." She laughs over her shoulder and walks ahead of me. There's a newborn ease to the swing of her hips and a looseness in her shoulders I don't recognize.

"You're relaxed," I tell her when we reach the veranda.

"How could I not be?" She points through the floor-to-ceiling window. "When that's my view?"

Crystalline water laps at the white sandy beach. Palm trees sway. Verdant, grassy mountains rise and fall along the coastline.

"It is beautiful," I agree. "I just wasn't sure you'd be able to put everything behind you long enough to unplug."

She pulls on my tie and grins up at me, shorter than usual in her bare feet.

"I'm not the one dressed like I'm on my way to a business meeting."

"Well, I *was* on my way to a business meeting, but now I'm done." I drop a kiss on her cheek and risk a hand at her waist. "For the rest of the week."

I kiss her lips lightly. "I'm all yours, if you want me."

We share a look that silently sizzles in the afternoon heat and draws tight in the balmy island air.

"Lucky me." Her laugh sounds nervous.

Or maybe not nervous. Tentative? Uncertain? I feel that, too. We practically broke Banner's desk having sex last week, but it feels like we are on the verge of our first kiss. Like there's some invisible line we are poised to cross. Whatever it is, it makes me hesitant, which I rarely am. I'm decisive and pursue what I want as soon as I want it. Maybe this feels fragile because it's been broken before. Something we've just pieced back together. The glue is still drying, and I don't want it to fall and break again.

"You don't want to know how the meeting went?" I ask, knowing that business is always firmer ground for us, even if we are on differ-ent sides of the field.

"We *are* on opposing teams," she says. "I don't want you to feel awkward about telling me anything."

"I signed him," I offer without reservation. I trust her.

"Oh my God!" Her eyes go saucer-wide, and her grin spreads. "Seriously? Huge, huge deal, Foster."

"Yeah, it is," I agree immodestly.

"This calls for a celebration." She clasps her hands together under her chin. "Should we go out?"

She's browned some from the sun, and my seven freckles sprinkle across her nose like flakes of cinnamon. With her bare face and feet and sporting her bikini, no one would think she's one of the NBA's most powerful agents. She's unadorned and in her own skin. Looking like this, she could bring me to my knees.

"What if we stay in?" I tug at the loose knot on her head, and the hair spills over her shoulder in a single line of silk. I toy with the ends, deliberately allowing my knuckles to brush the curve of her breast. "Could that work?"

A deep breath lifts her chest under the cover-up, and she swallows, lashes fluttering from the subtle contact with my hand. We haven't made love since her office, and I hope she wants it as badly as I do. She did ask for her own room, though. So maybe not.

"I forgot to ask how your room is," I say, dropping her hair and taking up with her hand, lacing our fingers together.

"It's, um, great." She looks from our joined hands to my face. "Beautiful actually. Thank you for this. For all of it. I needed it."

"So did I." I loop an arm at the small of her back and scoop her sun-warmed curves in to me.

She stiffens at first, and then I can almost see her make the decision. To relax. To enjoy. To let herself want me. I can't know for sure what the decision is, but she leans into me instead of away. The sun melts her expression into a smile, into pleasure. She props her elbows on my chest and works her fingers into the hair by my ears. It feels so good, I close my eyes and wait for more of her touch. She doesn't disappoint, walking her fingers to my temples and adding gentle pressure, coaxing a groan from me.

"That feels incredible." I slide my hands lower on the swell of her hips, lower still to cup her butt. "You have such a great ass, Banner. Have I ever told you that?"

She fixes her eyes on the tiles at our feet and licks those perfectly symmetrical lips, sinking her teeth into the bottom one.

"No, you haven't." The words come thin, like the breath has been sifted from them. "You don't think it's, um, too square?"

"Square?" I laugh at the unexpected question and squeeze the firm roundness overflowing my hands. "I have no idea what that means, but I want to bite your ass every time I see it, if that answers your question."

Banner's eyes widen, and then a deep-throated laugh unspools from her that reminds me how much I love to make that happen.

"Wow. Thanks." She gives a tiny shake of her head. "Leave it to you, Jared."

"Why'd you ask me that?" I squeeze her ass again just 'cause.

"It'll sound silly to you." She lowers her lashes and chews on the corner of her bottom lip. "There's this blogger who said…things about me when I started dating Zo. That's all."

The smile I've been wearing since I took her in my arms slowly falls apart.

"What kind of things?"

Rose-gold tints her cheeks as she toys with my tie, studying the pattern instead of looking at me.

"She said I was like the, um, the biggest Kardashian," she says softly, her smile less natural than before. "She called me Sponge Banner Square Pants because she said my ass was, well, square."

And August wonders why I hate people.

"I can usually brush stuff like that off," she says, looking up at me with that same stiff smile I can't stand. "I know. I'm a powerful woman and all that, right?"

Uncomfortable chuckle.

"I should be impervious to that shit." She twists her lips into a grimace. "But some of it sticks from time to time and kind of…"

She doesn't say the word "hurts," but it does. I can see that some stranger, some *person* who doesn't even know Banner—doesn't know that she speaks God knows how many languages by now, doesn't know she's the first to go to college in her family, doesn't know she charges into dangerous situations she has no business being in to rescue grown men who should know better, doesn't know that she sees potential in broken people like Quinn and refuses to give up on them even when they give up on themselves—some *person* has hurt this spectacular woman by saying her ass is square?

Fuck that.

I take her chin between my thumb and index finger and lift until her eyes meet mine.

"Listen to me, Banner," I say firmly. "Your ass is not square, but if it was, so the hell what?"

"I know that," she says hastily.

"Yeah, you're a strong woman. You're a lioness. Hear you roar. Got it, but no one likes things like that said about them in a conversation, much less tweeted to thousands of—"

"Millions," Banner interjects softly. "Tweeted to millions of people with a photo for reference."

"Tweeted to millions of people with a damn photo for reference," I say, futile rage testing my calm. "Humans, we suck. I know we have these bright, shining moments, but a lot of us just suck most of the time, and we say mean things to gain more followers. The worst of us exploit each other's pain to get something for ourselves, and then there are people like you."

"Jared, you don't have to—"

"People who get this human thing right. People who are actually kind. Actually have a conscience. Actually feel guilt when they hurt other people."

I'm on dangerous ground here because it's her guilt that keeps her across the hall instead of sleeping in my bed tonight, but this is more important than me getting laid. Which is saying something since few things take precedence over me getting laid most of the time.

"I've had beauty queens, porn stars, waitresses, strippers, lawyers," I list.

"Okay, Jared, I get the picture," she mutters, lips pressed together suppressing a laugh.

"Senators, ambassadors, stewardesses," I say. "Excuse me, flight attendants. I even had a princess, though I'm not allowed to talk about that."

"Oh my God." She rolls her eyes, but that beautiful mouth is no longer stiff, instead pliant and softened into a smile.

"And some were pretty, some were smart, some were funny. Some probably had square asses. I can't even remember now." I frame her face and hold her eyes with a look that goes serious so she'll know I mean it. "But none of them were you. There's only ever been one Banner, and her...I've never been able to forget."

Her smile falls away, and she swallows hard.

"This blogger bitch person has no idea who you are." I caress the silky skin covering one high cheekbone. "She has no idea that you've always been the girl I like most, and I don't even like people."

We stare at each other. I'm afraid to blink and shatter this unflinching moment. Everything I've laid out says so much about how I *feel* about her. I don't feel for women. I fuck them. I date them. I don't feel for them, not what I feel for Banner, and now she knows.

"I, um... Thank you." She clears her throat and pushes a swathe of hair back over her shoulder. "You probably want to get changed, right? To shower?"

Disappointment drains some of my fervor.

"Uh, yeah. Right." I drop my hands from her face and shove them into the pants of my suit. "And you probably want to shower."

"Yeah." She runs a palm over her arm. "Sunscreen is kind of sticky."

"Great." I start toward the stairs, and she joins me. "So we'll both shower and then maybe scrounge up something to eat?"

"The kitchen is fully stocked." She shoots me an almost shy look on the landing at the top of the stairs. "Fridge and pantry loaded."

"Great." I rock on my heels for a few seconds of awkward silence. "Well, we can come up with something for dinner and maybe eat out tomorrow?"

"Sounds great."

"Great," I say again and turn toward my bedroom. She turns to hers. "Have a good shower."

Have a good shower?

That's your parting shot, Foster? I ask myself once I'm under the stinging spray of the shower in my bathroom. How things got so awkward there at the end, I have no idea, but I was fumbling and stumbling like some college boy. No, in college I had more game than that. This was middle school–level awkward.

Keep the cards close to your chest.

That's Negotiation 101, but what did I do? Laid them all out on the table—and too soon. Banner's relationship just ended in an epically bad way because I couldn't keep my dick in my pants, per usual. She'll be dealing with the fallout, personally and professionally, for weeks, months. She needs time, but what do I keep doing? I keep pushing. I've always prided myself on knowing when to press and when to hang back, to let things come to me, but I don't have that with Banner. When she doesn't come to me, I chase her. When she needs space, I crowd her. I've always known how to get what I needed from women, and I'm realizing now it was because I needed so little: mutual physical satisfaction. This is different, much more complex than simply getting in Banner's pants.

I rest my head against the wall and fist my painfully erect cock.

Though getting in Banner's pants…I wouldn't turn it down right about now. I need more than that, though. And it's disconcerting because I've never needed more before.

I walk out of the shower, dry off. I'm pulling on briefs when the air changes in the room. The leftover steam shifts with the opening of my bathroom door. I glance up and couldn't be more shocked to see Banner standing there, wearing a white fluffy robe like the one hanging on the back of my door. Damp hair falls past her shoulders. I don't speak. I don't move toward her. I don't do anything but stare because I've screwed things up enough *doing things*. I want Banner to come to me.

The next move is hers to make.

CHAPTER 28
BANNER

"I don't need to be so full of myself that I feel I am without flaw. I can feel beautiful and imperfect at the same time. I have a healthy relationship with my aesthetic insecurities."
—Lupita Nyong'o, Oscar-winning actress

WHY ARE YOU HERE?

The perfectly reasonable question ricochets inside my head, a lonely echo bouncing around.

I'm just a girl standing in front of a boy asking him to… What do I want from Jared? We're well past just liking each other but not ready for the L-word. We've already bumped uglies—twice. I'm the one who insisted on my own room. So what exactly am I here asking him to do?

See me.

The answer whispers from behind the wall I've built around myself, a drawbridge I'm ready to lower. Why him? Why Jared, the guy I've made sure to hate through the years? I think I made sure to hate Jared because I liked him so much, and if he did what Prescott said he did, then he couldn't possibly have felt the same for me. My incredulity from that night in the laundromat when he kissed me, when he said he'd been thinking about it for a long time is only matched by my shock earlier when I told him about the blogger. I wondered how someone like Jared, with his parade of beauty queens and Cindys, would go so drastically "off brand" and choose someone like me. And tonight I heard the answer.

He *sees* me. Really sees me. Fifty pounds in either direction and the look in his eyes—that intensity, the longing, the desire—never changed.

If I asked myself why I'm standing here, Jared's curiosity is practically foaming at the mouth.

"That night was more traumatic for me than you probably realize," I say, starting in the middle instead of the beginning, taking up a thought that had no precedence and hoping he's following. "It was probably more traumatic than it should have been. I'm not the first girl caught naked in a room with a guy."

I laugh, even though nothing is funny. Jared watches me intently through lingering clouds of steam.

"But I was already self-conscious," I remind him.

"You wanted the lights out."

"Right." I lick my lips and fiddle with the belt of the fluffy white robe. "I had a boyfriend who was less than impressed with me when the lights were on and shared his opinion freely."

Jared steps toward me, muffling a curse, but I put my hand up to stop him. With only scraps of clothing between the two of us and all this steam and naked flesh just under the surface, if he comes too close this conversation will catch fire, and I need to get this out.

"Just…let me speak."

He pauses, leaning one hip against the marble counter, eyes trained on my face.

"I've always had a contentious relationship with food." I swallow the embarrassment that would choke this confession. "I've always struggled with my weight, and it got worse in college. I gained a lot in those years, but I was also in a relationship with a guy who used me. He pretended to be attracted to me so I could help him academically. He cheated on me."

Iron streaks through my hollow chuckle.

"Another reason I swore I would never cheat on anyone," I say. "I know how bad it feels. There were things he said that, even to this day, make me second- and third-guess myself. I hate that he and other people who didn't mean me well have had that much power in my life, but they have."

"Banner, you don't have to tell me all of this," Jared says, anger in his frown and the flat line of his mouth. "It makes me want to find them all and pound their faces in. They're blind and dumb."

A tiny smile lifts the corners of my mouth, lifts my heart.

"That's why I want to tell you." I break my own rule and walk over to him. I stop a few inches shy of sharing body heat, but our stares heat up, igniting the space left between us. "There's no differ-ence in the way you looked at me ten years and over fifty pounds ago and the way you looked at me by the pool."

"No," he agrees, the timbre of his voice deeper and richer the closer I come. "You were incredible then, and you're magnificent now. I've never met another woman like you, and I liked you from the first day of class."

"I know." I nod and then shake my head. "It was impossible to believe at first, but I know. That's why I bought Prescott's prank so easily. It made more sense, when the truth didn't. That you—"

"Wanted you," he interrupts softly.

"Yes." I hesitate and study the brick-red polish on my toes for a second. "After the things my ex had said and done, things that had been said all my life, it was hard to believe someone like *you* wanted *me*."

"But I did." He bridges the space separating us, reaching over to push a swathe of wet hair over my shoulder and cupping my neck. "I do. A lot."

He tugs me by my neck gently but firmly enough to pull me closer until my breasts, through the robe, brush his naked chest. I can't resist touching him, tracing the hard muscles and touching the stiff nipples with the tips of my fingers. His sharply indrawn breath doesn't stop me now that I've started. I round my hands on his shoulders, caressing the taut skin with my palms.

"You're so beautiful," I whisper, my hands addicted to the feel of him.

"It's only a shell," Jared says, his words seductive, his breathing more erratic. "I'll crack it open for you and pour everything out."

He slides the hand at my neck down to my shoulder, caressing the nakedness inside the robe.

"See, this is what I was afraid of," I say with a raspy chuckle. I step away from his hand, away from his perfectly sculpted chest and abs. "I had so many things I wanted to say."

"And then can we fuck?" Jared asks, impatient passion nipping at his words.

His coarse words may as well be a couplet, a sonnet, an ode considering how they make me feel. The consistency of how he wants me, how it never fluctuates, makes me want him more. More than the ridged terrain of his torso. More than the water-darkened gold hair curling at his neck or the stormy-sea-blue eyes and rugged masculine beauty of his face.

"Almost," I laugh and run my fingers nervously through my damp hair. "I shared all of that to say I've always been inhibited about my body. I've gotten better. Counseling and, I guess, living, maturing, becoming more confident. All of it has helped."

I grin up at him.

"And, no, the lights don't have to be off anymore."

A slow smile spreads across his lips, and his eyes still glow hot but are solemn.

"I have disciplines," I tell him. "Things I do to keep myself in a routine and consistent with my health goals. I count points. I work out. I have my apps."

I look at him as I tug at the belt of my robe.

"At least once a day, I look at myself completely naked."

Jared's hooded gaze scours my body, covered nearly head to toe in white terry cloth.

"Seeing you naked every day doesn't sound like much of a hardship," he says, voice braided with lust. "Sounds like my fantasy, actually."

I pause, my fingers caressing the soft fabric, my eyes caressing his face.

"The first time we made love," I say, resuming the work of my fingers at my waist, "I made you turn the lights off."

Jared's glance latches onto my waist, following the simple movements of my fingers.

"This time I want you to see me." I force the words past the anxious knot in my throat. "Not because I'm perfect—I'm still not—but because I trust you to want me just as I am."

Jared's hand covers mine at the belt of the robe. The other hand reaches up to cup my cheek, and his eyes lock with mine.

"I do, Ban," he says roughly, tenderly. "I've seen you. I know you've lost weight, but I'm more impressed with how you've *grown* than by what you've lost. You're more confident, more compassionate, more clever, more driven. You're more of all the things that drew me to you in the first place."

I blink back tears at the rightness of that. It's not that Zo didn't see me clearly. I know he did and that he loved me for who I am under my skin. But I tried to feel this for him, tried to want him the way I want Jared, and I never could. I don't know when thinking of him while I'm with Jared and thinking of Jared when I'm with Zo won't feel disloyal to them both. Right now it does, and I clear my mind of everything but the man standing in front of me.

Ten years ago, I demanded he kill the lights before we went any further. I wrapped layers of clothing around myself then to camouflage my flaws. To hide myself. Now I'm standing under bright, unforgiving lights in the bathroom, only a simple robe between Jared and my imperfections.

And I'm not concerned about the pounds I still need to lose.

I'm not wondering if anything will jiggle when he makes love to me.

I don't care about the last of the dimples in my thighs or if my hips are too wide.

I'm captivated by the acceptance in his eyes.

Seduced by the care in every touch, even more because I know he doesn't always care about people, can't tolerate everyone. But he said he likes me more than any other girl. I never imagined I'd fall for someone like Jared, so opposite of me. We both play by certain rules and are both each other's exception.

Whatever it is that binds us and has endured even through the hostility and deception compels me to do something I've never done with anyone else.

Eyes never leaving his, I completely loosen the belt of the robe. I shrug my left shoulder until one panel falls away, revealing my naked breast and glimpses of my waist and thigh. Jared inhales sharply though his nose and clenches a fist at his side. I shrug my right shoulder and the robe surrenders completely, falling to the floor in a white heap of clouds at my feet.

The tiny network of stretch marks at my waist and thighs, etched in my skin from the weight I've gained and lost... He sees those.

The discrepancy between my breasts—one slightly larger than the other—he sees that, I'm sure.

The stomach that never seems quite flat enough and pokes out if I even look at bread... He must see that. My eyes zero in on it every morning.

I'm sure he sees all my imperfections. I want him to see them and to want me anyway.

And he does.

"Can I touch you now?" His voice is scraped raw with hunger for me. The girl with the pencil in freshman orientation. The one he didn't see or even recall. That girl stands here showing him every-thing, trusts him with everything.

And feels completely seen.

I nod jerkily, breasts rising and falling with my choppy breaths.

His hands… God, his hands are so reverent when he strokes the curve of my jaw and then traces my face. He wanders down my neck, caressing the skin slowly like he's savoring every inch. He's watching the path his hands take, narrowing his eyes on my breasts cupped in his big hands. He bends and takes one nipple into the warmth of his mouth, stroking the other with his thumb.

I clutch the nearby counter, gripping it tightly and trying to stay on my feet while his mouth widens over my breast, sucking aggressively, and his other hand swipes down my side and palms my butt.

"This ass," he breathes over the dampened tip of my breast and moves his hand between my legs, palming me and sliding three eager fingers inside me without delay. He runs his finger to my ass and strokes the sensitive aperture, surprising me, overtaking me with unexpected sensations as he freely explores my body. "Have you ever been fucked in the ass?" he asks, running his thumb over the tiny hole, eyes burning with curiosity and lust.

"Yes," I breathe, realizing that I shed my inhibitions along with my robe. "I love anal."

His thumb stills, lingering and then probing the tiniest bit at the puckered hole but not delving inside. The look suspended between us spins a web of soon-to-be indulged fantasies.

"We're gonna get along just fine." He resumes the seeking, the stroking, the torture above the waist and below until I'm panting, desperate, quivering. Our breaths mingle. Our foreheads press together, and he rubs my back, my spine a conduit for the electric charge transmitted from his fingertips to the delicate column of nerves and muscles.

"It would be a shame if a bed is actually here this time," he says, "and we still don't use it."

He kisses me, our tongues parrying and thrusting, our moans meeting in the middle. I barely notice that he's slowly walking me backward into his bedroom. By the time the backs of my knees hit the firm mattress, I'm nearly delirious, twisting his hair in my fingers, scraping my nails down his back. There's a savagery in our kisses born of desire long denied. There's nothing sweet or gentle in it. A starving stroke of tongues, the sharp snap of teeth. Bared. Biting. The taste of blood mingles in the kiss, making it ferrous, feral. It's more than a kiss. It's a clash of titans.

"Wait." He grabs my hair, pulling my head back when I press into him, seeking more. "I want this slower."

"Jared." I reach between us and fist his cock. "We can do slower later."

"No." He chuckles and pushes my shoulder gently until I'm sitting on the bed. "Slower now."

I'm shocked when he gets down on his knees in front of me. Both times we made love, Jared put in work, eating me out like a starving man. I'm fully prepared and dripping wet for act three, but he surprises me yet again. Taking my foot in his hand, he kisses the arch. A frisson scuttles along my leg from the place he kissed me, and I twitch. He embarks on a journey that carries him up my leg, sucking the calf muscle and behind my knee, his tongue warm velvety torture. All the while his mouth worships me, he squeezes my hips, grips my waist, palms my breasts. By the time he christens the inside of my thighs with kisses, I'm thrashing, head flung back, heedless of my wet hair on the bed. The light caresses, the feathery kisses, the careful kneading of my flesh, he's doing it on purpose. A passionate provocation pushing me to beg. It's the best battle of wills, one where the end is already decided. Because he can go slow or fast, light or deep, but he will fuck me before this is over.

I win.

But I'm determined to resist as long as I can, gathering the fine linen of his sheets in my balled fists, pressing the tips of my toes into the cool stone floor, caging the moans and whimpers inside my teeth. Not giving him the satisfaction until he satisfies me.

And then the tide changes. Those gentle hands—the ones I want to ravage me, to dig into my ass while he barrels into my body—press my legs open. I tense, completely aware that I have no defense against that tongue, against the skill and patient hunger applied to the needy, weeping center of my body. I urge his head forward, deeper into the V of my legs, unashamed to ask for what I want. Prepared to demand it if he tries to go slow, to go easy.

"Banner," he says, still kneeling, his hair damp and cool against my thigh. "Watch me eat this pussy."

Barely hearing him over my heartbeat, I sit up on my elbows to follow his order. His eyes, blue fire, burn as he scoops his arms under my legs, lifting me, holding me immobile and open to him. Never looking away, he dips his head between my legs, and I watch his mouth on me. Watch the calm facade of his expression crack with hunger and fall apart with lust. I realize that in this battle of wills, his composure is as flimsy as mine. At the first swipe of his tongue in the wet folds, by mutual agreement we both lose all pretense of control. If this bed is our battlefield, we are two white flags surrendering to the demands of the other.

"Fuck, Ban," he mutters against my slick, wet mound. He jerks me closer to his mouth, and I watch as his tongue darts out furiously, flicking my clit. He drags his tongue from top to bottom, thoroughly enjoying every inch, every drop of me. I grunt, pulling his hair, pressing his head closer, bending my legs and sinking my heels into his shoulders. I'm a madwoman with no sense of propriety, no inhibition or pride. The need to join with him, to mate with him is paramount. I want to feel him aggressive and plunging into my body even more than I want to come, but I don't have to make that choice. In tandem, his fingers and mouth persist until I unravel. I come loose from all my bindings. Every insult, every criticism, every word spoken against me loses its power in the center of his perfect desire. To be wanted like this eclipses all the times I wasn't—all the times I felt unworthy. It billows from me, and I feel so completely free.

I'm still floating, drifting, when he joins me on the bed, scattering kisses over my shoulders, my neck, and the freckles on my nose. I smell myself on his face, and it spikes the frantic desire all over again. I clutch at his shoulders and urge him to position himself between my legs.

"Do I need a condom?" he asks, his voice urgent, hopeful.

"No." I pull his hair and squeeze the firm roundness of his ass. "Please fuck me."

"In a bed and with the lights on," he says. "How do you want it?"

I know immediately.

"I want to be on top."

It's not that I've never been on top, but the self-consciousness never really went away. Am I too heavy? Can he breathe?

"I'd love that," he replies.

"So you want me to ride you, Jared?" I ask playfully as he stretches out under me and I straddle his strong thighs.

"Do I want you to *ride?*" He challenges me with one cocked brow. "Hell no. If you're taking the top, you'd better drive."

We laugh like the kids in that laundromat, hearts free and minds clear. And for a handful of seconds, it's simple between us, but as I hover over him the humor evaporates. I'm on the threshold of something I'm not sure I'm ready for. Not him being inside me. I'm panting for that, but this intimacy with nothing between us. No secrets, no lies, no misunderstandings, no one else. The path to him is clear, and I'm afraid once I start down it, there is no turning back. Jared is a one-way ticket.

I take him in my hand and into my body, and the hot, tight clasp has us both gasping, foreheads smashed together. The first thrust gives me that almost-too-much feeling, that slight stretch I first mistake for pain, but it's actually the ache of my body begging for more. I'm wet, so I'm ready, but I'm not prepared to feel even more than I did before. I'm not prepared for the click in my soul, the key turning in my heart. I'm a door flung open when I rise and fall over him. He spans my back with his hands and buries his face in my neck, nuzzling me, licking me, biting me, growling and claiming like an animal. With every push in and pull out, he taps into something I didn't know was there. Something I didn't know needed to be found.

With one hand he brushes the damp hair back from my face, and with the other he grips me by the hip.

"You're so beautiful," he gasps. His face contorts with pleasure, and he pistons up into my body, his pace bruising. I lift my legs and hook my ankles at his back, needing him even deeper, even harder. Steadily invading and withdrawing, he finds my fingers, linking them with his and leaning into me until his lips brush against my ear.

"*Chinga*," he says, a salacious whisper, a memory from our first time together.

A breathless laugh escapes my lips, and I squeeze the fingers tangled with mine.

"*Chinga*," I whisper back.

Fuck.

We exchange the vulgar word like an endearment, passing it between us, incited by the sound of it on each other's lips. And then there are no words. Just our eyes holding as our bodies reunite—a sweet, sweaty merger. One heart slamming into the other. Breaths congregating between our mouths. The wills we both master with so much pride collapse, yield, give way. A détente between our bodies and a truce between our hearts. And with one final plunge, one last kiss, finally peace.

CHAPTER 29
JARED

Classic rule of negotiation: when the terms are more than you bargained for, consider abandoning the deal.

Banner Morales is more than I bargained for. We'd had sex twice in ten years and I remember every vivid detail of both encounters. Last night was…more. Her stripping down to nothing, dropping her robe and her guard, not just showing me her skin and the ripe curves of her body but showing me *herself*, she completely bared her inner self to me. The trust of that act heightened the intimacy between us in a way I've never experienced.

"I think I'll have steak." She smiles at me in the glow of lit candles. The restaurant, one of the island's finest, features a private terrace which hangs over the Caribbean with its gradated shades of blue, a startling blend of aquamarine, cerulean, and turquoise. The balmy breeze off the water toys with loose strands of Banner's hair and carries her clean scent across the table to me. If it weren't for the solicitous server checking on us every few minutes, I could imagine we are the only ones here. "Points be damned," she says with a laugh. "I'm on vacation. What are you having?"

I stare into those long-lashed, espresso-colored eyes, and all I can think of is how she looked down at me when I was between her knees, head buried in her pussy, slurping at her like one of the intoxicating island drinks that deceive you with their fruity sweetness.

That's Banner. She's so sweet, you don't realize how dangerous she is at first—that she goes to your head until you're reeling from the effects. You don't realize she's a beautiful snare, and once you're trapped, not only can you *not* get out, but you don't want to.

"Jared?" She shoots me an inquiring look over her menu. "What are you having?"

"Oh." I glance at the menu I've been holding for the last ten minutes but hadn't bothered reading. "The paella looks good."

"Oooh." She narrows her gaze on the menu and nods. "I've changed my mind. That does look delicious. I think I'll have that, too. It's one of my favorites to make."

"You cook much?"

It's when I have to ask these kinds of questions that I realize how much Banner and I don't know about each other. Despite feeling like I left irretrievable parts of myself inside her last night and that I'll carry the secrets of her body to the grave, we've missed a lot in the decade we were apart.

"I do actually." She shrugs, the olive skin of her shoulders gleaming sun-kissed and smooth in her strapless dress. "When I have time."

"Maybe you can cook something for me."

We stare at one another across the table, the possibility of an actual relationship—something we've never had the chance to consider—silently unfolding between us.

"Yeah," she replies. "I could make you my favorite dish."

"Which is?"

"Chicken enchiladas with mole sauce. I make it even better than my mama."

"You and your mom are close?"

"Yes, in the way mothers and daughters who are too much alike are close. Usually arguing after ten minutes together." She sips the fruity drink she ordered and grimaces. "I didn't realize this had pineapple. Blech."

I laugh at the face she makes. "I take it you don't approve?"

"I hate pineapple. Always have."

She sets the glass down on the table, and there's a tiny lull in our conversation. It doesn't feel like that awkward "so what do we talk about now" pause because there's so *much* to talk about we aren't sure where to start. I hesitate, unsure if I should say what I'm feeling, but then I remember her bravely sharing herself, her fears and insecurities, with me yesterday, and I know there is only forward for us. I'm not sure where we're going, but it has to be forward. I reach across the table for her hand, smiling at the wary look she offers. She's unsure, too.

"I feel like we have a lot to learn about each other," I tell her. "In some ways it feels like I've known you for years and can predict your next move before you think it, but in other ways I feel like I know nothing at all."

She squeezes my hand, a smile blooming on her mouth and rising on her cheeks. "You're right. I don't even know if you watch TV, much less what your favorite show might be."

"*Billions.*"

"I'm seriously not surprised." She smiles at me across the table. "Let me guess. Your favorite character is Bobby Axelrod, right?"

"Wrong," I come back, pleased that she mis-pegged me.

"Who, then?" she asks, eyes narrowed in speculation.

"Wendy Rhoades."

Her mouth falls open, and she leans forward, elbows on the table.

"I'm shocked you didn't say Bobby or at least Chuck. Why Wendy?"

Because she reminds me of you.

I don't say it. I can't shake every rule of negotiation. I can't give her *everything* up front.

"Bobby is the billionaire, and Chuck runs the city as the DA," I say. "But Wendy runs them both. They'd do anything for her. Bend their morals, break their rules. They'd even act against their own self-interest for her, which is antithetical for them both."

"You're so sure?"

"If there's one thing I know for sure," I laugh harshly, "it's selfish bastards, being one and all, and those two selfish bastards would do anything for Wendy. That's what ultimately drove Bobby's wife away. She knew she might be the wife, but Wendy was the queen."

"Yeah, I didn't see their divorce coming."

"I did," I scoff. "It's so obvious Bobby would fuck Wendy if she ever gave him any indication he had a chance."

I pause, capture, hold her gaze in the moonlight.

"That's what we selfish bastards do," I tell her. "We fuck the girl we want the first chance we get."

Static electricity crackles in the air, drawing us to one another even though neither of us moves an inch. It's invisible and inexorable, this pull, and I hope she's truly done resisting it.

"And how do you deal with the guilt?" she asks, her voice low and barely above a whisper. "The guilt of just taking and doing whatever you want?"

"What guilt?"

The truth lands on the table among our appetizers and silverware. Her heavy conscience and my lack thereof. Before she can probe any more, the server comes to take our dinner order. He walks away, and I shift the conversation instead of talking more about my general lack of morality.

"Favorite movie of all time?" I pick up where we left off before the interruption.

"*Shawshank Redemption.* You?"

"*The Godfather.*"

"Figures."

"Yeah, it does." We laugh together.

"Favorite food?" she asks.

"Lasagna." I sip my drink, a jalapeño margarita or some shit. I miss my Jameson. "Best lasagna I've ever had in my life was my mom's."

"I've never heard you talk about your mother," Banner says. "Only your stepmother."

There's a pain in my chest every time I think of my mother. Some emotions are so strong, some losses so essential that the heart—not your beating heart, your *feeling* heart—can't contain them, so the body absorbs the blow. That's how I grieve my mother.

"She died." I clear my throat and take another sip of my spicy margarita. "Breast cancer."

Banner has this way of making you feel like you're the only person in the room, maybe in the world. She doesn't blink, as if she might miss some vital detail of what you're saying if she does.

"How old were you?" she asks, her undrifting stare compassionate.

"Ten." I cough, less about the spices in my drink and more about how foreign it feels to talk about this, about her. "It was really fast. She was already stage four and..."

That's as far as I typically go, and I assume she'll do what other people do. Murmur condolences and move on. It's an old hurt, no place to linger, but Banner does what Banner does.

"Tell me about her," she says softly. "What was her name?"

"Angela." My laugh is short. Truncated. "Dad called her Angie. God, he yelled her name all the time. Yo, Angie, where are my socks? Angie, you pick up my dry cleaning? Angie, there's no beer in the fridge.'"

I pause to offer a knowing look.

"I can hear your thoughts from here," I tell her with a crooked grin. "And, yes, he did have some chauvinist tendencies my stepmother cured him of pretty quickly."

Her rich laughter and the warmth in her eyes ease the ache in my chest a little. I rarely talk about it because I hate feeling this way. Weak and helpless, like I can't make it hurt less and I can't ever bring her back, but I don't feel those things tonight. It feels right to tell one incredible woman in my life about the other.

"Mom wasn't a pushover, though." I toy with the cloth napkin wrapped around my silverware. "She just loved my dad so much.

Wanted to make him happy all the time. That's how she was. She always wanted everyone to be happy."

"Was your father still in the military then?"

I don't even remember telling Banner my dad was military, but I nod.

"Yeah. Army, so we lived all over when I was young." I shrug, dislodging the tightness creeping over my shoulders. "Dad got out soon after she died. Retired."

"He wanted to be there for you? I imagine that was such a tough time with you being so young."

I hadn't thought of it in those terms before. It never occurred to me that my father did that for me, but maybe he did. He wasn't around as much when he was in the army, and if he'd been deployed, I would have had to stay with relatives.

"Maybe." I look down at the table but don't see the white-linen tablecloth for a minute. I see, instead, my dad crying at my mother's grave. Feel him clutching my hand like a lifeline. "I guess that is when we started getting close."

"You have pictures?"

The question takes me off guard, and I stare at her like she asked me if I know where they buried Jimmy Hoffa.

"Uh, yeah. I do actually." It's the only physical photo I carry around. Everything else is digital, but this one I like to hold every once in a while. I dig out my wallet and pull the time-worn photo from the hidden pocket.

"Wow." Banner studies the photo I handed her. "She's gorgeous. That skin!"

"She was Italian. Guess it's why I'm a little darker, too. Little bit of year-round tan in the genes."

"That's the only difference between you and your dad." Banner raises wide eyes. "You guys could be twins otherwise."

My father was a little younger in that photo than I am now, and Banner's right. The likeness is uncanny.

"Was it hard for you?" She passes the photo back to me. "When your dad started dating your stepmother?"

"You know, it wasn't. Me and my dad had a few years, just the two of us, before she and August came along. I was a little older and frankly ready to have a woman back in the house. My dad couldn't cook for shit."

We share a chuckle, a lingering glance because talking about this stuff feels so…close. It feels like we're venturing into something new and deeper. The water's at my ankles, but for Banner, talking with her this way, with her looking this way, with her *being* this way, I'd wade in to the knees. Higher.

"So destiny brought the future basketball player and the future sports agent together under one roof, and the rest is history, huh?"

"Something like that." I look around for the waiter to refill my drink. "Sorry that got so heavy."

"I don't mind heavy," she says softly. "Life is heavy sometimes."

And there it is. She's one of those people who isn't uncomfortable with the pain of others. It's not awkward for her. She doesn't say those weird things, the pat phrases that don't actually mean anything, that don't do anything, like empty calories.

The server brings our food, and we dig in, both making appreciative noises instead of talking when the dishes first hit the table. We quiz each other over steaming plates and several more drinks. Banner finds a fruity one with no pineapple and plenty of alcohol. I begged the waiter for a Jameson and am on my third by the time we've excavated the last ten years of each other's lives and at least some of the things we never knew.

The air around us thickens with every drink we take and every secret we share. Our drinks must be spiked with lust, some aphrodisiac that has us both heavy-lidded, licking our lips, linking ankles under the table, stealing touches every chance we get. I'm torn between continuing the most stimulating conversation I've had in years and taking Banner home for the best sex of my life.

"So now that I know everything from your favorite color to your favorite movie," I say, "I think it's time to dig deeper."

"Deeper?" She relaxes into the seat, sipping the deceptively frothy concoction our server has plied her with all night. "Go on. Ask me anything."

"Strangest place you ever had sex."

The word "sex" planted in the air makes me hard. I read an answering flare of need in Banner's eyes. She tips her head back, draws in the fresh air off the Caribbean, and looks so much like she did last night: head tossed back, riding me, driving, controlling the pace of our bodies colliding. And the mark on her neck she didn't bother hiding, shaped like my mouth, ringed with my teeth, is yet another reminder of how we claimed each other.

"Hmm." She looks up at the ceiling like she has to think about it. "Well, I did have sex on a desk in my office last week."

"That cannot be the strangest place you ever had sex."

Her grin would border on bashful if she wasn't looking at me like she might crawl across the table and straddle me.

"I think it might be," she says, her laugh a little self-conscious. "I guess I just haven't been adventurous."

"Or maybe you haven't had the right lovers," I offer with a roguish grin. "You're welcome."

"Asshole." She rolls her eyes, predictably, but still smiles. "And what about you, Mr. Sex Anywhere?"

"The strangest? Let's see. Once backstage at a U2 concert."

"Damn, you *do* have good taste in music."

"Told you." I laugh and keep going. "Once in chambers. She was a judge. Aisle four of a grocery store. She was closing."

"Okayyyy." Her expression grows more curious and incredulous with each revelation. Since she's a Catholic, I think it best to omit my sexual encounter in a church confessional.

"A parent-teacher conference." I laugh at the horror on her face. "One of my clients was out of town and asked me to talk to the teacher."

"So I guess you enjoy the thrill of possibly getting caught?"

"No, I just like sex and have it whenever the mood strikes me." I shrug and shoot her a lopsided grin. "You should see your face right now. You're like *Green Eggs and Ham*, the Sex Edition."

"What?" She wrinkles her nose, obviously confused. "What does that even mean?"

"I would not do it here or there," I affect a droll accent, quoting Dr. Seuss. "I would not do it anywhere."

"Oh my God," she chuckles. "You're ridiculous."

"A train! A train!" I keep at it. "Could you, would you on a train? Not on a train. Not in a tree. Not in a car."

"Shut it!" she manages through her laughter. "I'm not a prude or anything. I just haven't been given the right opportunities."

"Ohhh, you haven't been *given* the right opportunities," I say, eager to provoke a response. "And here I thought you were the kind of woman who made her own."

Her eyes slit at my prodding, lit with a mixture of excitement and determination. She glances around the deserted terrace, and I'm not sure if I should be scared or aroused by her impish grin. I'm gonna go with aroused, since that seems to be my default with Banner.

"You know what," she says, tossing her napkin on the table. "You're right. That is the kind of woman I am."

She slides down her seat and disappears under the table.

"Banner, what—"

The sibilant hiss of my zipper jerking down shuts me right up. Her hands at my belt make me go still. I like where this is going.

"This is really happening?" I ask, afraid to hope.

"Uh-huh," she says, her voice muffled through the wood.

I slump in my seat and spread my legs. I want to make this as easy as possible for her.

She pulls me out, her hands firm and cool, her mouth hot and wet.

Holy fucking shit.

All the alcohol I've consumed starts boiling in my blood and rushes to the head below my belt. I'm going to enjoy every damn minute of this, and if our server comes back, I'll stab him with my steak knife.

"I like this done a very particular way," I say, striving not to sound breathless. "Do you need direction?"

"You tell me," Banner says, before taking my cock nearly to the back of her throat.

I grit my teeth and fist the tablecloth, determined not to moan. "You're doing just fine," I choke out.

"Mmmm," she hums, the vibration traveling from my dick to my toes. She drags me over her lips until only the tip is still in and then licks me like that vodka Popsicle. Thoroughly, greedily, like I'm worth a billion points and she can't get them down fast enough. I slam my hand on the table, disrupting the glass and china. Banner's laugh is steamy around me, and I almost lose it.

"Excuse me, sir?"

You have got to be kidding me.

"Uh, yeah." I compose myself enough to answer the server with some semblance of coherence as Banner rolls my balls in her hand.

"Dessert?" he asks.

Shit, I'm gonna come. I'm pretty sure my eyes are rolling in the back of my head.

"What?" I manage. "Huh?"

"Would you like dessert?" he repeats, casting a curious glance toward Banner's empty seat. "Or would the lady like something?"

"I don't know that I"—I spread my legs more and slide down, pushing another inch into her mouth—"saved room for anything else."

"The lady?" he asks again.

"She-she…" *God, she* excels *at this.* "Um, went to the bathroom."

At that very moment, Banner's enthusiastic bobbing below bangs her head on the table. The glasses and plates lift and clang. The server's eyes widen, and he clears his throat.

"Dude, double tip if you get the hell outta here," I rasp, on the verge of spilling my life down Banner's throat.

Without a word and with guaranteed discretion, he quickly leaves the terrace.

With him gone, I slide the table back enough to see Banner's pouty lips spread around my cock. An image to store away for future fantasies. I tangle my fingers in her hair, urging her to take more and faster. My other hand slips into the strapless dress to twist her nipple. Her breath stutters, disrupting the steady pace of her mouth on me, and I decide those are not the lips I want to see on my dick. I tug her hair until she has to release me. The look she sends up is leaded with passion, free of strictures and ready to give me whatever I want.

"Get up here," I command, only getting harder when she immediately raises from her knees to stand. I venture under her dress, finding her panties and working them down her legs. Our eyes never let go as the silk descends, and as soon as they ring her ankles, she steps out and positions herself over me. Her thighs rest on mine, and the bright-orange dress bunches at her waist. She leans in to kiss me, her mouth an open invitation, but pulls away just enough to make me chase her. My mouth strains to recapture hers. Husky laughter wafts over my lips with the Caribbean breeze while she reaches between us and guides me inside.

This must be how it feels to enter a temple. With eager devotion. With reverence. With the first thrust up into her body, the tenuous hold on my control snaps. I grip her hips, and the silk of her dress flows over the backs of my hands with our every undulation. She hooks one arm around my neck, and the other arm hangs limply at her side while she rides me with abandon, head flung back, eyes squeezed tightly shut, and the only sounds on the terrace our ragged breaths and grunts permeating the balmy air.

I can't take my eyes off her. Something inside irrationally taunts me that if I look away, she'll disappear. She's a storm I can't find the eye of. I need to hold her tightly, assure myself she won't get away—that she doesn't *want* to get away. Even with my arms locked at her waist, I can't contain her. I try to grasp her in parts, but her breast overflows my palm. Her ass spills past my hands. Everything is ripe. Everything is full, except my way in. My passage into her body is narrow and tight, allowing me only so much, but I take that path over and over, like a battering ram at a castle door, hell-bent on reaching the queen inside.

It's still not enough. Even with our bodies locked and grinding like gears, working each other into a frenzy, there's a gap, a space where doubt creeps in. Hunger for something deeper than physical possession gnaws at my gut. I thought this would satisfy me. It always has before, but I know instinctively that finishing now, I'd only want her again, still hunting for another entrance, for a way in deeper.

"Wait," I pant, and as much as it pains my cock, I clench my hands at her hips and stop the roll of our bodies together.

"What's wrong?" Banner's breath labors, her chest heaving, the bodice of her dress half-up, half-down, covering one breast and exposing the other.

I lift the dress more, ruched at her waist, exposing us to the cool air christening the place where our bodies join. "Look at us."

Confusion sketches a tiny furrow between her brows until she looks down and sees what I see, me disappearing inside her. Her body absorbing mine. I coax her hips into a gentle wave, and we watch the slick slide in and out, see her wetness, her juices coating my dick with each withdrawal. These are the pretty lips I wanted wrapped around my cock tonight. With one hand between her breasts, hoisting the skirt high, and one hand at her neck, I press my forehead to hers.

"You see yourself on me?" I ask. "You see how you take me in? How that greedy little pussy eats my dick?"

She nods against my forehead, her breath stuttering.

"Answer me, Banner," I say sharply.

"I see," she says, looking up to catch my eyes.

"I want to be inside you all the time," I say, urgency making my voice rough. "I want to be in your head."

I kiss her temple.

"To know what you're thinking." I press her away from me enough to kiss between her breasts and over her heart. "To know what you're feeling. To know what you need."

Our bodies take over, and I'm pounding up into her again despite my best intentions. The muscles of her legs clench on mine with every rise and fall. She kisses me, her tongue taunting mine. A sparring match of parries and feints.

"Okay," she breathes into our kiss.

I grip her face and solder our eyes together in a heated gaze.

"This is more than sex for me," I say. "Do you understand?"

Her eyes widen, darken with realization.

"I understand." She never looks away, even as the pace of our bodies increases. "It is for me, too."

Her whispered assurance starts filling that hole, that empty space having only her body doesn't touch. I kiss along her jaw, down her throat, inflict tiny bites on her collarbone.

"Mean it, Ban," I say fiercely into the scented cove behind her ear. "I need you to mean that."

"I do." Her breath chops up against my neck. Her fingers twine in my hair. Her knees tighten at my hips the harder and deeper and faster we fuck. "I promise it's more."

"I won't share you." I pull back and grasp her chin, forcing her to look at me. "I know it's hypocritical. I know I took you. I don't care. I won't share."

"You won't have to." The breathless promise tumbles past her lips and into that hole, filling it more. Soothing the empty ache of it. She takes me by surprise, grabbing my chin and clenching her inner muscles around my dick possessively, making me groan. "And I won't share you."

The idea that, with all the women I've fucked and never felt even a fraction of this intensity, I would jeopardize my connection to Banner is laughable, but I don't laugh because I see the same questions, the same need for reassurance, for more, in her eyes that I know is in mine.

"It's just you, Ban." I reach between us, stroking and pinching her clit as an electric bolt strikes from the base of my spine and down my legs, strangling my next words. "I promise."

That vow steals the last of my control, and every doubt, every hesitation leaves as I spill into the warm welcome of her body. My release triggers hers, and we both cry out, our voices loud and echoing on the empty terrace. We've forgotten the server could come back any minute. We don't consider some misguided diner possibly stumbling into our private space. There is only the Caribbean Sea, a sheet of blue-hued glass beneath us. Only the sweat-damp parts of us soaking up the breeze. There is only a promise we whispered before we both came, stronger than steel and as fragile as the beam of moonlight illuminating us.

CHAPTER 30
BANNER

"Did you save room for dessert?"

My question reminds me of our server who must have been horrified when he realized what we were doing on that terrace. Since I was under the table with Jared's dick in my mouth, I couldn't see his face. The memory burns my cheeks, but an irrepressible grin spreads across my lips.

"What's so funny?" Jared asks from his side of the table. "And I'm good for now on dessert. Stuffed actually."

"Okay." I rise from my seat, pick up my plate, and reach for Jared's.

"I got it," he says, gathering his plate, wine glass, and fork, and heads toward the kitchen. "Now what made you smile like the cat who ate the cream?"

An uncharacteristic giggle pops past my lips.

"Ironically, I was thinking about that poor waiter from the restaurant."

"He was anything but poor after that tip I gave him." Jared laughs and loads his plate into the dishwasher. "His eyes got bigger when he saw his gratuity than when he realized what you were doing under the table, believe me."

I cover the portion of the enchiladas we didn't eat and set down the *buñuelos* I prepared for dessert.

"These do look good," Jared says, plucking one of the doughnut-like sweetened balls from the basket I placed them in.

"They're so good." I breathe in their aroma and sigh. "Mama used to cook them for us all the time. I haven't had them in years."

Jared chews one, groaning his approval.

"Delicious." He grabs another one, biting half and offering me the other half. "Taste."

I hesitate, unable to turn off my inner calculator, tallying points.

"Just one bite," Jared persuades, rubbing the sweet fried dough across my bottom lip. "We're on vacation."

I nod and accept it, squeezing my eyes shut when the flavor explodes on my tongue along with a thousand memories from my childhood.

"So good," I say, swallowing the last of the dessert. "It's been forever since I had them. A few Christmases ago when Mama made them."

I look up and catch a thoughtful expression on Jared's face, the one I'm learning usually precedes a probing question.

"How do you think your family will react to you and Zo breaking up?" he asks.

I'd left that question with my points, checked at the door of this island villa, but now it intrudes. The closer we come to leaving, to returning to LA and dealing with the inevitable fallout of what we did, the harder it is to forget I have several difficult conversations awaiting me, including my family.

"They'll be surprised." I turn off the light in the kitchen, and we stroll back to the well-appointed salon. As we walk, Jared takes my hand, linking our fingers and drawing me in to his side. He touches me constantly, possessively. Each caress and kiss and touch subtly establishing ownership. I don't mind. I touch him the same way. I feel the same way, like I need to mark my territory even though there's no one here to threaten my claim.

"Surprised and upset?"

Jared flops onto the leather couch positioned prominently in the center of the room and pulls me onto his lap. There was a time I would sit tense and tight, wondering the whole time if I'm too heavy, if my weight is too much for him, but I relax, sitting sideways, my shoulder pressed into his chest and my head tucked into his shoulder.

"They will be upset. As I've thought about it, my family was part of the reason I ignored the little voice that kept telling me not to start with Zo. They've wanted us together for years." I toy with the collar of Jared's T-shirt and squeeze the hand linked with mine on my knee. "I can't sugarcoat it. They'll have a million questions, and I need to think about how I'm going to answer them."

"Honestly," he says. "Tell them about the doubts you had and the things that convinced you to ignore them. Tell them about us. I mean, you don't have to go into details about how we practically broke your desk."

I suppress a grin, not quite prepared to see any humor, but knowing one day I might be able to.

"And me?" he asks, a forced lightness to the question. "What will they think of me? Of us together? I know compared to Zo, I'm not exactly the boy you bring home to Mama."

I look up from my spot on his shoulder, studying his face for the things he's *not* saying. The tightness around his mouth. The concern in the eyes searching mine.

"I didn't think you would care what they think," I say and flatten my hand over the hard muscles of his stomach under his T-shirt.

"I don't. For me, I don't care. We're going to be together if the pope himself doesn't approve."

"I don't think our relationship requires papal approval." I laugh and caress his back. My hand freezes under the shirt as the word "relationship" lingers in the air. Even after all he said on the terrace, telling me he wanted more than sex, that he wouldn't share me and I wouldn't have to share him…it still feels like I'm assuming too much to call what we're building a relationship.

"Not papal," he agrees with an easy smile, obviously not nonplussed by the word. "Is 'mamal' a word? I think your mother will be the hardest to get on board."

"True." I nearly shudder thinking of the tongue-lashing in store for me over Zo.

"I know you love your family," Jared says soberly, reaching down to gently grip my jaw. "I love mine, too, but they have no say in this. No one does except us."

I search his face for perfidy or any duplicity, but there's only the same sureness I saw in him last night. Sureness about me and our *relationship*. I simply nod and lay my head back on his shoulder, content to listen to his heartbeat and the wash of waves a few yards beyond the villa door.

In the distance, a phone rings, shattering the comfortable quiet we've been lounging in.

"Ugh," I groan, shifting on his lap. "My phone."

"Leave it," he urges, kissing the curve of my neck. "Stay here and fuck. We've only had sex once today. Are we losing the magic already?"

I chuckle and kiss his cheek with finality.

"As tempting as that is, it's Cal's ringtone."

I haul myself to stand and rush toward the staircase and up the steps. I only told my boss that I needed a few days away, and my team is more than capable of holding down the proverbial fort while I'm gone. We've got a lot of off-season deals in the works, though. I can't ghost completely on my clients. This could be something I should handle myself.

Or maybe Zo told him he's leaving Bagley because I can't, in his words, keep my legs closed. That would be a much more embarrassing scenario, but I'm prepared for either.

"Hey, Cal," I reply, winded from racing to catch the call. "What's up?"

"Where the hell are you?" he demands immediately, discarding social graces.

"I told you I was taking a little time off." I pick up a pillow from the bed we've made love in so many times this week I've lost count. The pillow smells of Jared's clean, addictive scent.

"Yeah, well, it's really bad timing since your biggest client is in the hospital while you're off smelling the roses or whatever the hell you're doing."

I go stock-still, the pillow pressed to my face and Jared's scent still in my nose.

"What'd you say?" The question stumbles over my tongue and out of my mouth. "Which client? Who?"

"Alonzo Vidale. Who else would be your biggest client?"

"Zo?" I can barely breathe deeply enough to push out his name.

Jared appears at the door, leaning one shoulder against the frame with folded arms and a frown.

"Yes, Zo, Banner. Where the hell is your head?"

"What's... What's wrong? Where is he?"

"Like I said, he's in the hospital," Cal replies, a touch of impatience evident in his answer. "Has been for three days."

"Three days? In a hospital?" I shout, confusion, frustration, and anger infighting as I try to get answers. "Zo hates hospitals."

Ever since he sat in that waiting room while all his family members died one by one, he has avoided hospitals at all costs. The thought of him lying in a hospital alone for three days...

"What happened?" I demand.

"Apparently, he was up in Vancouver for some standard off-season stuff. They had him doing a stress test when he passed out."

Zo has never passed out in the ten years I've known him, not even from the excruciating pain of his torn ACL.

"The team thought we should know, so they called the office," Cal says.

"Why didn't they call me immediately?" Frustration sharpens my tone. "They're supposed to."

"Zo told them not to." Cal's curiosity crackles across the line.

"What the hell is going on, Banner? If you two are having some kind of lovers' quarrel, I don't need to know, but if this shit is affecting business, you need to fix it."

"I've got everything under control."

My reply sounds certain despite the chaos my life is spinning into. Jared's face is stone as he listens to my side of the conversation. Cal's questions, demands, and thinly veiled threats nip at me over the phone. And somewhere in a Vancouver hospital, my best friend has suffered alone in what he would consider his personal hell. Nothing is under my control, especially not my galloping heartbeat or the trepidation and anxiety roiling inside.

"You'd better," Cal warns. "Get up there, figure out what the hell is going on, and report back."

He hangs up, and I stare at the phone for a few seconds, immobilized by worry and shock.

"Zo's in the hospital?" Jared asks softly from his spot at the door.

"Yes." I swallow tears and choke back all the questions and fears fighting for a way out. Jared is not the person I should talk to about Zo. He can't be. I walk over to the closet, drag my suitcase out, and start tossing clothes in, not even paying attention to what I'm packing.

"Hey." Jared gathers my hands in his and forces me to stop long enough to look at him. "Tell me what's going on, Ban."

"He passed out." I close my eyes and try to block all the worst-case scenarios. "I'm sure there's a reasonable explanation, but he's been in the hospital for three days."

Helpless tears fill my eyes, and I want to be weak for a moment, but there's no time for weakness. Zo may have no time for my weakness. He'll need me strong. The worst part is that I'll have to convince him to let me help at all.

"So you're leaving?" Jared asks, a muscle flexing along the sharp angle of his jaw.

"I have to." I shake my hands loose to cup his face, staring into the concern and doubt in his eyes. "Zo hasn't told them yet that he's leaving. Cal didn't know about any of it."

"Maybe he doesn't plan to fire you after all," Jared murmurs, his full mouth in a humorless tilt. "I wouldn't if I wanted you back."

"This isn't about him wanting me back." I turn to the closet again and pull clothes off hangers and toss them carelessly, swiftly into my suitcase. "He's been there for three days already, and he hates hospitals."

"And you're off to the rescue, of course," Jared says. "I'm sure he has a spot at his bedside waiting for you."

I pause long enough to glare at him.

"That's not fair," I snap. "Could you just be human enough to care about someone other than yourself for one damn second?"

At my harsh words, a guard drops over Jared's face, like the visor of a helmet in battle, and he steps back, away from me.

"Jared, I didn't mean—"

"It's true, though, right?" His laugh is a mace swinging through the air, and I don't bother ducking. "I've said it myself. I'm a selfish bastard, but I won't pretend this doesn't bother me."

"I get that, but please believe what I told you last night." I reach for him, frame his handsome face in my hands, and let him look into my eyes so he can see that I mean what I'm about to say. "It's just you."

I can feel the tautly held muscles in his face relax under my touch. One arm scoops me in close, and the other buries his fingers in the hair at my neck. I can't say I've ever seen tenderness on Jared Foster's face, but the way he's looking at me now, it's the closest I think he's come.

"I didn't mean to be an asshole." He grimaces. "I mean, that is my naturally occurring state, but I know he's your client. He's your friend. Of course you'll go make sure he's okay."

"I have to."

"You have to," he agrees, nodding and tightening his hands on me. "Just remember us, okay? That we have something…"

He grapples for a second, searching for the word that is already on the tip of my tongue.

"Special?" I offer quietly.

He nods and bends to kiss the spray of freckles across my nose.

"Yeah. We have something special."

CHAPTER 31
BANNER

"Who the hell called you?"

Zo's angry question is the first shot fired as soon as I enter the hospital room. I set aside any distress I feel at seeing him, big and vulnerable. Too big for the hospital bed, too vulnerable to be the strong man who has been my best friend for the last decade.

"I think the better question is," I say, arranging my face into the implacable agent I need to be for him right now, "why didn't you call me?"

"Do you really want me to tell all these nice people why you would be the last person I call?" he asks, still in English.

I meet the curious stares of several doctors crowding around Zo's hospital bed. Ever since we started working together, Zo and I would retreat to Spanish when we needed to say things we didn't want others to know. Maybe rude, but we didn't care. We were a team. Clearly things have changed.

"I don't care what you tell them," I reply honestly because I'll air all our dirty laundry in front of strangers if that's what it takes. "But you're contractually obligated to notify your agent of any invasive medical procedures, preferably before they occur and definitely within twenty-four hours."

"Bullshit." Zo spits the word out, his eyes bitter slits in the striking face.

"Yes, I thought you might need reminding." I plop my Bottega Veneta Cabat bag at the foot of the bed, extract a copy of his contract, and extend the sheaf of papers to him. "Page forty-four."

He accepts the contract, flipping to the page I marked with a tiny red-flag sticky note.

"I don't care what the contract says." He tosses the contract back to me, and it lands at my purse. "I don't want you here."

"Tough." I plaster my negotiator's face over the hurt his words cause. "My career is inextricably tied to yours as long as I'm your agent, so anything that happens to that body happens to me."

"You're not my agent."

"According to this contract," I say, holding it up, "I am, and unless you can produce legal documentation proving that you have formally dissolved our agent–client relationship, not only do I have the right to be here, but it is my responsibility."

"Get out," he says harshly.

"No."

I cling to the calm facade and hide trembling hands in the pockets of my expertly tailored, wide-legged pants. The silk blouse, stilettos, diamond-stud earrings, expensive cologne, upswept hair… it's all professional armor I've wrapped myself in for this confrontation. He doesn't need a supportive girlfriend. He needs a fighter, and the flawless makeup I painstakingly applied is my war paint.

"Who's in charge here?" I ask, swinging my inquiry around the room.

"Apparently, you are," answers one white coat–clad man with a receding hairline and glasses.

"I need to be brought up to speed immediately," I say, ignoring his attempt at humor I don't have time for. "Doctor…what is your name?"

"Dr. Clintmore." He steps forward and shakes my hand.

"What is the status of my client?" I ask. "What has been done, and what is being considered? What do we know?"

Dr. Clintmore glances at Zo, silently requesting permission to share information before he divulges anything. Zo zips a look from the contract at the foot of the bed to my face and scowls but nods to go ahead.

"Mr. Vidale's blood pressure was dangerously low," Dr. Clintmore says. "He passed out during the stress test, but that wasn't his first time. He reported blacking out two other times over the last few weeks."

"What?" I can't help it. Concern slips through my mask, and I seek Zo's evasive eyes. "When? Why didn't you tell me?"

"Does it matter now?" Zo blows out a long breath.

"Yes," I answer, my voice unyielding. "Tell me."

"Once in the locker room near the end of the season," he says like the words are being dragged from him. "And a few weeks ago when I was in Argentina at the orphanage."

"And you didn't think to share this information?" I don't know if I want to shake him or hug him, but I'm spitting mad and scared as hell.

"I thought it was nothing." He hauls in a breath that stretches the muscles of his wide chest. "In the locker room, it was after a game when I played almost the whole time. I assumed I was probably exhausted and didn't hydrate enough. This summer, I had been working all day in the sun on the orphanage's new cafeteria."

Something flickers in his eyes when they meet mine. He's probably remembering that building the cafeteria was my suggestion the last time I accompanied him to the orphanage.

"So Mr. Vidale assumed those incidents and the weight loss were typical," Dr. Clintmore inserts.

I asked him about the weight he had lost, but he dismissed it as the intensity of the playing schedule. Why didn't I persist? How could this have escaped my notice? Guilt spears me right down the middle, but I try to focus on what the doctor is saying.

"We've run tests on his heart, his lungs," Dr. Clintmore continues. "All results have come back within range, except—"

"Except what?" I cut in, gripping the bed rail.

"The albumin levels in his blood are extremely high." The doctor spreads a cautious look between the other physicians in the room before going further. "There are many things that could be related to, so we won't speculate but will wait for the next results."

"What is albumin?" I ask.

Dr. Clintmore nods to one of the younger doctors to reply, and I realize the other doctors present are medical students.

"It's a protein your liver produces," the younger physician answers. "It helps keep fluid in your bloodstream and prevents it from leaking into other tissues."

"And what do high levels of it in the blood usually indicate?" I ask, tensing while I wait for his answer. He flicks an uncertain glance at Dr. Clintmore, who nods that he should continue.

"Alone, it's not conclusive enough for a formal diagnosis," he says. "When we biopsy his kidney—"

"Biopsy his kidney?" Surprise unhinges my jaw. "What does that involve exactly?"

"We'll drill a small hole in his back," Dr. Clintmore says, his eyes drifting between Zo's face and mine. "And extract a sample of his kidney to examine."

I gulp but keep my features straight and absorb everything I've learned since walking through the door.

"How long before we'll get those results?" Zo asks, the tiny twitch in his jaw the only tell of his concern. Otherwise he looks like we're discussing what he'll have for dinner.

"Just a few days."

"And can I go home in the meantime?" His shoulders tense while he waits for the doctor's reply. I know better than anyone how much he hates hospitals. He's probably been coming out of his skin the last three days.

"Of course," Dr. Clintmore says. "Wait here for the release paperwork. Take it easy. We'll call you to discuss results as soon as we have them."

"Sounds good." Zo flips long legs over the side of the bed and climbs out, straightening to his full six foot six. His dark hair has grown over the summer and waves past his ears. He walks to the closet, impervious of the audience viewing the taut muscles of his bare ass and back in the hospital gown. He spends half his life naked in locker rooms with other men, and God knows I've seen him naked enough that he shouldn't be self-conscious with me. The team of doctors clear their throats and head for the door. I quietly ask Dr. Clintmore to contact me directly when the results are in so I'm kept abreast.

I cross over to stare out the window, eyes fixed on the parking lot below but mentally synthesizing the information the doctors shared. A sense of foreboding spreads over my body like an invading army. My bravado, the false calm I armored myself in, the tough act... none of it will be enough if there is something really wrong with Zo, and I allow myself to feel helpless and afraid for the span of a few clipped heartbeats before wrapping myself in fake courage like chain mail and facing Zo again. He's fully dressed, tall and handsome and looking like he hasn't a care in the world. I know him well enough to spot the lie of his expressionless face.

"Why wasn't there anyone from the team here?" I ask, more to delay the things he'll say now that we're alone than out of real curiosity.

"They were here earlier," he replies. "They'd left by the time the doctor came with his news. Look, you and I both know this is ridiculous. I haven't had the chance to tell Cal I am leaving. Your presence here will only make things worse. I want you out of my life. I thought I made that abundantly clear."

I take the comment like a knife in the ribs but keep pressing forward.

"Call it my swan song." I grab my bag and look him in the eye like I would any other client, not like the good man I betrayed. I bury my shame so I can do my job as his agent and his friend.

"Well, I'm going home," he says. "I hope you have a hotel and don't plan to stay with me."

He pauses, uncharacteristic malice twisting his wide mouth.

"Unless that contract says I have to fuck you, too, until we are no longer contractually obligated?"

I bite my lip and blink back tears. It's not even that his words hurt. It's that he *means* them. That I did this. I made this good-hearted man, who lives to help, want to hurt.

"I have a hotel," I say softly, clutching my bag.

"Good," he says, turning his back to me while he waits for the final paperwork. "Use it."

"He has what?" Lowell asks with a heavy frown and through tight lips.

The Titans president of basketball operations sits in one of three chairs across from Dr. Clintmore. Zo and I occupy the other two. The fact that I don't yet understand what Zo has doesn't make me feel any better because he has *something*. Something, based on the grave set of Dr. Clintmore's face, very bad.

"We believe he has amyloidosis," the doctor repeats.

"It's a type of cancer?" Zo asks. I look at him, and I know he feels my eyes on him, but he doesn't look at me.

"Technically, no," Dr. Clintmore replies with the calm of a man well used to delivering life-ending news. "We call it a cousin of multiple myeloma, which is a cancer of the blood. A cancer of plasma cells. You'll often see the two conditions coexisting, sometimes one to a lesser degree than the other, but we categorize amyloidosis as a rare disease, not a cancer."

"You said you *believe* he has it," I say, homing in on any sliver of doubt, any chance that there is a mistake or that this is not serious. "So there's a chance he doesn't?"

"We would like to biopsy his bone marrow to confirm the diagnosis," the doctor replies, compassion leaking through his professional mask. "But we are fairly certain, given the results we already have."

"A bone marrow biopsy?" Zo frowns and swallows convulsively. "What are we talking about here? Like, what are my odds? What is the prognosis? When can I play again?"

With each question, Dr. Clintmore's marbled expression cracks a little more. The last question makes him sigh.

"I think playing is..." Dr. Clintmore pauses, obviously weighing his words. "A lesser concern considering the expectancy is generally six months to two years."

Expectancy?

"Do you mean life expectancy?" The question barrels from my mouth like a cannonball. "You're saying he has six months to two years to *live?*"

"This is not my specialty," Dr. Clintmore says hastily. "There are generalities and many variables that factor into each individual's prognosis. I wouldn't want to speak hastily. We need the biopsy results and to start treatment as soon as possible with a team of doctors who know more about this condition than I do. Immediate and aggressive treatment will improve whatever prognosis he has."

"What kind of treatment?" Lowell asks, rubbing his chin, a speculative look in his eyes. I know exactly what is running through his mind. He's thinking of his team, which has been built primarily around Zo. He's thinking of his upcoming season, in which Zo would have featured prominently.

"Even though it is not a cancer," Dr. Clintmore says, "it follows a similar course of treatment. Aggressive chemotherapy."

"Chemo?" Zo runs a hand through his lustrous hair. "Like, I'll lose my hair and be sick and can't play ball?"

That's it. I'm done with this shit. Lowell is over there silently scheming on how to cut his team's losses, and Zo is trying to figure out how to salvage the season and when he'll be back on the court.

"Fuck ball," I snap. "Did you hear the man, Zo? Six months to two years. The last thing I care about right now is when you'll get back on the damn court. You are in the literal fight of your life. Do you understand?"

"You think I don't know that?" he asks harshly, his dark eyes flashing fear and frustration. "That I don't realize how hard the road ahead is? But I need a goal, Banner. Something to help me at the end of that road. I need…"

You.

He doesn't say it. He wouldn't, but I know, even if he doesn't know it yet. Even if he won't say it. And a stony resolve builds itself brick by brick inside me. Hail Marys, prayers, rosaries, miracles… We'll do all those things, but what this will also require is someone determined that Zo won't die and foolish enough to believe it no matter what.

And that someone is me.

Jared flashes through my mind like lightning. Sharp and striking. Bright and dynamic. His sun-warmed body tangled in the luxurious sheets of our Caribbean villa. The golden stubble roughening his kisses first thing in the morning and the deep rumble of his laughter when we'd stay in bed and talk some mornings for hours, just digging around in each other's heads and delighting in the treasures we found. I already know what I have to do for Zo, even though it's gonna be a bitch convincing Zo to let me, and I don't know how Jared will feel about it.

But I do know that I have no choice.

Over the next hour, we hash out a plan. Based on information Dr. Clintmore gives me, I call the closest hospital with any real record of treating amyloidosis, Cedars-Sinai, but they cannot even see Zo for six weeks. Fortunately, Stanford has an actual Amyloid Center and clinical trials Zo may qualify for. Every door I knock on swings open to reveal more possibilities. I can see the road forming that could get him out of this alive, but it is not short, and it is not easy.

And I'll have to walk with him every step of the way.

Lowell is preparing to leave just as I'm starting another round of calls and making more arrangements.

"Banner, I'll be in touch about how we go forward," he says, measuring out just the right dose of compassion in the glance he offers Zo.

"Of course," I murmur, disconnecting the call before it goes through. "I'll walk you out."

As soon as we're outside the office and down the hall a few feet, I lay my cards on his table.

"Don't you think for one second about cutting him from the team," I say without preamble.

"Banner," he starts, shaking his head and looking at me like I'm the bane of his existence, which I have no problem being if necessary. "I have to act in the team's best interest. You know that. The league has excellent medical benefits, so he'll be taken care of, but I can't guarantee his spot will still be there in the end. Who knows what kind of shape he'll be in or if he'll even live through it?"

"Let me tell you something, Lowell," I say through clenched teeth. "He needs a goal. He needs something at the end of this to make him fight and keep going, and that is ball."

"I cannot guarantee that."

"Then you will lie."

"What?" His startled look transforms to disdain. "Even you can't force me to make that promise, especially one I'm not sure I can keep."

"I don't particularly care about your team or your season right now." I rest my fists at my hips and lift my chin. "Try to cut him and you'll have a PR shitstorm so thick you won't be able to see a foot in front of you. You'll be the team who kicked the league's patron saint ambassador when he was down, after all he's done for so many. After all he's done for *you*. By the time I'm done, not one sponsor will touch anything to do with your team or your arena."

I aim a hard look up at him.

"Test me."

His brows lower. Mine lift. In the hall we silently push and pull, but this is a tug-of-war I have no intention of losing. He knows I mean business and shakes his head as he walks toward the elevators. I stand outside Dr. Clintmore's office for just a second and let the full, dire weight of the situation fall on my shoulders. It's heavier than anything I've carried before, but I breathe through the knee-buckling pressure and adjust to the unaccustomed weight. Ignoring the tears that long to pour out of me and promising them they can have their way later when I'm alone, I reenter the office. Zo sits by himself on a couch by the window, shoulders slightly slumped and head in his hands. I walk forward, not sure what to prepare for. More of his biting anger, resentment, bitterness. Fear?

He looks up as I approach, and the tears standing in his eyes are almost my undoing. My steps falter as I'm faced with Zo's mortality, with his own belief that he will die. I steel myself against that. I cannot afford doubt, even from the one I'm believing for.

"Okay, so the team at Stanford is checking their open trials," I say, my tone businesslike, brisk, bordering on indifferent, though anyone who checked my pulse would know that to be a lie. "If they come back with a no, I'll find a way. In the meantime, you'll begin the chemo protocol there."

"Banner—"

"My real estate friend found us a townhouse in Palo Alto, not far from the hospital," I continue, afraid to let him speak. Afraid of what he'll say and how he'll try to make me stop. "We can stay the full three months while you're getting chemo. Longer if needed."

"Us? We?" His head jerks up, and his eyes search mine. "You're coming with me? To Stanford?"

"Of course I am." I dig around in my bag as if searching for something. "This will be harrowing. You can't do it alone."

"No, I can't," he agrees softly. He grabs my hand, gently tugging me away from my purse until I'm standing in front of him. "Bannini, *tengo miedo.*"

I'm scared.

His softly spoken admission cracks my facade like no angry words ever could, and for the first time since we heard the word *amyloidosis,* hot tears trickle down my cheeks. The riot of emotions I've been able to keep at bay roar to the surface and overtake me. They pull me under like a riptide, unexpected, unpredictable, unnavigable. I'm violently taken by a current beyond my control, and so is Zo. He pulls me down to the couch with him, beside him, and wraps his arms around me.

And we weep. We wet each other's clothes with our tears and clutch each other hard enough to bruise. I'll give myself this moment of weakness, but it will pass, and I will get up, and we will fight. I wipe the last of my tears and move to stand, but Zo catches my wrist to stop me. His hand tangles in my hair, and before I know his intentions, he's kissing me. Desperately, like the cure to the thing killing him lies just beyond my lips. I push at his chest, gently, firmly enough to put space between us.

"Zo, no." I pull away. "We can't."

"Why not?" he asks, bitterness creeping back into his voice. "Because of him?"

I freeze, shame shackling me to the seat.

"I can't do this right now, Zo," I say, and the tears I thought were done burn my throat again. "I have to focus on the next three months, on you getting better."

I look up at him and offer a watery smile.

"On you living," I say. "So just let me help you."

He tilts his head back, and a slight smile plays over his full lips.

"I will let you help me on one condition," he finally says.

Whatever he wants I'll give him, and he knows it.

"What?" I ask hesitantly, cautiously.

"Put it on hold, whatever you have with him. Don't take it any further."

I stare at him in shock long enough for him to go on without giving me a chance to respond.

"I know you, Banner," he says, squeezing my hands in his. "In ten years, you've never let me down. You're the most loyal person I know. And today, how you've stepped in, taken over, are sacrificing so much for me...I know this is what I want. *You* are what I want. What I need. Forever. I want to fight for you, but it seems I will be occupied for the foreseeable future fighting for my life. I cannot do both."

"Zo, I don't... I can't make any promises," I tell him as honestly as I can without being cruel. "I'm not sure we should ever have... Well, do you sometimes think that maybe we should have remained just friends?"

"That is my condition," he says, hardening his tone and ignoring my question. "I'm not expecting you to be in a relationship with me or to sleep with me, but you can't sleep with him either. He and I will both wait until I'm better and the fight is fair and the playing field is even."

All the air leaves my lungs. I thought he could ask anything of me and it wouldn't even be hard, but this is hard. I know this isn't what I want with Zo anymore. What I feel for and what I have with Jared is something already so deep and rich, and we've only scratched the surface of it, but what I told Lowell is true. Zo needs something he's fighting for. Simply fighting to live is not enough. He needs something he's fighting to live *for*.

We have something special.

Jared's last words echo in my head, caressing my thoughts and seducing my imagination. Hurting my heart.

Yes, Zo needs something to live for. He has ball.

And now he has me.

CHAPTER 32
JARED

"Iris, can you sit in on the Nike call?"

I glance up from the marketing plan on my iPad for the upcoming campaign and find my sister-in-law gaping at me with wide eyes.

"Me?" She points to herself, her mouth hanging open the smallest bit.

"Unless there's another Iris on our team," I say with a touch of sarcasm, looking away from her and moving right into the next agenda item.

I have to handle Iris carefully, never paying her special attention or granting her special favors. She's legitimately talented and has so much untapped potential, but she's also married to my brother, a silent partner in Elevation and an NBA all-star. I don't want her rise in this company, in this industry, to smack of nepotism. That would be a disservice to the badass she really is. She reminds me a lot of Banner, and I can see why Iris admires her so much. They'd be great friends, if given the opportunity.

And I plan to give them the opportunity. Knowing Banner, she'll want to be circumspect about our relationship, considering the public only recently found out about her and Zo. I have no idea how things will pan out after it leaks that Zo is leaving the Bagley Agency and that he and Banner aren't together. Until things settle, she'll want to be discreet. I can do discreet as long as it doesn't prevent us moving forward. I want my family to know, though. My parents' anniversary party would be a great time to introduce them to Banner. After they get over the shock of me actually bringing someone home, they'll love her.

Everyone loves Banner.

I've said every word but *love*. To her and to myself.

Fuck. Need. Want. *Mine*.

All great words to describe what we have but don't quite capture the depth of feeling. The intensity that has endured through years, through other relationships, through conflict. I set it aside when I couldn't have Banner, tried to ignore it while we built our separate lives and made our own way, but as soon as she was in my orbit again, she was like a string tied tightly around my finger, reminding me that there was someone out there who *fit* me in every way that matters. And I've searched for another word, a different word, a less committed word, less meaningful to describe what I feel for her, and I can't find it.

I've seen love, real love. I saw it between my father and mother. I've witnessed the miracle of my dad finding it again with my stepmother. I've seen it blossom under horrific conditions for August and Iris. I respect the word too much to use it lightly and have never even come close to using it with anyone else.

But Banner...she's not anyone else. There's only one Banner, and she's mine. I can admit that. I can say she's my match. That we belong together. She's my equinox.

But saying that word, for a guy like me, it's irrevocable—and, as corny as it sounds, sacred. I don't even *like* many people, for obvious reasons. Because they suck. They just annoy and disappoint me too often to even bother. Banner, someone I not only like more than everyone else but enjoy spending time with more than anyone else and want to fuck and claim to the exclusion of everyone else, is a tiny, glowing needle in a universe-sized haystack. I can't believe I found her, and I know how it feels to lose her. Until I know that won't happen again, that word just sits waiting for the perfect moment when I'm absolutely sure.

All these doubts and desires run on a back channel in my head during the staff meeting. My focus has been splintered ever since Cal summoned Banner to Vancouver. She and I haven't spoken much the last few days. We boarded separate planes, mine bringing me back to LA and hers taking her...to him. To Zo.

I'm paranoid for no reason. He's not like me. He's the good-hearted guy who's probably never seen an episode of *Billions*. Surely he doesn't eat game theory and dominant strategy for breakfast, lunch, and dinner the way I do. I know Banner. She has to fight for the people she cares about. She has to save, rescue. I've seen it with her clients, with her friends. And with Zo being her best friend, as she has reminded me maybe a million times, if he's really sick, I don't even want to think about what she would do for him.

The man's in the hospital. According to my last, albeit brief, call with Banner, he was supposed to get results yesterday. I'm emotionally evolved enough to know what a normal human would feel under these circumstances. I should feel sympathy. I should feel concerned. Instead, jackass that I am, I find myself wondering how he'll leverage this to get her back because that's what I would do.

My only hope is that he's a better man than I am.

"And Bill," I say, searching the faces gathered around our conference-room table until I find the junior agent. "That three-on-three tournament in Australia is the perfect chance to—"

My phone illuminates on the table, and Banner's name flashes across the screen.

"Hey, guys, I need to get this." Without looking up or missing a beat, I head for the door that leads to the hall. "Chyna, take over for me, will ya?"

"Sure thing, boss," she says.

I walk a few feet down the hall and lean against the wall before I answer.

"Hey."

"Hey," she replies, her voice low. "How are you?"

"I miss you." *I sound like such a pussy.* "When can I see you?" *Shit, it's getting worse.*

"I miss you, too. Um, can we talk?"

"Sure." I glance at my watch. "I'm wrapping up a meeting, but I—"

"I'm in your building," she cuts in. "I only have a few minutes. Can I come up?"

My heart races and slows. That built-in barometer that has navigated me through more than one difficult deal tells me a storm is brewing. The winds are shifting. I hear it in her quiet voice, a calm before the storm.

"Yeah," I say after a pause. "Come on up."

I'm waiting by the elevator when she arrives. She looks young and pretty, and my heart lurches at the sight of her. Even with her hair pulled back in a loose braid and wearing a simple patterned top, ripped-at-the-knee dark skinny jeans, and leather flip-flops, she exudes power. She's a woman who built herself from the inside out. The clothes are interchangeable, and her weight may fluctuate, but her strength is constant. She could stand here naked and be just as compelling.

I'd actually prefer her that way.

With a furtive glance at the conference room, where my team is pretending not to watch me fraternizing with the managing partner of our rival firm, I drag Banner by the hand into my office. As soon as we're inside, I pin her to the door. If my brain is sending a *slow down* signal, my hands aren't getting the message. Urgency marks every touch, my hand clasping her neck, freeing her hair, gripping her waist, squeezing her ass, sliding into her blouse to knead her breast. Her silky skin, the clean scent, the sweetness of her mouth, the deepest part down her throat...it all makes me desperate in a way I've never been desperate before. In a way I hate. Like I know this won't last and I can't keep her.

She reciprocates, straining up on her toes, chaining herself to me with arms around my neck. She grips my jaw, holds me still to have her way with my mouth. Carte blanche kisses, free-rein fondling, a no-holds-barred embrace with nothing off-limits.

"Ban," I whisper against her neck, my hand rhythmically rubbing her pussy through the thick denim. "Tell me we have time because I will fuck you up against this door right now."

She sighs, her fingers tightening in my hair, and kisses me slowly, thoroughly, until she pulls away to press her cheek to mine. Even as her hips rock into my touch, she shakes her head.

"No."

"No, we don't have time? Or just no?"

Her head dips lower so all I see is dark hair and slumped shoulders.

"Just no."

The rejection cools the southbound blood traveling to my dick and reduces my racing heart to a weighted thud in my chest.

"How's Zo?" I keep my voice even, though everything under the surface is disrupted. I'm disturbed. I know this is about him, that somehow she's telling me no because of him.

"Let's sit down." She doesn't wait for me but sits on the sleek leather couch in my office.

I sit beside her but lift her onto my lap, ignoring her protest.

"Jared, I'm too heavy," she says breathlessly, squirming.

"You're not." I link my fingers at her stomach and pull her back against my chest. "I held you like this on the island. Remember?"

I'm not just reminding her that she sat on my lap but that we took quantum leaps in the Caribbean. The things we entrusted to each other. The things I gave her and she gave me that we'd never shared with anyone before. Those count. Whatever is happening with Zo, however he is drawing her back to him, those days and nights I had with her *count*. They mattered, and I need her to remember that. She stills, relaxes into me, snuggles into me, and nods, her soft hair brushing my chin.

"That feels like another world," she says, caressing my fingers at her waist. "Like it was so long ago."

The only thing left of that serene time is our tans. The languid pace and liquid passion, flowing any way we chose, are restricted by whatever she is working up the nerve to tell me.

"It was only a few days ago." I give her a little shake. "Tell me what's going on."

She looks up, and the misery on her face clenches my heart into a fist.

"It's bad," she says, the words breaking on a sob. Tears leak over her smooth cheeks. "They say he has six months to two years."

Shock freezes all my synapses for a second, short-circuiting my thoughts.

"To *live*?" I tip my head back, angling so I can see her face. "You're saying Zo only has six months to live? Two years to live?"

The finely drawn line of her jaw flexes, and her sweet lips fall into a grim line.

"No, *they* say that." She narrows her eyes. "They're wrong. He's going to live a lot longer than that because I won't let him die."

I need to know if she's delusional, determined, or some hybrid of both.

"Tell me."

For the next few minutes, she unpacks everything the doctor told her and all that she's learned on her own.

"So it's not cancer?" I ask.

"There is *some* myeloma present," she answers. "But it's small compared to the big picture, the bigger problem. Amyloidosis often coexists with myeloma, but it's the one you never get rid of."

"So it's incurable?" I ask, tucking a chunk of hair behind her ear.

"Incurable, yes," she says. "But a lot of people are living with it for a long time. Stanford has this video on their site of a man, a doctor, whose condition was advanced, but he's still alive five years after his diagnosis. Skydiving, performing surgery, living a full life."

"Stanford? Is that where Zo will receive his treatments?"

She lowers her lashes and scoots off my lap, standing and facing me, hands shoved into her back pockets.

"Yeah, he has to live close to Stanford's Amyloid Center." She looks at me, shoulders tense and body held stiffly. "I already found a townhouse really close by. The chemo is slated for three months, so we'll stay there while he receives treatment."

She and I stare at each other, letting those words sink in. Words she knew would infuriate me.

"We?" I ask unnecessarily. "You'll be living with him in Palo Alto for the next three months? Did I hear you right?"

"You did." Defiance sparks in her eyes. "He has no one, Jared. His family, they're all gone. He won't be able to drive himself. Cook for himself. At some point, maybe even bathe himself."

"Wrong thing to say." I stand up to pace in front of the couch, driving impatient fingers through my hair. "You bathing Zo is not exactly winning me over to this idea."

"I don't have to win you over to it," she says, gentle, firm. "It has to be this way. You know that."

She touches my arm and waits for me to look down into the compassion filling her eyes.

"You know *me*, Jared. You know I would never let him do this alone."

I cover her hand on my arm and nod my understanding. I mean, come on. The guy is dying. Even I can't begrudge him that.

"Okay. So you'll be at Stanford for three months." I take her hand and pull her to me. "I get that. I don't like it, but of course I get it. When will we see each other?"

She draws a deep breath, loosens her fingers, and steps back.

"At first Zo was angry with me." She shakes her head and gnaws on her bottom lip. "Of course he was after what I did."

"Banner, when will we see each other?" I repeat, ignoring her detour.

"And he didn't want me there," she continues. "I literally had to use his contract and force him to let me stay."

I don't respond but fold my arms and wait for something I know I won't like.

"After we got the diagnosis and it was obvious how serious this is," she says, "things changed. He knew he needed my help, and he knows I'll do everything I can to get him all that he needs. He said he would allow me to help him on one condition."

"A condition?" I squeeze the bridge of my nose. "And what would that be?"

"I have to put things on hold," she says, her voice soft but steely. "Things with you on hold. Well, he doesn't know it's *you*, but he—"

"The fuck?" The expletive explodes from me before I think to check it. "He can't make you do that."

"He's not *making* me," she says, her voice controlled but quaking. "Jared, please don't make this any harder for me than it already is."

"Why?" I demand harshly. "Why do you think he made that his one condition, Banner? Don't you see he wants you back?"

"Yes." She looks at me unblinkingly. "He told me that."

"Oh, he did? What exactly did he say?"

"He said he wants to fight for me, but he has to fight for his life right now, and he can't do both."

Motherfucker. What am I supposed to do with that?

"He said that he wants a fair fight." She releases a heavy breath. "And an even playing field, and he can't have that while he's sick."

She already knows this is some shit.

"And I'm supposed to sit by patiently and wait while you live with him for the next three months?" I ask, swallowing down my rage and frustration. Struggling to appear reasonable. "That's how you see this happening?"

She runs a shaking hand over the hair I loosened when we kissed.

"I can't ask you to wait for me, Jared," she says wearily. "I know that. I understand it's a long time and you have...needs. I get that and wouldn't blame you for saying we're done. For finding someone else."

Finding someone else? The hell?

What she doesn't seem to realize is there isn't anyone else. I've tried all the "someone elses," and none of them simultaneously drive me wild and settle me inside the way Banner does.

"I didn't mean that I would find someone else." I hold her chin between two fingers and palm the curve of her waist. "I meant we'll see how long you last without me."

A slow smile dawns on her face with her realization, but it's a sun that sets before it fully rises. She frowns up at me and shakes her head.

"I won't lie to him," she says. "And I won't cheat. He specifically said we aren't to sleep together."

I don't have enough curse words for some son of a bitch, cancer or no cancer, telling me when I can or cannot fuck my girl. I don't care if I did steal her from him. *Mine now.* And I know how to keep her.

I hope.

"He specified that, did he?" I ask. "You know, I thought we were supposed to be the negotiators and the master strategists. Seems like Zo knows exactly how to get what he wants."

I press my palms over the curve of her ass, pressing until her breasts are crushed against my chest and she moans, dropping her head to my shoulder. If this is going to be torment for me, it's sure as hell going to be torment for her, too.

"The problem is," I whisper in her ear, as if we aren't the only ones here. As if we're nurturing a secret between our bodies and souls. "He wants something he can't have. And he can delay it for three months, but it won't make any difference."

"It won't?" She pants the words as I grind my erection into her belly. I want her wet and horny for me flying with him to their new townhouse in fucking Palo Alto.

"No." I squeeze each cheek, loving that my hands can't hold all that ass. "Because this ass is mine."

My beautiful, brilliant girl with her Julia Roberts lips and her lush ass. He thinks he can take her from me?

"I want you to do something for me, Ban." I feather kisses down her neck, and she tilts her head, baring her throat to me.

"What?" She's heavy-lidded, and if I slipped my fingers into her pants, she'd be soaked. My mouth waters, remembering those sweet juices flooding my mouth when she comes.

"Tonight in your new bed across the hall from Zo or wherever it is," I say, my voice husky, needy, "I want you to touch yourself."

Her breath catches, and she leans into me, cupping my neck with her cool palm.

"Touch yourself and think about me," I urge, taking her earlobe between my teeth. "I want you to slip your fingers in and think about how it's not enough. How it's not me."

"Jared," she gasps, her breath hitching.

"Think about how my mouth looked on your pussy. My head between your legs. Remember when you were on your knees under that table, choking on my dick."

"God, Jared." She shakes her head, her fingers trembling when she presses them to my chest. "This is already hard."

"Did you say hard?" I grab her hand and press it to the crotch of my suit pants. "This is how I'll be for the next three months."

I pull back to look in her eyes and run my thumb over her full lips.

"Waiting for you."

She tucks into my arms, her head on my chest, and I stroke her hair. We stay that way for the last few minutes we have together, before she has to go meet him, help him, be with him. Neither of us says *that* word, but if there's another word for the way I feel when she's close, for the way I miss her when she leaves, for the raging fear that someone would take her from me, then I don't know what it is.

It's only after she's gone and I'm back in the conference room, as though the most important person in my life didn't just traipse off to be at another man's side, that I realize what has happened. It's an irony that tilts my mouth into a smile of grudging respect.

I have to reassess my opponent. Zo may be dying, and who knows, he may only have a year or two left to live, but he is not done yet. And he may be a good man, but he is not above leveraging even the worst circumstances in his life to get what he wants.

That I can respect. He did something very few men have gotten away with.

Son of a bitch blocked my shot.

PART III

"i cannot love you gently,
it's not in me
to love in part,
so I will love You
completely,
and a little madly…"

—*Matt Spenser, poet*

CHAPTER 33
BANNER

WHEN YOU WALK THROUGH HELL WITH SOMEONE, YOU BURN, TOO.

The flames don't respect your privacy, your boundaries. They consume your time, torch your dignity, and turn your peace of mind to ashes. The last six weeks here in Palo Alto have been the most difficult of my life. I feel bad even saying that because compared to what Zo is enduring, I have nothing to complain about.

I cannot imagine him navigating this alone. It's not that Zo doesn't have friends. He does, many, but he's such a private man. Such a proud man, and this disease has stolen so much from him already. He hates that I see him this weak, much less that anyone else would.

"Banner," he calls from his bedroom.

I used to think mothers exaggerated when they said they could distinguish their babies' needs by a distinct cry, but I get it now. Not that Zo is a baby, but there is a certain note in his voice when he's dehydrated and a different one when he needs help getting to the bathroom. As a result of the chemo, he has the worst diarrhea. I'll never forget the day, after a particularly rough session, I walked in and found him crawling to the bathroom. His pajamas were already soiled. In the most stilted, painful silence, I helped him get clean and changed. He turned his head away from me, but I saw the tears adorning his cheeks. I'm glad he wasn't looking at me because he would have seen mine.

The note I hear in his voice now prompts me to grab the bottle of massage oil I keep by my bed. I walk swiftly to his room to see if I'm right. He smiles, eyeing the bottle in my hand, when I make it to his bedside.

"*Crees que me conoces tan bien,*" he says, his dark eyes large and pain-dulled in the gauntness of his face.

You think you know me so well.

I uncap the bottle and begin working the soothing oil into his size-fifteen feet.

"*Sí, lo se,*" I reply with a small smile.

I do.

We can go days without speaking or hearing English. Unless he has a chemo session at Stanford, he doesn't like to go out for various reasons. He hates being the face of something, a poster child. We are inundated with requests for interviews, special appearances, fundraisers. We accept the few he feels well enough to do and strongly enough about. Otherwise, we live quietly here on the periphery of the campus and hospital.

The media is grossly fascinated with his illness. As an agent, I understand fame. I know there's an exchange you make—your privacy for notoriety and success—but there are lines no one should cross, and we live in a time and in a culture that has erased those lines. We've become so conditioned to "following" and "tracking" that a man who wants to walk this hard road without spectators, without a TV special, without a podcast or a YouTube documentary, only piques their curiosity more.

Why can't we know everything?

"Are you hungry?" I ask in the companionable silence while I massage his hands and arms. One of the side effects of his treatment is tingling and pain. I'm not sure how much my massages help, but he likes being touched. The massages are painful for me because touching him, I can't deny how frail he has become. At six foot six, Zo has always been a tower of strength. His weight loss had already begun before, but we didn't realize the cause, and it wasn't as dramatic as it's become with the chemo. Over the last six weeks, the well-conditioned giant with the sculpted muscles has vaporized. His limbs have, in even such a short time, become almost spindly. They look too frail to support his tall frame. He's like a tree trunk walking on branches.

I finish the massage and cap the bottle. One glance tells me he is already drifting off. The fatigue is like a rain cloud dumping bouts of sleep on him throughout the day. I work while he sleeps, though there is almost as much to do for him as for my job. Between managing insurance and keeping notes organized from his doctors, I'm less and less involved in the day-to-day with the LA office.

God, it hurt to tell Cal he should find someone else to manage the office. I worked hard to earn that opportunity, but I couldn't do it well and give Zo my best here. Fortunately, I've been able to keep up with my client load. A nurse comes in a few times a week, which helps me keep my life afloat, but most of it falls to me. And I wouldn't have it any other way. Zo would do it for me. I'd do it for Mama, Camilla, Anna, or anyone I loved.

I'd do it for Jared, but I rein in my thoughts about him as much as possible. They always tell you to count the cost before you undertake a challenge. I can't allow myself to calculate what I may be losing with Jared by choosing to be here with Zo. Managing this, being here for Zo, requires complete focus. I don't have time for self-pity or second-guessing. Not when time is not on Zo's side.

As I figured he would, Zo falls asleep pretty quickly. He had chemo yesterday and is wiped. I'll take advantage of this time to look over a few contracts for Hakeem. But first, I check the app on my phone I use to manage Zo's myriad medications. Amyloids, the abnormal proteins produced in Zo's bone marrow, get deposited in multiple organs. Thank God they haven't reached his heart, but his kidneys, liver, digestive tract, and even central nervous system are all affected. Further down the line, he may require organ transplants and most certainly dialysis. For now, we're relying on a multidisciplinary team of specialists to manage all the various organs and affected areas. Since the proteins travel in the blood to latch onto the organs, his hematologist runs point and coordinates with the gastroenterologist, nephrologist, and neurologist who are also working with us. There are medicines for each organ, prescribed by each doctor. It's overwhelming. Thus the app.

I'm double-checking the new doses Zo's clinical trial implemented when I get a text.

> Quinn: Hey, stranger!
> Me: Hey, chica. How's the road treating you?

We made it official with AesThetics a few weeks ago, and they immediately put the Titanium Sweetheart to work as their new spokesperson. She's been going to conventions and doing trade shows and presentations all over the country. She heads to Europe next week.

> Quinn: Not too bad. I'm exhausted but can't complain. I'm headed into a meeting, but I'll call tonight so you can complain. Sound good?

I smile because she knows I won't complain. She's visited a few times but has been so busy herself it's hard to get up here.

> Me: Sure. Whatever you say. How's the book coming?
> Quinn: Ugh. You just don't let up EVER, huh?
> Me: LOL! This is not a new development. Answer the question.
> Quinn: What book? I'm not a writer.
> Me: No, you're a LIVE-er. You're a how-to manual on surviving hell. People will be inspired by your story. Write it so I can sell it. I have a short list of literary agents I think we should meet with.

Quinn: Of course you do. I'll think about it. Gotta go. Give Zo
my best and hang in there. I love you.

I blink at the tears that would spill over if I'd let them. I miss our talks. I miss having dinner with my friend and laughing about trivial stuff and all the things I took for granted when I *thought* I had a lot on my plate.

Me: Love you, too.

I'm just setting the phone down to get some work done when it rings.

Madre.

"Mama, *hola.*" I pop in my earphones and switch to Bluetooth so I can multitask.

"*Hola,*" Mama says. "How is he?"

I bite my lip before I answer. I hate worrying her. She sees Zo as a second son and flew up from San Diego when we first moved in to help me set up the house. She's been back a few times—but not since Zo's gotten so thin.

"He's good, Mama." I pull up Hakeem's shoe contract, scrolling to the section I need to modify.

"His hair? Has he lost his beautiful hair yet?"

"Uh, no." I cut and paste from a similar contract into Hakeem's. "I actually found these cold caps he wears to reduce hair loss. They seem to be working pretty well. It's minimal, but he went ahead and cut it close anyway."

"Did he get the rosary I sent?" Mama asks. "You know I used that rosary when your Aunt Valentina had breast cancer."

"I know, Mama. You told us."

"Every day I prayed. She ran a marathon last year," Mama says with supernatural satisfaction. "That's twenty-six miles, Bannini."

"I… Yeah, I know how long a marathon is, Ma."

"Remission." She says the word in triplicate, the three syllables like a prayer.

"There is no remission with amyloidosis," I remind her. "It's incurable. When Zo's clear of the proteins, he'll be in what they call response until they come back. And they will always come back."

"Not always."

"Yes, always, Mama. It's the nature of the disease."

"We'll see about that," Mama says with confidence. "And what about his sperm?"

I stop mid-type.

What the...?

"What about his sperm?" I laugh, a little taken off guard by the question.

"You will want to have children later, Banner," Mama says like she's talking to the village idiot. "Did he not put the sperm on ice?"

It hadn't occurred to me. It should have. I can't think of everything, but anything I miss gouges me with guilt. Even though Zo and I won't have children together, I should have thought to ask. Maybe he and the doctor discussed it privately, though Zo has so little privacy from me these days.

"I'll check on it." I dig back into the contract.

"Those are my grandbabies, Bannini," Mama says, her voice sorrowful. "Don't let them fry."

"Zo doesn't get radiology," I say absently. I don't add that his sperm are not her grandbabies. That would be as hard for her to process as Zo's illness. By tacit agreement, Zo and I don't discuss our relationship with each other or with anyone else. The media has basically dubbed him a martyred saint, and I'm the little woman standing by her man. He knows I've honored his request not to move forward with Jared, even though he doesn't know it *was* Jared.

Is Jared?

I haven't seen Jared in six weeks. I'm not sure if our tense is past or present anymore, but I miss him. I dream about him often.

Conversations we had, jokes we shared in the laundromat years ago, and, yes, I dream about us making love. All the time. It's so real, I almost expect my sheets to smell like him, expect to find golden hairs on my pillow. But my bed is cold and lonely. I can only hope his is, too. I know Jared's sexual appetite firsthand. I trust him when he says he'll wait for me, but I wouldn't blame him if he couldn't. It would gut me, but I wouldn't fault him, especially not when the woman you think of as "yours" everyone else celebrates as someone else's.

"So you will be back in time for the quinceañera?" Mama asks.

"Uhhh, yeah." I email the revised contract for Hakeem to look over. "We should be done with this round of chemo and back in LA by then, but I doubt Zo will be able to attend, Mama. After this, he has stem cell replacement. That'll strip his immune system, and he probably won't be out much for a long time."

The other end goes silent, which my mother never is.

"Ma?" I ask, closing my laptop and focusing on her completely. "Did you hear me?"

A muffled sob stabs me through the heart.

"When does it end?" Mama cries softly. "He's such a good man. For him to bear so much...*Dios ten piedad.*"

I can't do this. I can't be the one to comfort her, to listen to her pain. I have my own pain. And it is not time to indulge tears. There is too much road ahead of us for me to submit to tears right now. They're corked, and like a bottle of champagne, when that cork pops, they'll overflow.

"Mama, I have to go."

The silence again. This one stiff. Hurt.

"Banner, I know this is a lot for you, but you must talk to someone. You cannot be strong all the time. You will break."

Not yet, I won't. She didn't see his face creased with agony after the bone marrow biopsy. She hasn't caught him staring blankly at the stranger in the mirror with the shrunken frame or witnessed his helpless anger when the diarrhea is so bad he has to wear adult diapers just to leave the house. A man so proud, so regal, brought so low. I've seen Zo's cracks and know how close he is to breaking.

No, it's not time for me to cry. I don't get to break yet.

"Mama, I'm fine."

"You're not wavering, are you? I mean, in your love for him. I know it is hard to see the man you love so weak, but you are not a fragile woman."

"No, I'm not fragile." I leave the love alone. I do love Zo, probably more than I ever have, but I know what kind of love it is, what it should always have been.

"I'll come back up soon," Mama says. "I'll cook all his favorites."

"He can't keep anything down. I make him vanilla smoothies with a little pineapple. That's about all he can tolerate. Everything else just comes back up."

"He loves pineapple, and you hate it," she says with a little laugh. "Surely there's something I can make for him, or maybe I could…"

I feel her fix-it from here. I get it from her.

"Mama, just come," I say softly. "You don't have to *do* anything or try to make it better. Zo loves *you*. That's it. He doesn't get to see many people because his immune system is shot, and he would especially love to see *you*."

"I just want to do so much." Tears soak her voice. "He cannot die. I'm praying. I go to Mass. He is in God's hands. Tell me you believe he will be okay."

My faith is a coin toss. Heads. Tails. Fifty-fifty.

So I do for her what I do for myself every single day. I toss the coin in the air, hope for the best, and make myself sound certain of things over which I have no control.

"Mama, I believe."

CHAPTER 34
JARED

So this is what twenty years with the same woman looks like. With the right woman. My father and stepmother literally glow when they're together. I saw it the first time he brought her home, and twenty years later, they're just as bright.

I never resented Susan West marrying my dad. Losing my mother took something from him, made him sad in a way I thought would never go away. With Susan, he was happy again, and that was all that mattered to me.

Also, she made a mean pot roast.

"Oh, Jared," she gushes, one hand over her mouth and the other hand holding the tickets to Hawaii I gave them as an anniversary gift. "It's too much."

My dad catches my eye and silently mouths "It's not too much."

We share a smile, and I can't help but remember the conversation Banner and I had about my father that night at dinner. I'd never considered that he retired for me, but now I realize he probably did. I touch his arm to keep his attention before he goes back to opening more gifts from the pile in front of them.

"Hey," I say, waiting for him to look at me. "I just wanted to…"

He lifts thick fair brows in silent inquiry, waiting for me to do something I never do.

"Just…thanks for all you sacrificed for me," I mumble, dropping my hand from him and feeling like an idiot. I glance at Susan, who is smiling and tearing into a brightly wrapped box. "I'm glad you found her. You deserve to be happy."

I'm ready to move on, feeling awkward. Why am I so bad at being nice? My dad, though, excels at kindness, at connecting with people in a way, despite all my agent's charm, I never could. He clutches my shoulder, his eyes not brimming with tears but with emotion all the same.

"Nothing I ever did was a sacrifice, Jared," he said. "It was a privilege raising you, one I took very seriously."

I usually hate this burning sensation in my throat and this pricking behind my eyes, but tonight I don't. It's evidence of the love I have for my dad, of the love he has always made sure I felt from him. There is an understanding in the grin we share that maybe we've never shared. Probably because I never took the time, but having Banner in my life carved out something in me that wasn't there before. I'm not less of who I was, but she's added something. One of the things I love about Banner is how she flips things around so I see them in new ways.

One of the things I love about Banner is different from saying *I love Banner*. I'd be a fool to let myself say that with things as they stand right now. I haven't seen her in six weeks. We've barely talked. The whole world is planning her deathbed wedding to Zo. It's morbid. I can't stand it. I hate that they don't know she's *mine*. That everyone thinks she's some tragic heroine so deeply in love with Zo she would never leave his side—when she touches herself at night and thinks of me.

God, I hope she does.

Or am I alone in this pathetic farce, the one in which I don't even know the role I'm playing? Maybe I'm reciting my parts, hitting all my marks, the whole time thinking I'm the lead when I'm actually the chump pining for the girl, not the one who gets her in the end.

They open the rest of their gifts, and we cut a huge cake, and there's dancing, and it's all wildly romantic and the last thing I want to do. It's a reminder of my limited options. The woman I want isn't here meeting my family like I had planned, but she's in Palo Alto with her...boyfriend? I don't know what to call him. I don't know what they are.

What if he's won her back? I mean, six weeks in a house together, something has to happen, right? I wouldn't be in the same house with Banner for a day without bending her over something and fucking her from behind.

But that's just me.

I'm reminded every day that Zo and I are different people. He's the philanthropist. He's the patron saint. The goodwill ambassador. I'm not any of those things.

And I don't give a damn. She's still mine. Not Zo or all the commentators combined on *SportsCenter* and *Good Morning America* will convince me otherwise. But what about Banner? Does she remember whose she is? And that across the country in Maryland there is a blackhearted, horny motherfucker who by some miracle has convinced himself that he is hers?

I need some air or at least some space. I wander away from the herd of joyful partygoers and into the den, which is really my father's man cave. There is never a time when the television isn't on, and I've never seen it on any channel other than ESPN. I flop into the leather recliner usually reserved for His Royal Highness and settle in to check some scores.

Only it's not scores they're discussing.

"We have an update in the ongoing story of Alonzo Vidale," the commentator says, his face appropriately grave. "Who, as most know by now, is fighting a rare disease called amyloidosis."

"A few photos surfaced on Instagram from a fellow patient at the facility where he's being treated," the co-anchor says, blinking her false eyelashes like she's trying not to cry. "I think we all send Zo our best wishes and prayers."

As they're talking, the photos that were posted come on-screen. Again, people suck. Who does this kind of shit? Sees a man being treated and posts pictures of him at his lowest for the whole world to see? His face is gaunt in a way one immediately recognizes is due to illness. Obviously his height hasn't diminished, but when he and Banner walk out of the hospital, she seems to be holding him up, even though she's only holding his hand.

Why is she holding his hand? Is that really necessary?

I hate feeling this way. These thoughts are awful—even for me. He's fighting an against-all-odds, uphill battle for his life, and the only thing I can care about is the fact that he shouldn't be holding Banner's hand when I don't even get to see her.

"You okay in here?"

I glance up, pulling myself out of my selfish musings to nod at August.

"Yeah, just tired." I drop my head back against the recliner and close my eyes. "Long flight."

"Oh, good," he says. "I thought it might have something to do with Banner Morales and Zo Vidale."

I open my eyes and turn my head slowly in his direction.

"Excuse me?" I ask, eyes narrowed on August's face.

"Just a wild guess." He shrugs and offers me a Stella. "Want one?"

I accept the beer without further comment, and we fall into an uneasy silence. Uneasy because I know it won't last long.

"I only asked," he continues after a couple of sips, "because Iris mentioned seeing Banner at the office shortly before news came out about Zo. She thought things looked pretty intense between the two of you."

"That right?" I fix my eyes on the interview with Stephen A. speculating about the upcoming season.

"Yeah, and then I remember she told me you came to Banner's session at that conference and seemed really into what she was saying. That you guys knew each other in college."

"Wow, that Iris is *really* observant, huh?" I take a sip, still not looking at him.

"Look, if you need to talk to someone," August says, "and I suspect you do, you know you can talk to me. I won't judge you."

"Oh, so if I tell you I'm fucking Banner Morales, you won't think that's bad?"

His jaw drops, and then he snaps his mouth shut in a hard line.

"Bruh, I didn't think you'd taken it that far," he says with a heavy sigh. "Jared, you can't. You'll be a social pariah."

He leans over to peer into my face.

"And so would she," he says in a low voice. "You know that, right? That if word got out it would ruin her reputation. She'd be reviled."

"Right. I know that," I snap. "And you can rest easy. I'm not."

"But have you?" he presses.

I look back at him and say slowly, deliberately, "Many times."

"Dude." He squeezes the bridge of his nose. "Start from the beginning."

I walk him through my early friendship with Banner and the disaster with the Pride to reconnecting over the last few months and all the grinning and grinding in between.

"So you pursued her knowing she was in a relationship with Zo?" August asks, looking pained, which pisses me off.

"Yeah. You wouldn't know anything about going after a woman when she's with someone else, would you?" I ask, knowing damn well I'm being an asshole.

"Jared, stop." August shakes his head, disappointment in the look he gives me. "You know it was different with Iris. Caleb was a sociopath."

He really was. I rub my tired eyes and blow out a long breath.

"Yeah, that was fucked up, Gus. I just..." I growl and tunnel my fingers into my hair. "You want me to be sorry I took her, and I'm not. You want me to be better, and I won't be. I'm just going to be me. I'm not noble like you and Dad or a saint like Zo, and frankly, I have no desire to be."

August often felt like the odd one out in our small family. With my father and me being blond and Susan with her red hair and blue eyes, August's biracial gene pool made him look like he didn't belong, but I was the outlier. The one who saw things through smut-colored glasses and didn't want to save the world.

I wanted to run it.

"Dude, no one expects you to be like me or your dad or anyone else," August says. "And you're not as bad as you think you are."

"Well, however bad I am, she sees it and still wants *me*."

I point an accusatory finger at the wide-screen television mounted above the fireplace.

"And every time I see some story about her being Zo's rock or how they are made for each other or how she's standing by him through the hardest time of his life—"

"All of which is true," August interjects.

I just stare at him for a second, infuriated. He's my brother. He's supposed to be on my side, but he's too concerned about what he thinks is right. He's always so damn *good*. I can't stand it. I'm surrounded by paragons.

"It's not all true," I say after taking a semi-calming breath. "She doesn't belong with him. She belongs with me."

"The man is fighting for his life, Jared."

"She belonged with me before he got sick. You have your right." I pound my heart with my fist. "I have mine, and she is my right."

"Do you mean you're entitled to her or that she's right for you?"

"Both," I snap. "And I don't care if you judge me for it."

"You keep saying you don't care, but I think you do."

"Why? Because you would? We're brothers, Gus, but we're nothing alike, and that's not because we don't share blood. We are made differently fundamentally. I've never been like you and Dad.

Or like your mom. And you want me to change the way I am, the things I want, what I will do to get it, to satisfy your idea of what's right, and I won't do it."

"Except you *are* doing it," August counters softly. "For her, you're doing it."

I grit my teeth because that is true. If it were up to me, I'd be with Banner and damn everything else. It's not fair that Zo imposes this on her, on us, so that she can help him *live.*

"It's the most manipulative, unfair thing, what he's doing," I answer. "Yet he's the saint."

"More manipulative and more unfair than you leveraging the charity golf tournament to insinuate yourself with Banner, knowing she was in a committed relationship?"

"Yes, because I knew what she wanted and that it wasn't him."

"She told you that?"

"She didn't have to. If Banner loved Zo, I wouldn't be able to sway her. She wanted to be with me. She always has, and I've always wanted her. I was not going to let the wrong man keep me from finally having her."

"So you just take what you want?"

"Didn't you?"

"No, I didn't, and you know it," he says, a frown crashing his eyebrows brows. "I waited until Iris was ready, and I gave her time. Timing matters, Jared. If you force Banner into this and she can't do it the way that feels right to her, you could lose her forever."

"That won't happen." I make a conscious effort to unclench my fists.

"Or she could come to you, but all the things you love about her—the good, the compassion, the sense of right and wrong—could all be deconstructed and set aside for you. And then is she even the woman you love anymore?"

"I didn't say I love her."

His knowing look shuts me down.

"You didn't have to," he says. "And do you think Zo has trouble telling Banner he loves her? After all she's doing for him?"

I stand from the recliner and shove my hands into my pockets so I don't punch my brother. I walk around all the time wanting to punch something, to punch someone, but there's nowhere to direct my anger. No one to blame, other than Zo, and I can't make myself hate him. I resent this situation, which basically means I resent life—that it is uncaring, like a bird flying overhead and not even looking down to see where its shit landed. Shit happens to us all, indiscriminately.

I don't mind heavy. Life is heavy sometimes.

She said that in the Caribbean when we talked about my mother. It's not just *talk* with Banner. She means it. She's the kind of woman you can count on during life's most brutal storms. Not fainthearted.

Lionhearted.

"Look, I know it sounds like I'm against you," August says.

"Uh, yeah. It does."

"I want you to be happy. I want you to have what you want, who you want."

"That's Banner."

"But loving someone is the most selfless thing you can do," August says quietly. "It's not always about what you want *from* that person but what you want *for* them. What's best for them. What makes them the best version of themselves. I'm not saying you're not that for Banner. Hell, I hope you are. I was beginning to worry about you."

"Shut up," I say, relaxing enough to laugh.

"I'm just saying that's a different lens to look at it through, and it changes your perspective."

"You do know that I'm the older brother and am, by all rights, the one who should be doling out sage advice."

"Age ain't nothing but a number."

"Please let Aaliyah rest in peace."

"I will if you will."

"That doesn't make sense."

"Does it have to?"

"August, what?" I laugh because we've been having these point-less conversations most of my life and always when I need them.

"But does it?" He looks like he's pondering life's most important questions instead of some bullshit rabbit trail he's using to take my mind off this mess I'm in with Banner and Zo.

Thankfully, before I can answer, because who knows where that would take us, Susan, Iris, and my father join us in the den. Iris walks over and tucks under August's arm, looping her arms around his waist. My dad takes his usual seat in the recliner, and Susan sits on his knee. They hold hands, and the same tiny diamond he gave her twenty years ago still captures the light and manages to be blinding if it hits you in the eye just right.

"Where's Sarai?" August asks, dropping a kiss on Iris's hair.

"Torturing some stranger with a billion questions." Iris shrugs. "I was just too glad it wasn't me for five minutes. I'm pretty sure it was one of your cousins, though."

"You're *pretty sure*? So our daughter may be gagged and kidnapped by now, is that what you're saying?"

"Definitely gagged," I say, making everyone laugh. "If they take her, believe me, they'll bring her back."

Iris reaches over and punches my arm.

"You know it's true," I tell her, chuckling.

"Only I can talk about her that way." Iris mock-glares at me. "Even if she did ask me to sing 'The Star-Spangled Banner' backward today. That's normal, right?"

"I saw her," Susan interjects. "It was one of your cousins and her little girl. What Sarai needs is a little brother or sister."

"I'm ready," Iris says, widening her eyes meaningfully at August. "Your son is the holdup."

"You say you're ready," August replies, pushing the fall of dark hair away from her face. "Then you're complaining that you can't go to the conferences you want. Or run up to the LA office and do this or do that. We have time. We're young. There's no rush. Do everything you want to do."

"I *want* to have a baby," she says, stretching up on her toes to reach his cheek nearly a foot above her. "And do all of those things, too."

She looks over at me, and her smile dims a little.

"A really smart woman once said I should be unafraid to want it all," she says, grinning and searching my face for a clue to what is up with Banner and me. I'm sure August will fill her in since, apparently, they tell each other everything.

He's so whipped.

I remember Banner saying that at the Denver conference. That she wants to be the best in her field *and* have the husband and four kids. She wants it all, and God help anyone who tries to tell her she can't have it.

Shit. Four kids? Even one like Sarai would drive me out of my mind.

Why is she so Catholic?

What if Banner has those four kids with someone else? What if she ends up with Zo? With some other guy? A better guy?

I leave the room abruptly, suddenly feeling ill surrounded by couples who have the next fifty years all figured out. I haven't seen the woman I want in six weeks, and she's sleeping under the same roof with a guy who is madly in love with her. So in love he forgave her for *fucking* me. And damn it all if I wouldn't do the same because Banners don't just grow on trees. They broke the mold after they made her. I know. In ten years, I haven't found anyone even close, and now that I have a second chance, it feels like I'm losing her again. This Stella won't cut it. I need a real drink because if I think August is whipped, *feeling* this way, what am I?

CHAPTER 35
BANNER

JARED FEATHERS KISSES DOWN MY BACK, LICKING BETWEEN THE fine-boned links of my vertebrae. Barely there touches that tease my skin and whisper over my nerve endings. When he reaches the satin edge of my panties, he tugs them down with his teeth and presses his open mouth over the curves of my ass, suctioning the generous flesh into his mouth and moaning as he marks me. I match him moan for moan as my knees are wrenched apart and cool air hits me where I'm hot and wet between my legs.

I'm on all fours, my face buried in a pillow catching the guttural noises tumbling out of me. A heavy hand caresses my back, long fingers winding into the hair at the base of my neck. He spreads my cheeks, exposing me. I'm unprepared for the wet heat of his mouth at my puckered entrance. It feels too good for me to allow self-consciousness to interfere. Oh, no. I press back into the soft lips and greedy tongue lapping at me. He holds me in place when I squirm and takes his fill.

Pleasure curls around my spine, tightening and lengthening like a coil until the onslaught of sensations makes me spring. It hits me like the morning surf, lifting me so high that I crest and soar and meet the sun. Then I crash, panting for air as the water washes over me, sure that I'm drowning.

"God, Banner."

Jared's voice. It pours over me like hot oil, singeing my skin, leaving me slick.

"Banner."

"*Oh dios mío, sí,*" I mumble.

Oh my God, yes.

"Banner."

Something's off in his voice. It's the wrong kind of desperate. The worst kind of urgent. I claw my way through layers of consciousness until I break the surface of my sleep, groggy and disoriented with a pillow between my legs. I really hope I wasn't humping a pillow. That would be a new low.

"Banner."

It's faint, so faint, but Zo's voice drifts down the hall. The tone is distinct, but I can't place it, for once can't figure out what he needs and have never heard this in his voice. I throw off the covers and the last of my dream and rush down the hall in bare feet and the clothes I fell asleep in.

When I reach Zo's room, I leave my heart at the door, but my body rushes forward, and I think for just a moment I've lost my mind. He's on the floor, motionless.

I'm still asleep. I'm still asleep. I'm still asleep.

I repeat it in my head, like that will make this a horrible dream, but it's too real. The deathly pallor of his face. The pulse at his neck so faint it's crafted from butterfly wings. His breath so shallow it's barely there.

"Zo," I yell and shake him. "Wake up."

Unresponsive.

He's fainted before—extremely low blood pressure is a complication of this disease—but never like this.

"Zo, please wake up." Hearing the fright in my voice shatters my calm, and I'm screaming and shaking and trembling from head to toe. Hot tears, liquid sorrow scalds my cheeks and pools at my neck.

"*Levántate,*" I beg. "*Por favor. Despierta.*"

Get up! Please, wake up.

I look all around the room as if someone will suddenly appear to help me, but the room is empty. On his bedside table, I catch sight of the rosary my mother sent. The one that healed Aunt Valentina. And beside the rosary is Zo's cell phone.

I race to the bed and grab the phone, dialing on autopilot.

"Nine-one-one," the operator answers.

"*¡Ayuda!*" I beg for help, my mind scrambled with panic and relief. "*Por favor ayúdame.*"

"Ma'am, *no hablo español,*" the operator replies, her tone flat and calm. "Is there someone who speaks English?"

"I... I do. I'm sorry. I do. My friend. He's unconscious."

I try to answer all of her questions as calmly, as accurately as I can. Within minutes, the welcome wail of the siren approaches. Zo actually stirs the littlest bit, long eyelashes fluttering against his raw-boned cheeks.

"Banner?" His voice is more a breath than a whisper. He blindly extends his hand even though he doesn't see me, can't know I'm there.

But he does know I'm there and that I always will be.

———

"Banner, I'm fine." Zo's face clearly shows his exasperation. "You're hovering."

"I'm not hovering," I say, standing by the bed...hovering. "I just..."

I look around for something to do and settle on fluffing the pillows propped behind his back and head. What is even the point of fluffing these? I have no idea, but it gives me an excuse to stay in the room with him.

It's been three days since I found him unresponsive here in his bedroom. Between the attack on his kidneys and the constant diarrhea, he can easily become dehydrated. Beyond normal dehydration. He blacks out because his blood pressure drops so low. If not caught in time, it could kill him. I think my heart is still at the threshold of this bedroom where I left it when I ran to him. I fluctuate between paralyzing fear and numbness.

All the *what ifs* torture me. What if I hadn't heard him? What if we hadn't gotten him to the hospital in time? What if it happens again? The nurse was able to double her time here the last few days, but I still slept in here on top of the covers beside him, so afraid I wouldn't hear him calling me.

"At least try to drink a little more of the smoothie." I turn to grab the cup from the bedside table and catch him staring at my ass. "Really, Zo?"

The stern note I try to inject in my voice barely disguises the laughter. It feels like such a typical guy thing to do, and our life has been anything but typical the last two months.

"You're beautiful, Banner," Zo says, running his eyes over me in yoga pants and a tank top. "A man can look, yes?"

"Sure. Whatever." I roll my eyes and proffer the smoothie. "Drink some. You need to hydrate and haven't been eating enough."

"I would eat if I could. Believe me, and my taste buds are shot. Even the things I usually like taste like shit."

He sips some of the smoothie I hold for him. As I'm pulling it back, he surprises me by the move he makes and the strength behind it. With a finger tucked in the waistband of my pants, he pulls me toward him, throwing me off-balance. I fall on the bed, and he leans in to kiss me. Not a gentle kiss. A who-needs-to-breathe kind of kiss. It tastes of vanilla and pineapple. Most of all it tastes like Zo. For a moment I want to just lie back and let it happen, only because it feels familiar. It feels like our old life, the life we had before this disease razed our world, laid everything to waste. And before I broke his heart and betrayed his trust. But that time has passed, and this time isn't simple. It's hard, and even though this would be easy, I won't lie to him anymore.

"Zo," I mumble into the kiss, gently pushing his frail chest. "No. We can't."

He flops back on his pillow, wearing a frown, his jaw sharp with displeasure.

"Have you kept your end of our bargain?" he demands.

"What?" I stand by the bed, dumbfounded that he would even ask me that. "What do you mean?"

"I *mean,* are you fucking your other boyfriend?"

This happens from time to time, a side effect of the drugs. Wild mood swings. I don't know if it's the drugs or if he's just been holding that question back, waiting for the perfect chance to throw the infidelity in my face.

"Nothing to say, Bannini?" he asks, his voice stronger than I've heard it in weeks, reinforced with sarcasm.

"Yes, I have something to say. I don't have a boyfriend. I don't have sex. I don't have an office. I don't have a *life* right now, Zo."

I swing my arm around his bedroom in an angry arc.

"I have this. I have you, my best friend who hates me."

He grabs my hand, refusing to let go when I tug.

"I could never hate you," he says, his tone suddenly quiet and already repentant. "I shouldn't have kissed you. I shouldn't have said that. You've given up everything for me. I know this."

I let loose a frustrated breath. We may both be a little stir-crazy. Other than his appointments and treatments, we don't go out much. With Zo's immunity so compromised, there aren't many allowed in. His diarrhea has been crippling, and the only way he can leave the house is wearing a diaper, an indignity he can suffer only so many times. He's sick as fuck. I'm exhausted, and we're both stumbling through the flames of a hell we can't see the end of.

"There's nowhere else I'd rather be right now, Zo." I clamp my teeth together and stave off the tears I can't afford and that won't stop once they start. "You're my best friend. Nothing will change that."

He grins, even though his eyes are already drooping from the meds that make his nausea and pain bearable.

"It's probably good you stopped me," he slurs. "I would have fallen asleep at second base."

Our fight passes as quickly as it came. We've never been able to remain angry with one another for any amount of time. At least that hasn't changed.

I tiptoe out of the bedroom and close the door behind me. I can get some work done now. Maali is supposed to call in the next hour or so to discuss a few things I've left in her more-than-capable hands. When the phone rings, I assume it's her and don't even check the screen.

"Hello." There's silence on the other end for a beat or two. I'm ready to pull the phone away and check the caller when he speaks.

"Hey, Ban."

My poor, unsuspecting heart is unprepared for his voice. How it releases a fall of feathers in my belly and takes my breath hostage.

"Jared?" My voice sounds high and thin.

"Yeah." He hesitates before going on. "Is it okay that I called?"

God, yes.

"Sure." I bite my lip and search for my cool, my collected, but it's nowhere to be found. "It's good to hear your voice."

"I'm in town."

"Here?" I point to the floor. "In Palo Alto?"

"Yeah. I'd like to see you. Maybe we could meet?"

My hopes, my excitement sink. Fuck my life.

"I can't leave the house right now," I say quietly. "Zo had a rough couple of days, and the nurse isn't coming 'til tomorrow."

"Of course," he says too quickly, like he expected me to shut him down. "I get it. Maybe next time."

"Oh." My mind clamors for something to keep him on the phone a few minutes longer. "So you… You have business here? An appointment or something?"

It's quiet for too long, and for a second I think I've lost him.

"Jared?" I ask again. "You have business here?"

"Just you. I came to see you."

There's something so raw in his voice, and it's like he ripped a page from my heart and is reading it. That he aches with the same loneliness as I do. That maybe he dreams about me, too, and wakes up wishing for our island villa. For the sea breeze. Every night my skin relives his touch and my lips reminisce about his kisses.

"Zo's sleeping," I say softly, hopefully. "You could come over for a few minutes if you like?"

"I have some sponsor contracts for the golf tournament I could say I was dropping off since I was in town," he says. "But are you sure?"

I don't have a boyfriend. I don't have sex. I don't have an office. I don't have a life right now.

The hollow sound of my own words throbs in my ears. I'm closer than I've ever been to breaking. I'm cracking inside, and I'm so afraid of what will come out. Of what I can't hold. I need something.

I need him.

"Yeah," I answer. "Yeah. I'm sure."

CHAPTER 36
JARED

SHE MUST HAVE BEEN WATCHING FOR ME BECAUSE THE DOOR TO the townhouse swings open before I can ring the bell.

"I didn't want to wake Zo," she says by way of explanation.

We stare at one another, absorbing any changes the last two months have wrought. She's not pulled together. Not the boss I'm used to seeing with her suits and stilettos, but she's still Banner. I've seen several incarnations of this woman, but there is this steadfast strength to her, this obstinate light that refuses to dim. It's still easily detected under a messy bun, slightly stained tank top, and yoga pants. She's still my badass girl.

A gust of Northern California wind whips stray strands of dark hair across her face, and she shivers, crosses her arms against the cool breeze.

"Come on in." She steps back, and I follow her into a living room outfitted with a large sectional, low tables, throw rugs, and a mammoth mounted television.

"We have it month to month," she says, licking her pretty lips and looking around the room. "It came furnished."

"Oh yeah?" *Don't give a shit.*

"Yeah." She nods, rubs at the back of her neck, and points a thumb over her shoulder. "It's ideal because there's an office down here and a bedroom. The stairs would be hard for Zo some days. I sleep in the office down here so I'm close if he needs anything."

A shadow passes over her face, and I wonder what he has needed at night to cause that look. This separation has been hard on me, but I wonder, not for the first time, how hard this has all been for her. And I suspect it's worse than I imagined.

"So I work out of one of the upstairs bedrooms," she continues, her voice thinned with nerves. "It works. And I—"

"This isn't what I came for," I interrupt. "This banal thing you're doing. This small talk. All this conversation. It's not what I came for."

She blinks at me, her skin free of makeup, my freckles dusting her nose.

"It's not?" She slides her hands to where back pockets would be, only to grimace when she realizes she's wearing yoga pants. "Um, okay. What-what, then?"

I scope the layout of the room, spot a door leading to what might be a kitchen. I grab her hand and drag her in that direction. The door swings open and closed behind us. A pantry door is cracked enough to show a few shelves of food. I head there, still gripping her hand tightly in mine.

As soon as the pantry door shuts, I'm pressing her into a shelf, one hand at her ass, the other at her neck, holding her steady so I can get inside. I'm literally trembling like an untried boy, like an addict tasting his demon-drug. I'll take Banner any way I can get her. Snorted, smoked, shot in my veins. I want her with marrow-level hunger, the kind you have to dig inside your bones to satisfy. I suck her tongue too hard. I grip her waist too tightly. Every part of me fears this won't last. Knows it can't. And this kiss is not enough. These clothes are in my way. I growl, frustrated to finally have what I want and not be able to get it down fast enough. I shove her tank top up and push my hand under her bra, squeezing her breast, pinching her nipple, reminding her body how this works. How we feel together. I drag the yoga pants and her panties down over the delicious curve of her ass.

Skin. I need it.

I sink to my knees, turn her around, and bite one firm globe, spread her cheeks and swipe my tongue along the puckered ridge.

"Jared," she gasps, bangs her forehead to the shelf. "Jesus."

I follow the line of her ass with my fingers until I reach her pussy, wet and empty. Waiting. My mouth waters when I stroke her clit, when it grows plump and slick under my attention. Her muffled moans spur me on. She spreads her legs, silently begging me to penetrate. One finger. Two fingers. Three fingers pushing in, caressing her pussy walls while she humps my hand.

"Oh, God," she cries out. "We have to stop."

"No." I want to take her with him just yards away.

"Jared, please." Tears fill her voice. "I don't want to do this again. I can't lie to him. I can't hurt him. Not… Not now—"

Her words trail off, break.

"Please."

My fingers go still inside her, and with his usual bad timing, August's voice speaks in my head.

The things you love about her—the good, the compassion, the sense of right and wrong—will all be deconstructed and set aside for you.

And I can't do it. As much as the animal inside me wants to fuck her right under his nose, wants to punish Zo for keeping her from me, I can't do it. Because to do it to him is to do it to her, and I can't.

I rest my forehead against the bare curve of her ass and release a heavy sigh. Resignation. Deprivation. With one last kiss on her butt, my fingers slip out of her. She leans against the shelf, looking down at me with wet eyes, with spiky lashes.

"Thank you," she whispers, brushing away her tears.

I nod, but unable to resist one more sensual act of defiance, I shove three fingers, shiny and wet and pussy-scented, into my mouth and lick every drop of her from them, holding her eyes with mine the whole time until she closes hers, shuddering and biting her lip.

"I miss your pussy," I say abruptly.

Her eyes pop open, and a startled laugh floats past her kiss-swollen lips.

"You're not supposed to say that," she chides, adjusting her clothes, reluctant affection in her eyes.

I tug on her hand and bring her down to the pantry floor with me. I scoot until my back is against a wall and she's seated between my bent knees, her head resting on my shoulder.

"You're supposed to say romantic things," she continues, glancing up and grinning at me. "Not 'I miss your pussy.'"

"What kinds of romantic things should I say?" I lift the fine hairs curling at her temple. "Should I say that I think about you all the time?"

She goes still against me, long lashes lowered and painting shadows under her eyes.

"That would be a good start," she says.

"Or that I actually watched *An Affair to Remember* because it made me think of our night at the drive-in?" I confess. "That I dream about us waking up together? Or that every time I see a sunset, I think of that orange dress you wore the night we had dinner on the island?"

Wide, espresso-colored eyes find mine over her shoulder, and her smile grows.

Our stare holds until the moment smolders and the air grows smoky with lust and need and something much too tender for me to keep dismissing or misnaming it.

She tips back and presses a kiss to my lips, and it's so sweet, so pure, when she pulls back I palm her head and hold her there for a few seconds longer. Not to deepen it or to ask for more but to record it. To save the feel of her lips on mine just this way.

"You taste like pineapple," I say against her mouth. "You hate pineapple."

It's a silly thing to notice, and I'm not even sure why I said it or why she looks guilty, lowering her lashes with cheeks flushed.

"I… Yeah. I do hate pineapple."

"You made an exception?" I trace her thick brows with one finger.

"Um…not really." She blows out a quick sigh before meeting my eyes. "Zo likes pineapple in this smoothie I make for him."

I lift my brows, silently encouraging her to go on, to explain how this all fits together.

"He…well, he kissed me earlier."

My teeth clamp down, and my hand curls into a fist on the pantry floor.

"Jared, it's not what you think. It's a long story."

"One that ends with his tongue in your mouth?"

"Nothing's been going on," she assures me, pushing my hair back from my face, sinking her fingers in at the roots the way she knows I like. "It was a moment of weakness."

"His or yours?"

"Maybe both." She shrugs, her eyes weary. "Not me wanting him that way but feeling…I don't know, bad that I don't?"

"It doesn't help when you tell me shit like this." I rub my tired eyes.

"This is an impossible situation," she says softly. "But, Jared, what do you want me to do?"

"You don't want to know what I want, and I won't tell you because you'll think I'm mean and selfish."

She dusts her fingers over my cheeks, my chin, over my mouth like she's soothing me. I hate that if we sit here long enough, it'll start working. I trap her fingers against my mouth.

"Maybe not," she finally replies with a sad smile. "Sometimes when the day is filled with things I don't want to do, wouldn't choose but *have* to, I just look in the mirror and say out loud all the things I would do if it were up to me."

"And this helps?" *Because I doubt it.*

"It does. I just say it, even if it's awful, and I don't judge it. Then I go and do the right thing. I know it sounds silly."

"It does sound silly."

She leans forward, almost teasing me with a look—but not quite because this is so hard, and she probably senses how close I am to doing something stupid.

"But you haven't tried it," she says. "What could it hurt? Try it. Just tell me what you want. No matter how bad it sounds. I promise I won't judge."

"You don't get to judge?"

"No, I don't get to judge, but when you're done, when it's out of your system, we do the *have to* thing. The right thing."

"Okay. You want to hear what I want. Here goes. I want you to leave him and come to me. I'm not assigning right or wrong to it. I'm just telling you that every night when I'm in my bed alone, I keep hoping you'll show up at my door. And you'll tell me that I'm it for you. That nothing else is as important to you as I am. Because I'm saying that to you. I'm telling you that nothing else is as important to me as you are."

It's as close as I've come to confessing what's getting harder to deny every day, to keep calling it something else, but I'm still not ready to say it, not with Zo holding all these cards. All of the advantages.

"Oh, Jared, I—"

"No, listen. I want you to leave him and come to me, but the irony is I want you so badly because you never would. Your heart, integrity, strength of character... They draw me to you."

I pause to cup her face in my hands.

"And I..." I cough, clear my throat, and search for a word to settle on. "I *care* too much about you to corrupt that."

She scoots in closer and wraps her arms around me, tucking her head under my chin. She's so warm and soft and good and sweet, and she smells like her Pretty Pastel dryer sheets.

"I care about you, too, Jared," she says softly. "If I could do what I feel is right and still be with you right now, I would. I hope you believe that."

A distant ring robs me of my chance to answer. She scrambles to her feet, adjusting her yoga pants as she goes.

"That'll be Maali," she says, regret in her voice. "I have to catch this call. A couple of my guys have contracts on the bubble."

She opens the pantry door, letting the world back in.

"Okay." I haul myself to stand and follow her from the pantry and out of the kitchen.

"Give me a few minutes." She looks at me from the foot of the stairs, her expression uncertain. "Wait here?"

I nod my agreement and sit to stew in frustration. I tip my head back on the couch and try to evict images of him kissing her from my brain. I'm too tired, though, to exert that much mental energy, and I paint a full scene in my head with him touching her, taking her. A weary sigh is all I can manage. I wrapped up a shit-ton of stuff so I could afford the day off up here. I just got on a plane. Didn't call or ask in case she told me not to come. I've been going out of my mind missing her and being horny.

Okay. And jealous. Of a dying man. I know it's insanity, but hearing that he actually kissed her brings my concerns to life.

"Jared."

I open my eyes when my name is called. Zo is standing at the doorway leading down the hall. I fix my face, disguising my shock at how wasted away he has become. I've seen him on television and in a few photos since his diagnosis, but it's been a while. He's still tall, of course, a few inches taller than I am, but he's painfully thin. He holds a mask over the gauntness of his face and studies me with brows drawn together.

"Zo, hey." I sit up, but assume from the mask I shouldn't get too close.

"Why are you here?" he asks with, unless I'm mistaken, some underlying hostility. I'm not usually mistaken about someone wanting to kick my ass. I pick up on that kind of thing.

"Uh...I just dropped off some papers."

"From LA?" Skepticism and irritation clearly mark the visible half of his face.

"I was in town." I shrug and lean forward, elbows on knees. "Hope it isn't a problem."

His face relaxes. Maybe he realized he's scowling at me.

"No, of course not." He walks farther into the room, takes a seat a few feet away, and pulls the mask off. "After all, I understand you and Banner go way back."

I'm not sure what she's told him, so I just nod, keeping my face neutral.

"So how are you feeling?" I ask.

"Like each of my organs is systematically being attacked."

"Sorry." I twist my lips, self-deprecating. "I guess that was a dumb question. I can't imagine what you're going through."

"It would be a thousand times worse without Banner." A tiny smile crooks the sober line of his mouth. "She takes good care of me."

He watches me through a veil of thick lashes camouflaging his thoughts.

"I'd probably already be dead were it not for her. Loyalty like hers…" He shakes his head and looks down at his hands. "A woman like Banner comes once in a lifetime."

I don't acknowledge his statement with anything other than a steady stare, giving nothing away. Our eyes lock, and I drop mine first. Even I'm not interested in a staring contest with a dying man.

"So you were at Kerrington with Banner, yes?"

"Yeah. We were there together."

"I wish I could have seen her in college." His smile is easy and affectionate. "I met her as she was about to graduate, during her internship."

"With Bagley, right? When she signed you."

"It was more like I signed *her*," he says wryly. "I recognized her potential right away. Was she the smartest girl then, too? Back in college?"

My shoulders drop, the muscles relaxing at the prospect of an easy topic: Banner being awesome.

"Absolutely." I smile involuntarily, recalling Banner in college. So single-minded and earnest. "She was brilliant."

"She claims she was…what is the word?" He seems to search his mind. "I have chemo brain and sometimes can't find the right phrase when I need it. Frumpy? Is that it?"

"Frumpy?" I chuckle. "I guess you could say that. She dressed very differently, that's for sure."

"But that didn't make a difference to you, did it?" He sits back and links spindly fingers over his frail torso. "You didn't think she was frumpy, did you, Foster?"

The smile lingering from my amusement dries up, too, and we're left considering each other, both of us tight-lipped.

"No, I didn't think Banner was frumpy," I finally agree. "I thought she was…" I hesitate to go on, not sure what I'll reveal, give away.

"Beautiful?" he finishes softly.

I glance up to find him watching me closely.

"Yeah." I free my voice of emotion. "She was beautiful."

"So you wanted her then, too?"

I don't allow myself to respond for a moment but glance up the stairs, wondering how close Banner is and if she'll hear what's about to go down.

"Excuse me?" I ask.

"I said so you've always wanted Banner?" His face may be neutral, but his eyes proclaim anger.

I prefer gloves off anyway, so I won't bother lying to him. He wants this conversation, we can have it. It's overdue.

"Since the first time I saw her, I wanted her, yeah."

"And you're one of those men who just takes what he wants, huh? Even if she belongs to someone else?"

"Banner's never belonged to anyone else." I try to soften the declaration into an apology, but I want to be clear where I stand and what I believe. "Not really."

In case he's confused.

"I would beg to differ," he says stiffly. "Since she is my girlfriend."

Was!

I want to stand over him and shout the past tense.

I want to tell him I had her first and I've had her since and he was just the dash between. An ellipsis that should never have happened.

While we stare at one another, I don't think of his illness or his mortality or how pissed off Banner will be if I upset him. I only see a threat, an obstacle between me and what I want most.

"I know it was you, the one she betrayed me with." Even shrunken there is command in his voice, in the look he gives me. "You can't have her."

"I already have her," I answer simply, not even bothering to deny my role in their breakup.

Rage sparks in his tired eyes. "Fucking her once doesn't make her yours."

Once?

What about a dozen times? A dozen ways?

On every surface? In every corner?

Eating her pussy until she weeps?

What will it take, Zo, for you to accept that she's mine? Just tell me. I've probably already done it.

Would you like to taste her on my fingers right now?

I want to say it all but remain silent. It feels wrong sitting here discussing her with him. I don't want to be in his house, and I don't want Banner here either. At least one of us can go.

"Tell Banner I had to leave." I stand and head for the door. "I don't think it's the right time for this conversation."

"When should we have it?" he asks. "After I'm dead? Is that what you're hoping for? Biding your time, are you?"

I study his sunken eyes and his diminished frame. It sparks a memory, an unwanted one that I don't often revisit. My mother in bed, choosing to die at home with "her boys." With my father and me. I see her dragging herself to sit up against the pillows and check-ing my homework with her birdlike fingers and her scarf-wrapped head and her bloodless lips. That damn helplessness I always feel overtakes me for a nanosecond. Helpless then because I couldn't stop what was happening, and helpless now because nothing I do will ever be enough to bring her back. And I wonder if Zo feels helpless. He said he's in the fight of his life, and I see it. That battle-weary look, fighting off death itself, that's how my mother looked.

"No. I hope you beat this thing," I finally answer him, shrugging casually, my throat burning. He wouldn't appreciate my pity, so I say what I would want to hear. "We should make it…what did you call it? A fair fight?"

He laughs, a deep, vibrant sound that seems too big for his emaciated body.

"It drives you mad that I convinced her not to be with you, doesn't it? That she chose me over you. You're worried she'll choose me when it comes down to it, and you're right to worry because she will."

It comes rushing back, my resentment and anger. I grab it with eager hands, badly needing to feel something other than the old grief gripping my heart.

"I never would have pegged you as a man to exploit your sickness that way."

He sobers, his eyes going dull again.

"You think you are the only one who will do anything to keep her?"

He stands slowly, as if each inch off the couch pains him. I stop myself from reaching down to help. The proud set of his bony shoul-ders tells me his rival's assistance wouldn't be appreciated. I can't blame him. He follows me to the door and will probably be as glad to close it behind me as I will be to leave. I draw in a lungful of fresh air as soon as I'm on the porch.

"I would say may the best man win," I say with him standing in the door, waiting to shut me out. "But we both know you're a better man than I am, and I have no intention of losing her."

"Neither did I. Things change quickly. You should remember that." He glances back into the townhouse before looking back to me. "It would distress Banner to know I figured out it was you. What do you say we keep this between us?"

"How did you know?" I'm not making any promises about harboring a secret with him.

A wry grin quirks his mouth. "You came to the house that night with some trumped-up excuse about a meeting."

I frown, reviewing my actions. Every word I can remember from that visit and don't recall anything that would have given away my feelings. Or my intentions.

"It was the way you looked at her," he answers my unspoken question.

"How did I look at her?"

He slips the mask back over his face to keep the germs at bay, and his answer is muffled but to me crystal clear.

"You looked at her the way I do."

CHAPTER 37
BANNER

"I'M NOT SURE THIS IS A GOOD IDEA, ZO."

I consider the crowded auditorium, packed wall to wall with the best and brightest of the sports world.

"Bannini, I'm fine." He places my hand in the crook of his elbow. "Matter of fact, I feel better than I have in months."

It's probably true, but I don't trust it. Zo finished his three months of chemo. Our things are on their way back to LA from Palo Alto, but we came ahead by a few days to attend the Copeez, an awards show sponsored by SportsCo, the largest sports channel behind ESPN. They're honoring Zo tonight during the ceremony and have asked him to speak. He'll receive the Jimmy V Award for Perseverance at the ESPYs. He's already attended two fundraising dinners since we came back. It's a lot, and I just hope it's not too much too soon.

"You worry too much." Zo bends to kiss my hair. "Besides, we will show these people that I'm still alive."

"You don't have anything to prove to anyone."

He shrugs philosophically.

"Maybe I prove it to myself." He grins and runs appreciative eyes over me from head to toe, starting at my loose chignon, drifting over my tight dress, and ending on the expensive shoes that may kill me before this night is over. "If nothing else, it's a good excuse to show you off. We make a handsome couple, don't you think?"

I don't correct his use of the word "couple." Everyone here, everyone in the world assumes we're a couple, and we haven't corrected their misconception. Too complicated and no one's business but ours.

And Jared's.

I glance around the large room, eyes peeled for any sign of him. We haven't talked as much as I would have hoped the last month of our exile up at Stanford. When I came back down from my call with Maali, he was gone, and Zo was there. He said Jared had gotten an urgent call and had to leave. I didn't question it, and one of the few times I spoke with Jared after that, he confirmed that he was just pulled away by a client emergency. The two of them in a room together raised all my red flags. Something has felt different between Jared and me. I want to ask Zo if he and Jared talked at any length, if maybe he said something to him, but Jared is the last subject I want to discuss with Zo. Things are complicated enough.

"Do you see your family yet?" Zo asks, craning his neck to scan the crowd.

"No, but Mama called from the road to say they got stuck in traffic. A bad accident has lanes shut down, but they're on the way."

I glance at my watch and frown.

"They may miss your speech at this rate."

We start toward our seats, and it takes forever because everyone wants to stop and talk to us, to ask Zo how he's doing, tell him how good he looks, ask when he'll be back on the court. I just want to shoo them all away. His immune system is still recovering, and I pray being around this many people so soon doesn't make him sick.

I'm waiting for him to tactfully close a conversation with a journalist who has been hounding us for an interview when I spot Kenan coming from the direction of the greenroom. He probably walked the red carpet, which Zo and I opted not to do. Loath to leave Zo alone with this pushy hack, I wave Kenan over.

His stern features and imposing physicality lead most to believe he's a hard-ass. They're not wrong on many counts, but his heart—so tender.

"How are you?" I reach up for a hug. "I feel like we haven't talked all summer."

"You handed me over to that junior agent," he accuses with no heat. He was one of the clients I felt comfortable temporarily offloading. His contract is set for the next two years, and he intentionally pulled back from everything except the golf tournament to focus on the situation with his daughter and his ex-wife.

"How are things going with the custody battle?" I ask.

"Pretty good. Bridget has..."

Kenan stops mid-sentence, the intensity of his gaze fixed over my shoulder. I glance in that direction to see what has arrested his attention. It's not a what but a *who*. A beautiful woman stares back at him unblinkingly. She's slim, with skin like whipped cocoa. Her platinum-blond pixie cut and the bohemian flair to her formal dress distinguish her from everyone around her. She's not famous as far as I can recall, but there is something almost hypnotic about her presence. I tear my eyes away and look back to Kenan, who is still fixated on her. When I glance back over my shoulder, she has turned away and is talking to a little girl who looks vaguely familiar.

"Who is that, Kenan?" I punch his shoulder when he still doesn't answer. "Earth to Kenan. Who is that woman you were ogling?"

He narrows his eyes at me. Kenan isn't an easy guy to tease, but he allows me to do it every once in a while. "What woman?"

"Really?" I ask, slanting him a disbelieving look. "The little fairy over there you couldn't take your eyes off. Who is she?"

He stares at me for a few more seconds, like he's weighing if he'll regret whatever he shares.

"Her name is Lotus," he offers reluctantly.

"Well, she should either go out with you or file a restraining order."

His deep-timbered chuckle has me smiling, too. The smile slowly melts from his handsome face.

"She's not checking for me. Won't give me the time of day."

"Surely you won't let *that* stop you?" I challenge. "Not Kenan 'The Gladiator' Ross."

He rolls his eyes, but his stare drifts back in her direction. I hazard one more glance and lose all my air. The little girl with her who looked vaguely familiar is Sarai, August and Iris's daughter I met at the basketball game. Now August and Iris have joined her, along with Jared.

And his date.

Well, I assume the woman is his date. She is more Cindy than the original Cindy ever was. Blonder. Thinner. Prettier. Absolutely perfect. Jealousy claws through my veneer of civilization, and I want to tear her hair from its naturally blond roots. Her Scandinavian beauty taunts me, reminds me she fits his mold and is his type in a way I'll never be. I turn my head before he catches me staring at him and this dime-store goddess he picked up and brought in. We haven't talked much, but when we have, he was very clear about waiting. About still being there once Zo's chemo was done and we could assess where he stands. Zo's initial anger and bitterness have passed. I'm positive he'll let me help him where needed, even if I'm dating someone else, but maybe Jared has moved on and didn't know how to tell me.

"Ready?" Zo asks, then speaking to Kenan when he realizes I was in a conversation. "Kenan, good to see you."

They exchange pleasantries and catch up on Zo's health while I itch to run from this place screaming. If it weren't for Zo's speech, I would do just that. I don't look Jared's way, but even peripherally I can see them both gleaming and golden like the awards being handed out tonight, perfect under the bright lights. I've felt an awareness every time I've been in the same room with Jared, like we share some telepathic connection, even when I didn't want it to be that way. I don't feel that now, don't feel his attention. Maybe it's completely fixed on her.

"Can we go in now, Zo?" I ask, controlling my voice so it doesn't shake. "Please?"

"Of course." He takes my hand, and I don't even resist. I've been careful to draw the lines clearly when we are alone. The world can think what it wants about what we are to each other. Zo and I know that we are just friends now, even though he shows me he wants more every chance he gets. He and I know the truth.

And I thought Jared knew the truth. I thought he *was* my truth, but maybe it was all just a lie I told myself and he let me believe.

I sit through the first awards, numb and stiff, cognizant of Jared sitting with Cindy 2.0 a few rows ahead. He never once turns to look back at me. Or for me. Maybe he doesn't even know I'm here.

When they come to Zo's award, I afford him my complete focus, watching for signs of weakness or that he's tired himself out. He walks onstage obviously frail but regal, the league statesman he has always been and more. The audience is on its feet for a standing ovation that seems to go on forever before he says one word. The whole room is charged with emotion and support for this man who has done so much for so many.

He waves them down to their seats with a smile. He takes his place at center stage and talks about his journey, how important it was to remain positive, thanking everyone for their support, and even how it's not over and there is so much road ahead. I'm as proud as if it were me up on that stage.

And then it is.

"And I literally would not be here," Zo says after a few minutes, "were it not for Banner Morales."

My name from the stage startles me, and my face flames when I realize the camera and so many eyes have turned on me. I try to look natural, which never really works. *Trying* to look natural.

"Banner, come." Zo beckons me with a hand, his eyes burning with emotion and gratitude.

I want to shake my head vigorously like a kid refusing her

vegetables, but I cannot do that, not to Zo who stands bravely in front of all these people, literally a shell of himself, his body a husk for the boundless, soaring spirit still fighting inside. So I stand and I walk, gingerly picking my way down the row, conscious of the fact that I haven't been able to work out as regularly or as intensely and have put on a few pounds. Wondering how square and wide my ass might look with the wrong camera angle. Regretting that I didn't wear Spanx. Wishing I had worn something less revealing and wondering if the girls will stay safely tucked into the bodice of this form-fitting dress. And, of course, praying these high-ass heels don't fail me now and dump me unceremoniously on the stairs as I make my way to the stage.

The lights are so bright, and I'm reminded why I never wanted to be on this side of fame but have always been happy shoving others into the spotlight and onto center court.

"I would not be alive without this woman," Zo says, blinking at tears, a rare show of public emotion. "This award is ours, Bannini."

He never calls me that in public, and the word drips with intimacy because no one else in this building understands the significance of it. I study his face closely, and beneath the emotion lies calculation. He holds the trophy in one hand, but the other circles my waist possessively.

"I humbly accept this award on behalf of myself and the woman who has been my greatest blessing. Who has been my angel." He looks down at me from his great height. The chemo, the pain, the hell he has suffered left its mark on a face that has always been strikingly handsome. Now the lines of character etched there, the hard-won wisdom make him even more attractive even with a ravaged body. I see his spirit in his eyes and his passion for life.

For me.

"*Te amo*," he says, eyes fixed on me like I'm the light at the end of a very dark tunnel.

The room fills with "awwws" at his romantic declaration. A

public declaration he shouldn't be making, considering he and I both know the state of our relationship. This smile feels like drying plaster on my face, but I look up to meet his eyes, only to find him staring out at the audience, that same calculation sharpened to a point, loaded with dislike. I follow his stare to find out who has displeased him, who bears the brunt of that look.

It's Jared.

His eyes are glacial blue, iced with an answering look so loaded with malevolence I instinctively want to shield Zo from it. But I don't know whom to protect, him or Zo. They stare at one another like this is a contest of war instead of an awards ceremony. And then in sync, they both turn their eyes to me like I'm the prize.

Confusion, anger, hurt war under my serene expression. In a daze, I incline my head and smile appropriately through yet another standing ovation. Finally, Zo leads me backstage, still clutching both of his prizes: the award and me. As soon as we leave the glare of the stage and the scrutiny of thousands of people, I jerk away.

"*¿Qué fue eso?*" I ask in a voice low enough that the nearby stage-hands won't hear.

"What was what?" he replies in kind, but I know him so well. He knows exactly what I'm asking.

"How long have you known?" I ask, tears burning my throat. Shame choking me. Anger forcing me to speak.

"That it was Jared?" he asks softly.

Hearing him confirm it frees a sob from the cage of my throat. I cover my mouth to catch it, but it's loud in the close quarters backstage. Several people turn to look at me, to look at us. Zo guides us into a shadowy corner.

"I've always known it was him," Zo says in a voice of steel. "I knew it was him before it happened."

"Before it happened? What does that mean? What are you saying? Did you say something to him?"

"Does it matter?" Zo snaps. "If you have not noticed, he is

not alone here tonight. I knew the wait would kill his so-called feelings. He won't be faithful to you, Bannini. You must see that he is not for you. You and I, we make sense. You, him… It's not right. It never was."

His words only reinforce what the small, knowing voice has told me ever since freshman orientation when I offered Jared a pencil and he turned away without a second look. I blink up at Zo stupidly for a few seconds, processing too many things at once. What he did onstage. Him knowing about Jared. Jared showing up with my polar opposite. It's all too much. I grab the hem of my floor-sweeping dress and walk briskly away from him.

"Banner!" he calls after me.

"Don't." I put up a hand to ward him off without looking back. "Just give me a minute."

But I don't get a minute, no reprieve. As soon as I round the corner, Jared stands there waiting in his fits-like-a-glove tuxedo, hair brushed down and tamed to dull gold.

"Ban, we need to talk."

His voice, the very sight of him, fans hope in my chest for an instant—until I remember the Cindy he brought tonight and hear Zo's words again, yet another reminder that we don't belong together. Yet another time I'm not sure what to trust. Conscious of all the people around us, I press my lips tight to hold back the emotion threatening to spill over and march past him without saying a word.

The sign for restrooms hangs overhead, glowing like the North Star, and I follow the light toward the ladies' room. It's empty, but I don't stop until I'm in the last handicap stall. I lean against the wall and surrender to my tears. I can't even track their source. Is it the stunt Zo pulled, the public declaration of love from a saint which will only make it harder for me to leave him, will only invite public scorn? Is it the Cindy on Jared's arm tonight, looking like his perfect match? Is it the shame of Zo knowing I fucked Jared? Of him having a face, a name, a person to pair with my betrayal? Is it fear that, despite his strong showing tonight, I could still lose my best friend to an incurable death? It's all those things, and under the crushing weight, I sink to the bathroom floor and weep. Silent, hot tears springing from every problem, every hurt, every close call, every stolen kiss, every single thing in my life that has gone wrong—all at once. The cork pops, and as I knew they would, the tears overflow and won't stop.

"Banner."

Oh, God. Please not now.

"Ban, I know you're in here." Jared's voice is getting closer. I hear him opening stalls, searching for me. It's only a matter of time. Soon I'll see his feet in the space under the door. As best I can, I stuff the tears back into that black-hole bottle and pull myself up, braced for the battle I never seem to stop fighting. The battle to resist Jared Foster. When he flings the door open, I'm ready.

"This is the ladies' room," I say, glaring at him, clinging to the image of Cindy 2.0 on his arm. "I can't believe you followed me in here."

"I can't believe you thought I wouldn't." He locks the stall door, stalking toward me in the space shrinking with every inch he closes between us.

"You can't be here." I fold my arms under my breasts, conscious of how my cleavage is on display. His eyes drop to my chest, the glacial blue heating, wanting.

Hell no.

"I *am* here," he replies with a calm I know to be false. A muscle twitches in his jaw. His hands are knotted into fists in his well-tailored pants. "And you will talk to me."

"Go talk to your date," I snap, turning away from him, facing the diaper-changing station.

He grabs my arm and wrenches me around.

"No, you don't get to do that," he says, rage burning like a gas light in his eyes. "Not when I just had to sit through the league's patron saint telling the whole world he loves you. Had to watch him *claim* you in front of everyone and couldn't do a damn thing about it."

"Jared—"

"Haven't been able to do anything about it for months."

"Haven't fucked for months, don't you mean?" I fire back, jerking my arm from his grasp. "Isn't that what she's about? Your new Cindy? I said I didn't expect you to wait, but you could have at least told me so I didn't have to find out this way."

"Find out what exactly?" His voice drops to subzero, and his expression is the face of a cliff. "That I'm signing a Swedish soccer player who wanted to attend the awards tonight? Is that what I was supposed to tell you?"

My righteous indignation sputters, shrivels.

"What?" I ask dazedly, wondering if I've gotten it all wrong or if he's just that convincing.

"As for *fucking*," he grits out, "I haven't slept with another woman. Haven't wanted anyone else since you came back into my life. I haven't kissed anyone else. Can you say the same? 'Cause you tasted like him last time I saw you."

"I told you—"

"You haven't told me shit, Banner." With one impatient hand, he disrupts the neatness of his hair and paces in the small stall. "Except that you had to do this and I couldn't see you and he was more important."

"He was fighting for his life, Jared."

"I get that, but he used it to keep you close, to keep you away from me, and I resent him for it. He was playing his own game. He knew it was me all along. He told me so when I was there."

"I realized that tonight. Why didn't you tell me?"

He shrugs, discomfort twisting his expression.

"He said it would distress you, only make it harder, and I believed him. I knew you wouldn't leave him while he still needed you, and I agreed that it would only create more tension."

He cups my face between his hands, his eyes losing some of the ice, warming with affection, with passion.

"I should have told you," he says softly. "I wanted him to know from the beginning anyway."

I nod, leaning into the warm strength of his hands.

"I've always known how to play the game, Ban. Always calculated what every move would yield and how I would come out the winner." He shakes his head, helplessness foreign on his face. "But I didn't know how to do this, how to handle wanting you for so long and then losing you again to someone we both know deserves you more than I do."

And his words, so untrue, crystallize the truth for me.

We *are* a match, an unlikely perfect pair.

Neither of us fully seeing our worth. Not fully comprehending that our hearts were stitched together from the beginning with threads invisible to everyone else. With bonds that didn't make sense to anyone but us—and sometimes not even to ourselves. Me thinking he deserved someone with a better outside and him thinking I deserved someone with a better inside. When all along we deserved each other. And in that instant my heart puts words to this feeling that's been growing and evolving and persisting ever since I saw the most beautiful boy on campus at freshman orientation. My heart articulates something I've been afraid of because I thought he couldn't ever possibly fully reciprocate.

I love him.

Not in spite of his flaws. Not because he's handsome. Not *even though* he is a ruthless bastard. I just love him, exactly as he is. If he never changes. If he never sees things my way. If he never gets better. He is exactly what I want and how I want him right now. And the liberty of that, of not needing the one you love to be something else and *finally believing* that he wants you just as you are…that the constancy of his desire through years, fluctuating dress sizes, and barrier after barrier he keeps knocking down to get to you is real.

That you can trust his passion. That his desire is authentic and, even though he's sometimes a black-hearted man, what he feels for you is pure. Who would chase something as hard as Jared has chased me if he didn't want it badly?

"Kiss me," I whisper, training my eyes on him. "I want to taste like you."

A warning flare fires in his eyes.

"Banner, you can't say things like that to me wearing this dress and looking the way you do tonight."

God, and here I was fretting over my wide, square ass. Concerned about my Spanx-less jiggles, and he is looking at me like I'm his last supper. I turn my head to kiss one palm framing my face and then to kiss the other. I suck at the warm skin of his wrist, pulling the pounding pulse between my teeth, feeling his life blood throb against my tongue.

"Jesus, Ban," he rasps, sliding his other hand down to my waist, skimming over my well-rounded curves, cupping my ass. "I'm horny as hell right now. We probably shouldn't. I won't be able to stop."

I reach down to grip the rigid line of his cock in his pants.

"Who said you'd have to stop?"

"But Zo—"

"Knows it was you," I say, tipping up to kiss his neck. "He finished his chemo last week and will not stop me from helping him if I need to, no matter what comes next."

He swallows convulsively, shuts his eyes tightly.

"I don't want your reputation ruined," he says, concern sketched between his dark-blond brows. "I know I said I didn't care if you cheated, but I don't want people thinking you're anything other than the incredible woman you are. What you've done for Zo...I don't deserve you."

"But you'll have me anyway, right?" I remind him of his own words.

"I have no choice," he says hoarsely. "I love you."

That word. The one I just assigned to the desperate, persistent, stubborn passion lodged in my heart for him. Hearing it on his lips steals any doubts I have.

"And I love you, Jared Foster." I speak the words against his mouth, breathe them into him so he'll believe me. "Exactly as you are."

Hearing the same acceptance from me that I see in him, hear from him, opens the cage door on the passion he's checked, at my request, for the last three months.

"Exactly as I am, huh?" He dips to grab the hem of my dress and drags it up over my legs, the cool air electrically charged with every new inch of me he reveals. He thrusts sure fingers inside my thong. There's no fumbling or searching. Jared could find my clit in a cave. I'm already wet and swollen. He drops his forehead to mine, his breath heavy and hot over my lips.

"Hallelujah," he whispers. "This pussy has made a believer out of me."

My quick laugh bounces off the bathroom walls.

"You can't say that. It's borderline blasphemous."

"As long as we don't cross the line, and I think I've had about enough of you telling me what I can and cannot say about a pussy that is mine." He smiles down at me, the same wicked man he's been since our days at Kerrington, but there's a new contentment in his eyes.

"It is yours," I agree, my smile fading. "I am, too."

"Dammit," he mutters into my hair, slides his mouth over my jaw, down my neck. "I don't want anyone to catch us, for them to talk trash about you."

"You let me worry about my reputation." I chase his mouth until I catch it, kiss it. Own it the way he owns mine. We moan and growl into the kiss, with my hands tugging his shirt from the waistband of his pants. He digs his fingers into my upswept hair, and cool strands brush my bare skin as they fall. He hoists my skirt higher, and I hear a seam tear.

"Face the wall." His voice is harsh. Insistent.

"Oh, God, hurry." I turn, panting against the wall. I'm wet between my legs, and my nipples are like quarters, hard and round under the tight dress.

The sound of his zipper is Pavlovian, and my pussy drips like he pulled a lever, a conditioned response to the sensual prompt. My hands flatten on the wall, ass angled for him, so ready for him, when my fantasy morphs into my worst nightmare, frame by frame.

"Banner!" The voice comes stridently. "*¿Dónde estás?*"

This cannot be happening.

"Mama?" I bang my head on the bathroom wall.

"Your *mom?*" Jared hisses. He drops my dress and hastily zips his pants.

"*Sí, Madre.*" I'm blinking furiously, frantically righting my dress and running fingers through my half-up, half-down 'do. "How do I look?" I whisper.

He grimaces, rubs a thumb over my cheek like he's trying to remove a smear. "Like I already fucked you."

"Banner!" Mama says. "I know you are in here. I can hear you!"

Dios.

"I'm coming, Mama."

"So I heard," she says, accusation lacing the words.

I open the door to face my mirror image, thirty years older, several inches shorter, and forty pounds plumper. Fire and condemnation blaze in the dark eyes that flick from me to Jared.

"Who are you?" she demands.

Jared shoots me a quick glance. "I'm—"

"Not Alonzo," she snaps. "That's who you are. Banner, your fiancé needs you."

"Mama, you know we are not engaged," I say wearily. "Is he okay?"

"Oh, *now* you are concerned?" Her voice is a whip biting into my flesh. "*¡Dios mío!* What have I done? Where did I go wrong to raise a *puta* when Alonzo deserves a queen?"

The insult stings, but I don't let it sink all the way to my heart. I know she will regret it later. I inherited my temper from her. I'm intimately acquainted with the remorse that comes with cooler blood.

"What did she call you?" Jared asks, anger pulling his features tight. "What did you call her?"

"She is my daughter. I call her what I like."

"Not when I'm standing right here you won't," Jared fires back, undeterred and unaware that my mother is a brush fire in a fight and will burn you to the ground.

"Stop it, both of you." I press a hand to my forehead. "Zo, Mama. Is he okay?"

"He was feeling light-headed and tired."

Light-headed. The memory of him unresponsive on the bedroom floor splatters across my mind, and all my fears, all the *what ifs* I hoped were behind us, at least for now, with the last chemo treatment, come rushing back.

"Oh, God." I take off, jerking the hem of my dress up enough to shuffle-run from the bathroom.

I spot Zo standing a few feet away, surrounded by people who have no idea what is happening, but I know right away. The pallor of his skin. The sweat beading his brow.

"Bannini," he mutters, eyes rolling to the back of his head. He sways like a giant redwood tree, reaching for me blindly before he falls and hits the ground.

"No!" It bellows from somewhere outside me. I can't even place where that scream originated, even though my throat aches from the force of it. "Call 911! Now!"

I go down with him, cradling his head in my lap and counting each shallow breath. There's usually medical emergency staff on-site at events like this. I pray I'm right.

"Zo, wake up." I tap his cheek. "Come on. Please wake up."

"Ma'am, we've got him." A paramedic presses his way through the crowd. "What can you tell us?"

"It's his blood pressure," I say quickly, swiping the tears from my cheeks. "It's dangerously low. He just finished a round of chemo. He has amyloidosis, and he's dehydrated. He needs to be flushed with fluids immediately or his organs will start shutting down. He follows a very specific protocol at Stanford's Amyloid Center. Call ahead for his records."

I give him the name of Zo's hematologist, the lead doctor, and the paramedic nods as they heft Zo onto the stretcher.

"You're his wife?"

I look up and catch Jared standing in the circle, watching with undisguised concern.

"No, his best friend." I stand with them. "I'm coming with you."

"Okay," he says, the set of his mouth grim as he checks Zo's vitals.

"I'm coming, too," Mama says tearfully.

"Only room for one," he tells her briskly. "We're headed to Cedars-Sinai. You can meet us there."

I look over my shoulder one last time at Jared. He grips the back of his neck, nodding that he understands.

"Go," he mouths. "I love you."

I let that sink in, soothe the ache in my heart as I prepare myself for the next few hours. But can you ever really prepare to walk through hell?

CHAPTER 38
BANNER

THE SIREN SCREAMS, CLEARING OUR WAY THROUGH LA TRAFFIC, but it still feels like we're riding at a snail's pace to the hospital. Anxiety wraps its fingers tightly around my throat. My breathing is as shallow as Zo's. The words spoken urgently between the EMS techs garble around me.

Hypovolemic shock. IV resuscitation. Isotonic crystalloid.

None of it means anything, even though I've heard it all before.

"Banner," Zo gasps. He opens his eyes briefly, but they roll like a wild horse's. He waves a limp hand in the air, searching for something. Searching for me. "Bannini?"

I grab his hand. All my processes are delayed, shock and panic making the air thick and hot as soup.

"Sorry," he gasps, lips tinged blue, veins bulging in his neck.

"Do something," I scream, rivulets of hot, wet pain staining my cheeks and neck and chest. "You have to do something. He's… Oh, God, just…do…"

My words break on a sob.

"Ma'am, we're giving him fluids," one of the techs says. "We're limited in what we can or should do until we have a better assessment of what's actually going on. Especially considering the complexity of his condition, we might do more harm than good."

"Banner, listen," Zo says, his voice a wisp.

"Stop trying to talk." I press my fingers over his lips and lay my forehead to his. "Just... Just breathe, Zo. We're almost there."

"So sorry," he says again, barely audible. Tears trickle from his eyes and into his ears. "About Foster."

I pull in a startled breath to hear Jared's name on his lips. I don't know if the tears are for how he used his illness to keep Jared and me apart or because he hurts that I want Jared. Both possibilities drive a stake through my heart.

"No, no, no." I press my face to his chest, still frail beneath his tuxedo. "Don't be sorry. *En las buenas.*"

Through thick.

His eyes flicker open just long enough to catch and hold mine, a small smile playing on his wide mouth.

"*En las malas,*" he whispers.

Through thin.

His eyelids drop, like they're too weary for even one more second, and he's gone again.

"Zo!" I squeeze his hand and tap his face gently. "Don't you dare die, you selfish bastard. Don't you dare..."

Sobs consume my words, my eyes so blurred and burned with tears, I can't see in front of me. I wail like the siren overhead and shake with frustration and fear.

"We're here," one of them says.

Before, everything seemed slowed, time and motion gooped and dragging. Now it's greased and rapid. A flurry of activity, with every word quick and staccato. Every motion is a blur. They wheel Zo away within seconds of our arrival, and I'm left standing in the middle of the waiting room alone, incongruous in my dress and heels.

"Banner!" Mama comes into the waiting room, followed by my father, Anna my niece, and my sister Camilla. "Where is he?"

"They just took him." My throat closes, and I can't say anything more. My fears feel like boulders on my shoulders and pebbles in my belly.

Mama doesn't say anything, but the look she gives me repeats her insult from earlier.

Puta.

She and I stare at one another, knowing that the man fighting for his life is not the man I love. At least not the way Mama wants me to, but I don't live any part of my life to satisfy other people, and I'm damn tired of conducting my love life by the dictates of others.

"*Mi niña,*" Papa says, gathering me close.

I fall into his arms, into his familiar scent. If sawdust has a smell, my father carries it, from always being on his construction work sites. It reminds me of how hard he worked to provide the best life for us that he could. His arms remind me of how he has constantly supported my dreams, even when he couldn't see that high, couldn't imagine Ivy League colleges or living this fast-paced life surrounded by obscenely wealthy people talented beyond what the average person can comprehend. He supported me through everything. He supports me now.

I'm still buried in Papa's chest when my mother's voice cuts into the small slice of peace I've managed to find in the last hour's chaos.

"You have some nerve coming here," she snaps.

I lift and turn my head, shocked to see Jared standing in the waiting room, changed into jeans and a Wharton School of Business sweatshirt.

With studied patience, he holds my mother's stare and absorbs her harsh words without replying—a feat for him, I know.

"I, uh"—he clears his throat and extends a small bag to me—"thought you might like to change in case you're here for a while. Iris sent some things she thought might work."

My father triangulates a look between Jared, me, and finally the angry flush of my mother's face.

"Jared, hey. Thank you." I walk over and take the bag with a grateful smile. My body hums being this close to him. Not for sex. Just to be held and cared for by him. That'll have to wait.

"Papa, this is my friend Jared." I ignore Mama's scoff at the word *friend*. "Jared, my father Marco, sister Camilla, and niece Anna."

"Hi." Jared offers a slight smile and inclination of his head to each family member.

It's like we're inside a drum the air is so tight, charged with tension and questions. And from my sister, curiosity and appreciation. Her gaze, filled with interest, drags over Jared's tall, athletic frame and the chiseled lines of his face, the rumpled fairness of his hair. There was a time when I would have deferred, assumed that any man my sister expressed interest in would prefer her, but not with this one. And even though I have a lot to explain, I want her to know from the beginning that this one is off-limits. More than anything, I just need him to hold me, and that we cannot do in the open just yet.

"Jared." I place a hand on his arm to capture his attention. "Can I speak to you for a sec?"

He nods, looking slightly relieved.

"I'll be right back," I tell my family. I hold up my cell. "If the doctor comes in the next minute or so, just call."

Their speculation chases us down the hall, but at least for the next few minutes, I don't care. I duck into an empty hospital room, drag Jared in behind me by the hand, and close the door. As soon as we're inside, his arms surround me. I drop my head to the curve of his neck and fight back an onslaught of tears. It's been so much, for so long, and tonight seems to be nudging me over the edge. A few tears leak into the warmth of his skin, and one large hand cups my face and pushes my hair back.

"Hey, it's okay," he says, searching my face. "Let it go, Ban."

His words so considerate and him being here just like I need make it feel like for just a moment I *can* let go. That the burden I've been carrying for the last few months, the one that has cracked me in places and sometimes been too heavy, I can set aside.

"Oh, God, Jared." Tears drown my words for long moments

while I try to pull it together, but I can't stem the flow. "I was so scared in the ambulance. I thought he was going to…"

I can't say the word, the one I rarely allowed myself to even think for the last three months.

"He'll be okay," Jared assures me. "I know it. That man is not going out like that. He'll stick around if only to make my life miserable."

That coaxes a small smile from me as he knew it would. I link our fingers and look up at him, taking in the handsome face and the rare tenderness he reserves for pretty much only me.

"I think the two of you will be great friends one day," I tell him, and I mean it. Under the right circumstances and with some time, I could see them appreciating the differences in the other.

Jared conveys his skepticism about that with one lifted brow.

"I hope we'll get the chance." He turns me toward the small bathroom in the empty two-bed suite. "Go change so we can get back to your family. I have a hard enough road ahead with them."

That could be true, especially with my mother, but I want him to know that it won't affect the way I feel.

I'm poised to go change with my back facing the bathroom door.

"I love you," I tell him again and turn into the bathroom without waiting for a response, but Jared's not letting me off that easily. The door opens just as I'm unzipping my dress.

"You can't just say that and leave," he says, his voice uneven, his eyes lit with something wholly new. Something my words gave birth to. "I'm not used to it yet."

I slip the dress off, grateful that there is at least a strapless bra, and put on the T-shirt and yoga pants Iris sent. She's much smaller than I am, so I'm glad she chose stretchy clothes.

"Say it again." He advances deeper into the room until he stands right in front of me. "I need to hear it again."

"I love you," I say, my voice sober and honest. "I think I have for a long time."

He cups my cheek and kisses my hair.

"Me, too," he says, the look in his eyes belying the casual tone of his voice. "Since senior year, to be exact."

My phone rings, stealing our smiles. It's my mom.

"Hey, Mama. Any word?"

"The doctor just came out," she says, her voice stiff with disapproval. "If you can spare the time to hear what he has to say."

I don't even respond. Don't bother reminding her that sparing time is all I've done for the last three months. I don't have to defend myself to my mother or to anyone. The only person I need to completely understand is Zo, and I think now he does. I hope I'll get the chance to find out.

As soon as we rejoin my family in the waiting room, the doctor launches into his update.

"Who came in with him?" the doctor asks, looking over all the faces.

"Um, it was me," I say hastily. "I did all I could think to do. I thought he would be okay because he just finished his chemo, but I guess some of his organ functions are still compromised. It was too much, and I'm so sorry. If he—"

"You probably saved his life," the doctor cuts in, the look he gives me kind and a balm to some of the guilt that never seems too far away. "If we'd had to figure out all the things you gave us and hadn't gotten in touch with Stanford right away, we probably would have lost him. He was literally in the process of dying. His organs had begun shutting down."

I unconsciously grab Jared's hand at the doctor's words, at how close I came to losing my best friend. I force my breaths in and out slowly.

"We're flushing his body with a saline solution right now," the doctor continues. "He's resting and will be here for a few days recovering, but he should continue steadily improving."

"When can we see him?" I ask, needing to see for myself that Zo is okay.

"You can see him now." His glance roves over all the eager faces lined up. "Just two at a time, please."

I squeeze Jared's hand and let go, walking toward where the doctor said Zo was resting. I don't even check to see who the second person is who follows me but make my way straight to Zo's side. He's asleep, but I still have to talk to him.

"You scared me to death," I whisper and grab his hand, which is huge but still skeletal compared to its former size.

"Scared you so badly you ran off with your new boyfriend the first chance you got?" my mother asks in our native tongue from behind me.

I send her a quelling look over my shoulder.

"Mama, you don't know what you're talking about, and now is not the time."

"When will be the time, Bannini?" she asks, her eyes saddened, angry. "This man loves you."

"And I love him," I snap, turning to give her the full force of my expression. "Do you think I would have gone through the last three months if I didn't love him? That I would be prepared to do it again when he has stem cell replacement if I didn't love him?"

"Oh, that is your idea of love?" Mama expels a harsh laugh. "Cheating on him like a common whore?"

I'm quiet because I cannot fully deny her accusation. I did cheat on Zo, and as much as I love Jared, as sure as I am that we belong together, I will never condone what I did or how I hurt Zo.

"I see you have no defense," Mama continues. "You slept with him? With this *gringo*?"

"Yes, Mama," I answer softly, tears stinging my eyes. "I did."

"You admit it." She shakes her head, a layer of disappointment over her disapproval. "I raised you better than that. That you would shame our family, shame yourself this way is unacceptable."

"I know, Mama. I've apologized to Zo."

"He knows?" Mama asks. "So not just this disease but a broken heart, too?"

God, I'm not sure how much more of this I can take. Every word is like another heavy clump of dirt on a grave, burying me alive.

"Stop." The one word comes from behind me, from Zo. It's thin and weak, like him, but there is no mistaking the steel in it. "Don't talk to her like that."

"But, Zo," Mama says, making her way over to the bed. "She cheated on you? Was unfaithful to you?"

"Almost dying has a way of bringing things into focus," he says. "She's not in love with me."

A rueful smile tilts his beautiful mouth.

"I can admit that now," he says, sharing a look with me. "She may not be *in* love with me, but she loves me. She chose me when I needed her to. Tonight is not the first time she has saved my life, and I won't have anyone, not even you, Mama, speak against her."

He shifts his tired, intent stare from my mother to me.

"Good people may do bad things, wrong things," he says. "But they are *still* good people, still capable of doing amazing things, and Banner has more than proven that."

"Zo," I choke out. "You don't have to—"

"I have not always done the right thing, either, Bannini," he cuts in softly. "I forgive you. Forgive yourself, and then forgive me for keeping you from the one you do love. The one who loves you. I knew it as soon as he stepped foot in your house that night."

A harsh laugh briefly disrupts his shallow breathing.

"Hell, I don't think he even knew at that point how he felt," he says. "And in a way, I've been fighting it ever since."

I stuff down a sob. I didn't realize how much I needed this. How the burden of my infidelity was like a stone tied around my neck, something I've dragged around for months. The weight lifts, and I feel freer than I have in such a long time. And my heart swells with the same affection I have had from him from the beginning, from that first day in the Bagley office when he plucked me from obscurity and set me on a course that determined a future exceeding even what I had ever dreamed of.

"Thank you, Zo." I lean down to kiss his cheek. "For everything."

He is already drifting off again, succumbing to the medication they have given him to force rest on his body. I turn to find Mama watching me with wide, wet eyes. There is not forgiveness there, not yet, but at least now there is more understanding.

"We should go," I say stiffly. "Let him rest."

Mama slips a rosary from her purse, tagged with a silver cross, and wraps it around Zo's hand prone on the hospital bed. We walk out at the same time, both stopping when we see Jared seated on the floor against the wall facing the door. He pulls himself up, standing to his full, imposing height. I don't think about Mama beside me or even Zo on the other side of the door. I just know where I belong. I link my arms behind his neck and press myself into the familiar strength of his body, almost bursting into tears when he hugs me tighter, buries his head in the hair at my neck. We stay that way for long moments. I hear the quick steps of my mother's retreat, leaving us alone, but I don't pull away. Not yet.

"She's still not a fan of me, huh?" He laughs into the curve of my neck and rubs my back soothingly.

"She's not exactly a fan of me right now either, but she'll come around."

"I hope she does, but if she doesn't, we're still happening." His expression sobers. "Too many people, too many times, have come between us. Not again."

This man, this beautiful, unattainable man is mine. And he loves me like a Mack truck—the huge ones that just keep coming and don't stop for anything in their path. Being the object of such singular focus can be overwhelming, but it's also the best feeling in the world.

"Are you saying you want this for good?" I ask, more confident than I've ever been.

"For good?" He frowns and gives a quick shake of his head. "For good is too sanitized. I want your dirt and your pain and your darkness. Your weakness and your flaws."

He sprinkles kisses over my cheeks and nose, leaving adoration everywhere he touches me.

"I don't want you for good, Banner," he says. "I want you forever."

I gasp at hearing the future in his words, of the picture he's painting.

"I love you," he tells me again. "I didn't even think I was capable of saying that, much less feeling it, but I feel it for you."

He shifts to look down at me.

"I couldn't say that word even to myself for a long time because I thought I had to be absolutely sure of you."

"And are you?" I slip my arms around his waist. "Sure of me, I mean."

"Yes, but mostly I'm sure of myself. I love you, and even if you didn't love me back, I would still want what's best for you." He flicks a look over my shoulder at the closed hospital door. "I think that's the way he loves you. He loves you enough to let you go."

"And could you let me go?" I ask, mischief and hope twined around the question. "If I tried to get away?"

He looks down at me, those glacially blue eyes glinting with the possessiveness that I never thought I would want but from him turns me on.

"Why don't you try to get away from me again and we'll find out?"

We both laugh into a tender kiss because we know how much he enjoys the chase.

And that I'd let him catch me.

CHAPTER 39
BANNER

"Girl, you better wake up! The world is watching and waiting!"

Before I can grab my phone and silence the app, a muscled forearm reaches across me, plucks it off the bedside table, and hurls it against the wall.

"Uh...maybe not the best way to silence my phone," I mutter into my pillow.

"I thought it was quite effective." Jared's deep, sleep-roughened voice rumbles from his chest into my back. "Every morning with that damn app."

Shout-out to shatterproof cases.

"You're sleeping in," he says. Under the duvet, he pulls my back into his chest, anchoring us together.

"I need to get up." My protest is relatively weak because I'm exhausted and have worked out early every morning and worked late every night this week. Spending a Saturday morning in bed with Jared does hold some appeal.

"I think you should stay in bed," he says, his whisper finding its way through my hair into my ear.

An impish smile sprouts on my face, and I say the words that started it all for us more than ten years ago between spin cycles in a deserted laundromat.

"Convince me."

The husky chuckle breezing my neck holds sweet memories and makes dirty promises. He charts a course of kisses over my shoulder and arm. At my back, he lavishes me with his open mouth, licking gently down the shallow groove covering my spine. He shoves the duvet off the bed, and the cool air sprays goose bumps over my skin. He turns me to my back, kneeling and looking down at me.

It's just passing dawn, and early-morning sunlight filters through the windows. Not fully bright yet but enough light to illuminate the man above me. Enough to see the emotion I was afraid to name and so was he. His love is so evident. It's wordless but articulated in the reverent touch of his hand at my throat. It's passionate in the fingers gliding over my rib cage, stealing down my hip and across my thigh, making their inexorable way to my pussy.

"Oh." The one word precedes my indrawn breath as he strokes the tight knot of nerves budded inside.

Eyes never leaving mine, he finds my breast with his other hand, palming, squeezing, kneading, collaborating with the steady, sensual rhythmic torture between my legs. His fingers don't just thrust inside me. They search, seeking my pleasure and my secrets. Desire blossoms like a morning glory opening to the sun streaming through my bedroom window. In a matter of moments I come, shameless, stretching my legs wide, pulling my knees high, wantonly wringing every ounce of gratification from the orgasm that I can, exposing myself completely to his touch and his sight.

"I want you," I pant, snaring his eyes with mine as the wave recedes, ebbs. "Inside me."

He's discomposed. His breaths are ragged, heaving his chest with deep rises and falls just from touching me until I came. Simply from watching. Want and need twist, turn, gleam feral in his stare. The hunger there is a beast, and I am its singular focus. I feel the exhilaration of being hunted, pursued. The promise of being caught and taken. His control hangs by a gossamer strand, and when I reach up to grab his cock that control snaps.

He slides his thumb from my soaked folds to the tight, puckered hole below, lubricating me, preparing me.

"I want this." He growls it. Grits it between his teeth.

I nod. It won't be the first time he's taken me that way. It's always rough and rides the fine line of pain and bliss.

And I always beg for more.

Still on his knees, he stretches to the bedside table to grab the lube, and I take advantage of his preoccupation to lean up and take his cock into my mouth.

"Dammit, Ban." He squeezes the small bottle in one fist and tangles the other in my hair falling forward, curtaining the work of my lips around him. The bottle falls to the bed, discarded and forgotten. Both his hands cup my head as he pushes himself deeper into my mouth, down my throat. I choke a little from the aggressive thrust.

"Breathe," he commands but doesn't let up, doesn't pull back. He never does. He knows I don't want him to. I drop my jaw to accommodate the thickness, the raw thrust of his dick scraping inside my mouth and stretching the walls of my throat. He groans, drops his head back. Witnessing the abandoned pleasure on his face has me chasing my own high again. I slip my hands between my legs, stroking myself in sync with each of his powerful strokes.

"I don't want to come like this," he says, jerking out and leaning down to capture my jaw in one big hand. With his thumb, he rubs the faint trail of pre-cum into my swollen lips and then kisses me, sipping his own saltiness from my mouth. "Lie back."

I do. He grabs the lube again and drags me over the decadent cotton of our sheets to the edge of the bed. He stands at the foot, holding my stare while he anoints the tight hole with cool liquid. He pulls my legs straight up against his chest, stroking the sensitive skin inside my thigh.

"Tell me if it's too much."

His jaw clenches, the muscle pushing against the tanned, golden-stubbled skin. He eases into my ass by centimeters. The wide head forces its way in, and my breath catches. This is always the hardest part, that first breach. The thick, welcome intrusion. The pinch of pressure is a forerunner for the unbearable pleasure of his cock caressing the network of nerves cloistered in my ass.

"Oh my God." I swallow and arch my neck, begging the air for breath. He starts slowly, watching my face for signs of pain, discomfort. He begins cautiously, but every stroke in and out whittles his care, his consideration.

Until the beast just wants to fuck.

He's gripping my thighs to his chest and pounding into me with piston force. My body mourns even the millisecond he leaves to pull out and celebrates the fullness every time he slams back inside.

"Open it for me," he says, his voice desperate and commanding.

I know what he wants and cup my butt in both hands, stretching, pulling the cheeks apart to make his way easier.

"Shit," I gasp. It's intense. The penetration so deep, I shatter inside with every thrust.

Taking control, he pauses only long enough to drop my legs from his chest and let them fall open and pushes my knees up to my chest. He watches himself going in and out, biting his lip, gripping the inside of my thigh just below the knee. I know what's next, and I don't think I can take it.

His thumb revisits my pussy, gently at first, almost an apology for neglecting it, and then his jaw hardens and he presses his palm flat over the open lips, passing his hand across my clit over and over. I involuntarily close my legs against the devastating pleasure.

"Stop. Open," he orders abruptly, pressing my legs back wide and my knees back up. He strokes my clit and sinks his thumb into my pussy, all the while pounding into my ass. The orgasm rises from muscles coiled tight at the base of my spine and explodes over my back, a meteor shower raining down my legs, winnowing through my feet and toes. This feeling possesses me until I scream and thrash my head and grip the sheets.

"*Dios. Dios,*" I slur, spent, even as he maintains the vigorous pace. Sweat drips down the chiseled workmanship of his chest and abs. His damp hair curls.

How long has he been fucking me? I hope it never ends.

"God, I'm close," he grunts. "Fuck, fuck, fuck."

He pulls out and splashes a hot stream onto my ass and along the backs of my thighs, on my belly. His head flings back, proud and leonine, and then he looks at me, ownership in the gaze that takes in the creamy rivulets decorating my body.

And then he rubs it in.

I close my eyes, blocking all extraneous stimuli and every sense but touch. The world narrows to the ridges of his finger pads massaging his essence into my skin. He rubs it into the swollen lips between my legs and roughly over my nipples, melding us in the most primitive way. When the pleasure is too much to contain, I come again. Differently. Soundlessly. Noiselessly. My whole being sighs. My body with the release of such passion, it steals my voice. My heart for one devastatingly gorgeous moment stops, pauses in my chest in reverence. And my soul stills, quieted by the presence, the possession, of its mate.

———

"We're wrinkling."

I lift a bare, wet arm from the cooling bath water to show Jared my puckered fingertips. He's behind me in my claw-foot tub, his arms sheltering my shoulders and my head tucked into the curve of his neck.

"I see." He catches my fingers, briefly kisses the tips. He links his hands with mine on the lip of the tub. "What do you think about a hike today?"

"Oooh." I arch my neck to look at him over my shoulder. "That could be fun."

"Maybe Temescal Canyon?"

"I haven't done that one. I love the sound of that."

It feels strange sometimes that we...date. That we do normal things together like go to movies or the theater, eat dinner or walk on the beach. I grew up with the ocean close by, and I missed it when I lived in New York. Our schedules are so hectic, but when we snatch time to be together, it's to do simple things like that. Just breathing in ocean air and appreciating a majestic sunset and learning new things about each other all the while.

We've only been together a few weeks, and it's quiet. Not many know, only our closest family and friends. Zo and I released a joint statement explaining that our relationship had been platonic for months, but we had decided not to discuss it while we were navigating his illness. That put his "*te amo*" from the stage in a different light, that of a man appreciating his best friend for standing by him through hell. Which is what it was, what we are, even though it took Zo some time to accept it.

"Uh...what time were you thinking?" I ask, touching the powerful legs on either side of me.

His skin slides against mine behind me with a shrug.

"Two?" He pulls the wet hair from my neck and kisses the curve. "You have something to do?"

I'm quiet for a few seconds. I'm still involved with Zo's care now that we're back in LA. With chemo behind him, the medical team is monitoring his body's response. Preparing for the next stage, stem cell replacement, is a complex process that includes a battery of tests ensuring his organs are healthy enough for the procedure. Then follows a lengthy recovery that will largely isolate Zo, nearly quarantining him because of how the process will strip his immune system down to nothing. He'll have very few visitors.

But he'll have me.

"Yeah, I do have a few things to take care of." I clear my throat before going on. "I need to check on Zo."

It's quiet behind me, the only sound the water lapping against the tub with each slight subtle shift of our bodies.

"Does it bother you?" I finally ask softly. "That I'm still so involved with him? With his care?"

"Yes."

I try to be a no-judgment zone for Jared. We love each other deeply but are made so differently. We're both fiercely protective of the ones we love, but Jared has a tight filter for who gets in, for who gets loved. I'm glad I made the cut.

"Thank you for being honest with me." I turn in the tub so I'm facing him. "I can't abandon him."

"I know that." His lashes are lowered, screening his eyes from me. His face is implacable, chiseled into tight lines and sharp angles. "I don't want you to abandon him. That wouldn't be who you are, but it still bothers me because I know he's in love with you."

I can't deny that. It's an odd situation I have us in, but I'm not sure how to get out and live with myself. I know there will come a time when I'm less involved, but Zo is nowhere near out of the woods. With the stem cell process looming ahead, he is actually about to enter a deeper, darker forest in some ways. This would be the worst time to leave him.

"At least we're not living together," I say, my attempt to soothe the frown from his handsome face. "Me and Zo, I mean."

Our things are scattered between Jared's apartment and my house, but most nights we end up here.

He does grin at my hasty clarification and traces my lips, my cheekbones, leaving a damp trail in the wake of his finger.

"I knew what you meant." He kisses my nose. "My lease is up in a few months. We could discuss it, if you want."

My stomach lurches, and my breath hangs in my throat. My heart triple-beats.

"Sure, we can talk about it."

I glance down, studying the contrasting textures of our bodies in the water. My skin a little darker. His rougher, golden-hair dusted. There's no self-consciousness about my nudity, about my body. Yes, I'm in the best shape I've ever been, but it's not that. I'm still a double-digit girl in a single-digit town. I work out and eat right, but Mother Nature took her time spreading these hips and this ass. My curves are toned and firm, but they ain't going anywhere anytime soon, and I'm fine with that. I've grown to love that. Jared loves it, too. I used to think being with a man like him would make me more self-conscious. If anything, with his love as a constant, I'm more confident than ever.

"Hey." He tips my chin up so I meet his eyes, which are laughing, content, blue. "It would be a very short conversation. I want to live with you. To wake up with you every day. What do you say?"

His grin is teasing and infectious. As complicated as our careers, our lives are, it's simple when it's just us. And I love when it's just us.

"That'd be nice," I reply, leaning up to kiss him, long, slow, deep. When I pull away and turn back around, even though the water is getting chilly, I settle into his chest again.

"There's something, uh…else I wanted to discuss," he says.

Now I hear something in *his* voice, a reservation. A hesitation that has me grabbing his hand and linking our fingers at my waist.

"Shoot," I say. "What's up?"

He brushes his free hand over my hair and drops a kiss onto the wet strands.

"I have an offer to make," he says, watching my face closely. "I have a position for you at Elevation."

If you could hear a pin drop in bathwater, we would right now. It's not that I suspect he chased me for my clients, for what I could add to his agency. I'm clear on Jared's single-minded love for me. It's my brain working through the offer.

I separate myself from the woman stretched out against the man who owns her heart. That woman's ass still aches from how hard he fucked her. That woman wears stubble burns on her breasts and the insides of her thighs from his kisses. That woman's whole world fits inside this bathtub with the golden-haired man behind her. In an apocalypse, this would be all she needed.

But the world is not coming to an end, and I mentally take a few measured steps away from this tub and that girl and her man and examine the offer with objective distance.

"You say you have a position for me at Elevation?"

I turn and slide away until my back hits the other side and we're facing each other. I hang my arms over the lip of the tub, caught at the elbows.

"Yes." His lips twist, a smile suppressed because he feels the shift. The water isn't the only thing cooling. "A very generous offer, I think."

"You have a position for me at your agency. How would that differ from my current situation?"

"I'd beat whatever Cal pays you."

"Cal doesn't pay me." I relish the surprise in his eyes. "I negotiated a contract to waive my base salary in exchange for keeping even more of my commission."

I smile innocently and bat my lashes.

"It's actually quite a lot."

An amused breath passes his lips, and where I lean back, he leans forward, propping his elbows on the edges of the tub.

"So what would it take for you to come work for me?"

"I *won't* come work for you."

"You won't?" he asks, his frown quick, heavy.

"I know exactly how many clients Elevation represents, and I can guarantee that all of mine would follow me out the door if I left Bagley. That would double your client list." Now I lean forward, my naked breasts pushing through the water, and wait for him to raise his eyes from my nipples. "In a day."

"Double?"

"Double," I confirm. "I have autonomy at Bagley, by and large, and keep more of my money than I would anywhere else. Eventually, I'll strike out on my own but haven't wanted to take that step before. What you're describing would be a lateral move, at best, and doesn't interest me."

I raise one knee and watch his eyes drop between my legs.

"I won't come work for you," I reiterate. "But I would come work *with* you if the offer was right. Equal partner."

"Equal partner?" His mouth drops open, that strong jaw unhinged. "In the firm I built from nothing? You want to walk in the door and be handed an equal partnership?"

"Handed?" I tilt my head and compress my lips. "I can't remember the last time I was *handed* anything. I've worked my ass off for the last decade, just like you have. My reputation and results are just as good."

I give him a meaningful look and don't say the words aloud, but he hears them.

If not better.

He licks his lips and tucks them in, hiding a smile from me.

"I'd have to talk to August. He's a silent partner."

"You do that." I stand, naked and as confident as if we were wrapping up a negotiation at a boardroom table. I step out, tie a towel at my breasts, and offer my "closer" smile. "And get back to me."

EPILOGUE
JARED

"It is true what they say—When you know, you know."
—*Cindy Cherie, poetess*

"There's nothing to be nervous about," Banner says, chewing her thumbnail and scrunching her expression into a frown.

Looking nervous.

"Uh…okay." I pull into the parking lot of the villa where Banner's niece Anna's quinceañera reception is being held. "I'm not nervous."

She probably doesn't believe me, but I'm not. We've been together for six months, and I've been to the occasional dinner with her closest relatives, but this is the first time I'm attending a function with the entire sprawling family. Apparently, it's a big deal since she keeps telling me how *not* nervous I should be. We just left the Mass, which is traditionally held before the party. It was full-on Bible, rosary, priest, pomp and circumstance—the whole shebang. First time I've been to a church of any kind since…I literally cannot remember. I'm surprised lightning didn't strike.

"If my uncle Javier gets drunk," Banner says, "don't talk to him. Ignore him. He says crazy stuff when he's drunk."

"Don't we all?"

I get out, and so does she.

"And you already know not to engage with Mama." She checks

the hair bundled at the back of her head in a loose knot. "I really thought she would have come around by now."

Mama Morales has proved harder to win over than the public, whose perception of Banner as Zo's faithful Penelope was hard to banish but not as awkward as we anticipated. Banner definitely got props for taking care of Zo the way she did even when they weren't romantically linked. As much as I want to tattoo my name on her face so everyone knows, I do appreciate that it's best to take a more measured approach. When Banner left Bagley and came to Elevation, many assumed our relationship naturally developed there.

"Are you thinking about what Mama said last time?" Banner asks. "Is that why you're so quiet?"

"What'd she say last time?" I ask with a frown.

"Oh." She bites her lip. "Nothing. Never mind."

I roll my eyes and walk around to the passenger side of the car.

"You don't have to pretend your mother likes me." I loop my arms behind her lower back. "*She* doesn't pretend."

Banner reaches up to adjust my tie unnecessarily because my tie is always on point. She just needs something to do with her hands. If we didn't have to attend this reception, I'd give her something to do with her hands. Her mouth, too.

"But I want her to like you," she says with the slightest pout.

I bend and drop a kiss on her lips and on my freckles.

"Do *you* like me?" I ask by her ear.

"I more than like you." She turns her head to kiss my lips quickly. Too quickly for my taste. "I love you."

"Then you'll believe me when I say no one else's opinion really matters, not even your mother's."

She nods, but a frown dents between her brows. I smooth it away with my thumb.

"I mean it, Ban. It would be great if your mom liked me the way she loves Zo, but we both know that won't happen anytime soon."

"Oh, also." The frown is back. "Speaking of Zo..."

"Do we have to?"

"Jared, stop. He may be feeling well enough to come today." She glances up at me through long lashes.

"Don't even bother," I tell her. "That batting eyelash trick doesn't work on me."

"I'm well aware that you are immune to my charms," she says with a laugh, pulling out of my arms to walk ahead of me.

Her ass, though. That little sway of her rounded hips seduces me every time. The way that dress molds to the curve of her—

"Damn! You're doing it!" I say, realizing the lashes don't get me but I fall for that ass every time.

She's looking over her shoulder watching me watch her ass, mischief in her grin. I love that the woman who once asked if her ass was square feels confident enough in my love for her body exactly as she is to use that ass against me.

"You're so easy, Foster, and you think you're so hard." She laughs and loops her arm through mine. "Now, like I was saying about Zo, I need you to be nice."

I hate it when people *need* me to be nice because that means they know there's a strong possibility someone could set me off. After the way Zo kept us apart for months and then pulled her onstage in front of the whole world with all that *te amo* shit, knowing about us…

"Maybe we'll just avoid each other," I offer. "There are a lot of people here."

"No, I need you to try." She stops on the sidewalk leading up to the venue, her expression sobering. "You know what *he* means to me, and he knows what *you* mean to me. I want you both, at some point, to be okay with…each other."

"I'll try." My voice is curt. I don't mean to be, but just her saying "what he means to me" sets my teeth on edge.

"Thank you." She huddles in closer to my side. "This is gonna be fun. It's a really big deal. I remember my quinceañera. Such a special day for a girl."

"That ceremony at the church was cool."

"Yes, and now the real fun begins," she says. "Lots of drinking. Good food. A delicious cake. Anna will have the first dance with my papa."

"Sounds more like a wedding than a sweet...fifteen party."

"It is a lot like a wedding." She shoots me a knowing grin. "But it's not, so don't worry. I know how nervous weddings make single guys."

"Weddings don't make me nervous." I capture her hand and bring it to my lips just as we reach the entrance. "And I'm not single."

We share a long look, half questions, half unspoken answers, before her sister, Camilla, walks up to greet us.

"Everything is beautiful, Bannini," Camilla says, accompanying us to the foyer. She drops her eyes to the floor and then looks at Banner directly. "Thank you for this place. Anna feels like a princess here."

"She *is* a princess," Banner replies, hugging her sister. "We'll make sure she has all the things we never had and learns all the things we did."

"Yeah. Still." She gestures to the quaint villa where Anna's reception is being held. "You didn't have to."

"*Somos familia,*" Banner says, kissing her cheek.

"And thank you for bringing this one," Camilla says, turning a frankly admiring look my way. "I've been meaning to tell you that *he* is something else."

"Look, Milla," Banner says with a stiff smile. "You have one more time to look at my boyfriend like that. *¿Entiendes?*"

Camilla and I glance at each other for a few seconds before her laughter sputters past her lips. She pulls out a twenty-dollar bill and hands it over to me.

"You win." She shakes her head and grins. "Jared called it."

"Wait." Banner swings disbelieving eyes between her sister and me. "You set me up?"

She turns narrowed eyes on me.

"*You* set me up?"

"Just a friendly wager to see how jealous you'd get," I admit, pocketing the twenty. "It's pretty bad."

"And I suppose that twenty is for Anna's stash, yes?" Banner asks with arms akimbo.

"Of course," I mumble. "Most of it."

The three of us laugh at my joke, and I hand the twenty back. We make our way over to the table where there is more food than I have ever seen. A catered spread of tacos, enchiladas, barbacoa, salsa, guac, and so many dishes I've never seen but can't wait to taste. I grab a couple of the *biscohos*, a type of wedding cookie, and even spot some *buñuelos* like the ones Banner made for me in St. John.

As we eat, I absorb this new experience and relish seeing Banner with her family. She is louder and her hands are in constant motion, painting pictures in the air while she speaks with her cousins and aunts and childhood friends, more expressive than in the settings where I've seen her before. I love seeing this side of her that would only unfold here, with them. I can pick out a few words here and there when they lapse into a torrent of Spanish, but mostly I just enjoy the sound of their voices and the warmth of all the laugher interspersed with the lively music of the mariachi band. We have a good time when our family gets together, but this is chaos, and I'm glad I get to be a part of it.

A blond woman carrying a clipboard walks up as we're finishing our food.

"Ms. Morales," she says, glasses dangling at the tip of her nose. "I have a question regarding the contract and want to ask about the set up for the first dance."

"Oh, of course." Banner takes in the brightly colored palette of dresses and food, her rambunctious uncles laughing and drinking in one corner, her aunts boisterous and cackling in another, before turning her attention back to me. "You'll be okay for a few minutes?"

"I'm fine." I shake my glass. "I have punch, and I'm pretty sure it's spiked."

She nods and blows out a breathy laugh before following the coordinator.

I don't know many, and the few who know who I am to Banner aren't around right now. I refill my punch and am perfectly content to hold up a wall and people-watch, especially with so many new foods and traditions taking place around me. Anna is surrounded by the fourteen girls attending her today, or *damas* as Banner called them. They're giggling and adjusting her tiara and formal dress. Their dresses are a rainbow of colors and a flurry of satin and chiffon. Banner wants at least four kids? What if they're all girls? I think of Sarai and her billion questions and constant little-diva demands. God, what if they're as much work as my niece?

I'm still shuddering at that thought when Mama Morales invades my corner. We assess one another for a few silent seconds. We didn't have the most auspicious beginning, with me almost getting caught banging her daughter in the handicap stall.

"*Hola*, Señora Morales," I venture when the quiet turns awkward.

"You don't speak Spanish," she replies, not bothering to answer in her native tongue to see for sure.

"I speak enough to know you called Banner a whore." That still grates and she doesn't like me? *I* reserve judgment until she makes that right. Even though Banner shook it off, I know her mother's persistent disapproval bothers her.

"Ha! That's some big *cojones* you got there." The dark arch of brows Banner inherited elevates, and there's a twitch of the lips that look just like hers, too. "You speak enough Spanish to know what *that* means, *gringo?*"

The tense line of my mouth relaxes because she is so much like Banner, I have to like her just a little bit.

"You hurt Banner when you said that," I say, testing the temporary cease-fire between us.

"And you don't like seeing my daughter hurt?"

"No, I don't," I answer seriously, no smile in sight. "Not even by the people I know love her."

She searches my face for a moment before speaking again. "Do you have any idea how exceptional Banner is?"

She continues before I can answer.

"They said to me, 'Mrs. Morales, Banner is Mensa.'" She allows a glimmer of humor in her dark eyes. "I thought they were insulting my daughter. *Mensa* means 'stupid girl' in Spanish."

The slightest smile tilts one side of my mouth as I appreciate the irony.

"She was so different, so…" A helpless shrug lifts her shoulders. "I wasn't prepared for her."

"Neither was I," I agree wryly.

"The books she read, the languages she learned, the dreams she had, I couldn't teach her those things." The softened line of her lips cements. "But I did teach her honesty, loyalty, character. I taught her not to cheat."

The humor we'd briefly shared dissolves, leaving the warm early-evening air tense. I don't offer excuses or explanations because I don't owe anyone those. I take responsibility for my actions, and nothing she will say can make me regret that her daughter is mine.

"She's a good girl," Mrs. Morales says softly.

"I know that. If you're working up to telling me I don't deserve her, don't waste your time. I already know that, too."

"Zo is a good man." Her dark eyes never waver from my face, inspecting, assessing. "Are *you* a good man?"

I pause, examining her question and my response before answering.

"I'm good to your daughter. I would never hurt her and would kill anyone who tried."

That bold truth sits between the two of us for a few moments before she nods.

"Well, Banner has always known her own mind," she says. "And her mind is set on you."

Another smile twitches the corners of her mouth.

"I think she has set her heart on you, too."

"It's mutual," I assure her.

Her eyes don't leave my face, narrowing until she nods and seems satisfied by something she sees.

"Yes, well, my grandchildren will speak Spanish," she says brusquely. "And if you don't want us talking about you in your *face*, you will learn it and quickly."

"*Sí,*" I reply with a smile I don't try to hold back.

"So you're saying you *do* want to marry Banner, then?" she demands, dispelling the brief ease and crossing her arms over her chest exactly the way Banner does when she's reading me my rights.

"Uh…" This is taking a turn.

"What? You want to have the cow and the milk but not pay the farmer, eh? You want my grandchildren born out of wedlock?"

"No, you see, I was—"

"You have moved in, yes?" she asks, shifting her hands to her hips. "To my daughter's house? You live with her? You sleep with her every night?"

"Well, yeah, but we—"

"Then children will follow."

With her being such a devout Catholic, I'm not sure which might be more offensive, the fact that we have sex outside of marriage or that we use birth control. I wish Banner was here to answer these questions because I could screw this all up even worse. Fortunately, someone, a cousin if I recall correctly, calls for Mrs. Morales. With one searing look from my head to my toes, she leaves as abruptly as she came.

Well, that went well. I think. Maybe?

I could use some air after that. I step out onto the terrace and am thrilled to find it empty. The thrill is short-lived when I hear footsteps approaching. The last person I want to see is the only other person out here.

"Zo," I greet him evenly. "Good to see you."

His full-bodied laughter fits better now that he's getting some of his bulk back. His body has responded well to the stem cell replacement, though he is nowhere near ready for the court. You'd never know that by the stories Banner has planted. She has Sutton Lowell over a barrel with all the goodwill for Zo in the league. If they even hinted they were cutting him from the Titans, there would be public outcry. If he recovers enough to work out for them and if he proves he can still perform, his spot still waits.

"I thought you were more honest than that, Foster," he says with a microscopic smile.

"It *is* good seeing you, of course. I'm glad you're doing so well."

"It has been a lot, and Banner has been invaluable." He pauses. "Thank you for not making her choose or keeping her away from me."

"You mean the way you kept her away from me?" I can't resist asking.

That tiny quirk of his lips comes again. "I deserved that."

Yeah, you did.

"I was desperate to keep her," he says simply, looking me in the eyes. "I'm sure you can relate, can understand. I really appreciate you allowing her to help me these last few months."

"*Allow?*" I scoff. "You know I couldn't stop Banner doing what Banner wants to do if I tried. Believe me, I've tried. I wouldn't want to stop her. Banner is completely mine and wholly her own. I love that about her."

He nods, a smile of understanding tugging the corners of his mouth. We don't speak for a few moments, lost in our private thoughts. Lately, I've been tossing something around in my head that he may be the only person who can appreciate.

"Have you ever heard of multiple discovery?" I ask, leaning against the terrace wall.

"Can't say that I have," Zo replies, frowning.

"It's usually used for scientists or inventors. The phenomenon of two people discovering something in different places at essentially the same time," I say. "You'd be surprised how often it happens. Calculus, oxygen, the blast furnace...all multiple discoveries. Even Darwin's theory of evolution was postulated at the same time by someone else."

Zo lifts his brows, no doubt silently asking what my nerd talk has to do with the price of tacos in Mexico.

"I think that's what happened to us," I continue. "When we both met Banner, we saw something in her no one else saw yet. We made a spectacular discovery, and the rest of the world didn't recognize it. Couldn't see it when we could. It's like we shared a secret, the two of us."

"I get that," he says quietly, lifting a speculative gaze to mine. "And how is it resolved? When two discover something at the same time?"

I shrug, shove my hands into the pocket of my pants.

"It becomes a matter of who tells the secret first," I explain. "A rush to claim."

"So are you saying if I had met Banner first, she would have chosen me?" Dark humor fills his eyes.

"No, I don't think so," I answer. "Banner is my opposite, but she's my match."

My equinox.

"The only way Banner would have chosen you," I tell him frankly, honestly, "is if she'd never met me."

We are magnets who distracted ourselves with career, family, other people for a decade but ultimately couldn't resist the pull of one another.

"And you? You would have chosen someone else?" he asks, but I think he already knows the answer.

"Probably not," I answer quietly. "You'll find someone else, Zo. I know you will, but Banner's kinda my one shot."

He nods, maybe starting to understand why I fought so hard for her. Why I bulldozed him and anything in my path. I'm not an easy man to love, and finding someone I can love for the rest of my life would be nearly impossible. Banner is my miracle. Maybe he gets that and can forgive me one day for doing whatever it took to have her.

The woman in question strides out to the terrace, her confident gait briefly broken when she sees the two of us together. She doesn't voice the question written all over her face, but she's probably discreetly checking for blood.

"Zo, you're supposed to wear this." She holds up a facial mask. "A lot of good it's doing by the punch bowl when you're out here. I'm also not sure you should *be* out here. Sun's going down, and there's a little bit of a chill. Maybe you should—"

"Okay," he cuts in, lips twisted in exasperation. "Bannini, I got it."

Their eyes hold for a second. Hers concerned, his a little irritated but mostly indulgent.

"All right, but you need to *drink* this." She offers him a large cup and straw I hadn't noticed her holding. "None of that food in there is safe. You wouldn't be able to keep any of it down. This is sweet potato, lime, pineapple—"

"I need to tell you something," he interrupts, flicking a glance my way and then back to Banner before going on. "I hired a nurse to take care of me so you don't have to do so much or come over all the time."

Praise Jesus. I'm going to church every week from now on.

"A nurse?" Consternation wrinkles Banner's expression. "Why? I can—"

"No, you can't, Banner," he says gently, firmly. "I need you not to for a while."

She still looks confused, but I'm not. Zo needs to fall out of love with Banner and can't while she's there all the time being exactly the woman he wants.

"I personally think it's a great idea," I chime in, just in case they're wondering.

They both shoot me a wry "I bet you do" look and turn their attention back to each other.

"You have done more than enough," he says, taking her hand. "I couldn't have asked for a better friend."

"So you don't..." She swallows, and crystal tears bead the bottom row of her thick lashes. "You don't want me around? Is that what you're saying?"

He clears his throat, and my joy at this new development shrinks when I see tears in his eyes, too. His voice is still thick with emotion when he speaks. "For a while, I think it's best."

Banner and I have something he can't have with her, but he has something with her that is uniquely theirs. I scour my heart for jealousy, but there is none. How could there be? Banner is so pure in her motives, in her heart for him. He and I both recognize she would do anything for him *as his friend*. I don't envy him the task ahead...getting over her.

I never could.

He puts the mask she brought him over his face and loops the strings over his ears.

"There." The mask muffles the word. "You happy now?"

Her smile up at him clears some of her tears.

"I'll be happier," she says, "if you drink some of this. You need your..."

Her voice peters out, and she shakes her head, worry disrupting the smooth lines of her face.

"At least let me go over everything with the nurse," she says. "There's an app to keep up with your meds. And I have a regularly scheduled call with the hematologist who manages the multidisciplinary team. It's a lot, and I just want to make sure the, um...transition is seamless."

He simply nods, lifts the mask long enough to take a pointed sip of the concoction she brought over.

"I'll make sure she speaks with you," he says. "Now I'm going to go drool over all the food I cannot eat yet."

He runs a glance over her face, lingering on each feature like he's memorizing it, his eyes dark and sober over the white mask.

"Goodbye, Banner," he says.

She just nods and watches him leave the terrace. It's quiet for a bit except for the laughter and music floating out to us from inside. I give Banner a moment to swipe a finger under her eyes.

"You want to dance?" I ask finally, softly.

Her eyes are still bright with tears, but she smiles and steps into my arms. We sway to the faint strains of a mariachi band playing something thankfully more mellow. The last time we danced, Sixpence None the Richer was singing "Kiss Me." That night, I did kiss her, and everything changed.

"I'm sorry I was upset that he's getting a nurse," she says after a few minutes of our quiet sway. "It's not… It's just—"

"I'm not mad." I reach for her chin, lifting it so she meets my eyes. "I get it."

Relief chases the worry from her face.

"I do think it's a good idea, though," I tell her, as if she didn't know. "You need to devote as much time as possible to your job, considering I hear your new boss is a hard-ass."

Her deep-throated laugh drowns out everything else for a second.

"Boss?" She loops her arms around my neck, slipping her fingers into my hair. "I'm pretty sure my contract says I'm an equal partner at Elevation. I *did* deliver on my promise to double your client list when I left Bagley."

"That you did." A smile stretches across my face, the kind I'm sure the Cheshire Cat leaves hanging in Wonderland.

"You sure you don't just want me for my clients?" She smiles up at me, the question free of sting. Her face, everything about her, so clearly confident in herself, in my love.

We've come far. Who *were* we at the beginning of this road? Two ambitious, lost kids who found each other. God, we were so careless, as we often are when we're young. We don't value the things most precious, assuming the rare is common. But it's not. We weren't common. In all the years that followed, Banner was my yardstick, and no one else ever measured up. No one ever will. There are many amazing women around. I know that. I've met some, but it's not just who Banner *is* but who we are together. Who I am with her. I'd never fit with anyone the way I do with Banner, even though from the outside looking in we might not make sense.

"Do I want you for your clients?" I repeat the question as a whisper in her ear. "Should I dance you into the shadows over there and show you what I really want from you?"

She pulls back to stare up at me, her dark eyes a warning and a dare.

"We can't," she says, her voice firm but her eyes salacious. "We've made love in a lot of places and gotten away with it, but I think my niece's quinceañera would be pushing it *even for us*."

I dance her into said shadows, under an overhang of palm trees, a reprieve from what remains of the sun, and gently push her against the wall.

"Did you say push?" I press my erection into her. "This sounds more and more like an invitation."

She expels a short breath, bites her lips, and closes her eyes as she subtly gives my dick an answering grind.

"I said no," she says breathlessly.

"Scared your mom'll catch us again?" My laugh is huskier now with the sweet curve of her hips against me. "I would not do it here or there. I would not do it anywhere."

Her giggle is pure appreciation for my dirty Dr. Seuss.

"St. John's was such a good trip." She sighs, a rueful twist to her mouth. "Not sure when we'll get away again. The season's in full swing, and we'll be at playoffs in a few weeks."

I wish I could disagree, but our vacations will have to wait. I suspect the San Diego Waves will finally make the playoffs, so August could be negotiating the first postseason play of his NBA career. No way I'll check out for any of that. And Banner will keep an eye on Kenan, too, and the other players we manage.

"We may not be able to go back to our island anytime soon," I say, slipping my hands down to cup as much of her butt as I can hold. "But I'm gonna fuck you in that orange dress when we get home."

She nods a little jerkily, straining up to lick my neck. I want her to bite me, ring my throat with teeth marks so everyone at this party knows I'm hers, but she won't. For all her wildness in bed, Banner's too circumspect to shock her family. She has to keep us both in line because she knows I don't give a damn.

"Are you sure we can't just…" I grasp the hem of her dress, sliding it along the sleek line of her thigh. "In and out. Quick, I promise."

"As titillating as the thought of you quickly taking your satisfaction and me not having time to come sounds"—she rolls her eyes and laughs—"it's a firm no."

"When have I ever left you unsatisfied?" I kiss the velvety, scented curve of her neck.

"Never." She lays her head on my chest, placing one hand over my heart. "You satisfy me completely, Jared."

My hands tighten on her butt and slide up to her waist, drift into her hair. I want to take it down. I love seeing her hair liberated, loose. Maybe that's left over from an entire semester wondering how long it was, how it would feel in my hands.

"Blame this dress," I tell her. "It shows off the sexiest parts of you."

"Let me guess." Her laugh rumbles into me. "The ass?"

I caress the dramatic curve from her back to her butt, rubbing my hand along her spine.

"No, this is the sexiest thing about you." The laughter leaves my voice. "This gorgeous backbone."

She pulls back to study my face in the shadows. With the sun setting, soon we'll have to pick each other out in the dark like we did the first time we made love.

"Your strength," I continue, pressing my fingers along the delicate bones strung up her back. "And this."

I skim the curve of her breasts but don't stop there, not until I reach the skin left bare by the neckline of her dress. Until my hand rests on her heart.

"This heart of yours." My laugh is full of self-deprecation. "This heart that you somehow miraculously have given to me, it's the other sexiest thing about you."

She traces the line of my eyebrows, the slant of my cheekbones, my lips. I know what she sees. A good-looking guy with a not-always-good heart. Not a heart like hers.

"That's just about the most perfect thing anyone's ever said to me," she says.

All my life I've been driven, in constant motion to always achieve the next thing. Right now, I find a rare moment of contentment just holding her and considering the stunning horizon on the verge of sunset. The golden hour always takes me back to dancing with Banner months ago, green-peaked mountains on one side, aquamarine ocean on the other. We weren't merely dancing with our bodies but were negotiating the steps of our past, our present, our future. Figuring out how it would all come together. We were *battling*, our wills clashing as she tried to do what she thought was right and me dragging her in the direction of what I knew couldn't be wrong. I have that ability to "just know," and it hasn't failed me yet.

And standing here with Banner in the golden hour, the early evening is completely still. There's not even a breeze, but I'm a weather vane and I feel the winds shifting. I "just know."

"I have another offer for you." I make my voice sure when for once I'm not.

"Is it an offer I can't refuse?" she asks, toying with my tie, a playful smile on those beautifully symmetrical lips.

"Uh, you could say no, I guess."

"Jared." She laughs and shakes her head. "*The Godfather?* Your favorite movie? 'I'm gonna make you an offer you can't refuse.'"

She waves her hand, dismissing the joke I should have gotten.

"Never mind. You know I'm bad at jokes."

"You are." I exhale a sharp, nervous breath. "I'm usually quicker than that, though. Sorry. Uh, seriously. I have an offer."

"Okay. I'm all ears."

I've convinced teams to take risks on players they thought two, three, four times about signing. I've persuaded brands to pay twice what they intended in a matter of one meeting, but I can't come up with the words to convince Banner Morales to marry me? This is the most important pitch of my life.

"So we have a lot, right?" I ask.

"I think we have everything we need." She laces her fingers into the short hair at my neck.

"Not everything," I say, taking advantage of the opening. "A wise woman once said I should be unafraid to want it all."

"*Technically*, I was addressing a roomful of women who average about a third of their male counterparts' salaries, and you're a rich white American male," she teases. "So you *have* just about everything, but you were saying?"

I let out a short laugh.

"Did you just *rich white male* me?"

"I *did* just *rich white male* you," she chuckles unrepentantly.

"I'll let you get away with it just this once." I shake my head at her and try to remember where I was. "So like I was saying, I want it all."

I reach into her hair and find one of the pins anchoring it, taking it out. A thick, dark lock spills over her shoulder.

"Jared!" She touches the hair still pulled up.

"I want to wake up with you every morning." I steal another pin, freeing another section of hair.

"Which you already do." She gives up and just angles a look up at me that is part deep love, part perennial exasperation.

"I want to kiss you every day." Another pin gone. More hair falls. "Make love to you every day."

"Also what you already do...every day. Sometimes a few times a day. No complaining. I'm totally here for that."

I grasp the final pin, slide it free, and watch the last of her thick hair fall around her shoulders. Enough of her makeup has worn off that I see her freckles. She looks so much like my girl from the laundromat.

"I want my ring on your finger."

Even over the mariachi band still going strong inside, I hear her gasp. I feel her shock. She doesn't speak but just stares at me with wide eyes.

"I want four kids with you," I continue but hastily modify. "Though if that number is negotiable, I could go down. Like, *way* down."

"Uh, no, Jared, I—"

"Okay, four then. Whatever," I concede with a frown, rushing on before she can tell me no or not now or I'll think about it. Or any shit that isn't what I want her to say. "Look, I know I'm a risk. I'm not..."

Him.

"I'm not Zo," I continue softly, looking from the terrace floor back up to her shell-shocked face. "Or August or my dad. I'm not nice and selfless and considerate. I know how to *charm* people but can't figure out how to like them. I get it."

I regret all the times I told her I had no moral compass, nothing to anchor my conscience, because who in their right mind marries a guy who admits that?

"I know I said my compass spins." Emotion makes it hard to get the words out. "But not with you."

I push the hair I've freed back from her face.

"Banner, I'm set on you," I continue. "And if you'll have me, I promise you won't regret it. I'll love you every day for the rest of my life."

That's all I've got. I just gave her more of myself than any other person on the planet has. I hold my breath and wait to see what she does with it.

She licks her lips and tucks a chunk of hair behind her ear before looking back to me. She cried for Zo earlier, but there's no comparison to what I see standing in her eyes right now. The love, the devotion and unconditional acceptance I feel for her, looking in her eyes, I see it returned under a sheen of tears.

"That's some offer," she says, her voice deepened with the emotion redolent in her eyes. "And I have your answer."

She reaches up and cups my face between trembling hands and, in the dying light of the golden hour, has never been more beautiful to me.

"I don't deserve you, Jared Foster," she says softly, surely. "But I'm going to have you anyway."

BONUS EPILOGUE
BANNER

"You bring my heart
beautifully
to its knees…"

—*Matt Spenser, poet*

Pop!

The sound cracks open the morning quiet in my bedroom, accompanied by a sharp sting to my ass through satin sheets.

"Ow," I mumble into the pillow and reach behind me to rub the spot Jared smacked. "That hurt."

"Rise and grind." He rips the sheet away, exposing my back and butt to the cool air. "Isn't that what your app usually tells you to do?"

My tank top and boy-cut underwear don't cover much, but I'm well past self-consciousness about his rear view of my butt. If he can bite this ass, he can see it in the harsh morning light, dimples, dips, and all.

"Time to make the doughnuts," he says, quoting that old Dunkin' Donuts commercial.

Did he say doughnuts?

There's this little spot on my way to work with the best dough-nuts. Strawberry-cream filling. I could just pull right in and…eat all my points before nine a.m. What am I thinking? I've practically built up an immunity to pastries. What the hell?

Wait a minute.

1. Cravings.

2. Slight abdominal cramping.

3. Irritability...which could just be because Jared unceremoniously disturbed the best sleep I've had all week.

But the other signs suggest my period should start soon. Probably today.

"Ugh."

"Ugh?" Jared asks, sitting on the bed beside me, the chiseled lines of his face coming into view. "Is that any way to greet your fiancé first thing in the morning?"

If the tiny wings fluttering in my belly are anything to go by, even after four months I'm still not used to being Jared Foster's fiancée.

"Not *ugh* to you." I flip to my back and squint up at him, unsure if the gold light surrounding his head is sunlight streaming between the cracks separating my shades or if his wide smile is literally making him glow. "What's wrong with you? Why are you so happy?"

"Banner, can't a man have joy?" he asks with a straight face.

"Joy?" I snort into a yawn. "You?"

"I resent that." A single brow lifted, he accessorizes his crisp, blindingly white shirt with arrogance. "We're getting married in a week. The real question is why don't *you* have joy? What was that *ugh* about?"

"My period."

His hand freezes on one shiny cufflink.

"Like, menstruation?"

"Yes."

"Like, the every month cycle?"

"That's the one."

"When?" He looks genuinely distressed. "Isn't there a pill you can take or something to stop it?"

"Why would I take that pill?"

"Our honeymoon?" He tilts his head and side-eyes me. "We don't want to…negotiate around your period on our honeymoon."

"Why?" I sit up, pulling my knees to my chest and pressing my back into the headboard. "You have some freaky shit planned for our honeymoon?"

A wolfish grin tips one side of his mouth and doesn't bother with the other. "No more than the usual freaky shit. Just with rings and vows."

I forgot horny. My period also makes me horny. My cousin's coming to town for sure. I hope my body doesn't give off some pheromone to alert Jared because he'll start something we'll have to finish and we'll be late for work.

I speak from experience.

"My period should be long gone by our honeymoon, so we can do it on a train, on a plane, in a tree. Whatever the heck you want."

"You know we can never read *Green Eggs and Ham* to our kids, right?"

"Oh!" I clasp my hands under my chin and widen my eyes innocently. "Are you ready to discuss kids already?"

I think he might be sick.

"Uh, what's the rush?" He avoids my eyes and stands quickly as if I might force myself on him for the sole purpose of impregnation. "We're not even hitched yet."

"Right." I rest my chin on my knees and provoke him with a grin. "You can go toe to toe with the NBA commissioner if necessary without batting an eyelash, but I mention kids and you're scurrying."

"I'll leave the batting eyelashes to you," he says wryly. "And I'm not scurrying. Why would the thought of my own offspring make me scurry?"

"You tell me."

"How about *you* tell *me* why you're still in bed? Every other morning, I wake up in a dark room with your phone screeching at me."

"I caught it pre-screech and went back to sleep." I cover my mouth when another yawn takes over my whole face. "Sorry. Stayed up so late working on that sports drink thing for Hakeem."

"You've been working hard." Jared frowns and comes back to the bed. He lifts my chin and scrutinizes my face. "You look tired."

"Gee, thanks," I reply with a grimace.

"You didn't let me finish." He leans down, his just-brushed minty-fresh breath fanning my lips. "You look tired *but* beautiful."

He dips and captures my lips between his. I should spare him the stale breath o' morning, but he tastes so good. I cup the perfect angle of his jaw and thread my fingers into his hair. God, he feels and smells so damn good.

"Hmmmmm." We moan in unison, and he runs his thumb over my nipple. It peaks through my tank top. His hand at my waist coaxes me down over the pillows until I'm flat on my back and he is, suit and all, on the bed and thrusting between my legs.

"Jared, we have to stop." I force myself to pull away. "We'll be late."

"Shit." He sucks my earlobe, and I swear I can *feel* my ovaries quiver. Must be the period. "You're right. I've got that meeting with marketing about Tillman's new shoe."

He peers down at me, his eyes loving as they wander over my face, feature by feature.

"I was hoping we could ride to the office together," he says. "We still can if you get up now."

I lay one last kiss on his lips, lingering to carry this with me all day, but then give him a gentle shove so I can sit up.

"I would, but I have a meeting, too."

As soon as my feet hit the floor, all the things I need to accomplish today inundate my mind. The lassitude flees, and my natural drive kicks in. I walk to the closet and shed the tank top and underwear. I'm tossing them into my hamper when Jared appears at the door.

"Damn, you look good," he mutters, his eyes crawling over my naked body. "We barely saw each other yesterday. We *have* to fuck today. Like, have to."

"Jared." I can't help but laugh at the earnest expression on his face. I walk past him to start what will have to be a very quick shower. "You make it sound like a world summit."

"Priorities, Ban." His hungry glance makes a thorough journey over the curves I'm taking underwater. "Some people want world peace. I want you."

"I want you, too." I smile and squirt shampoo into my palm. "But speaking of priorities, don't you have a meeting?"

"Yeah." He glances at his watch. "You sure you can't be ready in, say…fifteen minutes so we can ride together?"

"I have my own meeting. My own schedule. My own office." I give him a chiding look. "And do not come in there today looking for a quickie on my desk."

"There go my lunch plans," he deadpans. "You want a lot of your *own* things considering we're getting married. What about your own name? You still want that?"

He makes his question sound light, but I've known this man for more than a decade now. I know when something bothers him.

"Okay, Foster," I say, rinsing shampoo from my hair and rubbing in some conditioner. "Let's have it. You don't want me to keep my last name. Am I right?"

He rubs the back of his neck and slides the other hand into his well-tailored slacks. *Ave Maria, that man in a suit is just about criminal.*

"I wouldn't say that." He leans against the bathroom counter.

"Hey." I push the water from my face and grab my bodywash. "Judgment-free. Tell me. Please?"

The firm line of his mouth yields a little. His heavy sigh is all hesitation and resignation before he goes on.

"If I tell you, you'll think I'm prehistoric and misogynistic and patriarchal and—"

"And it won't be the first time or the last," I interrupt. A laugh slips past my lips before I catch it. I straighten out my face, tuck away my amusement.

"You can't call judgment-free and then laugh before I even tell you," he says, bending a stern look on me through the steam. Or as stern as it can be when he keeps staring at my breasts.

"I'm not laughing." I press my lips together and hastily rinse off. "And we'll both be late if we don't hurry up."

"You're saying you didn't laugh? I made that up?"

"I may have chortled a little," I say and stretch out my arm. "Towel, please."

Jared pauses to give me a pointed look before grabbing the fluffy white towel.

I reach for it, but he withholds it.

"Let me do that for you," he says, his voice dropping, his eyes heating up. He dries my shoulders and arms brusquely but slows down when he reaches my breasts.

"Jared." I swallow, fighting the desire his touch incites, at once a rush of adrenaline and a languorous crawl through my blood. I touch the dripping hair hanging down my back. "I'll get you wet."

"I think I'm getting *you* wet." He passes the soft towel over my butt and then slips it between my legs. He pinches my clit, and even though the towel is between his fingers and my bare pussy, I feel the touch to my toes.

"Jared," I groan a weak protest. "I can't be late for this meeting."

He casts one last lava-hot look over my damp, naked skin but wraps the towel around my shoulders, pulling me closer by the edges.

He meets my eyes and finally shows me the unapologetic, ruthless bastard I've come to love.

"I don't want you to keep your last name because I want people to know you're mine."

He doesn't look away but lets me see the unreasonable possessiveness in his implacable stare.

"I know that," I say softly. "But every room we're in together, you make it very clear who I belong to."

He smiles a little because he knows it's true. Hugging me from behind. A hand on my hip or at my neck. Playing with my hair. He's all over me all the time.

I fucking love it.

"And if my ring doesn't scream *this girl is taken,*" I say, holding up my hand to wiggle my fingers between us, "I don't know what does."

We chose it together, the advantage of Jared spontaneously proposing. He didn't have a ring already chosen. It's bigger than what I would have expected to like but still classy. Not gaudy. An emerald-cut black diamond set in platinum, surrounded by diamonds. It's a bold ring. Unique and unforgettable.

Like the man who gave it to me. The one looking at me like I'm a mystifying theorem.

"Jared, our last names aren't the same now, and I'm yours."

"True." He doesn't look convinced.

"And with that line of thinking, how does anyone know *you* belong to *me* if you don't carry *my* last name?"

"You want me to take your name?"

"Not necessarily. I just don't want to lose mine." I shift the towel from around my shoulders to wrap my torso, knotting it between my breasts. "My father doesn't have Morales males to carry on his name. I'm proud of my name. Of my heritage. Of where I come from. Of my parents and my family. I don't want all of that to be lost in—"

"Me? You don't want all of that lost in me?"

"Don't think of it that way." I shake my head. "It's not like that, or maybe it is, but it's not a reflection of what I *don't* want of you. It's a reflection of what I want to *keep* of myself."

He's quiet for a few seconds, absorbing my words before he nods.

"I get that." He bends to fit his mouth to mine, cups my neck, deepens the kiss, and just when I'm ready to say screw this day and drag him back to the bed, he pulls away.

"Not fun, is it?" He drops a light kiss on my hungry lips. "To be left hanging."

I chuckle and walk into the closet to select what I'll wear today, a simple kelly-green dress that will mold my curves but still leave me room for comfort. It's a long day ahead.

"I love that color on you," Jared says from the closet door.

I turn to catch his glance and smile, holding the dress up to me. "You do?"

He nods, but he's in his head now, and I only have half his attention. While I blow-dry my hair, he leans against the bathroom wall, silent, contemplative. He's still thinking about me keeping my name. I can practically see my words gain footing in his thoughts. I can visualize my views clinging to the inside of his brain. I love how he listens to me. Intently. Actively, like something I say could change his mind at any moment or further convince him how wrong I am. Even when we're on opposite sides of an issue, in the thick of a debate, I don't mind. I just love sharing my thoughts, hearing his, exchanging ideas. It's true stimulation like I've never had with anyone else. Not even my longest relationship before this one.

Which reminds me…

"Hey, my appointment this morning is with Zo," I say after brushing my teeth. "But I'll get to the office in time for our weekly update meeting with the staff."

It's quiet for a few moments. I look up to find him watching me, his expression at ease but his eyes alert.

"At his house?" he asks, and there are about three questions tucked into that one.

"Yeah."

Jared trusts me, and he knows for sure nothing would happen between Zo and me, but he still has some discomfort about the closeness that exists between us. Maybe he always will.

I put on the dress and turn my back to Jared, pulling my hair aside and displaying my unzipped dress. "Help a sister out?"

He pulls the zipper up to the middle of my back and then stops, slipping one large hand in under the dress, spreading his fingers over my rib cage and just under my breast. He draws me back into his chest and tucks his head into the curve of my neck, his silky hair caressing my sensitive skin.

"I don't like feeling this way, Ban," he says, his voice low.

My head tips back and turns so I can see his profile.

"Feeling what way? Jealous?"

"No, not exactly jealous." He frowns. "I wouldn't say that. More like…did you ever have trouble sharing your toys when you were growing up?"

"No," I answer immediately. "Never."

"Of course you didn't." He chuckles into the freshly blown hair hanging around my shoulders. "So there was this kid in my neighborhood."

"What was his name?" I turn to face him, but his hand doesn't leave my skin. Just slides to caress my back while we talk.

"Does that really matter?"

"You don't remember his name," I tease with a grin.

"It's been twenty-five years, Ban. You can't expect me to remember the name of every person who has passed through my life. It was a long time ago."

"And the new receptionist? Who's been at Elevation for over a month, what's her name?"

"Like I was saying," he continues, ignoring my question and threading laughter through his words. "There was a kid in my neighborhood."

He squeezes one eye closed, concentrating.

"Okay. Steven. Maybe his name was Steven. Anyway, we both wanted this bike a guy up the street was selling. I had a lemonade stand, mowed lawns, busted my ass to buy that bike. He was busting his ass, too, but I got it first."

He huffs a short laugh, shakes his head.

"Every time I rode my bike," he says, snapping his brows together, "he'd stop what he was doing and just stare."

"And you didn't like that," I offer softly, unnecessarily.

"I hated it," Jared confirms with a smile that mocks his own pettiness. "One day we'd left the garage door up, and I walked in. There he was looking at my bike."

"Do you think he was going to take it or something?"

"I don't know that he would have actually taken it, but he *wanted* it."

"Maybe you could have offered to let him ride it sometimes?" The horror on Jared's face makes me laugh. "I mean, since he wanted it so badly."

"That would have been *your* response," Jared says with the smallest smile. "I, however, told him if I caught him around my bike again I was gonna punch him in the face."

"Harsh but not surprising."

"That's how it feels with Zo sometimes."

My smile fades by inches until it's gone completely.

"Jared, no." I reach up to cup his face, hold his eyes with mine. "It's not like that anymore."

"Not for you, but for him..." He shrugs, a muscle flexing along his jaw. "He still wants you."

"I don't think so," I reply as honestly as I can, even though he cocks a skeptical brow. "No, really. We haven't seen each other as much lately now that he has his nurse. I'm not involved with his care. Things have been on hold with his career while he's recovering from stem cell replacement. Today will be the first time we've seen each other in weeks. You know that."

"But he has to still want you."

"How can you be so sure?"

"Because I could never stop," he admits.

And...I'm jelly.

I tip up on my toes and loop my arms around his neck, kissing along his neck and up to his jaw.

"Screw it," I mumble against his cool skin. "We can do it really fast."

"See, you waited too late to say yes." He laughs into a kiss that doesn't go long or deep enough and slides my zipper up the rest of the way. "Now I really will be late if I don't go."

It's a good thing we take turns being reasonable or we'd be in bed all day every day.

"You're right. I'll be late, too." I grab my makeup bag from under the sink. "I'll have to do my face in the car as it is."

He bends to kiss my nose like he does at least once a day.

"Before you cover my freckles," he says with a smile. "I love you."

I can't help but smile, too, and sometimes I can't believe this is us. The hardened cynic and his tenderhearted rival, grinning foolishly at each other a mere week before our wedding.

"I love you, too." I step away reluctantly, missing the hard press of his body already. Missing the hard press of his unwavering focus already. Jared was intense before, but now that we live and work together, it's even more and all the time. His eyes, his attention, his hands on me all the time.

I wouldn't have it any other way.

I'm grabbing the bag that carries everything from my tampons to my iPad when he catches up to me at the door, suit jacket on and his face already cast into the unreadable lines he shows the world. Only I get to see him vulnerable, unsure. *Trusting.* What an amazing privilege.

We reach our cars in the garage at the same time, and I'm juggling my coffee and bag when he gets my attention.

"Hey, Ban."

I glance over my shoulder, our eyes meeting across the roof of his convertible.

"That new receptionist," he says with a grin. "Her name is Joanna."

I didn't lie to Jared. I never would. Zo and I haven't seen each other in weeks, but I didn't tell him I'm sometimes as unsure of where things stand between us as Jared is. In hindsight, I know Zo was right to hire a nurse. We needed that space to recalibrate our boundaries, to adjust our relationship.

We spent our first Christmas apart in ten years. Jared and I went to visit his parents in Maryland. I exchanged gifts with my family the night before we left. Despite his low tolerance for people in general, Jared *knows* people. He understands them and charms them until they're eating from his hand. My family is no different, no less susceptible to his charisma, except for my mother. She has softened significantly toward him, though, and I've repaired my relationship with her. She knows I'm happy in a way I never was with Zo, but he's like the son she never had. And with him sick, I wanted him to have her, too, especially for the holidays.

So I experienced my first Christmas with snow instead of palm trees. Sitting by a fire instead of by the pool. Jared's family is amazing. August and Iris, his stepmother Susan and his father. Spending time with them eased the ache of being away from my people some, but I did miss my family. And I did miss Zo.

My finger hovers over the doorbell of Zo's stately new Calabasas home when the door swings open. His nurse, Brittany, rushes past me, speaking quickly into her cell phone.

"I'm on my way," she says, barely sparing me a glance, her tone anxious. "His medication should be on the bathroom counter. It's the Accupril."

"He's home?" I whisper and point a thumb over my shoulder into the house. I don't want to interrupt her call, but I need to make sure it's okay to go inside.

She gives me the briefest of glances and nods, unlocking her car, still talking as she gets behind the wheel and pulls off without an actual word to me. Obviously, there's an emergency. She and I usually chat about Zo's progress, if he's taking his meds, his diet. The whole gamut.

His diet.

It's been so long since I made him one of those smoothies he loves. I lock the door Brittany left standing open and survey the marble-tiled foyer. I have to tip my head all the way back to find the top of the ceiling, it's so high. I've only been here a few times since Zo purchased this new house. With him on leave from the Titans, there wasn't any reason to stay in Vancouver. He's closer to his medical team and the only family he has—mine—living here in LA.

"Kitchen?" I mumble to myself, considering the passageway that forks to the right. Zo could be in there, but even if he isn't, I can whip up one of his smoothies.

Only it sounds like someone has beaten me to it.

The familiar whir of the blender mixes with a soft, melodious voice singing in Spanish, a song I've heard once before. When I enter the kitchen, I'm surprised to find a petite woman, her body a circuit of gorgeous curves, ebony hair hanging thick and straight to her waist. The Vancouver Titans T-shirt she wears only reaches the middle of her deeply tanned slim thighs.

"*Gracias a la vida que me ha dado tanto,*" she sings, her pretty voice barely audible over the blender.

Thanks to the life that has given me so much.

"*Me ha dado la risa y me ha dado el llanto,*" she continues, the words clearer when the blender stops.

Life has given me laughter and tears.

"Gracias a la Vida," I say, naming the song she's singing.

She jumps a little and turns to face me. Dark, wide eyes are fringed by lashes fake lashes would envy. Her face somehow manages to be simultaneously delicately boned and strongly featured. She's beautiful. Not a face you'd soon forget.

"Graciela?" I ask. I'm assembling information slowly. The song. Her face. Her voice. I've heard her sing before. "San Nicolas, right? You're the director of the orphanage there?"

"*Sí. Hola.*" Her pouty lips widen in a genuine smile, which doesn't last long. "Oh, Banner. *Lo siento...*"

She glances down at her bare legs and feet, tugs at the hem of the shirt before darting a look up the back stairs leading to the next floor.

"You're visiting?" I continue in Spanish, not remembering how much English she speaks.

"Uh, yes." Her eyes slide away from meeting mine directly. "Alonzo said you and he were…not together anymore. I'm sorry if—"

"We aren't." I cover my heart with my hand. "Oh. No, we aren't. See, I'm engaged."

I toss up my hand to show her my ring, and we exchange uncertain smiles.

"*Felicidades*," she murmurs, continuing in Spanish.

"*Gracias*," I reply.

The awkward silence between us doesn't have long to bloom, broken by heavy steps descending the staircase leading into the kitchen.

"Did you find what you needed, Gracie?" Zo asks, his voice reaching us before the rest of him does.

When he appears at the bottom of the stairs, I'm taken aback. He's wearing only sweatpants. Bare feet. Bare chest.

A well-developed chest!

Gone is the frail torso the disease had reduced him to before his stem cell replacement. He's still not as heavily muscled as before, but it's obvious he's been working out again and that it's paying off.

"Banner," he says, brows lifting. He glances at a clock on the wall. "Our meeting. I'm sorry. I didn't realize how late it was."

His eyes drift to the skimpily dressed woman by the blender, and a tiny smile quirks the corner of his mouth. "You remember Graciela, yes?"

"Of course." My lips feel stiff, but I bend them into a smile and force myself to meet his eyes. "We were just…um, of course."

Graciela and I half-smile at one another. I fiddle with my earrings and run a nervous hand through my hair. She rests one small foot on the other, shifting restlessly. For a few seconds, the hand of the clock ticking is the only sound in the kitchen. This is just weird. Before Zo and I started dating, I ran into women leaving his house all the time. I helped him choose gifts for them. He'd ask for advice and confide intimate things about his love life. So it's not that I've never seen him with another woman, even "the morning after." It's just the first time since we became...an us. I imagine it was even more difficult for him watching me with Jared.

Guilt harpoons my heart, stealing my breath for a second. I'm deliriously happy with Jared. We fit in every way. Our minds, opposing, convening, collaborating. Our bodies, joined in passion, in unconditional love. Our hearts, so different and imperfectly interlocked. I will never regret choosing to spend my life with Jared, but I will *always* regret hurting Zo. I'll never forget the agony of confessing my sin, telling him I had broken our faith. A part of me will always be ashamed, but we've come a long way and have been through hell together. Seeing him look so healthy, look so much like himself again, makes me happier than I can articulate. Seeing him with another woman makes me...

"Gracie, could you give us a few moments?" Zo asks, breaking the chain of my thoughts. He's beside her now, his big hand cradling her hip. "It won't take long. Just business."

The word *business* lands on me heavily at first but lightens as I absorb it. I *am* business. We'll always be friends, but he's redrawn the boundaries, and standing beside the woman he spent the night with, he's making it clear to her—and to me—that this is business and she has nothing to worry about.

I approve.

She melts into him for a moment like she's forgotten I'm here, drawing in a breath of his scent, the bodywash I remember well. She's so much smaller, but nothing about her is weak. There's a strength running through her like a ribbon of steel. I've seen it in action, seen *her* in action directing the San Nicolas orphanage with compassion and ruthless efficiency.

"*Espérame arriba,*" he says into her hair, his voice low and intimate.

Wait for me upstairs.

Round two, maybe? Zo's muscles aren't the only things coming back. That libido seems to be making quite the recovery, too.

Heat simmers between them, the kind of heat I never felt with him and, if Zo is honest, maybe he never felt with me. I swallow and rub the back of my neck, eager to finish our conversation and get the hell out of their way.

She nods but pulls away to pour the smoothie from the blender into a large cup.

"I made this for you," she says, her voice sweet and husky. "Just as you like it, I hope."

He takes a quick sip, and the orange froth lingers on his lip. She reaches up to wipe it away and licks it from her finger.

Okay.

I clear my throat, and they both glance at me, her a little abashedly, him with some amusement.

"It was good seeing you again, Banner," Graciela murmurs and turns to go.

Zo's hand drops from the small of her back, but his glance follows her up the steps before returning to me. The affection that has always been in his eyes when he looks at me miraculously still remains. I don't deserve it. Nor the respect he still affords me every time we see each other, when he speaks of me in interviews or speeches. No one would ever know how I injured him. He's never spoken a harsh word publicly about me or Jared. For a moment, I'm overcome by how close I came to losing Zo, how close we *all* came to losing such an extraordinary human. Next comes worry that we still will.

"We need to discuss the doctor's reports," I say more abruptly than I'd planned.

His brows lift, and he leans against the counter, his arms, well-muscled again, folded across his chest.

"Just dive right in, eh?" he asks. "Nothing to say about Graciela?"

"Sorry." I frown and push a chunk of hair behind my ear. "I didn't mean to skip pleasantries, but we need to talk."

I glance up and smile.

"Besides, what am I supposed to say about a beautiful woman in your bed? Congratulations?"

His short bark of laughter loosens the air between us even more. I walk over to him and start clearing the fruits and vegetables Graciela used for his smoothie. I gather the carrots, a bundle of kale, a tomato, and a sweet potato.

"No pineapple?" I ask, heading toward the refrigerator.

"Graciela thinks it's too harsh."

I stiffen mid-bend to replace the items in the crisper, straighten quickly, and face him.

"Too harsh?" I demand. "I cleared pineapple with your team dietician. What makes her think my smoothie is too harsh? How would *she* know?"

Zo watches me over the rim of his cup as he takes a leisurely sip of his "less harsh" smoothie.

"And I guess therein lies the essence of why it didn't work between us," he says, his lips pressed together against a smile.

"Excuse me?" I ask, still irritated by Graciela's derision of my smoothie recipe. "What do you mean?"

"You don't give a damn that I slept with her, but you're jealous she's the one making my smoothies. Maybe you only wanted to be my nurse all along."

I hazard a glance up and find his dark eyes smiling at me.

"I mean, it's pineapple," I mutter and grab a bowl of grapes. "What harm can pineapple do?"

I cross back over to lean with him against the counter.

"So is it serious?" I ask, placing the bowl on the counter and popping a grape into my mouth.

"I like her a lot. She likes me. We are good together." He shrugs, takes another sip of his smoothie. "The doctor finally cleared me for a brief trip out of the country, so I flew down to check on the orphanage. She and I reconnected there."

"I'm happy for you."

"*Gracias.*"

"Well, I'm sure the kids were glad to see you, too." I smile, remembering our work down there a few summers ago. I've rarely seen him happier. Not even when he won a championship. "And you were glad to see them."

"*Sí*, it is very special to me," he says, his mouth falling into a sober line. "I, too, am an orphan. I understand how it feels to be alone in the world."

A painful knot burns my throat. He's been through so much in his life, and so much struggle with this damn amyloidosis still lies ahead. That I brought him even an ounce of pain in an already-trial-filled life sickens me. I bite my lip and blink back tears.

"But you changed all that, Bannini," he says softly.

"What?" I look up, startled by his words while I'm castigating myself. "Changed all what?"

"I wasn't alone in this world for long." He stares into his smoothie, eyes unfocused or focused on the past, something I can't see. "That was the worst day of my life, losing them all at once."

"I know." I touch his wrist and squeeze. "I know it still hurts."

"Yes, but the day I walked into Cal's office and met you," he says, covering my hand with one of his, smiling at me. "That was one of the best days."

"No." I shake my head, weighted by my own guilt. "I haven't been the friend to you I should have, Zo. I... You know what I did."

"Yes, I do know what you did." He tips up my chin. "You navigated me into wealth I never could've imagined. You gave me a second family when mine was gone. When I was sick..."

Our stares connect, and I know, like me, he's recalling the ER visits, the close calls, the chemo, the diarrhea, the fear of death hovering over us for months. He's remembering the hell we walked through together. If I close my eyes, I can still feel the flames licking at my faith, still smell my hope, charred when he was close to death. I can taste my secret tears as I watched him fighting for his life. As I fought with him.

"When I was sick," he starts again, swallowing and drawing a breath. "You wouldn't let me give up. You wouldn't let the doctors give up. You took no prisoners. That's what you do for everyone you care about, but I like to think I am special."

My lips twitch in spite of the tears those memories burned into my eyes.

"You're very special to me, Zo," I say, my voice thickened by emotion. "You know that."

"But I'm not him," he says softly but not sadly. There's an acceptance in his eyes I haven't seen before. An understanding, a new contentment. Maybe Graciela gave him that. Maybe time has, or perspective.

I was naive to think we could conduct this conversation without Jared coming up, but there was a tiny part of me that hoped we could because *he* will always be the one I choose. Over Zo. Over my mother's approval. I'll choose Jared over even my own *judgment* and over everything I hold dear. He will always be the one I hold *dearest*. I will always choose him.

Before I can respond, Zo goes on, asking me something even more awkward.

"Are you excited about the wedding?"

I've always been honest with Zo. Even when I knew what I had to tell him would make him think less of me and would break his heart, I told him the truth.

"Yes," I answer simply, staring at, twisting the stunning ring Jared put on my finger. "Very."

"I'm happy for you."

His words, spoken softly but with such apparent sincerity, break the last of my restraint, and tears slip over my cheeks.

"Oh, Zo, you don't have to—"

"I am," he cuts in. "How it happened, no. I would not choose that, and it hurt. You know that. It hurt badly."

I just nod because words won't come out.

"But you never looked at me the way you look at him."

"I'm sorry." My words wobble.

"And maybe I never looked at you the way he does."

My head snaps up so I can meet his eyes.

"I thought I did," he continues. "Being with Graciela...I don't know. There is something else there that maybe we never had, yeah? You know?"

A tiny smile pulls my lips out of their misery because I *do* know. That fire. That heat I sensed between them, once you taste it, nothing less ever satisfies.

"Who knows where this will go between us," he says. "I mean, who wants to start something lasting with a dying man?"

"Don't say that," I snap, outrage in the look I give him. "Your body's in response. You're getting better every day. The last doctor report said they couldn't believe your progress. That they've never seen anyone do as well with this condition as you're doing."

"That same report advised against resuming an eighty-two-game schedule playing professional basketball."

I drop my eyes to the floor at the reminder of why I'm actually here: to discuss a future that once shone so brightly and now looms uncertain.

"You are too thorough to have missed that," he says, the soulful eyes that struck me the first time I saw him again tinged with sadness, with regret. "It's over, Banner. I have to retire."

"Zo, maybe we could—"

"You know it," he interrupts and grabs my hand. "I have made peace with it. I have my *life*. I have more money than I can ever spend. I have my philanthropic efforts. The orphanage."

He pauses to chuckle and glance up the staircase Graciela took a few minutes earlier.

"I have a woman crazy enough to want a relationship with me, even knowing I have an expiration date."

"Don't joke about it, Zo." Tears clog my throat. "The thought of losing you…of you…"

Even saying that word could diminish my hope, my faith, so I don't say it.

"We'll all die someday," he says philosophically. "I just have to spend more energy than most making sure I stick around as long as I can. The rest of the report really is encouraging. They speculate that the excellent condition my body was in before my sickness accounts for how it is responding now."

He lets my hand go and flexes the impressive muscles in his arms.

"And in case you hadn't noticed, I'm getting my form back."

I laugh and roll my eyes.

"Show-off," I say playfully. "Vain bastard."

"No, that would be your fiancé."

"Ohhh!" I laugh and shake my head, leaning against the counter again to consider him. "You just couldn't resist."

"No, I couldn't." His smile softens, and he takes my hand again. "Let's talk about the part of my future we *can* actually control. We started this adventure together over a decade ago against the odds. You ready to do it with me again?"

"You know I always have your back." I grin, already strategizing, visualizing Zo's next chapter. "And I also have a plan."

"That's my girl," he says, his smile free of all the things that could have ruined us, could have ended us for good.

"*En las buenas,*" I say the words I haven't dared say to him since he almost died in the ambulance months ago.

Through thick.

His smile dies off, but not in anger or disappointment or any of the things I dreaded seeing in his eyes forever. His smile disappears, and what remains is what should have been there all along. The unwavering, unconditional love of one friend for another.

"*En las malas,*" he replies.
Through thin.

I'm really late.

In my haste to make our staff meeting, I park a little crookedly and practically run into the building that houses Elevation. This is the one meeting Jared cannot stand for any of us to miss. I'm an equal partner, which means he will be as equally snappy to me as to anyone else if I miss this meeting. I board the elevator and pull my phone from my purse to check the time, ignoring the Girl, You Better alert reminding me I didn't work out today and skipped a meal. The last thing I want to hear about is the metabolic implications of not eating on the regular, not when I need to get into my wedding dress next week.

Which reminds me. Quinn and I are supposed to have one last fitting for our dresses. She and Camilla are my two maids of honor. No other bridesmaids. It will be a simple wedding in the small San Diego chapel where I received my first communion. Where, growing up, I confessed to Father López, who will perform the ceremony. I'm texting Quinn a reminder when the elevator doors open.

The office is eerily empty because everyone is meeting in the conference room. Great. No way to slip in undetected. When I open the door, everyone looks my way except Jared. His eyes never stray from the oversized ad markup he's holding.

"Ms. Morales," he says, eyes narrowed on the ad copy in his hands. "How nice of you to join us."

"Sorry I'm late." I spread a smile around the room to all the friendly faces of our staff. They accepted me as Jared's equal immediately, and I've been pleased by the respect not only the women but also the men have shown me. "I had a meeting."

"Oh, I'm aware," Jared drawls, his dark-blond brows snapping together. "Of your meeting, I mean."

The staff knows he can be an asshole. They also know I don't take shit from him. Inevitably, two such strong personalities leading a firm like this, we clash from time to time. Sometimes epically, but we make up as quickly. The first time we had makeup sex in my office, the entire staff must have heard us. For weeks they teased us about the "metaphorical lunch" we had in our office. My cheeks flame at the memory, even though there is nothing sexy about the sharp look Jared aims over the dark rim of his glasses.

Okay. Maybe it is a little bit sexy.

"Bill," he says, addressing one of our junior agents but watching me as I sit beside him at the head of the table. "Tell us about that scouting trip you took to North Carolina."

I feel Jared's eyes on me the entire time Bill is talking. I glance up to catch his stare, lifting my brows to silently ask him what the hell. Bill wraps up his recruitment report, and Jared sighs heavily, taking off his glasses and squeezing the bridge of his nose.

"Thanks, Bill." He glances at his watch. "Anyone else have a client update?"

"I do," I say, meeting his intense cerulean-blue eyes.

"Oh, yes." Jared leans back in his chair and links his fingers over the taut abs covered by his crisp shirt. "Do tell. How is Mr. Vidale?"

Everyone knows I dated Zo. And everyone knows I'm marrying Jared next week. And everyone hears the sarcasm, the tightness in his voice when he asks the question.

"You're being ridiculous," I whisper to him.

"Am I?" he whispers back.

"We can talk about it over lunch," I whisper.

"I wonder if that means another metaphorical lunch?" Bill whispers to the girl next to him, but not quietly enough.

"And I wonder if you'd be metaphorically unemployed," Jared snaps. "Or just kind of not work here anymore."

In the lengthening silence, with the staff wondering whose head the boss will chop off next, I decide to soothe his unreasonable… whatever this is.

"So like I said," I tell him and the rest of the room, "I have a client update. Zo's latest report showed great progress."

"That's good," Jared says, his tone, his eyes softening some. "I'm glad to hear he's doing better."

I offer him the slightest smile, but he looks down at the notepad in front of him.

Idiot.

"He has decided to retire, though."

Gasps, murmurs, sounds of dismay fill the conference room. Zo is beloved everywhere and by everyone. The entire league has been rooting for him since his diagnosis. It would be easy to view his early retirement from the NBA as a defeat.

But I'm not having that.

"I'm relieved actually," I say, blowing out an extended breath and waiting for the questions to start so I can spin this to them the way I will to the rest of the world.

"Relieved?" Bill asks. "One of your biggest clients is retiring so young and you're relieved? Why? Because it's better for his health?"

"Well, now he can focus on the book we've been planning to document his journey," I say, studying my nails.

"Ah, yes. The book," Jared says, a smile starting at the edges of his mouth and growing. "Novel idea, pun intended."

"Thank you." I slide a look over to him from the corner of my eye. "I thought so. He'll announce his retirement at a press conference next week, but I spoke to Robin on my way here about an exclusive interview soon after."

"Robin?" Jared asks, knowing amusement spreading over his face, making its way into his eyes.

"Roberts," I say, feigning impatience. "From *Good Morning America*, of course. Keep up, Foster. I've also preliminarily contacted a speaker's bureau about Zo joining their circuit."

"It sounds like you have everything under control." Jared nods, looking slightly less tense. "Well, if no one else has—"

"Oh," I cut in. "One more thing about Zo."

"Yeah?" The muscle along his jaw tightens while he waits.

"He got a new...*bike*," I say.

Jared's glance flicks to mine, narrows.

"A new bike?" he asks, picking between the lines of what I'm saying.

"Yes, a beautiful bike with gorgeous curves. Imported! Perfect for him."

"You don't say." Jared's smile spreads across his full lips, and he reaches under the table to take my hand, caressing the finger adorned with his ring. "A bike of his very own, huh?"

"Yup."

Jared stares into my eyes for an extra few seconds while everyone else waits to be dismissed. "Well, I know what it's like to have a beautiful bike with gorgeous curves. You cherish that."

"I feel like this could be another metaphor," Bill whispers.

"I'm glad he got his own bike," Jared goes on, holding my eyes with his, ignoring Bill. "I'm happy for him."

With my best friend healthier than he's been in a long time, with Elevation flourishing, and with my pending wedding to the man I started falling for as soon as he asked to borrow a pencil, I feel lighter than I've ever felt.

"Yeah, I'm happy for him, too."

JARED

"Think you'll cry?"

August's absurd question catches me off guard while we wait in a small room to take our places at the altar.

"Cry?" My laugh bounces off the rectory walls. I think this is a rectory. I can't keep all the names people have for churches straight. We could get married at a Safeway for all I care, as long as at the end of this day Banner is Mrs. Jared Foster.

Or Mrs. Banner Morales-Foster.

Whatever.

As long as she's mine.

"Why the hell would I cry?" I try to loosen the collar of the shirt, only to realize this is as loose as it gets. "I'm not you. I'm *pretty* sure your heart has a pussy, Gus."

"An asshole to the very end, huh?" He grins and shakes his head. "You'll see. There's something about that moment when she comes down the aisle and you realize she's yours forever."

"But I already know Banner's mine forever."

August gives me a long-suffering look. And he has been suffering me for a long time. Since we were kids. I did this for him on his wedding day, and miraculously, improbably, I actually found someone I could tolerate for the rest of my life, and he's doing it for me on mine.

Only I more than tolerate Banner. I *have* to have her. I want every moment with her I can squeeze out of this life. And if there is an afterlife, I'll chain us together in that, too.

Though I really don't know how I feel about all that afterlife crap. Let's just get through this life in one piece, shall we?

Banner knows I'm not religious. Or traditional. Or Catholic. Or Mexican.

I was willing to go through any motions, any traditions she wanted for the ceremony, but she only wanted to do things that would hold meaning for us both. So we are keeping it pretty simple but have written our own vows.

I *am* slightly nervous about that.

Those vows will be my moment to declare to the whole world that I do indeed believe in miracles. How else could I explain finding someone like Banner, much less someone like her choosing someone like me? How else to explain that when I saw her as my equinox, as my match, that she saw it, too?

God, I wish I'd really understood it all those years ago. Maybe I would have fought harder to make her understand what happened that night. But we were so young, and maybe the ten years we spent apart were not years wasted but years *needed*. We both had so much growing to do, so much to achieve and become on our own. Who knows if we would have lasted if we'd begun in college after our one night together. But we're beginning now. They say today is the first day of the rest of our lives. I'm not one for sentiment, but I'll take that one.

August peeks around the corner and turns back to me, his eyes lit with anticipation.

"It's time," he says. "You ready?"

The reality of this moment, the gravity of what I'm about to do slams into me, and I draw a deep breath, catching, feeling the weight of it.

"Yeah, I'm ready."

I follow him out, and we take our places at the altar. The family is being seated, and I catch Señora Morales' eyes as she's ushered in to take her seat. We exchange a real-deal smile. We're in a good place. Does she love me the way she does Zo? Probably never. Does she know without a doubt that I love her daughter more than anything in this world?

I've made sure she does.

But even if she doesn't, I'm marrying Banner anyway.

When it comes to Banner, I'm on some *SorryNotSorry* shit. We are happening no matter what, but I know what Banner's family means to her, so I'm glad she and her mother have restored their relationship.

I mentally run through my vows while Quinn and Camilla walk gracefully up the aisle, assuming their place across from us. Thank

God. That means Banner's next, and we can finish this and then the reception. And then the honeymoon. I'm ready to have Banner to myself for two weeks with no work and no one else. I'm ready to get this over with.

But as soon as the first strains of "Wedding March" fill the church and the doors open to reveal my bride, my impatience drains away.

And I just want to slow everything down. I want to savor this moment. Freeze it for posterity. Steal it from time and hold it in my heart forever.

I've never seen anything more beautiful than Banner on our wedding day. Her dress is the color of buttercream whipped against her olive-toned skin. Her shoulders are bare, and the silk dress molds the curves of her breasts, her waist, and hips. She's veil-less, which I requested. Her hair spills loosely around her shoulders and down her back. I didn't request that, but she knows I love her hair that way.

And I get it. I know why August thought I might cry. It's not the dress or the guests' *oohs* and *ahhs* or the music and pomp and circumstance. It's not even the church that makes these moments sacred. It's *her*. The love shining from Banner's eyes. The fact that she's trusting me with her life, joining her future with mine, and I might not be worthy of it. Might not be worthy of *her*, but I can't imagine life without her.

The urge to kiss her singes my lips, and as soon as she reaches me, I lean down to cup her cheek and take her lips between mine. She's as sweet in front of all these people as she was the first time I kissed her in a laundromat by ourselves. A guest in the audience gasps, shocked that I breached some made-up rule about when I can kiss my girl during our wedding ceremony.

Fuck that.

She laughs against my lips, kisses me back briefly before pulling away.

"You look beautiful." I whisper the words over her lips, and don't give a damn if everyone has to wait all day for her to answer.

"You look beautiful, too. You always do," she whispers back. "But should we…?"

She tips her head toward the waiting priest.

I turn to find Father López gaping at us a little, staring at me like I stole the communion wafers.

"Sorry, Father," Banner whispers. "We can start now."

After "Dearly Beloved," his words start fading into the background, articulating all the things he thinks marriage means. My chest gets tighter and tighter as we approach the vows and I'll have to tell Banner what it means to *me*. I'm glad she goes first.

"Banner and Jared have written their own vows," Father López says and nods for Banner to begin.

"Jared," she starts.

And I have to focus really hard on what she says next because those espresso-colored eyes, those same-size lips, have never looked more stunning. She even left my seven freckles uncovered because she knows how much I love them.

"Ours has been a long road," she says. "Not an easy one. We aren't easy people."

She pauses to shoot me an impish grin. "Especially you. There's nothing easy about you, Foster."

The guests laugh, and I look away from her long enough to spare them a wry grin.

"But who wants easy?" she asks, her smile melting away. "When I'm with you, I feel truly alive. It sounds cliché, but when I'm with you, life, everything is more vibrant. Easy doesn't challenge, doesn't stretch. *You* do those things. *You* challenge me. *You* stretch me. You never settle for less, and I love that about you. I love how high your standards are for people. For yourself. So high that sometimes you don't even see what a good man you are."

She blinks those long lashes, and a tear slides over her cheek.

"But I see it," she says, her voice huskier, softer. "I have high standards, too. And you meet and exceed every one of them. You *are* a good man, and you're the one I choose to spend the rest of my life with. You're my standard, Jared. Trial, triumph, good days, bad days. I want to walk with you through every circumstance, and I want to spend every day for the rest of my life loving you. *Te amo.*"

Her words, so sincere, so miraculous—that she could see me that way—ease the tightness in my chest. She has given me the greatest gift—a commitment in front of everyone that what I feel, she feels it, too. I hear sniffles in the audience. People cry at weddings, and my throat burns, too, but I stave off tears because it's my turn and I can't screw this up. It's too important that I get it right, say it right.

"Banner," I say. "*No me enamoré de ti a la vez.*"

"*I didn't fall for you all at once,*" Camilla translates in English as we arranged.

At my first words in Spanish, Banner's startled glance locks with mine. The tears gathering in her eyes make all the Rosetta Stone I've been sneaking in worth it.

"*Me enamoré de ti en pedazos.*"

I fell for you in pieces.

"*Primero fue tu voz.*"

First it was your voice.

"*Confiado y fuerte, audaz y fuerte.*"

Confident and strong, bold and loud.

"*Lo que me llevó a tu mente, fuerte y brillante.*"

Which led me to your mind, sharp and brilliant.

"*Y luego vi tu cara, tu cabello, tu cuerpo.*"

And then I saw your face, your hair, your body.

"*Una hermosa capa que cubría lo que más me atraía.*"

A beautiful layer covering the thing that drew me most.

"*Tu corazón.*"

Your heart.

"*Un corazón tan ancho, tan profundo.*"

A heart wide enough, deep enough.

"*Para compartir la alegría, el dolor de aquellos a tu alrededor.*"

To share the joy, the sorrow of those around you.

I press my palm to her heart and my forehead to hers, swallowing against the emotion burning through every fiber of my body so I can get this out.

"*Un corazón tan abierto para dejarme entrar.*"

A heart open enough to let me in.

"*Y nunca me voy a ir.*"

And I'm never leaving.

I knot my fingers into a fist over the thunderous pounding of her heart.

"*A través de los buenos tiempos, a través de los tiempos difíciles.*"

Through good times, through hard times.

"*Aquí es donde me quedaré.*"

This is where I'll stay.

The sniffles are even louder now, the *awwwws* and *oooohs* more abundant, but I block them all out and tune every sense, every thought and sensation to Banner. I thought hearing my vows in the language she loves most would be special for her, and I was right. There's a richness in the air between us, a tensile thread that only we can see and feel tied between our hearts. And I realize that it wasn't the Spanish that did that. We did that with a love only we can feel this deeply and in a language spoken from my soul to hers that only we understand. It affects me, and for a second I really do think I'll lose my shit and fall at Banner's feet and beg her to never see me the way everyone else does. To never take off the blinders that fool her into thinking I'm good enough for someone with a heart like hers.

She's affected, too. The tears streak through her makeup, and she doesn't even check them. And she does something unexpected. The thing I love about her, how she feints left when I anticipate right. My little rule follower, the queen of doing things as they're supposed to be done, the standard bearer for crossed "t's" and dotted "i's" grabs the back of my neck, tips up on her toes, doesn't wait for Father López to pronounce us anything. She shows the world what we already are.

A match.

And she kisses me.

"I think we scandalized Father López," I say, raising my voice so Banner hears me in the bathroom. "Two unauthorized kisses in one ceremony."

Her deep laugh reaches me in the bedroom.

"I know. My aunt Valentina probably has rosaries dedicated to us now."

We could have gone anywhere in the world for our honeymoon, but we came back to the villa on St. John's. It holds significance for us, a turning point in many ways. It seemed the perfect place to start this new chapter of our lives together.

"She did seem concerned for my eternal soul." I tie the knot on my sleep pants. I'm usually a sleep-naked kind of guy, but it felt weird to be all *bam* on our honeymoon the first time we make love as man and wife. And my assumption is she'll come out of that bathroom in something special that I'll probably rip off with my teeth in five seconds. But I can at least begin the night civilized.

"Aunt Valentina is concerned with everyone's eternal soul," Banner replies with a laugh, her voice coming closer. "I think you won her over, though, delivering your vows in Spanish. You won me over, too."

She appears at the door, and my mouth literally drops open. I expected some kind of gown or virginal-white lingerie. Not sure why. I've done my part to ensure she's far from virginal, but her choice for tonight is absolutely perfect. It's a black teddy, cut high at the hips, cinched at her waist with a silk bow. Patches of silk are strategically placed, but it's mostly lace, and her skin glows through the openings. The dusky discs of her nipples are clearly visible through the lace molding her breasts. Long and firm, her legs glimmer with the lotion or oil or whatever she put on them. Whatever it is, it's damn sexy and makes me want her thighs wrapped around my head while I devour her pussy.

I mean, I always want that, but the glimmer levels it up.

Thick, dark hair streams down her back, and tiny curls flower around her hairline. She's left her face exactly the way I like it. Free of makeup, the way I first fell for her. Nothing but her naturally pretty lips, seven freckles, and a dimple that tells me when I make her laugh.

"Wow," I say, once I can form words. "Um, you look…"

I swallow whatever inadequate shit I was about to say to describe the perfect mixture of pure and sensual standing in front of me. I give up on words and walk over to her. From the neck down, she's all confidence and firm, full curves. When I look into her eyes, there's an unexpected shyness that only makes me want her more. I have one more thing I need to do before I let myself have her.

"I, um… I have something for you." I reach into the pocket of my sleep pants and draw out a gold coin.

"Is that an *arra?*" Her wide eyes find mine, a pleased smile christening her lips.

"Yeah, uh, I heard it's tradition for the groom to give the bride thirteen of these on the wedding day."

She takes it from between my fingers, studying it for a few seconds, and then says, "It's engraved with today's date."

"I thought we could kind of make our own tradition and every year add another one with a new anniversary date. Not just for thirteen years but…"

Forever.

Self-consciousness steals the word from me.

"It was a stupid idea," I say after a moment of silence. "We don't have to—"

"I love it," she whispers, cupping my cheek. "Thank you."

It was a simple thing, but I'm glad it holds meaning for her the way I hoped it would. And I've been imagining these next moments all day, certain that making love to Banner once we're married will hold meaning, too. She looks so beautiful, I want to see her from every angle.

"Turn around for me," I say, my voice husky, pleading.

"Jared." She laughs, her glance skidding away from mine, off to the side. She bites into the pillowed softness of her bottom lip, lifts her lashes to study my face, to see if I'm serious.

"Ban, please. Show me."

Holding my stare, she nods and starts turning slowly. As soon as she's facing away from me and I see her ass, I take her shoulders, stopping the circuit. It's a thong. Both ass cheeks are just…there, swelling out from the curve of her waist and back. How can I not…

I sink to my knees, bite the left cheek, and then soothe the sting with my tongue.

"Oh, God, Jared," she gasps.

I repeat the bite and soothe on the other cheek. Her ass is so full and round and firm. God, all that work pays off. There is no body I'd prefer over hers. No one I'd rather see than this woman, my wife. I scatter open-mouth kisses over her bottom and reach around to touch her stomach. My hand inches down until I reach the lace between her legs. One finger slides under the fabric, moves down to caress her clit.

"Jesus." She reaches around behind her to clench her fist in my hair. "Yes."

I stroke her clit over and over until it's swollen and wet and continue the sucking kisses all over her ass. Her hips take the rhythm of my finger, and as I speed up my strokes, she becomes more frantic.

"Oh, God," she cries out, close to orgasm, but I'm not ready for that, so I stop.

"No." Her voice breaks. "Jared, please."

"Trust me, Ban." I stand and turn her around to face me again. I bend to kiss her, and she whimpers against my lips, on the edge of something I more than want to give her. I lead her by the hand over to the bed and gently push her shoulder so she's sitting on the bed.

"Open your legs." It's said softly but it's a command, one she's more than happy to follow. She spreads her legs immediately, and I stare at the soaked lace bisecting her pussy. My mouth waters at the sight, at the thought of my tongue on her, of my face buried there. I take my place on my knees in front of her and bow between her thighs.

At first, I content myself with tasting her through the lace, allowing the scrape of it across my tongue to heighten the sensation. My mouth never leaving her pussy, I reach up to untie the silk bow at her waist. The panels fall open and her breasts spill out. I pull the lace aside so there's nothing between my lips and her pussy.

"Rub your nipples," I say against the wet, silky lips.

Panting, she nods, reaching up to pinch and roll her nipples while I open her up and suck her clit.

"Ahhh." She thrusts into my face, still rolling her nipples. "Dammit, Jared."

I scoop her legs onto my shoulders and lick into the folds, slip my tongue inside, pull the lips between mine.

"*Dios, dios, dios,*" she pants, her hips moving faster over my face, her hands urgent on her breasts. "Please, please. *Por favor.*"

I lift under her thighs, bringing her ass higher to my mouth, and shift my lips to her asshole, running my tongue over the puckered surface.

"Oh, shit," she screams.

I dig my tongue into the tight hole and reach up to stroke her clit.

"No, no, no," she sobs. "I can't... Jared, you have to."

I don't have to do shit but stay right here until she squirts all over my thumb, which is my goal. I pinch her clit and push my thumb into her pussy, which contracts helplessly around me. I lick into her ass deeper until she squeezes my head between her knees and screams. Her juices run from her pussy down the seam of her ass. I try to lick leisurely, but I want it too badly, and my tongue chases every drop until I'm grunting and squeezing her thighs and spreading her ass cheeks to lick it all out.

When I'm sated, I look up to find Banner laid back on the bed, arms stretched above her head, breasts free of the bodice. Tears slip from the corners of her eyes, and she's muttering, begging me in Spanish under her breath to fuck her. I stand, shuck the sleep pants off, and fist my cock, which is painfully erect. I'm going to fuck my wife like an animal, so I hope she's ready. She slits her eyes open, catching my starving stare. She slips the teddy off, lifts her feet to the bed, widening her knees, spreading her thighs, to receive me.

She's ready.

I crawl up on the bed between her legs and don't even pretend I want more foreplay or another caress. I want inside this pussy right fucking now, and she knows it. I align our bodies and, without further ado, charge in.

"Ahhhh." Her pussy rips that sound of deepest pleasure from my throat. "Dammit, Banner, what is your pussy made of?"

She laughs a little.

"Don't talk," she says huskily. "Fuck."

I can't even go fast enough, get deep enough. I hook an arm under her thigh for leverage, to tunnel in farther. Her hands come up to loop around my neck, her fingers threading into my sweat-dampened hair. She presses one hand over my heart and holds my eyes.

"I'll stay right here," she whispers, repeating my vow to her from the ceremony. "I love you so much."

God, she can't say that to me right now. Something tight in my chest starts dissolving.

"I love you, Ban," I tell her, setting my forehead to hers. I rain kisses over every inch of her face.

God, she's precious. The best thing that has ever happened to me. So much more than I deserve. And then I know what August means. It didn't happen for me at the altar. Not the one in a church with people staring at us, inspecting us. No, for me it happens at *my* altar. Inside her body, where *I* worship. The tears prick my eyes and burn my throat. They finally run from my eyes, over my cheeks, onto her neck. I adorn her body with my sweat, with my tears. This body, this heart, this soul, this *woman* is the only thing I truly revere. And as my body joins with her again and again, as my heart, so sullied, meets hers, so pure, I know how it must feel to be the horizon. To live at that precise point where heaven meets earth.

I come on a roar, driving my cock into her again and again with branding force, claiming her body from the inside. The irony, of course, is that Banner owns *me*. I'm hers and probably have been since the day I met her. It's like I said. I fell for her in pieces, and she takes more of me with every touch, every kiss, every word, every act of kindness.

And tonight, now, I'm irrevocably all hers.

When we're both coherent again and I'm breathing like a human instead of a raging locomotive, we slip under the silky sheets and fold our arms around each other in the silence that follows religious experiences. That's what making love to Banner as my wife for the first time felt like. And I've been robbed of words. If it's always like this, I don't know if I'll survive it, but it is decidedly a wonderful way to go. I'm drifting off to sleep when something warm and velvety swipes my neck. Funny how something so simple can instantly transport you to another moment in time. To the moment she licked me just like that after we made love for the first time. Only we were just kids. And it was in the back room of a deserted laundromat. And it was in the dark.

"*Dijiste tus votos en español,*" she says, pulling me from the past.

My brain, still sludge from our lovemaking, can barely process but manages to figure out she's speaking to me in Spanish. She wants to know how much I know.

You said your vows in Spanish.

"*Sí*," I reply with definite smugness because this may be the best gift I could have given her on our wedding day.

"*¿Cuánto entiendes?*" she asks.

How much do you understand?

"*Alguna cosa*," I reply drowsily.

Say something.

"*Y te aviso si entiendo.*"

And I'll let you know if I understand.

It's quiet, she's quiet for a moment, and then she speaks, her voice a command she knows, when it comes down to it, I will follow.

"*¿Cuándo puedo tener tus bebés?*"

When can I have your babies?

I grin in the dark that she has the audacity to ask me this on our wedding night. But this is the woman I love. Banner is a bold declaration. She's a living dare that I'll accept every time.

"*Cuando quieras*," I answer.

Whenever you want.

CHECK OUT THE *BLOCK SHOT* PLAYLIST:

http://bit.ly/BlockShotSpotify

Read on for a sneak peek at the
next book in the series, *Hook Shot*

LOTUS

THEY SAY IF YOU CAN MAKE IT HERE, YOU CAN MAKE IT ANYWHERE.
New York City is a beautiful bitch dipped in glitter, giving you
the finger while walking the runway in her Louboutins. The best,
brightest, and beastliest grind here.

When I moved from Atlanta to New York two years ago, it felt
like I was embarking on an improbable adventure to an open frontier.
I was like that Pioneer Woman on television, but instead of churn-
ing my own butter, I made clothes from scratch. My bare neces-
sities were three garbage bags stuffed with all my belongings, my
great-grandmother's sewing machine, and a knockoff Louis Vuitton
Neverfull bag. I fancied myself Carrie Bradshaw. The girls eating
lunch with me in Bryant Park right now? They're my Charlotte,
Miranda, and Samantha, all rolled into two.

"So I've got some news," Billie says, her eyes darting between me
and my roommate, Yari. "Paul's getting a divorce."

I give something dark in my grilled chicken salad an investiga-
tive poke to make sure it doesn't move but otherwise don't respond.
Yari, looking inappropriately unimpressed, slurps the last of her
Pellegrino through a straw.

"Uh, *bitches...*" Billie says, disappointment darkening her green
eyes. The flush climbing her cheeks is embarrassment, anger, or
ninety-five degrees of New York summer. Either way, her temperature

is rising.

"Oh, sorry. That's great," I finally say, not bothering to inject much enthusiasm or faith into my words.

"Doesn't he get a divorce like every month?" Yari asks, fake curiosity on her face. "Seems like he decides to get one every time you give him a blow job."

If anything, Wilhelmina Claybourne, Billie to her friends, of which we are the closest, blushes even redder.

"No, he doesn't," Billie replies, suddenly preoccupied with the turkey roll on her Styrofoam plate.

"Were you or were you not balls to jaws last night?" Yari's eyes are serious, but her lips twitch at the corners.

"I don't see what that has to do with any—"

"Balls to jaws. I rest my case." Yari bangs her water on the table like a gavel. "I think it's sad that I understand Paul better than you *and* his wife do."

"It's not a real marriage," Billie protests weakly.

"That must be why he never gets a real divorce." I stand and gesture for them to do the same. "Come on. We need to get back to work or we'll be late for the meeting."

The green umbrella covering our table sheltered us from some of the unrelenting sunshine, but as soon as we toss our trash and start walking the few blocks to our office, it beats on our heads.

"They don't even sleep together," Billie tries again.

"Why would he need to sleep with his wife when he's fucking you?" I ask, keeping my tone nonchalant. I actually get pissed as hell every time we have this revolving door of a conversation.

"Forget I brought it up." Billie sighs, walking between us with her eyes trained forward.

"I'm sorry, Bill, but you're having an affair with another woman's husband," Yari says, taking the elastic band from her wrist and pulling her long, dark hair into a messy bun. "This is the circle of trust and truth, and we're your best friends. If we don't call you on your ratchet ways, who will?"

Billie looks over at me, waiting for me to weigh in. Like she doesn't already know where I stand.

"She's right," I say. "You're thinking with your heart and your vagina."

"Gimme a break. You like sex more than Yari and me combined," Billie fires back.

I don't unleash on her because I know we're riding her hard and she needs to score a point. "I actually think I'm done with dick for a while," I say a little too casually.

My words create a tiny cone of stunned silence even as the frenetic urban soundtrack continues playing around us.

"Sorry." Yari bangs an imaginary hearing aid. "This damn thing doesn't always pick up bullshit. What'd you say?"

The three of us laugh, but I sober with each step that takes us closer to the design studio where we work in the Garment District.

"I'm serious," I tell them. "I love dick, true, but I feel like I need…I don't know, a break."

How do I explain how complex sex is for me? I've always compartmentalized it into a purely physical connection. I scratched the itch on my terms, letting men into my body but allowing no real intimacy. Lately, though, not only has it left me unsatisfied, but it's left me depressed. Empty. Bleak. Something in me wants more than what I've had, but true intimacy is a risk I'm not willing to take.

Not to mention the fear. The last time I had sex…

How do I explain to my friends what I don't fully understand myself? Nothing I've been feeling makes sense. And telling them now would be like starting in the middle of a story they've never heard before. Maybe I could at least *try* talking to them about it.

"Whoa." Billie stares at her phone with her mouth hanging open. "Did we know there's a *Hi, Felicia* Bitmoji?"

Okay. Maybe not talk to my friends about this.

"Sorry," she says, sidestepping a construction worker. "What were you saying about swearing off dick, Lo?"

"I think I want to take a sex break."

Both of them stare at me as we approach the entrance to JPL Maison, the design studio where we work.

"I don't understand the words that are coming out of your mouth," Yari finally replies.

"I don't know," I say with a shrug. "It feels…empty."

"Then find a bigger dick," Billie says. "One that'll fill you up."

The three of us share a grin in the lobby of the renovated loft that houses our offices.

"I'm serious. I think this"—I gesture to my pelvic area—"needs to be man-free for a while."

"Remember that time I tried to quit smoking and gnawed through the strap of my purse?" Billie asks. "I feel like that's how you'll be if you don't come on a regular basis. You might also gain ten pounds. I did."

"Who said anything about not coming?" I ignore Yari's snort. "I have a diverse and quite capable fleet of vibrators."

The garage door of the elevator lifts, and we walk onto a floor displaying bolts of vibrant fabric, several tables with seamstresses and sewing machines, and rack after rack of expensive clothing in various stages of completion.

"What about Chase?" Yari says of our boss's favorite photographer and my latest fuckboi. "He won't be happy about your little sex break."

"Already told him, and you're right. He wasn't happy." I snort. "What can I say? I got a golden pussy. It's a curse."

They laugh as I knew they would, distracted by the sass I use to cover my confusion. It was that last time having sex with Chase that pushed me to this decision.

"But Chase knows he's got about as much say over my body as he has over the price of tea in Chinatown," I continue. "He'll be fine."

We climb the iron stairwell to the top floor housing our offices and the conference room. I take my spot at the long table, a slab of repurposed slate unearthed from an old quarry. In every meeting, I sit immediately to the right of Jean Pierre Louis, founding designer of JPL Maison.

Two paths couldn't have been more unlikely to cross than mine and my boss's. I stepped in to style a shoot for a friend at the last minute in Atlanta. I wasn't even officially working in fashion. It was a side hustle to help get me through college. My major at Spelman was business, but I often considered opening my own store or doing something in fashion later.

JP and I hit it off right away. I was the only one who understood his tirade of French when he saw the "blasphemy" of his creation being so poorly styled. I stepped in, fixed the hot mess the stylist had made, and soothed the savage beast with the Louisiana French MiMi taught me. Apparently, it was good enough because by the end of the day he was telling me dirty jokes in French and offering me a job.

We've only gotten closer over the last two years. He recommended that I enroll at FIT, which is not far from the studio. It kicked my ass, getting my associate's degree in fashion design while working full-time and often *overtime* at the atelier, but it was worth it. I've been at JP's right in every meeting for a long time now.

"Wearable wonder," JP says without preamble, his French accent thick. "That is our theme for this season."

He gestures for everyone at the table to gather around him and his sketch pad. He could design digitally and share it so we all looked on our iPads, but JP is surprisingly old school. His fingers are often smudged with charcoal from his pencils, and the notepad perennially tucked under his arm is always full.

"Feast your eyes," he says with a dramatic flourish, "on spring."

READING GROUP GUIDE

1. At the beginning, Jared wants to get into the Pride to secure his future, but once its members insult Banner, he pulls out. Have you ever had to walk away from something you really wanted because you realized it didn't represent your morals?

2. How do Banner's past experiences with men make it hard for her to trust that Jared actually has feelings for her? What do her reactions say about the effect that cruel words can have on someone's confidence?

3. Kennedy Ryan has said it is essential in many of her second chance romances that while the couple are apart, the woman is establishing herself, pursuing her dreams and learning what is most important to her happiness beyond a romantic relationship. How do you see Banner doing this in the ten years she and Jared are apart?

4. What does Banner mean when she says "the daughter of a lion is still a lion"? Banner's speech discusses how women are pushed around in the sports industry, but how do her words apply to women everywhere?

5. Jared doesn't just *hope* to win Banner back—he *promises* he will and doesn't regret helping Banner cheat on her boyfriend. Do you find that sort of commitment to love admirable, or should Jared have let Banner go? What would you want if you were Banner?

6. Why is Banner so reluctant to let Jared win her over, even outside of her relationship with Zo? Do you agree with Jared that she's trying to convince herself Jared has bad intentions so that she doesn't have to face the truth of their connection, or are her reservations more complicated than that?

7. Banner agrees to not take things further with Jared while she helps Zo through his battle with illness, claiming Zo "needs something he's fighting to live for" even though she knows her feelings for him are platonic. Was this the right thing to do? Is there any "right" thing to do in a situation like this?

8. August tells Jared that "loving someone is the most selfless thing you can do." How does hearing that change the way Jared thinks about the situation with Banner and Zo?

9. How did you feel about both Jared and Zo defending Banner to her mother? Have you ever had to stand up to your own family before, and how would you feel if someone did so on your behalf?

10. Banner and Jared often talk about whether they "deserve" each other. Is it truly possible for anyone to deserve another person? Why or why not?

AUTHOR Q&A

Your author's note details that you wrote *Long Shot* after seeing a poor portrayal of domestic abuse in the media. Can you tell us more about your inspiration for this book and for the Hoops series as a whole? What message do you hope to bring to the women who read these books, whether they be survivors or not?

An elevator surveillance video of a football player hitting his girlfriend went viral. She was knocked unconscious and he dragged her through the doors like it was nothing. The ensuing disturbing cultural narrative revolved around the repercussions for his career, the responsibility of the team, how long they knew about the tape, and speculation about her as a gold digger. There was far too little actual concern about her as a human being and the private terror she might be navigating. My chief hope was compassion for survivors. I wanted readers to see how it could happen to someone who, on the surface, should be able to avoid the often-insidious traps laid by violent partners. I also wanted them to recognize how complex it can become to "just leave" especially when children are involved; that when you leave, your chances of death increase astronomically, and the care and planning it usually takes to do so successfully. So much of Iris's journey would have looked different in the context of a legal system designed to actually protect women and children, to listen to women, and to consistently prosecute abusers. As a whole, there is a thread of women's empowerment that runs through each book in the Hoops series. It looks different for each character—Iris, Banner and Lotus—but they all, in the process of overcoming their unique obstacles, become stronger and more sure of their place in the world. I want women reading this series and my books in general to find their power, exercise their gifts, and create space for themselves in a world that often tries to shrink and silence them.

Basketball is such a huge component of *Long Shot* and the Hoops universe. Do you have a personal connection to the sport, or what was the reason for centering the series around it?

I LOVE basketball. I grew up in North Carolina, home of the biggest sports rivalry in college basketball: UNC v. Duke. The home of the G.O.A.T Michael Jordan (argue with your mama. LOL). When my husband and I first met, we didn't have an instant romantic connection. We were friends and bonded around our mutual love of the sport. He was a former college baller before being injured. I'm not a huge sports fan in general, but I know basketball, and it felt like a comfortable place for me to set this universe where I knew I'd be having really difficult discussions. Side note, my husband was the one who explained to me what it meant to "play someone at the five," so he gets some of the credit for that! Plus he's 6'5", and I love a tall guy, so I think I'll keep him ;-)

Why is it so important to you to not only tackle difficult content in Hoops, such as domestic abuse, sexual assault, and illness, but to put those graphic, painful experiences directly on the page? Do you feel this is something important to portray in romance novels in particular?

I think the only book I would consider "graphically depicted" is *Long Shot*, and I did want the reader to have a visceral response to Iris' journey. It's singular in my catalogue and was not undertaken lightly. I interviewed several survivors, and would cry after our conversations. Hearing what they endured to survive, not only for themselves but for their children, moved me more than anything had until that point, and I would hazard to say even since. What was consistent was how the system worked against them. I didn't want Iris to be someone who believed her abuser loved her. There are women working through that falsehood, and I have compassion for them, but Iris is someone who at the first blow wants out and runs. I needed readers to see how at every turn, a patriarchal system was working against her with absolutely devastating effect. The things Iris goes through were inspired by real women who lived to tell me their stories, and I chose not to gloss over their harrowing experiences. I wanted readers to feel as compelled and as compassionate as I did. Several survivors read the book as I was writing and helped me decide what to include. This book will be too difficult for some, and I hope the content warnings help readers determine if it's a journey they want to start. If they start and it's too hard, I hope they'll stop reading because their mental well-being is more important to me than them reading my book. For those who decide to read, I want them to know research and real conversations are the bedrock of this story. I had no desire to romanticize abuse. I *did* want to encourage women who survive hell that they may one day find a happily ever after. And I wanted those of us who encounter them to think before we judge, and to ask ourselves what we as a community can do to help.

The Hoops books were originally published several years ago. Did you make any updates from the previous versions, or did you think about these stories in a different way when working on them a second time?

I didn't update very much at all. These stories still hold true. I think the only thing now is that I know many readers feel seen in these pages, whether because they've experienced similar things, or just because they love seeing women of color at the center of stories that esteem their pleasure, success, and happiness. I look forward to more readers meeting Iris, Banner, and Lotus, and hope a new wave of women will feel inspired by their journeys.

Your author's notes talk about the people you've interviewed to portray your characters' experiences authentically. How do you choose which experiences you want to portray, and how do you go about finding sources for your research and turning them into the vibrant characters of the Hoops world?

My background is in journalism, and I approach writing fiction similar to how I approach writing an article. I find sources. I talk to people. I do research and interpret that information for my purposes. I actually often start with my readers. I have a sizeable reader group on Facebook, and I'll sometimes post in there asking if anyone has experience with this or that. I usually get more responses than I can use. I schedule interviews with them, but I also go down research rabbit holes and reach out to specialists I find. I always have "experts" beta reading for me who know much more than I do. My first goal is to do no harm, and having sensitivity and expert beta readers is a huge part of ensuring, to the best of my ability at the time, that my stories uplift, not hurt. For Hoops, I interviewed many therapists, social workers, shelter workers, and even a beautiful woman diagnosed with the condition Zo has in *Block Shot*. I talked with a woman who ran a support group like the one Lotus finds in the basement of a church. Reading books, listening to podcasts, and having conversations is probably at least 60% of my writing process, and is actually the most fun part to me. Taking all of that information and synthesizing it into a story and characters that will challenge and entertain, that's the hard part, but is also the joy of what I get to do.

ACKNOWLEDGMENTS

I never know where to start with acknowledgments. That's a good problem to have. It means there are so many people who have supported me that this part of the book proves almost as challenging as writing it. (Not really. No. LOL!) But it's hard! Hard because I'll inevitably, inadvertently leave someone out. I know I'll inadequately express my gratitude even to those I include, but here goes.

Thank you to Jane, who taught me most of what I know about amyloidosis. You relived a painful time in your life with me so I could write authentically about Zo's journey. Your fighting spirit and bottomless faith are like nothing I've ever seen. I love you so much, and you have my prayers as you continue your fight, you WarriorAngel.

To my beta readers, who offered their constructive honesty, their bibliophile enthusiasm, and their listening ear. Tijuana, Shelley, Terilyn, Sarah, Serena, Yamara, Margie, Azailia——thank you! I loved sharing Banner and Jared's journey with you from the "needs work" beginning to the "much better" end. And Joanna, for enduring all the rereads, the vmails, the persistent questions, the same question asked in five different ways. For being the fine-tooth comb through every strand of each book I write. You're my #SafetyNet! I love you (said with a British accent! LOL).

Thank you to my PA Melissa! Girl, you know I'm a handful

and I always have another idea and another thing I need. You never complain, and I appreciate your heart as much as I do your hands. You're a great part of my team. Thank you for everything.

And to all the girls out there like Banner and like ME, the double-digit girls in a single-digit world——GET IT! Chase it! Take it! Shine! Stand proud and do what Banner did. Build yourself from the inside out. Don't let anyone convince you that you aren't beautiful. Not for *a girl your size*. Not if you were *a few pounds lighter*.

Beautiful.

End. Of.

And it's often hard to know where to start, but I always know where to end. With my boys! To the best husband a girl could ask for. My #LifetimeLovah who inspired "I'd play you at the five" in *Long Shot* and "I want to make you laugh like that every day" in *Block Shot*. Because you do. Even when things are dark and hard, you'll pull a laugh out of your hat of magic tricks. I could write Jared, who loved Banner at any size, because that is how you have loved ME! You've always seen me, pounds up or pounds down. You've shown me what unconditional love looks like. And to the most fantastic special son, you are my greatest responsibility, highest privilege, and best inspiration. Both of you lend me to a world you cannot see and the words in my head you can't hear every time I write a book. Thank you for still believing me when I say "I'll make it up to you" and loving me even if I don't.

ABOUT THE AUTHOR

A RITA Award winner and *USA Today* bestseller, Kennedy Ryan writes for women from all walks of life, empowering them and placing them firmly at the center of each story and in charge of their own destinies. Her heroes respect, cherish, and lose their minds for the women who capture their hearts.

Kennedy and her writings have been featured in *Chicken Soup for the Soul*, *USA Today*, *Entertainment Weekly*, *Glamour*, *Cosmo*, *TIME*, *O Mag*, and many others. She has a passion for raising autism awareness. The cofounder of LIFT 4 Autism, an annual charitable book auction, she has appeared on *Headline News*, *Montel Williams*, NPR, and other media outlets as an advocate for ASD families. She is a wife to her lifetime lover and mother to an extraordinary son.

Connect with Kennedy!

Website: kennedyryanwrites.com
Facebook: @kennedyryanauthor
Instagram: @kennedyryan1
TikTok: @kennedyryanauthor
Twitter: @kennedyrwrites